Meg Cabot is the autho[illegible] ful *The Princess Diaries* [illegible] copies sold around the [illegible] the US and UK best-s[illegible] [illegible] weeks and won several awards. Two movies based on the series have been massively popular throughout the world.

Meg is also the author of the best-selling *All American Girl*, *All American Girl: Ready or Not*, *Teen Idol*, *Avalon High*, *Nicola and the Viscount*, *Victoria and the Rogue* and *The Mediator* series as well as several other books for teenagers and adults. She lives in Florida with her husband and one-eyed cat, Henrietta, and says she is still waiting for her real parents, the king and queen, to restore her to her rightful throne.

Visit Meg Cabot's website at www.megcabot.co.uk

Also by Meg Cabot

The Princess Diaries
The Princess Diaries: Take Two
The Princess Diaries: Third Time Lucky
The Princess Diaries: Mia Goes Fourth
The Princess Diaries: Give Me Five
The Princess Diaries: Sixsational

The Princess Diaries Guide to Life
ThePrincess Diaries Princess Files
The Princess Diaries Guide to Christmas

All American Girl
All American Girl: Ready or Not

Avalon High

Teen Idol

Nicola and the Viscount
Victoria and the Rogue

The Mediator: Love You to Death
The Mediator: High Stakes
The Mediator: Mean Spirits
The Mediator: Young Blood
The Mediator: Grave Doubts

Look out for

The Princess Diaries: Seventh Heaven

The Mediator: Heaven Sent

For older readers

The Guy Next Door
Boy Meets Girl
Every Boy's Got One

The PRINCESS DIARIES

Books 5 & 6

Meg Cabot

MACMILLAN

First published 2003 as *The Princess Diaries: Give Me Five* and
2004 as *The Princess Diaries: Sixsational* by Macmillan Children's Books

This edition published 2006 by Macmillan Children's Books
a division of Macmillan Publishers Limited
20 New Wharf Road, London N1 9RR
Basingstoke and Oxford
www.panmacmillan.com

Associated companies throughout the world

ISBN-13: 978-0-330-44274-9
ISBN-10: 0-330-44274-0

1 3 5 7 9 8 6 4 2

A CIP catalogue record for this book is available from
the British Library.

Typeset by Intype Libra Ltd
Printed and bound in Great Britain by
Mackays of Chatham plc, Kent

The author wishes to express her gratitude to the people who contributed in so many ways to the creation and publication of these books: Beth Ader, Jennifer Brown, Barb Cabot, Sarah Davies, Laura Langlie, Abby McAden, Michele Jaffe, David Walton and especially Benjamin Egnatz.

The PRINCESS DIARIES

Give Me Five

'It's true,' she said. 'Sometimes I do pretend I am a princess. I pretend I am a princess, so that I can try and behave like one.'

A Little Princess
Frances Hodgson Burnett

The Atom

The Official Student-Run Newspaper of Albert Einstein High School
Take *Pride* in the AEHS Lions

Week of May 5 *Volume 456/Issue 27*

Science Fair Winners Announced

by Rafael Menendez

Science students entered 21 projects in the Albert Einstein High School Science Fair. Several projects advanced to the New York City regional competition, which will be held next month. Senior Judith Gershner received the grand prize for slicing a human genome. Earning special honours were senior Michael Moscovitz for his computer program modelling the death of a dwarf star, and freshman Kenneth Showalter for his experiments in gender transfiguration in newts.

Lacrosse Teams Win

by Ai-Lin Hong

Both the varsity and junior varsity lacrosse teams beat their competitors this past weekend. Senior Josh Richter led the varsity team to a stunning defeat of The Dwight School 7–6 in overtime. The JV defeated Dwight by a score of 8–0. These exciting games were marred by a peculiarly aggressive Central Park squirrel that continuously darted out on to the field. Eventually it was chased away by Principal Gupta.

AEHS's Princess Spends Spring Break Building Homes for Appalachian Poor

by Melanie Greenbaum

Spring Break was a working holiday for AEHS freshman Mia Thermopolis. Mia, who, it was revealed last fall, is actually the sole heir to the throne of the principality of Genovia, spent her five-day vacation helping to build homes for Housing for the Homeless. Said the princess of her sojourn in the foothills of the Smoky Mountains, 'It was OK. Except for the whole "no bathroom" thing. And the part where I kept hitting myself in the thumb with my hammer.'

Senior Week

by Josh Richter, Senior Class President

The week of May 5–10 is Senior Week. This is the time to honour this year's AEHS graduating class, who have worked so hard to show you leadership throughout the year. The Senior Week Events Calendar goes like this:

Mon	Tues	Wed	Thurs	Fri	Sat
Senior Awards Banquet	Senior Sports Banquet	Senior Debate	Senior Skit Nite	Senior Skip Day	Senior Prom

A Note From Your Principal:

Senior Skip Day is not an event sanctioned by school administration. All students are required to attend classes Friday 9 May. In addition, the request made by certain members of the freshman class to lift the sanction against underclassmen attending the prom unless invited by an upperclassman is denied.

Notice to all Students:

It has come to the attention of the administration that many pupils do not seem to know the proper words to the AEHS School Song. They are as follows:

Einstein Lions, we're for you
Come on, be bold, come on, be bold, come on, be bold
Einstein Lions, we're for you
Blue and gold, blue and gold, blue and gold
Einstein Lions, we're for you
We've got a team no one else can ever tame
Einstein Lions, we're for you
Let's win this game!

Please note that at this year's graduation ceremony, any student caught singing alternative (particularly explicit and/or suggestive) words to the AEHS School Song will be removed from the premises. Complaints that the AEHS School Song is too militaristic must be submitted in writing to the AEHS administrative office, not scrawled on toilet doors or discussed on any student's public access television programme.

Letters to the Editor:

To Whom it May Concern:
Melanie Greenbaum's article in last week's issue of *The Atom* on the strides the women's movement has

made in the past three decades was laughably facile. Sexism is still alive and well, not only around the world, but in our own country. In Utah, for instance, polygamous marriages involving brides as young as eleven years of age are thriving, practised by fundamentalist Mormons who continue to live by traditions their ancestors brought west in the mid-1800s. The number of people in polygamous families in Utah is estimated by human rights groups at perhaps as many as 50,000, despite the fact that polygamy is not tolerated by the mainstream Mormon church, and also that the enforcement of tough penalties in the case of underage brides can sentence a polygamous husband or church leader arranging such a marriage to up to fifteen years in prison.

I am not telling other cultures how to live, or anything. I am just saying take off the rose-coloured spectacles, Ms Greenbaum, and write an article about some of the real problems that affect half the population of this planet. The staff of *The Atom* might well consider giving some of their other writers a chance to report on these issues, instead of relegating them to the cafeteria beat.

Lilly Moscovitz

AEHS Food Court Menu

compiled by Mia Thermopolis

Monday	Tuesday	Wednesday	Thursday	Friday
Potato Bar	Soup & Sand.	Taco Salad Bar	Asian Bar	Bean Bar
Fr. Bread Pizza	Chicken Pattie	Burrito	Chicken Parm.	Grilled Cheese
Fish Fingers	Tuna in Pitta	Corndog/Pickle	Corn/FF	Curly Fries
Meatball Sub	Indiv. Pizza	Deli Bar	Pasta Bar	Buffalo Bites
Spicy Chix	Nachos Deluxe	Italian Beef	Fish Stix	Soft Pretzel

**Take out your own personal ad!
Available to AEHS students at 50 cents/line**

Happy Ad
Happy Birthday, Reggie!
Sweet Sixteen At Last!
The Helens

Found: one pair glasses, wire frames, the Gifted and Talented classroom. Describe to claim. See Mrs Hill

Happy Ad
Go to the prom with me, CF?
Please say yes.
GD

Lost: Spiral notebook in caf., on or about 4/27. Read and DIE! Reward for safe return. Locker No. 510

Happy Ad
Happy Birthday in advance, MT!
Love,
Your Loyal Subjects

Happy Ad
Shop at Ho's Deli for all your school supply needs! New this week: ERASERS, STAPLES, NOTEBOOKS, PENS. Also Yu-Gi-Oh cards, *Slimfast* in Strawberry

For Sale:
One Fender precision bass, baby-blue, never been played. With amp, how-to videos. $300. Locker No. 345

Looking for Love:
Female frosh, loves romance/reading, wants older boy who enjoys same. Must be taller than 5'8", no mean people, non-smokers only. NO METALHEADS.
Email: Iluvromance@aehs.edu

Happy Ad
Personal to MK from MW:
My love for you
Like a flower grows
Where it will stop
No one knows.

Wednesday, April 30, Bio.

Mia – Did you see the latest issue of The Atom*?*

I know, Shameeka, I just got my copy. I wish Lilly would stop mentioning me in her letters to the editor. I mean, as the only freshman on the newspaper staff, I have to pay my dues. Lesley Cho, the editor-in-chief, got her start on the cafeteria beat. I am TOTALLY FINE with covering the lunch menu every week.

Well, I think Lilly just feels if your goal really is to be a writer someday, you aren't going to get there writing about Buffalo Bites!

That is not true. I have made some very important innovations in the lunch column. For instance, it was my idea to capitalize the 'i' in Individual Pizza.

Lilly is only looking out for your best interests.

Whatever. Melanie Greenbaum is on the girls' basketball team. She could fully slam-dunk me if she wanted to. I don't think Lilly antagonizing her is in my best interests.

So . . .

So what?

So has he asked you yet?????

Has who asked me what?

HAS MICHAEL ASKED YOU TO THE PROM???????

Oh. No.

Mia, the prom is in less than TWO WEEKS! Jeff asked me a MONTH ago. How are you going to get your dress in time if you don't find out soon whether or not you're going? Plus you have to make an appointment to get your hair and nails done, and get the boutonnière, and he has to rent the limo and his tux and make dinner reservations. This is not pizza at Bowlmore Lanes, you know. It's dinner and dancing at Maxim's! It's serious!

I'm sure Michael is going to ask me soon. He has a lot on his mind, what with the new band and college in the autumn and all.

Well, you better light a fire under him. Because you don't want to end up having him ask at the last minute. Because then if you say yes it'll be like you were waiting around for him to ask.

Hello, Michael and I are going out. It's not like I'm going to go with somebody else. As if anybody else would ask me. I mean, I'm not YOU, Shameeka. I don't have all these senior guys lined up at my locker, just waiting for a chance to ask me out. Not that I would. Go out with another guy, I mean. If one asked. Because I love Michael with every fibre of my being.

Well, I hope he asks you soon, because I don't want to be the only freshman girl at the prom! Who will I hang with in the Ladies' Room?

Don't worry. I'll be there. Oops. What was that about ice-worms?

They differ from earthworms in that they . . .

The Ice-Worm
by
Mia Thermopolis*

Contrary to popular opinion, glaciers do not just support life above and below them, but also within them.

Recently, scientists discovered the existence of worms that live *inside* ice – even mounds of methane ice on the floor of the Gulf of Mexico. These creatures, called ice-worms, are one to two inches long and live off the chemosynthetic bacteria that grows on the methane, or are otherwise living symbiotically with them . . .

*Mr Sturgess, the notes Shameeka and I were passing were fully class-related. I *swear*. But whatever.

Only 70 words. 180 to go.

HOW CAN I THINK ABOUT ICE-WORMS WHEN MY BOYFRIEND HASN'T ASKED ME TO THE PROM???????

Wednesday, April 30, Health and Safety

M – Why do you look like you just swallowed a sock?

Because, Lilly, the Bio sub caught Shameeka and me passing notes and assigned us both a 250-word paper on ice-worms.

So? You should look at it as an artistic challenge. Besides, 250 words is nothing for an ace journalist like yourself. You should be able to knock that out in half an hour.

Lilly, has your brother mentioned the prom to you?

Um. What?

Prom. You know. Senior Prom. The one they are holding at Maxim's a week from this Saturday. Has he mentioned to you whether or not he's, um, planning on asking anyone?

ANYONE? Just who do you mean by ANYONE? His DOG?

You know what I mean.

Michael does not discuss things like the prom with me, Mia. Mainly what Michael discusses with me is whether or not it is my turn to empty the dishwasher, set the table, or take the wadded-up tissues down the hall to the incinerator chute after Mom and Dad's Adult Survivors of Childhood Alien Abduction group therapy meetings.

Oh. Well, I was just wondering.

Don't worry, Mia. If Michael's going to ask anyone to the prom, it will be you.

What do you mean IF Michael's going to ask anyone to the prom?

I meant WHEN. OK? What is WITH you?

Nothing. Only that Michael is my one true love and he's graduating and so if we don't go to the prom this year I'll never get to go. Unless we go when I'M a senior, but that won't be for THREE YEARS!!!!!!!!!!

And besides, by that time Michael might be in graduate school. He might have a beard or something!!!!! You can't go to the prom with someone who has a BEARD.

I can see that you're very emotional about this. Are you premenstrual or something?

NO!!!!!! I JUST WANT TO GO TO THE PROM WITH MY BOYFRIEND BEFORE HE GRADUATES AND/OR GROWS EXCESSIVE AMOUNTS OF FACIAL HAIR!!!!!!!!! IS THERE ANYTHING WRONG WITH THAT??????

Whoa. You fully need to take a Midol. And rather than asking me whether or not I think my brother is going to ask you to the prom, I think you should ask YOURSELF something, and that's why a completely outdated, pagan dance ritual is so important to you.

It's just important to me, OK????

Is this because of that time your mom wouldn't buy you the Prom Queen Glamour Gown for your Barbie, and you had to make your own out of toilet paper?

HELLO!!!! Lilly, I would think that you might have noticed that the prom plays a key role in the socialization process of the adolescent. I mean, look at all the movies that have been made about it:

Movies That Feature The Prom As Prominent Plot Device

by Mia Thermopolis

Pretty in Pink: Will Molly Ringwald go to the prom with the cute rich boy or the poor weird boy? Whichever one she goes with, does she really think he's going to like that hideous pink potato sack of a dress she makes?

Ten Things I Hate About You: Julia Stiles and Heath Ledger. Was there ever a more perfect couple? I think not. It just takes the prom to prove it to them.

Valley Girl: Nicholas Cage's first starring role in a movie ever, and he plays a punk rocker who crashes a suburban mall rat's prom. Who will she ride home with in the limo, the guy with the Members Only jacket, or the guy with the Mohawk? What happens at the prom will decide it.

Footloose: Who can forget Kevin Bacon in the immortal role of Ren, convincing the kids in the town with the no-dancing ordinance to rent a place outside of city limits so they can assert their independence by tripping the light *fant-astique* to Kenny Loggins?

She's All That: Rachael Leigh Cook has to go to the prom in order to prove that she is not as big a nerd as everyone thinks she is. And then it turns out she still is, but – and this is the best part of the whole thing – Freddie Prinze Junior loves her anyway!!!!!

Never Been Kissed: Girl reporter Drew Barrymore goes undercover to crash a masquerade prom! Her friends dress as a strand of DNA, but Drew knows better and wins the heart of the teacher she loves by dressing as, what else, a princess (Oh, OK, Rosalind. But it looks like a princess costume).

And who can forget:

Back to the Future: If Michael J. Fox doesn't get his parents together by the prom, he might not ever be BORN!!!!!!!!! Proving the importance of the prom from both a societal as well as a BIOLOGICAL point of view!

What about Carrie*? Or do you not count buckets of pig blood as essential to the adolescent socialization process?*

YOU KNOW WHAT I MEAN!!!!!!!!!

OK, OK, calm down, I get your point.

You're just jealous because Boris can't ask you because he's still just a freshman like us!

I am making sure you get some protein at lunch because I think your vegetarianism has finally short-circuited your brain cells. You need meat, now.

Why are you minimalizing my pain? I have a legitimate concern here, and I think you need to consider the fact that it has nothing to do with my diet or menstrual cycle.

I seriously think you need to lie down with your feet above your head to get the blood flowing back into your brain because you are suffering from severe cognitive impairment.

Lilly, SHUT UP! I am way stressed right now! I mean, tomorrow is my fifteenth birthday, and I am still nowhere close to becoming self-actualized. Nothing is going right in my life: my father is insisting that I spend July and August with him in Genovia; my home life is completely unsatisfactory, what with my pregnant mother's incessant references to her bladder, and her insistence on giving birth to my future brother or sister at home, in the LOFT, with only a midwife – a midwife! – in attendance; my boyfriend is graduating from high school and starting college, where he will constantly be thrust into the presence of large-busted co-eds in black turtlenecks who like to talk about Kant, and my best friend doesn't seem to understand why the prom is important to me!!!!!!!!!!!

You forgot to complain about your grandmother.

No, I didn't. Grandmere has been in Palm Springs having a chemical face peel. She won't be back until tonight.

Mia, I thought you prided yourself on the fact that you and Michael had this open and honest relationship. Why don't you just ask him yourself if he plans on going?

I CAN'T DO THAT! I mean, then it will sound like I am asking him to ask me.

No, it won't.

Yes, it will.

No, it won't.

Yes, it will.

No, it won't. And not all co-eds have large breasts. You really ought to speak to a mental health specialist about this absurd fixation you have with the size of your chest. It's not healthy.

Oh, there's the bell, THANK GOD!!!!!!

Wednesday, April 30, Gifted and Talented

IT IS NOT FAIR. I mean, I know my friends have more important things on their minds than the prom – Michael is busy with graduation and Skinner Box, his band; Lilly's got her TV show which, even if it is still only on the public access channel, continues to break new ground in television news journalism every week; Tina's still looking for a guy to replace her ex, Dave Farouq El-Abar, in her heart; Shameeka's got cheerleading, and Ling Su has Art Club and all.

But, HELLO!!!!!!! Isn't ANYONE thinking about the prom? ANYONE AT ALL, besides me and Shameeka??? I mean, it is next week, and Michael hasn't asked me yet. NEXT WEEK!!!! Shameeka is right, if we are going, we really have to start planning for it now.

Only how am I supposed to ask Michael whether or not he is planning on asking me? You can't do that. That fully ruins the romance of the thing. I mean, it's bad enough that my own mother was the one who had to propose when she found out she was pregnant. When I asked her how Mr G popped the question, my mom said he didn't. She said the conversation went like this:

Helen Thermopolis: 'Frank, I'm pregnant.'

Mr Gianini: 'Oh. OK. What do you want to do?'

Helen Thermopolis: 'Marry you.'

Mr Gianini: 'OK.'

HELLO!!!!!!!!! Where is the romance in THAT???? 'Frank, I'm pregnant, let's get married.' 'OK.' AAAAACKKKK!!!!

What about:

Helen Thermopolis: 'Frank, the seed from your loins has sprung to fruition in my womb.'

Mr Gianini: 'Helen, I have never heard such joyous news in all of my thirty-nine years. Will you do me the very great honour of becoming my bride, my soul mate, my life partner?'

Helen Thermopolis: 'Yes, my sweet protector.'

Mr Gianini: 'My life! My hope! My love!'
(KISS)

That's how it SHOULD have gone. Look at the difference. It is so much better when the guy asks the girl instead of the girl asking the guy.

So obviously, I can't just walk up to Michael and be all:

Mia Thermopolis: 'So are we going to the prom or what? 'Cause I need to buy my dress.'

Michael Moscovitz: 'OK.'

NO!!!!!!!!! That will never work!!!!!!! Michael has to ask ME. He has to be all:

Michael Moscovitz: 'Mia, the past five months have been the most magical of my life. Being with you is like having a refreshing ocean breeze blowing constantly

	against my passion-fevered brow. You are my sole reason for living, the purpose for which my heart beats. It would be the greatest honour of my life if I could escort you to the Senior Prom, where you must promise to dance every single dance with me, except the fast ones that we will sit down during because they are lame.'
Mia Thermopolis:	'Oh, Michael, this is so sudden! I simply wasn't expecting it. But I adore you with every fibre of my being, so of course I will go to the prom with you, and dance every single dance with you, except the fast ones because they are lame.' (KISS)

That's how it should go. If there is any justice in the world, that's how it WILL go.

But WHEN? When is he going to ask me? I mean, look at him over there. He is so clearly NOT thinking about the prom. He is arguing with Boris Pelkowski over the rhythm of their band's new song, 'Rock Throwing Youths', a searing criticism of the current situation in the Middle East. I am sorry, but someone who is worrying about the situation in the Middle East is HARDLY LIKELY TO REMEMBER TO ASK HIS GIRLFRIEND TO THE PROM.

This is what I get for falling in love with a genius.

Not that Michael isn't a perfectly attentive boyfriend. I mean, I know a lot of girls – like Tina, for instance – are totally jealous of me for having such a hot and yet so incredibly supportive life mate. I mean, Michael ALWAYS sits next to me at lunch, every single day, except Tuesdays and Thursdays when he has a Computer Club meeting during lunch. But even then he gazes at me longingly from the Computer Club table on the other side of the caf.

Well, OK, maybe not longingly, but he smiles at me sometimes when he catches me staring at him from across the cafeteria, trying to figure out who he looks like the most, Josh Hartnett or a dark-haired Heath Ledger.

And OK, so Michael doesn't feel comfortable with public displays of affection – which is no big surprise seeing as how everywhere I go I am followed by a six-foot-five Swedish expert in krav maga – so it's not like he ever kisses me in school or holds hands in the hallway or sticks his hand in the back pocket of my overalls when we are strolling down the street or leans his body up against mine when we're at my locker the way Josh does to Lana . . .

But when we are alone . . . when we are alone . . . when we are alone . . .

Oh, all right, so we haven't got to second base yet. Well, except for that one time during Spring Break when we were building that house. But I think that might have been a mistake on account of my hammer was hanging by its claw from the bib of my overalls and Michael asked to borrow it and I couldn't hand it to him because I was busy holding up that sheet of dry wall so his hand sort of accidentally brushed up against my chest while he was reaching . . .

Still. We are perfectly happy together. More than happy. We are *ecstatically* happy.

SO WHY HASN'T HE ASKED ME TO THE PROM?????????????????

Oh, my God. Lilly just leaned over to see what I was writing and saw that last part. That is what I get for using capital letters. She just went, 'Oh, God, don't tell me you're *still* obsessing over that.'

As if that weren't bad enough, Michael looked up and went, 'Obsessing over what?'!!!!!!!!!!!

I thought Lilly was going to say something!!!!!!!!!! I thought she was going to go, 'Oh, Mia's just having an embolism because you haven't asked her to the prom yet.'

But she just went, 'Mia's working on an essay about methane ice-worms.'

Michael said, 'Oh,' and turned back to his guitar.

Trust Boris to go, 'Oh, methane ice-worms. Yes, of course. If they turn out to be ubiquitous on shallow sea-floor gas deposits, they could have a significant impact on how methane deposits are formed and dissolve in seawater, and how we go about mining and otherwise harvesting natural gas as a source of energy.'

Which, you know, is good to know for my essay and all, but seriously. Why does he even know this?

I don't know how Lilly puts up with him. I really don't.

Wednesday, April 30, French

Thank God for Tina Hakim Baba. At least SHE understands how I feel. AND she totally sympathizes. She says that it has always been her dream to go to the prom with the man she loves – like Molly Ringwald dreamed of going to the prom with Andrew McCarthy.

Sadly for Tina, however, the man she loves – or once loved – dumped her for a girl named Jasmine with turquoise braces. But Tina says she will learn to love again, if she can find a man willing to break down the self-defensive emotional wall she has built-up around herself since Dave Farouq El-Abar's betrayal. It was looking like Peter Hu, whom Tina met over Spring Break, might succeed, but Peter's obsession with Korn soon drove her away, as it would any right-thinking woman.

Tina thinks Michael is going to ask tomorrow, on my birthday. About the prom, I mean. Oh, please let that be true! It would be the best birthday present anyone has ever given me. Except for when my mom gave me Fat Louie, of course.

Except I hope he doesn't do it, you know. In front of my family. Because Michael is coming out with us on my birthday. We are going to dinner tomorrow night with Grandmere and my dad and Mom and Mr Gianini. Oh, and Lars, of course. And then on Saturday night, my mom is having a big blow-out party for me and all of my friends at the Loft (that is, providing she can still walk by then, on account of her you-know-what).

I haven't mentioned Mom's problem with her you-know-what to Michael, though. I believe in having a fully open and honest relationship with the man you love, but seriously, there are some things he just doesn't need to know. Like that your pregnant mother has problems with her bladder.

I only invited Michael to both the dinner and the party. Everyone else, including Lilly, is just invited to the party. Hello, how unromantic would *that* be, to have your birthday dinner with your mom, your stepdad, your real dad, your grandma, your bodyguard, your boyfriend and his sister. At least I was able to narrow it down a little.

Michael said he would come to both, the dinner and the party, which I thought was very brave of him and further proof that he is the best boyfriend that ever lived.

If I could just nail him down on this prom thing, though.

Tina says I should just come out and ask him. Michael, I mean. Tina is a staunch believer in being very up front with boys, on account of how she played games with Dave and he fled from her into the arms of the turquoise-toothed Jasmine. But I don't know. I mean, this is the PROM. The prom is special. I don't want to mess it up. Especially since I'm only going to be able to see Michael for like another month or so before my dad drags me off to Genovia for the summer. Which is so totally unfair. 'But you signed a contract, Mia,' is what he keeps saying to me. My dad, I mean.

Yeah, I signed a contract, like a *year* ago. OK, eight months ago. How was I supposed to know then that I would fall madly and passionately in love? Well, OK, I was madly and passionately in love back then, but hello, it was with somebody totally different. And the real object of my affections didn't like me back. Or if he did (he says he did!!!!!!!!!), I didn't exactly know it, did I?

And now my dad expects me to spend two whole months away from the man to whom I have pledged my heart?

Oh, no. I don't think so.

It is one thing to spend Christmas in Genovia. I mean, that was only thirty-two days. But July *and* August? I'm supposed to spend two whole *months* away from him?

Well, it is so not happening. My dad thinks he's being all reasonable about it, since originally he was going to make me spend the WHOLE summer in Genovia. But since Mom's due date is in June, he's acting like it's this big concession to let me stay in New York until the baby's born. Oh, yeah. Thanks, Dad.

Well, he is just going to have to exhale, because if he thinks I am spending the last two months of the first summer of my life with an actual boyfriend *away from* said boyfriend, then he is in for a very big surprise. I mean, what is there even to *do* in Genovia in the summer? NOTHING. The place is lousy with tourists (well, so is New York, but whatever, New York tourists are different, they are much less repulsive than the ones who go to Genovia) and Parliament isn't even in session. What am I going to *do* all day? I mean, at least here there'll be the whole baby thing, once my mom hurries up and has it, which I actually wish would be sooner than June because it is like living with Sasquatch. I swear to God, all she does is stomp around and grunt at us, she is in such a bad mood on account of all the water weight and the pressure on her you-know-what (my mom shares WAY too much information sometimes).

Whatever happened to pregnancy being the most magical time in a woman's life? Whatever happened to being full of the wonder and glory of creation?

Clearly my mom has never heard of either of those things.

The point is, this is Michael's last summer before he leaves for college. And OK, the college he is going to is just a few subway stops uptown, but whatever, I am not going to see him at school any more after this. For instance, he is no longer going to be swinging by my Algebra class to give me strawberry gummy worms like he did this morning, to the wrath of Lana Weinberger, who is just jealous because her boyfriend Josh NEVER surprises her with gummy worms.

No. Michael and I should be spending this summer together, having lovely picnics in Central Park (except that I hate having picnics in public parks because all the homeless people come around and look longingly at your egg-salad sandwich, or whatever, and then you have to give it to them because you feel so guilty about having so much when others have nothing and they are usually not even grateful, they usually say something like, 'I hate egg salad,' which is very ungracious if you ask me) and seeing *Tosca* on the Great Lawn (except that I hate opera because everybody dies all tragically at the end, but whatever). There's still strolling through the San Gennaro festival and Michael maybe winning me a stuffed animal at the air-rifle booth (except that he is ethically opposed to guns, as am I, except if you are a member of law enforcement or a soldier or whatever, and those stuffed animals they give away at fairs are fully made by children in Guatemalan sweatshops).

Still. It could have been totally romantic, if my dad hadn't gone and ruined it all.

Lilly says my father clearly has abandonment issues from when his father died and left him all alone with Grandmere and that's why he is being so totally rigid on the whole spending-my-summer-in-Genovia thing.

Except that Grandpere died when my dad was in his twenties, not exactly his formative years, so I don't see how this is possible. But Lilly says the human psyche works in strange and mysterious ways and that I should just accept that and move on.

I think the person with issues might be Lilly on account of how it's been almost four months since her cable access television programme *Lilly Tells It Like It Is* was optioned by the producers who made the movie based on my life and they still haven't managed to find a studio willing to tape a pilot episode. But Lilly says the entertainment industry works in strange and mysterious ways (just like the human psyche) and that she has accepted it and moved on, just like I should about the whole Genovian thing.

BUT I WILL NEVER ACCEPT THE FACT THAT MY DAD WANTS ME TO SPEND SIXTY-TWO WHOLE DAYS AWAY FROM THE MAN I LOVE!!!! NEVER!!!!!!!!!!!!!

Tina says I should try to get a summer internship somewhere here in Manhattan, and then my dad won't be able to make me go to Genovia, on account of how that would be shirking my responsibilities here. Only I don't know of any place that would want a princess for an intern. I mean, what would Lars do all day while I was alphabetizing files or making photocopies or whatever?

When I walked in before class started, Mademoiselle Klein was showing some of the sophomore girls a picture of this slinky dress she is ordering from Victoria's Secret to wear to the prom. She is a chaperone. So is Mr Wheeton, the track coach and my Health and Safety teacher. They are going out together. Tina says it is the most romantic thing she has ever heard of, besides my mom and Mr Gianini. I have not revealed to Tina the painful truth about my mom being the one to propose to Mr Gianini, because I don't want to crush all of Tina's fondest dreams. I have also hidden from her the fact that I don't think Prince William is ever going to email her back. That's on account of how I gave her a fake email address for him. Well, I had to do something to get her to quit bugging me for it. And I'm sure whoever is at princew@windsorcastle.com is very appreciative of her five-page testimonial on how much she loves him, especially when he is wearing his polo jodhpurs.

I sort of feel bad about lying to Tina, but it was only to make her feel better. And someday I really will get Prince William's real email address for her. I just have to wait until somebody important dies, and I see him at the state funeral. It probably won't be long – Elizabeth Taylor is looking pretty shaky.

Il me faut des lunettes de soleil.
Didier demand à essayer la jupe.

I don't know how someone who is as deeply in love with Mr Wheeton like Mademoiselle Klein is supposed to be can assign us so much homework. Whatever happened to spring, when the world is mud-luscious and the little lame balloon-man whistles far and wee?

Nobody who teaches at this school has a grain of romance in them. Ditto most of the people who go here, too. Without Tina, I would be truly lost.

Jeudi, j'ai fait de l'aerobic.

Homework

Algebra: pages 279–300
English: *The Iceman Cometh*
Biology: Finish ice-worm essay
Health and Safety: pages 154–160
Gifted and Talented: As if
French: *Ecrivez une histoire personnelle*
World Civ.: pages 310–330

Wednesday, April 30, in the limo on the way home from the Plaza

Grandmere fully knows there is something up with me. But she thinks it's because I'm upset over the whole going-to-Genovia-for-the-summer thing. As if I don't have much more immediate concerns.

'We shall have a lovely time in Genovia this summer, Amelia,' Grandmere kept saying. 'They are currently excavating a tomb they believe might belong to your ancestress, Princess Rosagunde. I understand that the mummification processes used in the 700s were really every bit as advanced as ones employed by the Egyptians. You might actually get to gaze upon the face of the woman who founded the royal house of Renaldo.'

Great. I get to spend my summer looking up some old mummy's nasal cavity. My dream come true. Oh no, sorry, Mia. No hanging out at Coney Island with your one true love for you. No fun volunteer work tutoring little kids with their reading. No cool summer job at Kim's Video, rewinding *Princess Mononoke* and *Fist of the North Star*. No, you get to commune with a thousand-year-old corpse. Yippee!

I guess I must be more upset about the whole Michael thing than even I thought, because midway through Grandmere's lecture on tipping (manicurists: $3; pedicurists: $5; cab drivers: $2 for rides under $10, $5 for airport trips; double the tax for restaurant bills except in states where the tax is less than 8 per cent; etc.) she went, 'AMELIA! WHAT IS THE MATTER WITH YOU?'

I must have jumped about ten feet into the air. I was totally thinking about Michael. About how good he would look in a tux. About how I could buy him a red-rose boutonnière, just the plain kind without the baby's breath because boys don't like baby's breath. And I could wear a black dress, one of those off-one-shoulder kinds like Kirsten Dunst always wears to movie premieres, with a butterfly hem and a slit up the side, and high heels with laces that go up your ankle.

Only Grandmere says black on girls under eighteen is morbid, that off-one-shoulder gowns and butterfly hems look like they were made that way accidentally, and that those lace-up high heels look like the kind of shoes Russell Crowe wore in *Gladiator* – not a flattering look on most women.

But whatever. I could fully put on body glitter. Grandmere doesn't even KNOW about body glitter.

'Amelia!' Grandmere was saying. She couldn't yell too loud because her face was still stinging from the chemical peel. I could tell because Rommel, her mostly hairless miniature poodle who looks like he's seen a chemical peel or two himself, kept leaping up into her lap and trying to lick her face, like it was a piece of raw meat or whatever. Not to gross anybody out, but that's sort of how it looked. Or like Grandmere had accidentally stepped in front of one of those hoses they used to get the radiation off Cher in that movie *Silkwood*.

'Are you listening to a single word I've said?' Grandmere looked peeved. Mostly because her face hurt, I'm sure. 'This could be very important to you someday, if you happen to be stranded without a calculator or your limo.'

'Sorry, Grandmere,' I said. I *was* sorry, too. Tipping is totally my worst thing, on account of how it involves maths and also thinking quickly on your feet. When I order food from Number One Noodle Son back home I always have to ask the restaurant while I am still on the phone with them ordering how much it will be so I can work on calculating how much to tip the delivery guy before he gets to the door. Because otherwise he ends up standing there for like ten minutes while I figure out how much to give him for a seventeen dollar and fifty cent order. It's embarrassing.

'I don't know where your head's been lately, Amelia,' Grandmere said, all crabby. Well, you would be crabby too if you'd paid money to have the top two or three layers of your skin chemically removed. 'I hope you're not still worrying about your mother, and that ridiculous home birth she's planning. I told you before, your mother's forgotten what labour feels like. As soon as her contractions kick in, she'll be begging to be taken to the hospital for a nice epidural.'

I sighed. Although the fact that my mother is choosing a home birth over a nice safe clean hospital birth – where there are oxygen tanks and candy machines and Dr Kovach – *is* upsetting, I have been trying not to think about it too much . . . especially since I suspect Grandmere is right. My mother cries like a baby when she stubs her toe. How is she going to withstand hours and hours of labour pains? She was much younger when she gave birth to me. Her thirty-six-year-old body is in no shape for the rigours of childbirth. She doesn't even work out!

Grandmere fastened her evil eye on to me.

'I suppose the fact the weather's starting to get warm isn't helping,' she said. 'Young people tend to get flighty in the spring. And, of course, there's your birthday tomorrow.'

I fully let Grandmere think that's what was distracting me. My birthday and the fact that my friends and I are all twitterpated, like Thumper gets in springtime in *Bambi*.

'You are a very difficult person for whom to find a suitable birthday gift, Amelia,' Grandmere said, reaching for her Sidecar and her cigarettes. Grandmere has her cigarettes sent to her from Genovia, so she doesn't have to pay the astronomical tax on them that they charge here in New York, in the hopes of making people quit smoking on account of it being too expensive. Except that it isn't working, since all of the people in Manhattan who smoke are just hopping on the PATH train and going over to New Jersey to buy their cigarettes.

'You are not the jewellery type,' Grandmere went on, lighting up and puffing away. 'And you don't seem to have any appreciation whatsoever for couture. And it isn't as if you have any hobbies.'

I pointed out to Grandmere that I do have a hobby. Not just a hobby, even, but a *calling*: I write.

Grandmere just waved her hand, and said, 'But not a *real* hobby. You don't play golf or paint.'

It kind of hurt my feelings that Grandmere doesn't think writing is a real hobby. She is going to be very surprised when I grow up and become a published author. Then writing will not only be my hobby, but my career. Maybe the first book I write will be about her. I will call it, *Clarisse: Ravings of a Royal*, A Memoir, by Princess Mia of Genovia. And Grandmere won't be able to sue, just like Daryl Hannah couldn't sue when they made that movie about her and John F. Kennedy Junior, because all of it will be one hundred per cent true. HA!

'What DO you want for your birthday, Amelia?' Grandmere asked.

I had to think about that one. Of course, what I REALLY want, Grandmere can't give me. But I figured it wouldn't hurt to ask. So I drew up the following list:

What I would like for my 15th birthday, by Mia Thermopolis, aged 14 and 364 Days

1. End to world hunger
2. New pair overalls, size eleven
3. New cat brush for Fat Louie (he chewed the handle off the last one)
4. Bungee cords for palace ballroom (so I can do air ballet like Lara Croft in *Tomb Raider*)
5. New baby brother or sister, safely delivered
6. Elevation of orcas to endangered list so Puget Sound can receive federal aid to clean up polluted breeding/feeding grounds
7. Lana Weinberger's head on a silver platter (just kidding – well, not really)
8. My own mobile phone
9. Grandmere to quit smoking
10. Michael Moscovitz to ask me to the Senior Prom

In composing this list, it occurred to me that sadly the only thing on it that I am likely to get for my birthday is item number 2. I mean, I *am* going to get a new brother or sister, but not for another month, at the earliest. No way was Grandmere going to go for the quitting smoking thing or the bungee cords. World hunger and the orca thing are sort of out of the hands of anyone I know. My dad says I would just lose and/or destroy a mobile, like I did the laptop he got me (that wasn't my fault. I only took it out of my backpack and set it on that sink for a second while I was looking for my Chapstick. It is not my fault that Lana Weinberger bumped into me and that the sinks at our school are all stopped up. That computer was only underwater for a few seconds, it fully should have worked again when it dried out. Except that even Michael, who is a technological as well as musical genius, couldn't save it).

Of course the one thing Grandmere fixated on was the last one, the one I only admitted to her in a moment of weakness and should never have mentioned in the first place, considering the fact that in twenty-four hours, she and Michael will be sharing a table at Les Hautes Manger for my birthday dinner.

'What is the prom?' Grandmere wanted to know. 'I don't know this word.'

I couldn't believe it. But then, Grandmere hardly ever watches TV, not even *Murder She Wrote* or *Golden Girls* reruns, like everyone else her age, so it was unlikely she'd ever have caught an airing of *Pretty in Pink* on TBS or whatever.

'It's a dance, Grandmere,' I said, reaching for my list. 'Never mind.'

'And the Moscovitz boy hasn't asked you to this dance yet?' Grandmere wanted to know. 'When is it?'

'A week from Saturday,' I said. 'Can I have that list back now?'

'Why don't you go without him?' Grandmere demanded. She let out a cackle, then seemed to think better of it, since I think it hurt her face to stretch her cheek muscles like that. 'Like you did last time. That'll show him.'

'I can't,' I said. 'It's only for seniors. I mean, seniors can take underclassmen, but underclassmen can't go on their own. Lilly says I should just ask Michael whether or not he's going, but—'

'NO!' Grandmere's eyes bulged. At first I thought she was choking on an ice cube, but it turned out she was just shocked. Grandmere's got eyeliner tattooed all the way around her lids like Michael Jackson, so she doesn't have to mess with her make-up every morning. So when her eyes bulge, well, it's pretty noticeable.

'You cannot *ask him*,' Grandmere said. 'How many times do I have to tell you, Amelia? Men are like little woodland creatures. You have to *lure* them to you with tiny breadcrumbs and soft words of encouragement. You cannot simply whip out a rock and conk them over the head with it.'

I certainly agree with this. I don't want to do any conking where Michael is concerned. But I don't know about breadcrumbs.

'Well,' I said. 'So what do I do? The prom is in less than two weeks, Grandmere. If I'm going to go, I've got to know soon.'

'You must hint around the subject,' Grandmere said. '*Subtly*.'

I thought about this. 'Like do you mean I should go, "I saw the most perfect dress for the prom the other day in the Victoria's Secret catalogue?"'

'Exactly,' Grandmere said. 'Only of course a princess never purchases anything off the rack, Amelia, and NEVER from a catalogue.'

'Right,' I said. 'But Grandmere, don't you think he'll see right through that?'

Grandmere snorted, then seemed to regret it, and held her drink up to her face, as if the ice in the glass was soothing to her tender skin. 'You are talking about a seventeen-year-old boy, Amelia,' she said. 'Not a master spy. He won't have the slightest idea what you are about, if you do it subtly enough.'

But I don't know. I mean, I have never been very good at being subtle. Like the other day I tried subtly to mention to my mother that Ronnie, our neighbour who Mom trapped in the hallway on the way to the incinerator room, might not have wanted to hear about how many times my mom has to get up and pee every night now that the baby is pressing so hard against her bladder. My mom just looked at me and went, 'Do you have a death wish, Mia?'

Mr Gianini and I have decided that we will be very relieved when my mom finally has this baby.

I am pretty sure Ronnie would agree.

Thursday, May 1, 12:01 a.m.

Well. That's it. I'm fifteen now. Not a girl. Not yet a woman. Just like Britney.

HA HA HA.

I don't actually feel any different than I did a minute ago, when I was fourteen. I certainly don't LOOK any different. I'm the same five foot nine, thirty-two-A-bra-size freak I was when I turned fourteen. Maybe my hair looks a little better, since Grandmere made me get highlights and Paolo's been trimming it as it grows out. It is almost to my chin now, and not so triangular shaped as before.

Other than that, I'm sorry, but there's nothing. Nada. No difference. Zilch.

I guess all of my fifteeness is going to have to be on the inside, since it sure isn't showing on the outside.

I just checked my email to see if anybody remembered, and I already have five birthday messages, one from Lilly, one from Tina, one from my cousin Hank (I can't believe HE remembered. He's a famous model now and I almost never see him any more – no big loss – except half-naked on billboards or the sides of telephone booths, which is especially embarrassing if he's wearing tighty-whities), one from my cousin Prince René and one from Michael.

The one from Michael is the best. It's a cartoon he's made himself, of a girl in a tiara with a big orange cat opening a giant present. When she gets all the wrapping off, these words burst out of the box, with all these fireworks: HAPPY BIRTHDAY, MIA, and in smaller letters, Love, Michael.

Love. LOVE!!!!!!!!!!!

Even though we have been going out for more than four months, I still get a thrill when he says – or writes – that word. In reference to me, I mean. Love. LOVE!!!!! He LOVES me!!!!!

So what's taking him so long about the prom thing, I'd like to know?

Now that I am fifteen, it is time that I put away childish things, like the guy in the poem, and begin to live my life as the adult that I am striving to become. According to Carl Jung, the famous psychoanalyst, in order to achieve *self-actualization – acceptance, peace, contentment, purposefulness, fulfilment, health, happiness and joy* – one must practise *compassion, love, charity, warmth, forgiveness, friendship, kindness, gratitude and trust.* Therefore, from now on, I pledge to:

1. Stop biting my nails. I really mean it this time
2. Make decent grades
3. Be nicer to people, even Lana Weinberger
4. Write faithfully in my journal every day
5. Start – and finish – a novel. Write one, I mean, not read one
6. Get it published before I turn 20
7. Be more understanding of Mom and what she is going through now that she is in the last trimester of her pregnancy
8. Stop using Mr G's face-razor on my legs. Buy my own razors
9. Try to be more sympathetic to Dad's abandonment issues while also getting out of having to spend July and August in Genovia
10. Figure out way to get Michael Moscovitz to take me to the prom without stooping to trickery and/or grovelling

Once I've done all this, I should become fully self-actualized and ready to experience some well-deserved joy. And really, everything on that list is fairly doable. I mean, yes, it took Margaret Mitchell ten years to write *Gone With the Wind*, but I am only fifteen, so even if it takes me ten years to finish my own novel, I will still only be twenty-five by the time I get it published, which is only five years behind schedule.

The only problem is I don't really know what I'm going to write a novel about. But I'm sure I'll think of something soon. Maybe I should start practising with some short stories or haikus or something.

The prom thing, though. THAT is going to be hard. Because I truly do not want Michael to feel pressured about this. But I have GOT TO GO TO THE PROM!!! IT IS MY LAST CHANCE!!!!!!!

I hope Tina is right, and that Michael intends to ask me tonight at dinner.

OH PLEASE GOD LET TINA BE RIGHT!!!!!!!!!

Thursday, May 1, MY BIRTHDAY, Algebra

Josh asked Lana to the prom.

He asked her last night, after the varsity lacrosse game. The Lions won. According to Shameeka, who hung around after the junior varsity game, at which she'd cheered, Josh scored the winning goal. Then, as all the Albert Einstein fans poured out on to the field, Josh whipped off his shirt and swung it around in the air a few times, à la Mia Hamm, only of course Josh wasn't wearing a sports bra underneath. Shameeka says she was astounded by the lack of hair on Josh's chest. She said he was in no way Hugh Jackman-like in the goody trail department.

This, like the trouble my mother is currently having with her bladder, is really more than I want to know.

Anyway, Lana was on the sidelines, in her little sleeveless blue-and-gold AEHS cheerleading micro-mini. When Josh whipped his shirt off, she went running out on to the field, whooping. Then she leaped into his arms – which, considering that he was probably all sweaty, was a pretty risky endeavour, if you ask me – and they Frenched until Principal Gupta came over and whacked Josh on the back of the head with her clipboard. Then Shameeka says that Josh put Lana down and said, 'Go to the prom with me, babe?'

And Lana said yes, and then ran squealing over to all her fellow cheerleaders to tell them.

And I know that one of my resolutions now that I am fifteen is that I am going to be nicer to people, including Lana, but really, I am having a hard time right now keeping myself from stabbing my pencil into the back of her head. Well, not really, because I don't believe violence ever solves anything. Well, except for when it comes to getting rid of Nazis and terrorists and all. But really, Lana is practically

GLOATING. Before class started, she was fully on her mobile, telling everyone. Her mother is taking her to the Nicole Miller store in SoHo on Saturday to buy her a dress.

A black, off-one-shoulder dress, with a butterfly hem and a slit up one side. She's getting high heels that lace up the ankles, too, at Saks.

No doubt body glitter as well.

And I know I have a lot to feel grateful for. I mean, I have:

1. A super, loving boyfriend who, when the royal limo pulled over to pick him and Lilly up on the way to school today, presented me with a box of cinnamon mini-muffins, my favourites, from the Manhattan Muffin Company, which he'd gone all the way down to Tribeca really early in the morning to get me, in honour of my birthday.
2. An excellent best friend, who gave me a bright-pink cat collar for Fat Louie with the words *I Belong to Princess Mia* written on it in rhinestones that she'd hot-glue gunned on herself while watching old *Buffy the Vampire Slayer* reruns.
3. A great mom who, even if she does talk a little too much lately about her bodily functions, nevertheless dragged herself out of bed this morning to wish me a happy birthday.
4. A great stepdad who swore he wouldn't say anything in class about my birthday and embarrass me in front of everyone.
5. A dad who will probably give me something good for my birthday when I see him at dinner tonight, and a grandmother who, if she won't actually give me something I like, will at least WANT me to like it, whatever heinous thing it ends up being.

I seriously don't mean to be ungrateful for all of that, because it is so much more than so many people have. I mean, like kids in Appalachia – they are happy if they get socks for their birthday, or whatever, since their parents spend all their money on hooch.

But HELLO. IS IT TOO MUCH TO ASK THAT I GET THE ONE THING FOR MY BIRTHDAY THAT I HAVE ALWAYS WANTED – and that is ONE PERFECT NIGHT AT THE PROM??????????????? I mean, Lana Weinberger is getting that, and she is not even striving to become self-actualized. She probably doesn't even know what self-actualization *means*. She has never been kind to anyone in her whole entire life. So why does SHE get to go to the prom?

I am telling you, there is no justice in the world.

NONE.

Expressions with radicals can be multiplied or divided as long as the root power or value under the radical is the same.

Thursday, May 1, MY BIRTHDAY, Gifted and Talented

Today, in honour of my birthday, Michael ate lunch at my table, instead of with the Computer Club, even though it's a Thursday. It was actually quite romantic, because it turns out that not only had he paid that little visit to the Manhattan Muffin Company this morning, but he also ditched fourth period and snuck out to Wu Liang Ye to get me the cold sesame noodles I like so much and can't get downtown, the ones that are so spicy you need to drink TWO cans of Coke before your tongue feels normal again after you eat them.

Which was totally sweet of him, and was actually even a bit of a relief, because I have been quite worried about what Michael is going to give me as a birthday present, because I know he must feel like he has a lot to live up to, seeing as how I got him moon rocks for his birthday.

I hope he realizes that, being a princess and all, I have access to moon rocks, but that I truly do not expect people to give me gifts that are of moon rock quality. I mean, I hope Michael knows that I would be happy with a simple, 'Mia, will you go to the prom with me?' And, of course, a Tiffany's charm bracelet with a charm that says *Property of Michael Moscovitz* on it that I could wear everywhere I go and so the next time some European prince asks me to dance at a ball I can hold up the bracelet and be all, 'Sorry, can't you read? I belong to Michael Moscovitz.'

Except Tina says even though it would be totally great if Michael got this for me, she doesn't think he will, because giving a girl – even his girlfriend – a chain that says *Property of Michael Moscovitz* seems a little presumptuous and not something Michael would do. I showed Tina the collar Lilly had given me for Fat Louie, but Tina says that isn't the same thing.

Is it wrong of me to want to be my boyfriend's property? I mean, it's not like I'm willing to usurp my own identity or take his name or anything if we got married (being a princess, even if I wanted to, I couldn't, unless I abdicated). In fact, chances are, the guy I marry is going to have to take MY name.

I just, you know, wouldn't mind a LITTLE possessiveness.

Uh-oh, something is going on. Michael just got up and went to the door to make sure Mrs Hill was firmly ensconced in the Teachers' Lounge, and Boris just came out of the supply closet, but the bell hasn't rung yet. What's up with that?

Thursday, May 1, still MY BIRTHDAY, French

I guess I needn't have worried about what Michael was going to get me for my birthday, because just now his band showed up – yes, his band, Skinner Box, right here in the G and T room. Well, Boris was already here because he is supposed to practise his violin during G and T, but the other band members – Felix, the drummer with the goatee, tall Paul the keyboardist and Trevor the guitar-player – all cut class to set up in the G and T classroom and play me a song Michael wrote just for me. It went:

> Combat boots and veggie burgers
> Just one glance gives me the shivers
> There she goes
> Princess of my heart
>
> Hates social injustice and nicotine
> She's no ordinary beauty queen
> There she goes
> Princess of my heart
>
> Chorus: *Princess of my heart*
> *Oh I don't know where to start*
> *Say I'll be your prince*
> *Till this lifetime ends.*
>
> *Princess of my heart*
> *I loved you from the start*
> *Say you love me too*
> *Over my heart you so rule.*
>
> Promise you won't execute me
> with those gorgeous smiles you shoot me

There she goes
Princess of my heart

You don't even have to knight me
Every time you laugh you smite me
There she goes
Princess of my heart

Chorus: *Princess of my heart*
Oh I don't know where to start
Say I'll be your prince
Till this lifetime ends.

Princess of my heart
I loved you from the start
Say you love me too
and then together we will rule.

And this time there was no question the song was about me, like there was that time Michael played me that 'Tall Drink of Water' song he wrote!

Anyway, the whole school heard Michael's song about me because Skinner Box had their amps turned up so loud. Mrs Hill and everybody else who was in the Teachers' Lounge came out of it, waited politely for Skinner Box to finish the song, then gave the whole band detention.

And, OK, on Mademoiselle Klein's birthday, Mr Wheeton had a dozen red roses delivered to her in the middle of fifth period. But he didn't write a song just for her and play it for the whole school to hear.

And yeah, Lana may be going to the prom, but her boyfriend – not to mention his friends – never got detention for her.

So really, except for the whole having-to-spend-July-and-August-in-Genovia thing – oh, and the prom thing – fifteen is looking pretty good so far.

Homework

Algebra: You would think my own stepfather would be nice and not give me homework on MY BIRTHDAY, but no
English: *The Iceman Cometh*
Biology: Ice-worm
Health and Safety: Check with Lilly
Gifted and Talented: As if
French: Check with Tina
World Civ.: God knows

Thursday, May 1, still MY BIRTHDAY, the ladies' room at Les Hautes Manger

OK, this is so my best birthday ever.

I am serious. I mean, even my mom and dad are getting along with each other – or trying to, anyway. It is so sweet. I am so proud of them. You can totally tell my mom's maternity tights are driving her crazy, but she isn't complaining about them a bit, and Dad totally hasn't said anything about the anarchy symbols she's wearing as earrings. And Mr Gianini put Grandmere right off her lecture about his goatee (Grandmere cannot abide facial hair on a man) by telling her that she looks younger and younger every time he sees her. Which you could tell pleased Grandmere no end, since she was smiling all through the appetizers (she can move her lips again now that the inflammation from her chemical peel has finally died down).

I was a little worried that Mr G's observation would cause my mom to go off on the beauty industry and how they are ageist and are constantly trying to propagate the myth that you can't be attractive unless you have the dewy skin of someone my age (which doesn't even make sense since most people my age have zits unless they can afford a fancy dermatologist like the one Grandmere sends me to, who gives me all these prescription unguents so that I can avoid unprincesslike breakouts), but she totally refrained in my honour.

And when Michael showed up late on account of having been in detention, Grandmere didn't say anything mean about it, which was such a relief, because Michael looked kind of flushed, as if he'd run the whole way from his apartment after he'd gone home to change. I guess even Grandmere could tell he'd really tried to be on time.

And even someone who is totally immune to normal human emotion like Grandmere would have to admit that my boyfriend was the handsomest guy in the whole restaurant. Michael's dark hair was sort of flopping over one eye, and he looked SO cute in his non-school-uniform jacket and tie, which is part of the mandatory dress code at Les Hautes Manger (I warned him ahead of time).

Anyway, Michael's showing up was kind of the signal I guess for everyone to start handing me the presents they'd got me.

And what presents! I am telling you, I cleaned up. Being fifteen RULES!

DAD

OK, so Dad got me a very fancy and expensive-feeling pen – to use, he said, to further my writing career (I am using it to write this very journal entry). Of course I would have rather had a season pass to Six Flags Great Adventure theme park for the summer (and permission to stay in this country to use it) but the pen is very nice, all purple and gold, and has *HRH Princess Amelia Renaldo* engraved on it.

MOM and MR G

A mobile phone!!!!!!!!!!! Yes!!!!!!!!! Of my very own!!!!!!!!!

Sadly the mobile phone was accompanied by a lecture from Mom and Mr G about how they'd only bought it for me so that they can reach me when my mom goes into labour, since she wants me to be in the room (this is so not going to happen due to my excessive dislike of seeing anything spurt out of anything else, but you don't argue with a woman who has to pee twenty-four hours a day) while my baby brother or sister is born, and how I'm not to use the phone during school and how it is a domestic-use-only calling policy, nothing transatlantic, so when I am in Genovia don't think I can call Michael on it.

But I didn't pay any attention, because YAY! I actually got something on my list!!!!!

GRANDMERE

OK, this is very weird because Grandmere actually gave me something else from my list. Only it wasn't bungee cords, a cat brush or new overalls. It was a letter declaring me the official sponsor of a real live African orphan named Johanna!!!!!!! Grandmere said, 'I can't help you end world hunger, but I suppose I can help you send one little girl to bed every night with a good dinner.'

I was so surprised, I nearly blurted out, 'But, Grandmere! You hate poor people!' because it's true, she totally does. Whenever she sees those runaway teen punk rockers who sit outside Lincoln Center in their leather jackets and Doc Martens, with those signs that say *Homeless and Hungry*, she always snaps at them, 'If you'd stop spending all your money on tattoos and naval rings, you'd be able to afford a nice sublet in NoLita!'

But I guess Johanna is a different story, seeing as how she doesn't have parents back in Westchester who are sick with worry about her.

I don't know what is going on with Grandmere. I fully expected her to give me a mink stole or something equally revolting for my birthday. But getting me something I actually *wanted* . . . helping me to sponsor a starving orphan . . . that is almost *thoughtful* of her. I must say, I am still in a bit of shock over the whole thing.

I think my mom and dad feel the same way. My dad

ordered up a Martini after he saw what Grandmere had given me, and my mom just sat there in total silence for like the first time since she got pregnant. I am not kidding, either.

Then Lars gave me his gift, even though it is not correct Genovian protocol to receive gifts from one's bodyguard (because look what happened to Princess Stephanie of Monaco: her bodyguard gave her a birthday present, and she MARRIED him. Which would have been all right if they'd had anything in common, but Stephanie's bodyguard isn't the least bit interested in eyebrow threading, and Stephanie clearly knows nothing about ju-jitsu, so the whole thing was off to a rocky start to begin with).

Anyway, you could tell Lars had really put a lot of thought into his gift, because it was:

LARS

An authentic New York Police Department Bomb Squad baseball cap, which Lars got from an actual NYPD bomb squad officer once when he was sweeping Grandmere's suite at the Plaza for incendiary devices prior to a visit from the Pope. Which I thought was SO sweet of Lars, because I know how much he treasured that hat, and the fact that he was willing to give it to me is true proof of his devotion, which I highly doubt is of the matrimonial variety, since I happen to know Lars loves Mademoiselle Klein, like all heterosexual men who come within seven feet of her.

But the best present of all was the one from Michael. He didn't give it to me in front of everybody else. He waited until I got up to go to the bathroom just now, and followed me. Then just as I was starting down the stairs to the ladies', he went, 'Mia, this is for you. Happy birthday,' and gave me this flat little box all wrapped up in gold foil.

I was really surprised – almost as surprised as I'd been over Grandmere's gift. I was all, 'Michael, but you already gave me a present! You wrote that song for me! You got detention for me!'

But Michael just went, 'Oh, that. That wasn't your present. This is.'

And I have to admit, the box was little and flat enough that I thought – I really did think – it might have prom tickets in it. I thought maybe, I don't know, that Lilly had told Michael how much I wanted to go to the prom, and that he'd gone and bought the tickets to surprise me.

Well, he surprised me, all right. Because what was in the box wasn't prom tickets.

But still, it was almost as good.

MICHAEL

A necklace with a tiny little silver snowflake hanging from it.

'From when we were at the Non-denominational Winter Dance,' he said, like he was worried I wouldn't get it. 'Remember the paper snowflakes hanging from the ceiling of the gym?'

Of course I remembered the snowflakes. I had one in the drawer of my bedside table.

And, OK, it isn't a prom ticket or a charm with *Property of Michael Moscovitz* written on it, but it comes really, really close.

So I gave Michael a great big kiss right there by the stairs to the ladies' room, in front of all the Les Hautes Manger waiters and the hostess and the coat check girl and everyone. I didn't care who saw. For all I care, *US Weekly* could have snapped all the shots of us they wanted – even run them on the front cover of next week's edition with a caption that says *Mia Makes Out!* – and I wouldn't have blinked an eye. That's how happy I was.

Am. That's how happy I *am.* My fingers are trembling as I write this, because I think, for the first time in my life, it is possible that I have finally, finally reached the upper branches of the Jungian tree of self-actual—

Wait a minute. There is a lot of noise coming from the hallway. Like breaking dishes and a dog barking and someone screaming . . .

Oh, my God. That's *Grandmere* screaming.

Friday, May 2, midnight, the Loft

I should have known it was too good to be true. My birthday, I mean. It was all just going too well. I mean, no prom invitation or cancellation of my trip to Genovia, but, you know, everyone I love (well, almost everyone) sitting at one table, not fighting. Getting everything I wanted (well, almost everything). Michael writing that song about me. And the snowflake necklace. And the mobile phone.

Oh, but wait. This is ME we're talking about. I think that, at fifteen, it's time I admitted what I've known for quite some time now: I am simply not destined to have a normal life. Not a normal life, not a normal family and certainly not a normal birthday.

Granted, this one might have been the exception, if it hadn't been for Grandmere. Grandmere and Rommel.

I ask you, who brings a DOG to a RESTAURANT? I don't care if it's normal in France. NOT SHAVING UNDER YOUR ARMS IF YOU ARE A GIRL IS NORMAL IN FRANCE. Does that maybe TELL you something about France? I mean, for God's sake, they eat SNAILS there. SNAILS. Who in their right mind thinks that if something is normal in France, it is at all socially acceptable here in the US?

I'll tell you who. My grandmother, that's who.

Seriously. She doesn't understand what the fuss is about. She's all, 'But of course I brought Rommel.'

To Les Hautes Manger. To my birthday dinner. My grandmother brought her DOG to MY BIRTHDAY DINNER.

She says it's only because when she leaves Rommel alone, he licks himself until his hair falls out. It is an Obsessive Compulsive Disorder diagnosed by the Royal Genovian vet, and Rommel has prescription medication he is supposed to take to help keep it at bay.

That's right: My grandmother's dog is on Prozac.

But if you ask me, I don't think OCD is Rommel's problem. Rommel's problem is that he lives with Grandmere. If *I* had to live with Grandmere, I would totally lick off all my hair. If my tongue were long enough, anyway.

Still, just because her dog suffers from OCD is NO excuse for Grandmere to bring him to MY BIRTHDAY dinner. In a Hermes handbag. With a broken clasp, no less.

Because what happened while I was in the ladies' room? Oh, Rommel escaped from Grandmere's handbag. And started streaking around the restaurant, desperate to evade capture – as who under Grandmere's tyrannical rule wouldn't?

I can only imagine what the patrons of Les Hautes Manger must have thought, seeing this eight-pound hairless miniature poodle zipping in and out from beneath the tablecloths. Actually, I know what they thought. I know what they thought, because Michael told me later. They thought Rommel was a giant rat.

And it's true, without hair he does have a very rodent-like appearance.

But still, I don't think climbing up on to their chairs and shrieking their heads off was necessarily the most helpful thing to do about it. Although Michael did say a number of the tourists whipped out digital cameras and started shooting away. I am sure there is going to be a headline in some Japanese newspaper tomorrow about the giant rat problem of the Manhattan four-star restaurant scene.

Anyway, I didn't see what happened next, but Michael told me it was just like in a Baz Luhrmann movie, only Nicole Kidman was nowhere to be seen: this busboy who apparently hadn't noticed the ruckus came hustling by, holding this enormous tray of half-empty soup bowls. Suddenly Rommel, who'd almost been cornered by my dad over by the seafood bar, darted into the busboy's path, and the next thing everyone knew, lobster bisque was flying everywhere.

Thankfully, most of it landed on Grandmere. The lobster bisque, I mean. She fully deserved to have her Chanel suit ruined on account of being stupid enough to bring her DOG to MY BIRTHDAY dinner. I so wish I had seen this. No one would admit it later – not even Mom – but I bet it was really, really, really funny to see Grandmere covered in soup. I swear, if that's all I had got for my birthday, I'd have been totally happy.

But by the time I got out of the bathroom, Grandmere had been thoroughly dabbed by the maître d'. All you could see of the soup were these wet parts all over her chest. I completely missed out on all the fun (as usual). Instead, I got there just in time to see the maître d' imperiously ordering the poor busboy to turn in his dish towel: he was fired.

FIRED!!! And for something that was fully not his fault!

Jangbu – that was the busboy's name – totally looked as if he were going to cry. He kept saying over and over again how sorry he was. But it didn't matter. Because if you spill soup on a dowager princess in New York City, you can kiss your career in the restaurant biz goodbye. It would be like if a gourmet cook got caught going to McDonald's in Paris. Or if P. Diddy got caught buying underwear at Wal-Mart. Or if Nicky and Paris Hilton got caught lying around in their Juicy Couture sweats on a Saturday night, watching *National Geographic Explorer*, instead of going out to party. It is simply Not Done.

I tried to reason with the maître d' on Jangbu's behalf, after Michael told me what had happened. I said in no way could Grandmere hold the restaurant responsible for what HER dog had done. A dog she wasn't even supposed to have HAD in the restaurant in the first place.

But it didn't do any good. The last I saw of Jangbu, he was heading sadly back towards the kitchen.

I tried to get Grandmere, who was, after all, the injured party – or the allegedly injured party, since of course she wasn't in the least bit hurt – to talk the maître d' into giving Jangbu his job back. But she remained stubbornly unmoved by my pleas on Jangbu's behalf. Even my reminding her that many busboys are immigrants, new to this country, with families to support back in their native lands, left her cold.

'Grandmere,' I cried in desperation. 'What makes Jangbu so different from Johanna, the African orphan you are sponsoring on my behalf? Both are merely trying to make their way on this planet we call Earth.'

'The difference between Johanna and Jangbu,' Grandmere informed me, as she held Rommel close, trying to calm him down (it took the combined efforts of Michael, my dad, Mr G and Lars to finally catch Rommel, right before he made a run for it through the revolving door and out on to Fifth Avenue and freedom on the miniature-poodle underground railroad), 'is that Johanna did not SPILL SOUP ALL OVER ME!'

God. She is such a CRAB sometimes.

So now here I am, knowing that somewhere in the city – Queens, most likely – is a young man whose family will probably starve, and all because of MY BIRTHDAY. That's right. Jangbu lost his job because I WAS BORN.

I'm sure wherever Jangbu is right now, he is wishing I wasn't. Born, that is.

And I can't say that I blame him one little bit.

Friday, May 2, 1 a.m., the Loft

My snowflake necklace is really nice, though. I am never, ever taking it off.

Friday, May 2, 1:05 a.m., the Loft

Well, except maybe when I go swimming. Because I wouldn't want it to get lost.

Friday, May 2, 1:10 a.m., the Loft

He loves me!

Friday, May 2, Algebra

Oh, my God. It is all over the city. About Grandmere and the incident at Les Hautes Manger last night, I mean. It must be a slow news day, because even *The Post* picked it up. It was right there on the front cover at the news-stand on the corner:

A Royal Mess, screams *The Post.*

Princess and the Pea (Soup), claims *The Daily News* (erroneously, since it wasn't pea soup at all, but lobster bisque).

It even made the *Times*! You would think that the *New York Times* would be above reporting something like that, but there it was, in the Metro section. Lilly pointed it out as she climbed into the limo with Michael this morning.

'Well, your grandmother's certainly done it this time,' Lilly says.

As if I didn't already know it! As if I wasn't already suffering from the crippling guilt of knowing that I was, even in an indirect manner, to blame for Jangbu's loss of livelihood!

Although I do have to admit that I was somewhat distracted from my grief over Jangbu by the fact that Michael looked so incredibly hot, as he does every morning when he gets into my limo. That is because when we come to pick him and Lilly up for school, Michael has always just shaved, and his face is looking all smooth. Michael is not a particularly hairy person but it is true that by the end of the day – which is when we usually end up doing our kissing, since we are both somewhat shy people, I think, and we have the cover of darkness to hide our burning cheeks – Michael's facial hair has gotten a bit on the sandpapery side. In fact, I can't help thinking that it would be much nicer to kiss

Michael in the morning, when his face is all smooth, than at night, when it is all scratchy. Especially his neck. Not that I have ever thought about kissing my boyfriend's neck. I mean, that would just be weird.

Although as far as boys' necks go, Michael has a very nice one. Sometimes on the rare occasions when we are actually alone long enough to start making out, I put my nose next to Michael's neck and just inhale. I know it sounds strange, but Michael's neck smells really, really nice, like soap. Soap and something else. Something that makes me feel like nothing bad could ever happen to me, not when I am in Michael's arms, smelling his neck.

IF ONLY HE WOULD ASK ME TO THE PROM!!!!!!!!! Then I could spend a whole NIGHT smelling his neck, only it would look like we were dancing, so no one, not even Michael, would know.

Wait a minute. What was I saying before I got distracted by the smell of my boyfriend's neck?

Oh yes. Grandmere. Grandmere and Jangbu.

Anyway, none of the newspaper articles about what happened last night mention the part about Rommel. Not one. There is not even a hint of a suggestion that the whole thing might possibly have been Grandmere's own fault. Oh no! Not at all!

But Lilly knows about it, on account of Michael having told her. And she had a lot to say about it.

'What we'll do,' she said, 'is we'll start making signs in Gifted and Talented class, and then we'll go over after school.'

'Go over where?' I wanted to know. I was still busy staring at Michael's smooth neck.

'To Les Hautes Manger,' Lilly said. 'To start the protest.'

'What protest?' All I seemed to be able to think about was

whether my neck smells as good to Michael as his does to me. To tell the truth, I cannot even remember a time when Michael might have smelt my neck. Since he is taller than me, it is very easy for me to put my nose up to his neck and smell it. But for him to smell mine, he would have to lean down, which might look a bit weird, and could conceivably cause whiplash.

'The protest against their unfair dismissal of Jangbu Pinasa!' Lilly shouted.

Great. So now I know what I am doing after school. Like I don't have enough problems, what with:

a) My princess lessons with Grandmere
b) Homework
c) Worrying about the party Mom is having for me Saturday night and the fact that probably no one will show up and even if they do it is entirely possible that my mom and Mr G might do something to embarrass me in front of them, such as complain about their bodily functions or possibly start playing the drums
d) Next week's menu for *The Atom* being due
e) The fact that my father expects me to spend sixty-two days with him in Genovia this summer
f) My boyfriend still not having asked me to the prom

Oh no, let me just FORGET ALL ABOUT all of THAT stuff and worry about Jangbu.

I mean, don't get me wrong, I am totally worried about him, but hello, I have my own problems, too. Like the fact that Mr G just passed back the quizzes from Monday, and mine has a big red C minus on it and a note: *SEE ME.*

Um, hello, Mr G, like I didn't just see you AT BREAKFAST. You couldn't have mentioned this THEN?

Oh my God, Lana just turned around and slapped a copy of *New York Newsday* on my desk. There is a huge picture on the cover of Grandmere leaving Les Hautes Manger with Rommel cowering in her arms, and bits of lobster bisque still stuck to her skirt.

'Why is your family so full of FREAKS?' Lana wants to know.

You know what, Lana? That is a very good question.

Friday, May 2, Bio

I cannot believe Mr G. The *nerve* of him, suggesting that my relationship with Michael is DISTRACTING me from my schoolwork! As if Michael has ever done anything but try to help me to understand Algebra. Hello!

And OK, so Michael comes in to visit me every morning before class starts. So what? How is that harming anyone? I mean, yeah, it makes LANA mad, because Josh Richter NEVER comes in to see HER before class, because he is too busy admiring his own highlights in the men's room mirror. But how is THAT distracting me from my schoolwork?

I am going to have to have a serious talk with my mother, because I think the impending birth of his first child is turning Mr G into a misanthrope. So what if I got a sixty-nine on the last quiz? A person can have an off day, can't she? That does NOT mean that my grades are slipping, or that I am spending too much time with Michael, or thinking about smelling his neck every waking moment of the day, or anything like that.

And Mr G suggesting that I spent the entirety of second period this morning writing in my journal is completely laughable. I fully paid attention to his little lecture about the polynomials towards the last ten minutes or so of class. PLEASE!

And that thing where I wrote HRH Michael Moscovitz Renaldo seventeen times at the bottom of my worksheet was just a JOKE. God. Mr G, what happened to you? You *used* to have a sense of humour.

Friday, May 2, Bio

So . . . did he ask you last night? At your birthday dinner. S

No.

Mia! There are exactly nine days until the prom. You are going to have to take matters into your own hands and just ask him.

SHAMEEKA! You know I can't do that.

Well, it's getting to be crunch time. If he doesn't ask you by the party tomorrow night, you aren't going to be able to say yes if he DOES ask you. I mean, a girl has to have some pride.

That is very easy for someone like you to say, Shameeka. You are a cheerleader.

Yeah. And you're a princess!

You know what I mean.

Mia, you can't let him take you for granted in this way. You have to keep boys on their toes . . . no matter how many songs they write for you, or snowflake necklaces they give you. You've got to let them know YOU'RE in charge.

You sound just like my grandmother sometimes.

EEEEEEEEEEWWWWWWWWWWWW!

Friday, May 2, Gifted and Talented

Oh my God, Lilly will NOT shut up about Jangbu and his plight. Look, I feel for the guy, too, but I am not about to violate the poor man's privacy by trying to track down his home phone number – especially not using a certain royal's BRAND-SPANKING-NEW MOBILE PHONE.

I have not even been able to make ONE call from it. Not ONE. Lilly has already made five.

This busboy thing is totally out of control. Lesley Cho, *The Atom*'s editor-in-chief, stopped by our table at lunch and asked if I could do an in-depth story on the incident for Monday's paper. I realize that now at last I have been given my entrée into real reporting, and not just working the cafeteria beat, but does Lesley really think I am the most appropriate person for this job? I mean, isn't she running the risk of this story being less than completely prejudice-free and unbiased? Sure, I think Grandmere was wrong, but she's still my GRANDMOTHER, for crying out loud.

I am not sure I really appreciate this peek into the seedy underbelly of school newspaper reporting. Working on a novel instead of writing for *The Atom* is starting to look more and more appealing.

Since it is Friday and Michael was up at the bean bar getting me a second helping, and Lilly was otherwise occupied, Tina asked me what I am going to do about Michael's not having asked me to the prom yet.

'What CAN I do?' I wailed. 'I just have to sit around and wait, like Jane Eyre did when Mr Rochester was busy playing billiards with Blanche Ingram and pretending like he didn't know Jane was alive.'

To which Tina replied, 'I really think you should say something. Maybe tomorrow night, at your party?'

Oh, great. I was kind of looking forward to my party – you know, except for the part where Mom was sure to stop everyone at the door and tell them all about her Incredible Shrinking Bladder – but now? No chance. Because I know Tina will be staring at me all night, willing me to ask Michael about the prom. Great. Thanks.

Lilly just handed me this giant sign. It says, LES HAUTES MANGER IS UN-AMERICAN!

I pointed out to Lilly that everyone already knows Les Hautes Manger is un-American. It is a French restaurant. To which Lilly replied, 'Just because its owner was born in France is no reason for him to think he does not have to abide by our nation's laws and social customs.'

I said I thought it was one of our laws that people could pretty much hire and fire who they wanted to. You know, within certain parameters.

'Just whose side are you on in this, anyway, Mia?' Lilly wanted to know.

I said, 'Yours, of course. I mean, Jangbu's.'

But doesn't Lilly realize I have way too many problems of my own to take on an itinerant busboy's as well? I mean, I have the summer to worry about, not to mention my Algebra grade, and an African orphan to support. And I really don't think I can be expected to help get Jangbu's job back when I can't even get my own boyfriend to ask me to the prom.

I gave Lilly her sign back, explaining that I won't be able to come to the protest after school, as I have a princess lesson to attend. Lilly accused me of being more concerned for myself than for Jangbu's three starving children. I asked her how she knew Jangbu even had kids, because so far as I knew this had not been mentioned in any of the newspaper articles about the incident, and Lilly still hadn't managed to get hold of him. But she just said she meant figuratively, not literally.

I am very concerned about Jangbu and his figurative children, it is true. But it is a dog-eat-dog world out there, and right now, I've got problems of my own. I'm almost positive Jangbu would understand.

But I told Lilly I'd try to talk Grandmere into talking the owner of Les Hautes Manger into hiring Jangbu back. I guess it's the least I can do, considering my presence on earth is the reason the poor guy's livelihood was destroyed.

Homework

Algebra: Who knows
English: Who cares
Biology: Whatever
Health and Safety: Please
Gifted and Talented: As if
French: Something
World Civ.: Something else

Friday, May 2, in the limo on the way home from Grandmere's

Grandmere has decided to act like nothing happened last night. Like she didn't bring her poodle to my birthday dinner and get an innocent busboy fired. Like her face wasn't plastered all over the front of every newspaper in Manhattan, minus the *Times*. She was just going on about how in Japan it is considered terrifically rude to poke your chopstick into your rice bowl. Apparently, if you do this, it is a sign of disrespect to the dead, or something.

Whatever. Like I am going to Japan anytime soon. Hello, apparently I am not even going to my own PROM.

'Grandmere,' I said, when I couldn't take it any more. 'Are we going to talk about what happened at dinner last night, or are you just going to pretend like it didn't happen?'

Grandmere looked all innocent. 'I'm sorry, Amelia. I can't think what you mean.'

'Last night,' I said. 'My birthday dinner. At Les Hautes Manger. You got the busboy fired. It was all over the papers this morning.'

'Oh, that.' Grandmere innocently stirred her Sidecar.

'Well?' I asked her. 'What are you going to do about it?'

'Do?' Grandmere looked genuinely surprised. 'Why, nothing. What is there to do?'

I guess I shouldn't have been so shocked. Grandmere can be pretty self-absorbed, when she wants to be.

'Grandmere, a man lost his job because of you,' I cried. 'You've got to do something! He could starve.'

Grandmere looked at the ceiling. 'Good heavens, Amelia. I already got you an orphan. Are you saying you want to adopt a busboy, as well?'

'No. But, Grandmere, it wasn't Jangbu's fault that he spilt soup on you. It was an accident. But it was caused by your dog.'

Grandmere shielded Rommel's ears.

'Not so loud,' she said. 'He's very sensitive. The vet said—'

'I don't care what the vet said,' I yelled. 'Grandmere, you've got to do something! My friends are down at the restaurant picketing it right now!'

Just to be dramatic, I switched on the television and turned it to New York One. I didn't really expect there to be anything on it about Lilly's protest. Just maybe something about how there was a traffic snarl in the area, due to rubberneckers peering at the spectacle Lilly was making of herself.

So you can imagine I was pretty surprised when a second later, a reporter started describing the 'extraordinary scene outside Les Hautes Manger, the trendy four-star eatery on 57th Street,' and they showed Lilly marching around with a big sign that said LES HAUTES MANGER MGMT UNFAIR. The biggest surprise wasn't the large number of Albert Einstein High School students Lilly had managed to talk into joining her. I mean, I expected to see Boris there, and it wasn't exactly astonishing to see that the AEHS Socialist Club was there as well, since they will show up to any protest they can find.

No, the big shocker was that there was a large number of men I'd never seen before marching right alongside Lilly and the other AEHS students.

The reporter soon explained why.

'Busboys from all over the city have gathered here in front of Les Hautes Manger to show their solidarity with Jangbu Pinasa, the employee who was dismissed from Les

Hautes Manger last night after an incident involving the Dowager Princess of Genovia.'

In spite of all of this, however, Grandmere remained completely unmoved. She just looked at the screen and clacked her tongue.

'Blue,' she said, 'isn't Lilly's best colour, is it?'

I seriously don't know what I am going to do with the woman. She is completely IMPOSSIBLE.

Friday, May 2, the Loft

You would think in my own house I would find a little peace and quiet. But no, I come home to find my mom and Mr G in a raging fight. Usually their fights are about the fact that Mom wants a home birth with a midwife and Mr G wants a hospital birth with the staff of the Mayo Clinic in attendance.

But this time it was because my mom wants to name the baby Simone if it's a girl, after Simone de Beauvoir, and Sartre if it's a boy, after – well, some guy named Sartre, I guess.

But Mr G wants to name the baby Rose if it's a girl, after his grandma, and Rocky if it's a boy, after . . . well, apparently after Sylvester Stallone. Which, you know, having seen the movie *Rocky*, isn't necessarily a bad thing, since Rocky was very nice and all . . .

But my mom says over her dead body will her son – if she has a son – be named after a practically illiterate prize-fighter.

Still, if you ask me, Rocky is better than the last name they came up with if it's a boy: Granger. Thank God I went and looked up Granger in the baby-name book I bought them. Because once I let them know that Granger means 'farmer' in Middle French, they totally cooled on it. Who names their baby Farmer?

Amelia doesn't mean anything in French. It is said to be derivative of Emily, or Emmeline, which means 'industrious' in Old German. The name Michael, which is old Hebrew, means 'He who is like the Lord'. So you see that, together, we make a very nice pair, being industrious and lord-like.

But the fight didn't end with the whole Sartre versus

Rocky thing. Oh no. My mom wants to go to B.J.'s Wholesale Outlet in Jersey City tomorrow to buy the supplies for my party, but Mr G is scared terrorists might set off a bomb in the Holland Tunnel, trapping them in there like Sylvester Stallone in the movie *Daylight*, and then Mom might go into labour prematurely and have the baby with the water from the Hudson River gushing all around.

Mr G just wants to go to Paper House on Broadway to buy Queen Amidala birthday plates and cups.

Hello, I hope they know I am fifteen years, not months, old, and that I can perfectly understand everything that they are saying.

Whatever. I put on my headphones and turned on my computer in the hopes of finding some solace away from all the raised voices, but no such luck. Lilly could only have just got home from her protest thingy, but she's already managed to send around a mass email to everyone in school:

Fr: WomynRule

ATTENTION ALL STUDENTS OF ALBERT EINSTEIN HIGH: Your help and support is vitally needed by the Students Against The Wrongful Dismissal Of Jangbu Pinasa Association (SATWDOJPA)! Join us tomorrow (Saturday, May 3) at noon for a rally in Central Park, and then a protest march down Fifth Avenue to the doors of Les Hautes Manger on 57th Street. Show your disapproval over the way New York City restaurateurs treat their employees! Do not listen to the people who argue that Generation Y is the Materialistic Generation! Make your voice heard!

Lilly Moscovitz, President
SATWDOJPA

Hello. I didn't know my generation was the Materialistic Generation. How can that even be? I hardly own anything. Except a mobile phone. And I've only had that for like a day.

There was another message from Lilly. It went:

Fr: WomynRule

Mia, missed you today at the rally. You should have been there, it was totally AMAZING! Busboys from as far away as Chinatown joined our peaceful protest. There was such a feeling of camaraderie and warmth! Best of all, you'll never guess who showed up . . . Jangbu Pinasa himself! He came to Les Hautes Manger to pick up his last pay cheque. Was he ever surprised to see us all there, picketing on his behalf! He was really shy at first and didn't want to talk to me. But I informed him that, though I might have been brought up in an upper-class household, and my parents are members of the intelligentsia, at heart I am as working class as he is, and have only the best interests of the common man at heart. Jangbu is coming to the march tomorrow! You should come, too, it's going to be awesome!!!!!!!!

Lilly

PS You didn't tell me Jangbu was only eighteen years old. Did you know that he is a Sherpa? Seriously. From Tibet. Back in his home country, he already graduated from high school. He came here searching for a better life because agricultural trade in his homeland has been brought to a standstill by the politics of the Chinese occupying power, and the only non-agricultural job young Sherpas can get is serving as porters and guides in the Himalayas. But Jangbu doesn't like heights.

PPS You also didn't tell me he was so HOT!!!! He looks like a cross between Jackie Chan and Enrique Inglesias. Only without the cheek mole.

It really is quite exhausting to have geniuses as both your best friend as well as your boyfriend. I swear I can hardly keep up with the two of them. Their mental gymnastics are totally beyond me.

Fortunately there was also an email from Tina, whose intellectual capacity is more equal to my own:

Iluvromance
Mia, I've been thinking it over, and I've decided that the best time for you to ask Michael whether or not he is going to ask you to the prom really will be tomorrow night at your party. What I think we should do is organize a game of Seven Minutes in Heaven. (Your mom won't care, right? I mean, she and Mr G aren't going to actually BE THERE during the party, are they?) And when you are in the closet with Michael, and things get hot and heavy with him, you should pop the question. Believe me, no boy can say no to anything during Seven Minutes in Heaven. Or so I've read.

Jeez! What is with my friends? It is like they live in a completely different universe from me. Seven Minutes in Heaven? Has Tina lost her mind? I want to have a NICE party, with Coke and Cheetos and maybe the Time Warp if I can get Mr G to help me move the futon couch. I do

NOT want a party where people are going off in the closet to make out. I mean, if I want to make out with my boyfriend, I will do it in the privacy of my own room . . . except of course that I'm not allowed to have Michael over when no one else is home, and when he is over I have to leave the bedroom door open at least four inches at all times (thanks, Mr G. You know, it totally sucks having a stepfather who is also a high-school teacher, because who is better equipped to rain on a teenager's parade than a high-school teacher?).

I swear, between my grandmother and my friends, I don't know who causes me the most headaches.

At least Michael left a nice message:

```
LinuxRulz
You seemed pretty quiet during G and T today. Are
you OK?
```

Thank God my boyfriend can be counted on to always be supportive of me. Except, of course, when he neglects to ask me to the prom.

I decided to ignore Lilly's and Tina's emails, but I wrote back to Michael. I tried to implement some of that subtlety Grandmere was talking about the other day. Not that I approve of Grandmere right now, or anything. Still, it must be stated that she has had a lot more boyfriends than I have.

```
FtLouie
Hey! I'm fine. Thanks for asking. I just can't shake
this feeling lately that there's something I've for-
gotten. I can't quite put my finger on what it is,
though. Something to do with this time of year,
though, I think . . .
```

There! Perfect! Subtle, yet pointed. And Michael, being a genius, was sure to get it.

Or so I thought, until he wrote back . . . which he did right away, since I guess he was online as well.

```
LinuxRulz
Well, judging by the C you got on that quiz today,
I'd say what you're forgetting is everything we've
been going over these past few weeks in Algebra. If
you want, I'll come over on Sunday and help you with
Monday's assignment.
```

Oh my God. Did any girl ever have a boyfriend so totally clueless? Except possibly Lilly? Except that I think even Boris Pelkowski would have seen through my artless ploy.

I am so depressed. I think I am going to go to bed. There is a *Farscape* marathon on, but I am not in the mood to watch other people's space adventures. My own are upsetting enough.

Saturday, May 3, DAY OF THE BIG PARTY

My mom poked her head in bright and early and asked me if I wanted to go with her and Mr G to B.J.'s for party supplies. Normally I love B.J.'s, on account of the cavernous warehouse filled with oversize stuff, and the free cheese samples and the popcorn and everything. Not to mention the drive-through liquor store Mr G likes to hit on the way home, where they open your boot and fill it with six-packs of Coke without your ever even having to get out of the car.

But for some reason today I was too depressed even for the drive-through liquor store. So I just stayed under the covers and asked my mom weakly if she minded going by herself. I said I had a sore throat and thought I should stay in bed until it was time for the party, just to make sure I was well enough actually to attend it.

I don't think my mom really fell for the whole sick act, but she didn't say anything about it. She just went, 'Suit yourself,' and left with Mr G. Which, considering the mood she's been in lately, is actually letting me off pretty lightly.

I don't know what's wrong with me. I am such a failure. I mean, I have all these problems. I want to go to the prom with my boyfriend, only he hasn't asked me, and I'm too afraid he'll think I'm being pushy to discuss it with him. I don't want to spend my summer in Genovia, but I signed a stinking contract saying I would, and now I don't think I can get out of it. My best friend is trying to do all this good for mankind and everything, and I can't be bothered to lift so much as a piece of posterboard to help her out, even though the person she's trying to help is someone whose misfortunes are all my fault in the first place. And my grade is starting to slide in Algebra again, and I don't even care.

Really, with all that weighing on my shoulders, what

choice do I have but to turn on the Lifetime Movie Channel for Women? Maybe if I watch some movies about real-life women who've surmounted near impossible obstacles, I might find the courage to face my own.

Hey, it could happen.

Saturday, May 3, 7:30 p.m. half an hour before my party is to begin

I don't think turning on the Lifetime Movie Channel for Women was such a hot idea. All it did was make me feel inadequate. Really, I don't know who could watch movies like that and not feel bad about themselves. I mean, here is just a sample of what some of these women endured:

The Taking of Flight 847:
The Uli Derickson Story

The Bionic Woman's Lindsay Wagner saves all but one of the passengers in this true story of a plane hijacking in the mid-eighties. In the movie, Uli convinces the hijackers to spare the lives of the passengers by singing a touching folk song, causing the hijackers' eyes to well up.

Unfortunately I don't know any folk songs, and the songs I do know – such as Bif Naked's 'I Love Myself Today (Uh-Huh)' – probably wouldn't soothe anyone, especially a hijacker.

The Abduction of Kari Swenson

Michael J. Fox's wife Tracey Pollan stars in the true story of an Olympic biathlete who gets kidnapped by hillbillies who want to make her their bride. Ew! As if camping isn't bad enough. Imagine having to camp with people who've never bathed. But Kari gets away and goes on to win the gold, and the bad guys go to jail, where they make them shave every day and brush their teeth.

However, I am no biathlete. I am not even an athlete. If I were kidnapped by hillbillies, I would probably just start crying until they let me go in disgust.

Cry for Help: the Tracey Thurman Story

Facts of Life's Jo get brutally assaulted by her husband while the cops are watching, then successfully sues the police for failing to protect her, striking a blow for victims of stalking everywhere.

But I have a bodyguard. If anybody tried to assault me, Lars would hit them with his stun gun.

Sudden Terror: The Hijacking of School Bus#17

Maria Conchita Alonso, fresh from her role as Amber in *The Running Man*, plays Marta Caldwell, the brave driver of a Special Ed. bus which is hijacked by a guy who is mad at the IRS. Her calm and gentle demeanour keeps the hijacker still long enough for a SWAT officer to shoot him in the head through the bus window, much to the horror of her Special Ed. charges, who are hit with the guy's blood spatter and brain tissue.

But I take a limo to school, so the chances of this happening to me are moot.

She Woke Up Pregnant

This is the true story of a woman whose dentist has sex with her while she is under anaesthesia for a root canal. Then the dentist has the nerve to say he and the patient had an affair and that she's making up the rape thing so her husband won't get mad about the new baby . . . until, that is, a female cop goes undercover as a patient and the cops use a lipstick camera to catch the dentist in the act of taking her shirt off!

But this would never happen to me as I have nothing in the chestal area that would be of interest even to a psychopathic dentist.

Miracle Landing

Connie Sellecca plays First Officer Mimi Thompkins, who manages successfully to land Flight 243 after its roof is ripped off mid-flight due to metal fatigue. She is not the only brave one on that flight, since there was also a flight attendant who kept checking on the people in the front of the plane where there was no roof, and telling them they were going to be fine even though they had giant pieces of aeroplane carpet stuck to their heads.

I would so never be able either to land a plane or tell people with massive head wounds that they were going to be fine, due to the fact that I would be barfing too hard.

Seriously, I don't know how anyone can be expected to just hop out of bed after viewing movies like that and feel all good about themselves.

Even worse, I happened to catch a few minutes of *Miracle Pets*, and I was forced to admit that as a pet, Fat Louie is pretty much bottom of the barrel, intelligence-wise. I mean, on *Miracle Pets* they had a donkey that saved its owner from wild dogs; a parrot that saved its owners from a house fire; a dog that saved its owner from dying of insulin shock by gently shaking her until she ate some gumdrops, and a cat that noticed its owner was unconscious and sat on the auto-dial 911 button on the phone and miaowed until help arrived.

I am sorry, but Fat Louie would be no match for wild dogs, would probably hide in a fire, wouldn't know a gumdrop from a hole in the wall, and wouldn't know to sit on the 911 button if I were unconscious. In fact, if I were unconscious, Fat Louie would probably just sit by his food bowl and cry until Ronnie from next door finally went insane and got the superintendant to let her in to shut the cat up.

Even my cat is a failure.

Worse, Mom and Mr G had a fabulous time without me at B.J.'s. Well, except for the part where Mom totally had to pee but they were stuck in the middle of the Holland Tunnel, so she had to hold it until they came to the first Shell station on the other side, and when she ran to the ladies' room it turned out to be locked so she nearly ripped the arm off the gas station attendant grabbing the key from him.

But they found tons of Queen Amidala stuff on sale, including panties (for me, not the party guests, of course). My mom poked her head into my room when they got home to show me the Amidala panty six-pack she picked up, but I just couldn't work up any kind of enthusiasm about it, though I tried.

Maybe I have PMS.

Or maybe the weight of my new-found womanhood, seeing as how I'm fifteen now, is simply too much to bear.

And I really should be happy, because Mr G hung all these Queen Amidala streamers up all over the Loft, and strung flashing white Christmas lights all through the pipework on the ceiling and put a Queen Amidala mask on Mom's lifesize bust of Elvis. He even promised not to jam on his drums along with the music (a carefully selected mix put together by Michael, which includes all of my favourite Destiny's Child and Bree Sharp releases, even though Michael can't stand them).

WHAT IS WRONG WITH ME???? Is this all just because my boyfriend hasn't asked me to the prom yet? Why do I even care? Why can't I be happy with what I have? WHY CAN'T I JUST BE GLAD I EVEN HAVE A BOYFRIEND AND LEAVE IT AT THAT?

This party was such a bad idea. I am so not in a party mood. What was I even thinking, having a party? I AM

AN UNPOPULAR NERD PRINCESS!!!!! UNPOPULAR NERD PRINCESSES SHOULD NOT HAVE PARTIES!!!!!!!!! NOT EVEN FOR THEIR UNPOPULAR NERD FRIENDS!!!!!!!!! No one is going to come. No one is going to come, and I'm going to end up sitting here all night with the twinkling Christmas lights and the stupid Queen Amidala streamers and the Cheetos and the Coke and Michael's mix, BY MYSELF.

Oh God, the buzzer just went off. Someone is here. Please God give me the strength to get through this night. Give me the strength of Uli, Kari, Tracey, Marta, that dental patient lady, Mimi and that flight attendant. Please, that's all I ask of you. Thanks.

Sunday, May 4, 2 a.m.

Well. That's it. It's over. My life is over.

I would like to thank all of those who stood by me during the hard times – my mother, back before she became a one hundred and eighty pound quivering mass of bladderless hormones; Mr G, for attempting to salvage my GPA, and Fat Louie for just being, well, Fat Louie, even if he is totally useless when compared to the animals on *Miracle Pets*.

But nobody else. Because everybody else I know is obviously part of some nefarious plot to drive me to madness, just like Bertha Rochester in *Jane Eyre*.

Take Tina, for example. Tina, who shows up at my party and, first thing, grabs me by the arm and drags me into my room, where everybody is supposed to be leaving their coats, and tells me, 'Ling Su and I have got it all worked out. Ling Su'll keep your mom and Mr G busy, and then I will announce the game of Seven Minutes in Heaven. When it's your turn, get Michael in the closet and start kissing him and when you've reached the height of passion, ask him about the prom.'

'Tina!' I was really annoyed. And not just because I thought her plan was totally weak, either. No, I was miffed because Tina was wearing body glitter. Really! She had it smeared all over her collarbones. How come I can't even seem to find body glitter in the store? And if I did, would I have the coolness to smear it on my collarbones? No. Because I am too boring.

'We are not playing Seven Minutes in Heaven at my birthday party,' I informed her.

Tina looked crestfallen. 'Why not?'

'Because this is a nerd party! My God, Tina! We are nerds. We don't play Seven Minutes in Heaven. That is the kind of thing people like Lana and Josh play at their parties. At nerd parties, we play things like Spoon, or possibly Light as a Feather, Stiff as a Board. But not kissing games!'

But Tina was totally adamant that nerds DO play kissing games.

'Because if they don't,' she pointed out, 'then how do you think little nerds get made?'

I suggested that little nerds get made in the privacy of nerd homes after nerds marry, but Tina wasn't even listening any more. She flounced out into the main room to greet Boris, who'd actually, it turned out, arrived a half-hour before, but since he hadn't wanted to be the first one at the party had stood in my vestibule for thirty minutes, reading all of the Chinese menus the delivery boys shove under the door.

'Where's Lilly?' I asked Boris, because I would have thought the two of them would arrive at the same time, seeing as how they are dating and all.

But Boris said he hadn't seen Lilly since the march on Les Hautes Manger that afternoon.

'She was at the front of the group,' he explained to me as he stood by the refreshment table (really our dining table) shoving Cheetos in his mouth. A surprising amount of orange powder got trapped between the spokes of his orthodontic brace. It was oddly fascinating to watch, in a completely gross way. 'You know, with her megaphone, leading the chants. That was the last I saw of her. I got hungry and stopped for a hot dog, and next thing I knew, they had all marched on without me.'

I told Boris that that is, actually, the point of a march . . . that people are supposed to march, not wait for members of the group who'd stopped for hot dogs. Boris seemed kind of shocked to hear this, which I guess is not surprising, since he is from Russia, where marching of any kind was outlawed for many years, except marches for the glorification of Lenin, or whatever.

Anyway, Michael showed up next with the mix for the CD player. I'd thought about having his band play for my party, since they are always looking for gigs, but Mr G said no way, as he gets in enough trouble with our downstairs neighbour Verl just for playing his drums. A whole band might send Verl over the edge. Verl goes to bed promptly every night at 9 p.m. so he can be up before dawn to record the activity of our neighbours across the way, whom he believes are aliens sent to this planet to observe us and report back to the mother ship in preparation for eventual interplanetary warfare. The people across the way don't look like aliens to me, but they *are* German, so you can see why Verl might have made such a mistake.

Michael, as usual, looked incredibly hot. WHY does he always have to look so handsome, every time I see him? I mean, you would think I would get used to how he looks, seeing as how I see him practically every day . . . a couple of times a day, even.

But each and every time I see him, my heart gives this giant lurch. Like he's a present I'm just about to unwrap, or something. It's sick, this weakness I have for him. Sick, I tell you.

Anyway, Michael put the music on, and other people started to arrive, and everyone was milling around, talking about the march, and last night's *Farscape* marathon – everybody except for me, who hadn't taken part in either. Instead, I just ran around taking people's coats (because even though it was May it was still nippy out) and praying that everybody was having a good time and that no one would leave early or overhear my mother telling anyone who would listen about her Incredible Shrinking Bladder . . .

Then the doorbell rang and I went to answer it, and there was Lilly, standing with her arms around this dark-haired guy in a leather jacket.

'Hi!' Lilly said, looking all bubbly and excited. 'I don't think you two have met. Mia, this is Jangbu. Jangbu, this is Princess Amelia of Genovia. Or Mia, as we call her.'

I stared at Jangbu in shock. Not because, you know, Lilly had brought him to my party without asking first, or anything. But because, well, Lilly had her arm around his waist. She was practically hanging on him, for crying out loud. And her boyfriend Boris was right there, in the next room, trying to learn the electric slide from Shameeka . . .

'Mia,' Lilly said, stepping inside with a look of annoyance. 'Don't say hi, or anything.'

I said, 'Oh, sorry. Hi.'

Jangbu said hi back, and smiled. The truth was, Jangbu WAS incredibly good-looking, just like Lilly had said. In fact, he was way better looking than poor Boris. Well, I hate to admit it, but who isn't? Still, I never thought Lilly liked Boris for his looks, anyway. I mean, Boris is a musical genius and, as I happen to know, given the fact that I myself go out with one, they are not easy to find.

Fortunately Lilly had to let go of Jangbu long enough for him to take off his leather jacket when I offered to put it in the bedroom for him. So when Boris finally saw that she'd arrived and went over to say hello, he didn't notice anything amiss. I took Jangbu and Lilly's jackets and wandered, in a daze, back towards my bedroom. I ran into Michael along the way, who grinned at me and said, 'Having fun yet?'

I just shook my head. 'Did you see that?' I asked him. 'Your sister and Jangbu?'

Michael looked towards them. 'No. What?'

'Nothing,' I said. I didn't want to cause Michael to blow

up at Lilly the way Colin Hanks did when he caught his little sister, Kirsten Dunst, kissing his best friend in the movie *Get Over It*. Because even though I have never really noticed Michael harbouring protective feelings towards Lilly, I am sure that is only because she has been dating Boris all this time, and Boris is one of Michael's friends and a mouth-breather, besides. I mean, you are not going to get too upset over your little sister going out with a mouth-breathing violinist. A hot, newly unemployed Sherpa, however . . . now that might be a different story.

And though you wouldn't know it to look at him, Michael is very quick-tempered. I once saw him glare quite formidably at some construction workers who whistled at me and Lilly down on Sixth Ave. when we were coming out of Charlie Mom's. The last thing I needed at my party was for a fist fight to break out.

But Lilly managed to keep her hands off Jangbu for the next half-hour, during which I attempted to put aside my depression and join in on the fun, especially when everyone started jumping around, doing the Macarena, which Michael had jokingly put in the mix he'd made.

It's too bad there aren't more dances, other than the Time Warp and the Macarena, that everybody knows. You know how in movies like *She's All That* and *Footloose*, everybody starts doing the same dance at the same time? It would be so cool if that would happen sometime in like the cafeteria. Principal Gupta could be on the sound system, reading off the announcements, and suddenly somebody puts on the Yeah Yeah Yeahs or whatever and we all start dancing on the tables.

In olden times, everybody knew the same dances . . . like the minuet, and stuff. Too bad things can't be like olden times.

Except, of course, I wouldn't want to have wooden teeth or the pox.

Anyway, things were finally starting to look up, and I was actually having a pretty good time fooling around, when all of a sudden Tina was like, 'Mr G, we're out of Coke!' and Mr G was like, 'How can that be? I bought seven flats of it at the drive-through liquor store this morning.'

But Tina insisted all the Coke was gone. I found out later she'd hidden it in the baby's room. But whatever. At the time, Mr G honestly thought there was no more Coke.

'Well, I'll run down to Grand Union and buy more,' he said, putting on his coat and going out.

That's when Ling Su asked my mom if she could see her slides. Ling Su, being an artist herself, knew exactly the right thing to say to my mother, a fellow artist, even if since she's been pregnant she's had to give up oils and work only in egg tempera.

No sooner had my mom whisked Ling Su into her bedroom to break out her slides than Tina turned off the music and announced that we would now be playing Seven Minutes in Heaven.

Everybody looked pretty excited about this – we certainly had never played Seven Minutes in Heaven at the last party we'd all been to, which had been at Shameeka's house. But Mr Taylor, Shameeka's dad, wasn't the type to fall for the 'Out of Coke' or 'Can I see your slides?' thing. He is way strict. He keeps the baseball bat he once hit a home run with in one corner of the room as a 'reminder' to the boys Shameeka dates of just what, exactly, he's capable of, should they get fresh with his daughter.

So the Seven Minutes in Heaven thing had everybody way stoked. Everybody, that is, except for Michael. Michael is not a big fan of Public Displays of Affection, and it turns out he is even less of a fan of being locked in a closet with his girlfriend. Not, he informed me, after Tina had gigglingly shut the closet door – closing the two of us in with Mom and Mr G's winter coats, the vacuum cleaner, the laundry cart and my wheelie suitcase – that he had anything against being in a dark enclosed space with me. It was the fact that, outside the door, everybody was listening that bugged him.

'Nobody's listening,' I told him. 'See? They turned the music back on.'

Which they had.

But I sort of had to agree with Michael. Seven Minutes in Heaven is a stupid game. I mean, it is one thing to make out with your boyfriend. It is quite another to do it in a closet, with everybody on the other side of the door knowing what you are doing. The ambiance is just not there.

It was dark in the closet – so dark I couldn't even see my own hand in front of my face, let alone Michael. Plus, it smelt funny. This, I knew, was on account of the vacuum cleaner. It had been a while since anybody – namely, me, since my mom never remembers, and Mr G doesn't understand our vacuum cleaner, on account of it being so old – had emptied the vacuum bag, and it was filled to the brim with orange cat fur and the pieces of kitty litter Fat Louie is always tracking across the floor. Since it was scented kitty litter, it smelled a little like pine. But not necessarily in a good way.

'So we really have to stay in here for seven minutes?' Michael wanted to know.

'I guess,' I said.

'What if Mr G gets back and finds us in here?'

'He'll probably kill you,' I said.

'Well,' Michael said. 'Then I'd better give you something to remember me by.'

Then he took me in his arms and started kissing me.

I have to admit, after that, I kind of started thinking Seven Minutes in Heaven wasn't such a bad game after all. In fact, I sort of began to like it. It was nice to be there in the dark, with Michael's body all pressed up to mine, and his tongue in my mouth, and all. I guess because I couldn't see anything, my sense of smell was that much stronger, or something, because I could smell Michael's neck really well. It smelt super nice – way better than the vacuum-cleaner bag. The smell sort of made me want to jump on him. I can't really explain it any other way. But I honestly wanted to jump on Michael.

Instead of jumping on him, which I didn't think he'd enjoy – nor would it be socially acceptable . . . plus, you know, all the coats were sort of impeding our ability to move around a lot – I tore my lips from his, and said, not even thinking about Tina, or Uli Derickson, or even what I was doing, but sort of lost in the heat of the moment, 'So, Michael, what is up with the prom? Are we going, or not?'

To which Michael replied, with a chuckle, as his lips nuzzled my own neck (though I highly doubt he was smelling it), 'The prom? Are you crazy? The prom's even stupider than this game.'

At which point, I sort of broke our embrace and took a step backwards, right on to Mr G's hockey stick. Only I didn't care, because, you know, I was so shocked.

'What do you mean?' I demanded. If it hadn't been so dark, I so would have run my searching gaze across Michael's face, looking for some sign he was joking. As it was, however, I just had to listen really hard.

'Mia,' Michael said, reaching for me. For somebody who thought Seven Minutes in Heaven was such a stupid game, he seemed to be kind of into it. 'You've got to be kidding. I'm not exactly the prom type.'

But I slapped his hands away. It was hard, you know, to see them in the dark, but it wasn't like there was much chance of missing. The only other thing in front of me, besides Michael, was coats.

'What do you mean, you're not the prom type?' I wanted to know. 'You're a Senior. You're graduating. You have to go to the prom. Everybody does it.'

'Yeah,' Michael said. 'Well, everybody does lots of lame stuff. But that doesn't mean I'm going to, too. I mean, come on, Mia. Proms are for the Josh Richters of the world.'

'Oh, really?' I said, sounding very cold, even to my own ears. But that was probably on account of how super attuned they were to everything, seeing as how I couldn't see. My ears, I mean. 'What, then, do the Michael Moscovitzes of the world do on prom night?'

'I don't know,' Michael said. 'We could do more of *this*, if you want.'

By *this*, of course, he meant making out in a closet. I did not even credit that with a response.

'Michael,' I said, in my most princessy voice. 'I'm serious. If you don't plan on going to the prom, just what, exactly, do you intend to do instead?'

'I don't know,' Michael said, sounding genuinely baffled by my question. 'Go bowling?'

BOWLING!!!!!!!!!!!!!!!!! MY BOYFRIEND WOULD RATHER GO BOWLING ON HIS PROM NIGHT THAN GO TO THE PROM!!!!!!!!!!!!!

Does he not have an ounce of romantic feeling in his body? He must, because he got me that snowflake necklace . . . the necklace that I haven't taken off, not even once, since he gave it to me. How can the man who gave me that necklace be the same man who would rather go *bowling* on his prom night than go to the prom?

He must have sensed that I was not taking kindly to this news, since he went, 'Mia, come on. Admit it. The prom is the corniest thing in the world. I mean, you spend a ton of money on some rented penguin suit you can't even get comfortable in, then spend a ton more money on dinner somewhere fancy that probably isn't half as good as Number One Noodle Son, then you go and stand around in some gymnasium—'

'Maxim's,' I corrected him. 'Your Senior Prom is taking place at Maxim's.'

'Whatever,' Michael said. 'So you go and eat stale cookies and dance to really, really bad music with a bunch of people you can't stand and who you never want to see again—'

'Like me, you mean?' I was practically crying, I was so hurt. 'You never want to see me again? Is that it? You're just going to graduate and go off to college and forget all about me?'

'Mia,' Michael said, in quite a different tone of voice. 'Of course not. I wasn't talking about you. I was talking about people like . . . well, like Josh and those guys. You know that. What's the matter with you?'

But I couldn't tell Michael what was the matter with me. Because what was the matter with me was that my eyes had filled up with tears and my throat had closed up and I'm not sure but I think my nose had started to run. Because all of a sudden I realized that my boyfriend had no intention of asking me to the prom. Not because he was going to ask someone more popular instead, or anything. Like Andrew McCarthy in *Pretty in Pink*. But because my boyfriend, Michael Moscovitz, the person I loved most in the whole world (with the exception of my cat), the man to whom I had pledged my heart for all eternity, had absolutely no interest at all in attending HIS OWN SENIOR PROM!!!

I really can't say what would have happened next if Boris hadn't suddenly ripped the closet door open and yelled, 'Time's up!' Maybe Michael would have heard me sniffling and realized I was crying and asked me why. And then, after he'd drawn me tenderly into his arms, I might have told him in a broken voice, while resting my head against his manly chest.

And then he might have sweetly kissed the top of my head and murmured, 'Oh, my darling, I didn't know,' and sworn then and there that he would do anything, anything in the world, to see my doe eyes shine again, and that if I wanted to go to the prom, well then by God, we'd go to the prom.

Only that's so not what happened. What happened instead was that Michael blinked at all the sudden light, and held up an arm to shield his eyes, and so never even saw that my own eyes were tear-filled and that my nose might possibly have been running . . . although this would have been horribly unprincesslike and probably didn't even happen.

Besides, I nearly forgot my grief, I was so astounded by what happened next. And that was that Lilly went, 'My turn! My turn!'

And everyone got out of her way as she went barrelling towards the closet . . .

Only the hand she reached for – the man whom she chose to accompany her for her Seven Minutes in Heaven – was not the pale, soft hand of the violin virtuoso with whom, for the past eight months, Lilly had been sharing furtive French kisses and Sunday morning dim sum. The hand Lilly reached for was not one belonging to Boris Pelkowski, mouth-breather and sweater tucker-inner. No, the hand

Lilly reached for belonged to none other than Jangbu Pinasa, the hot Sherpa busboy.

Stunned silence roared through the room – well, except for the wailing of the Sahara Hotnights on the stereo – as Lilly thrust a startled Jangbu into my hall coat closet, then quickly went in after him. We all stood there, blinking at the closed door, not knowing quite what to do.

At least, *I* didn't know what to do. I looked over at Tina, and I could tell by the shocked expression on her face that *she* didn't know what to do, either.

Michael, on the other hand, seemed to know what to do. He laid a sympathetic hand on Boris's shoulder and said, 'Tough break, man,' then went and grabbed a handful of Cheetos.

TOUGH BREAK, MAN?????? That is what boys say to one another when they see that their friend's heart has just been ripped from his chest and tossed upon the floor?

I couldn't believe Michael could be so cavalier. I mean, what about the whole Colin Hanks thing? Why wasn't he tearing that closet door open, hauling Jangbu Pinasa out of it, and beating him to a bloody pulp? I mean, Lilly was his little sister, for God's sake. Didn't he have an ounce of protective feeling towards her?

Completely forgetting about my despair over the whole prom thing – I think the shock of seeing Lilly's eagerness to lock lips with someone other than her boyfriend had numbed my senses – I followed Michael to the refreshment table and said, 'That's it? That's all you're going to do?'

He looked at me questioningly. 'About what?'

'About your sister!' I cried. 'And Jangbu!'

'What do you want me to do about it?' Michael asked. 'Haul him out and hit him?'

'Well,' I said. 'Yes!'

'Why?' Michael drank some 7-Up, since there wasn't any Coke. 'I don't care who my sister locks herself into the closet with. If it were you, then I'd hit the guy. But it's not you, it's Lilly. Lilly, as I believe she's amply proved over the years, can take care of herself.' He held a bowl out towards me. 'Cheeto?'

Cheetos! Who could think of food at a time like this?

'No, thank you,' I said. 'But aren't you at all worried that Lilly's—' I broke off, uncertain how to continue. Michael helped me out.

'Been swept off her feet by the guy's rugged Sherpa good looks?' Michael shook his head. 'Looked to me like if anybody is being taken advantage of, it's Jangbu. The poor guy doesn't seem to know what hit him.'

'B-but . . .' I stammered. 'But what about Boris?'

Michael looked over at Boris, who had slumped down on to the futon couch, his head cradled in his hands. Tina had rushed over to him and was trying to offer sisterly balm to his wounded feelings by telling him that Lilly was probably only showing Jangbu what the inside of a real American coat closet looked like. Even I didn't think she sounded very convincing, and I am very easily convinced by almost anything. For instance, in convocations where we are forced to listen to the debate team, I almost always agree with whichever team is talking at the moment, no matter what they're saying.

'Boris'll get over it,' Michael said, and reached for the chips and dip.

I don't understand boys. I really don't. I mean, if it had been MY little sister in the closet with Jangbu, I would have been furious with rage. And if it had been MY Senior Prom, I'd have been falling all over myself in an effort to secure tickets before they were all gone.

But that's me, I guess.

Anyway, before any of us had a chance to do anything more, the front door to the Loft opened and Mr G came in, carrying bags of more Coke.

'I'm home,' Mr G called, putting the bags down and starting to take off his windbreaker. 'I picked up some ice, too. I figured we might be running out by now . . .'

Mr G's voice trailed off. That's because he'd opened the hall closet door to put away his coat and found Lilly and Jangbu in there, making out.

Well, that was the end of my party. Mr Gianini is no Mr Taylor, but he's still pretty strict. Also, being a high-school teacher and all, he is not unfamiliar with games like Seven Minutes in Heaven. Lilly's excuse – that she and Jangbu had gotten locked into the closet together accidentally – didn't exactly fly with him. Mr G said he thought it was time for everybody to go home. Then he got Hans, my limo driver, who we'd arranged beforehand to take everybody home after the party, to make sure that when he dropped off Lilly and Michael, Jangbu didn't go inside with them, and that Lilly went all the way into her building, up the elevator and everything, so she didn't try to sneak down and meet Jangbu later, like at Blimpie's or whatever.

And now I am lying here, a broken shell of a girl . . . fifteen years old, and yet so much older in so many ways. Because I know now what it is like to see all of your hopes and dreams crushed beneath the soulless heel of despair. I saw it in Boris's eyes, as he watched Lilly and Jangbu emerge from that closet, looking flushed and sweaty, Lilly actually *tugging on the bottom of her shirt* (I cannot believe Lilly got to second base before I did. And with a guy she'd known for a mere twenty-four hours, as well – not to mention the fact that she did it in MY hallway closet).

But Boris's eyes weren't the only ones registering despair tonight. My own have a distinctly hollow look to them. I noticed tonight as I was brushing my teeth before bed. It is no mystery why, of course. My eyes have a haunted look to them because I am haunted . . . haunted by the spectre of the dream of a prom that I know now will never be. Never will I, dressed in off-one-shoulder black, rest my head upon the shoulder of Michael (in a tux) at his Senior Prom. Never will I enjoy the stale cookies he mentioned, nor the look on Lana Weinberger's face when she sees that she is not the only freshman girl besides Shameeka in attendance.

My prom dream is over. And so, I am afraid, is my life.

Sunday, May 4, 9 a.m., the Loft

It is very hard to be sunk in the black well of despair when your mother and stepfather get up at the crack of dawn and put on The Donnas while making their breakfast waffles. Why can't they go quietly to church to hear the word of the Lord, like normal parents, and leave me to wallow in my own grief? I swear it is enough to make me contemplate moving to Genovia.

Except, of course, there I would be expected to get up and go to church as well. I guess I should be thanking my lucky stars that my mother and her husband are godless heathens. But they could at least turn it DOWN.

Sunday, May 4, Noon, the Loft

My plan for the day was to stay in bed with the covers up over my head until it was time to go to school on Monday morning. That is what people who have had their reason for living cruelly snatched from them do: stay in bed as much as possible.

This plan was unfairly destroyed, however, by my mother, who just came barrelling in (at her current size, she can't help but barrel everywhere she goes) and sat down on the edge of the bed, nearly crushing Fat Louie, who had slunk down underneath the covers with me and was snoozing at my toes. After screaming because Fat Louie had sunk all his claws into her rear end, right through my duvet, my mom apologized for barging in on my grief-stricken solitude, but – she said – she thought it was time we had A Little Talk.

It is never a good thing when my mom thinks it is a time for A Little Talk. The last time she and I had A Little Talk, I was forced to listen to a very long speech about body image and my supposedly distorted one. My mother was very worried that I was contemplating using my Christmas money for breast-enhancement surgery, and she wanted me to know what a bad idea she thought this was, because women's obsession with their looks has got completely out of control. In Korea, for instance, thirty per cent of women in their twenties have had some form of plastic surgery, ranging from cheekbone and jawbone shaving to eye slicing and calf-muscle removal (for slimmer calves) in order to achieve a more Western look. This as opposed to three per cent of women in the US who have had plastic surgery for purely aesthetic purposes.

The good news? America is NOT the most image-obsessed country in the world. The bad news? Too many women outside our culture feel pressured to change their looks to better emulate ours, thinking Western standards of beauty are more important than their own country's, because that is what they see on old reruns of shows like *Baywatch* and *Friends*. Which is wrong, just wrong, because Nigerian women are just as beautiful as women from LA or Manhattan. Just maybe in a different way.

As awkward as THAT chat had been (I was not contemplating using my Christmas money for breast-enhancement surgery: I was contemplating using my Christmas money for a complete set of Shania Twain CDs, but of course I couldn't ADMIT that to anyone, so my mom naturally thought it was something to do with my boobs), the one we had today really takes the cake as far as mother/daughter talks go.

Because of course today was THE mother/daughter talk. Not the 'Honey, your body is changing and soon you'll have a different use for those sanitary napkins of mine you stole to make into beds for your Star Wars action figures' talk. Oh no. Today was the 'You're fifteen now and you have a boyfriend and last night my husband caught you and your little friends playing Seven Minutes in Heaven and so I think it's time we discussed You Know What' talk.

I have recorded our conversation here as best I could so that when I have my own daughter I can make sure NEVER, EVER to say any of these things to her, remembering how INCREDIBLY AND UTTERLY STUPID THEY MADE ME FEEL WHEN MY OWN MOTHER SAID THEM TO ME. As far as I'm concerned, my own daughter can learn about sex from the Lifetime Movie Channel for Women, like everybody else on the planet.

Mom: Mia, I just heard from Frank that Lilly and her new friend Jambo—

Me: Jangbu.

Mom: Whatever. That Lilly and her new friend were, er, kissing in our hall closet. Apparently, you were all playing some sort of make-out game, Five Minutes in the Closet—

Me: Seven Minutes in Heaven.

Mom: Whatever. The point is, Mia, you're fifteen now. You're pretty much an adult, and I know that you and Michael are very much a couple. It's only natural that you'd be curious about sex . . . perhaps even experimenting—

Me: MOM!!!! GROSS!!!!!!!!!

Mom: There's nothing gross about sexual relations between two people who love one another, Mia. Of course I would prefer it if you waited until you were older. Until you were in college, maybe. Or your mid-thirties, anyway. However, I know only too well what it is like to be a slave to your hormones, so it's important that you take the appropriate precau—

Me: I mean, it's gross to talk about it with my MOTHER.

Mom: Well, yes, I know. Or rather, I don't know, since my own mother would have sooner dropped dead than have mentioned any of this to me. However, I think it is important for mothers and daughters to be open with one another about these things. For instance, Mia, if you ever feel that you need to talk about birth control, I can make you an appointment with my gynaecologist, Dr Brandeis—

Me: MOM!!!!!!!!!!!!! MICHAEL AND I ARE NOT HAVING SEX!!!!!!!!!!!!!!!!!

Mom: Well, I'm glad to hear that, honey, since you are a bit young. But if the two of you should decide to, I want to make sure you have all your facts straight. For instance, are you and your friends aware that diseases like AIDS can be transmitted through oral sex as well as—

Me: YES, MOM, I KNOW THIS. I AM TAKING HEALTH AND SAFETY THIS SEMESTER, REMEMBER?????

Mom: Mia, sex is nothing to be embarrassed about. It is one of the basic human needs, such as water, food and social interaction. It is important that if you choose to become sexually active, you protect yourself.

Oh, you mean like *you* did, Mom, when you got knocked up by Mr Gianini? Or by DAD?????

Only of course I didn't say this. Because, you know, what would be the point? Instead I just nodded and went, 'OK, Mom. Thanks, Mom. I'll be sure to, Mom,' hoping she'd finally give up and go away.

Only it didn't work. She just kept hanging around, like one of Tina's little sisters whenever I'm over at the Hakim Babas' and Tina and I want to sneak a look at her dad's *Playboy* collection. Really, you can learn a lot from the *Playboy* adviser, from what kind of car stereo works best in a Porsche Boxter to how to tell if your husband is having an affair with his personal assistant. Tina says it is a good idea to know your enemy, which is why she reads her dad's copies of *Playboy* whenever she gets the chance . . . though we both agree that, judging from the stuff in this magazine, the enemy is very, very weird.

And oddly fixated with cars.

Finally my mom ran out of steam. The Little Talk just kind of petered out. She sat there for a minute, looking around at my room, which is only minorly a disaster area. I am pretty neat, overall, because I always feel like I have to clean my room before I can start on my homework. Something about a clear environment making for clear thinking. I don't know. Maybe it's just because homework is so boring I'll take any excuse to put off doing it.

'Mia,' my mom said after a long pause. 'Why are you still in bed at noon on a Sunday? Isn't this when you usually meet your friends for dim sum?'

I shrugged. I didn't want to admit to my mom that dim sum was probably the last thing on anybody's mind this morning . . . I mean, seeing as how apparently Lilly and Boris were broken up now.

'I hope you aren't upset with Frank,' my mom went on, 'for ruining your party. But really, Mia, you and Lilly are old enough to know better than to play silly games like Seven Minutes in Heaven. What on earth is wrong with playing Spoon?'

I shrugged some more. What was I going to say? That the reason I was so upset had nothing to do with Mr G, and everything to do with the fact that my boyfriend didn't want to go to the prom? Lilly was right: the prom is just a stupid pagan dance ritual. Why did I even care?

'Well,' my mom said, climbing awkwardly to her feet. 'If you want to stay in bed all day, I'm certainly not going to stop you. There's no place else I'd rather be, I'll admit. But then, I'm an old pregnant lady, not a fifteen-year-old.'

Then she left. THANK GOD. I can't believe she tried to have a sex talk with me. About *Michael.* I mean, doesn't she know Michael and I haven't gotten past first base? No one I know has, with the exception, of course, of Lana. At least I assume Lana has, judging by what got spray-painted about her across the gymnasium wall over Spring Break. And now Lilly, of course.

God. My best friend has been to more bases than I have. And *I* am the one who is supposed to have found my soulmate. Not *her*.

Life is so unfair.

Sunday, May 4, 7 p.m., the Loft

I guess it must be Check on Mia's Mental Health Day, since everybody is calling to find out how I am. That was my dad on the phone just now. He wanted to know how my party went. While on the one hand this is a good thing – it means neither Mom nor Mr G mentioned the whole Seven Minutes in Heaven thing to him, which wouldn't have made him too ballistic or anything – it was also kind of a bad thing, since it meant I had to lie to him. While lying to my dad is easier than lying to my mom, because my dad, never having been a young girl, doesn't know the kind of capacity young girls have to tell terrific whoppers – and apparently isn't aware that my nostrils flare when I lie, either – it is still sort of nerve-racking. I mean, he IS a cancer survivor, after all. It seems sort of mean to lie to someone who is, basically, like Lance Armstrong. Except without all the Tour de France wins.

But whatever. I told him the party went great, blah blah blah.

Good thing he wasn't in the same room with me. He'd have noticed my nostrils flaring like crazy.

No sooner had I hung up the phone with my dad than it rang again, and I snatched it up, thinking it might be, oh, I don't know, MY BOYFRIEND. You would have thought Michael might have called me at some point during the day, just to see how I was. You know, whether or not I was crippled with grief over the whole prom thing.

But apparently Michael is not all that concerned for my mental health, because not only has he not called, but the person on the other end of the phone when I eagerly snatched it up was about as far from being Michael as you can get.

It was, in fact, Grandmere.

Our conversation went like this:

Grandmere: Amelia, it is your grandmother. I need you to reserve the night of Wednesday the seventh. I've been asked to dine at Le Cirque with my old friend the Sultan of Brunei, and I want you to accompany me. And I don't want to hear any nonsense about how the Sultan needs to give up his Rolls because it is contributing to the destruction of the ozone layer. You need more culture in your life, and that's final. I'm tired of hearing about *Miraculous Pets* and the Lifetime Channel for Stay at Home Mothers or whatever it is you're always watching on the television. It's time you met some interesting people, and not the ones you see on TV, or those so-called artists your mother is always having over for girls' Bingo night, or whatever it is.

Me: OK, Grandmere. Whatever you say, Grandmere.

What, I ask you, is wrong with that answer? Really? What part of *OK, Grandmere. Whatever you say, Grandmere* would any NORMAL grandmother find suspicious? Of course, I'm forgetting my grandmother is far from normal. Because she was all over me, right away.

Grandmere: Amelia. What is wrong with you? Out with it, I haven't much time. I'm supposed to be dining with the Duc di Bormazo.

Me: Nothing's wrong, Grandmere. I'm just . . . I'm

a little depressed, that's all. I didn't get such a good grade on my last Algebra quiz, and I'm a little down about it . . .

Grandmere: Pfuit. What is it REALLY, Mia? And make it snappy.

Me: Oh, all RIGHT. It's Michael. Remember that prom thing I told you about? Well, he doesn't want to go.

Grandmere: I knew it. He's still in love with that housefly girl, isn't he? He's taking her, is he? Well, never mind. I have Prince William's mobile phone number here someplace. I'll give him a ring, and he can take Concorde over and take you to the little dance, if you want. That will show that unappreciative—

Me: No, Grandmere. Michael doesn't want to take someone else. He doesn't want to go at all. He . . . he thinks the prom is lame.

Grandmere: Oh . . . for . . . the . . . love . . . of . . . heaven. Not one of those.

Me: Yes, Grandmere. I'm afraid so.

Grandmere: Well, never mind. Your grandfather was the same way. Do you know that if I had left it up to him, we'd have been married in a clerk's office, and gone to a *coffee shop* for lunch afterwards? The man simply had no understanding of romance, let alone the public's need for PAGEANTRY.

Me: Yes. Well. That's why I'm a little down today. Now, if you don't mind, Grandmere, I really have to start on my homework. I have a story due to the paper in the morning, too . . .

*

I didn't mention that it was a story about HER. Well, more or less. It was the story about the incident at Les Hautes Manger. According to the *Sunday Times*, the restaurant's management was still refusing to take Jangbu back on. So Lilly's march had been for nothing. Well, except that it had apparently gotten her a new boyfriend.

Grandmere: Yes, yes, get to work. You have to keep your grades up, or your father will give me another one of his lectures about forcing you to concentrate too much on royal matters and not enough on trigonometry or whatever it is you seem to be having so much trouble with. And don't worry too much about the situation with *that boy*. He'll come around, same as your grandfather did. You just have to find the right incentive. Goodbye.

Incentive? What was Grandmere talking about? What kind of incentive would make Michael come around to the idea of going to the prom? I couldn't think of a single thing that might make him get over this obviously deeply rooted prejudice he had against it.

Except possibly if the prom were a combo prom/*Star Wars*/*Star Trek*/*Lord of the Rings*/computer convention.

Sunday, May 4, 9 p.m., the Loft

I know why Michael never called. Because he emailed me instead. I just didn't check my messages until I turned on my computer to type up my story for *The Atom.*

LinuxRulz

Mia – Hope you didn't get in too much trouble over the closet thing from last night. Mr G is a cool guy, though. I can't imagine he was too upset, after his initial blow-up.

Things have been pretty tense here, what with the whole Lilly/Boris break up. I am trying to stay out of it, and I strongly recommend, for your sanity's sake, you do the same. It's their problem, NOT OURS. I know how you are, Mia, and I really mean it when I say you're better off staying out of it. It's not worth it.

I'll be around all day if you want to give me a call. If you aren't grounded or whatever, maybe we can get together for dim sum? Or if you want, I can come over later to help with your Algebra homework. Just let me know.

Love – Michael

Well. Judging from the tone of THAT, I guess Michael isn't feeling too bad about the whole prom thing. It's almost as if he doesn't KNOW he's ripped out my heart and torn it into little pieces.

Which, considering the fact that I didn't exactly tell him how I felt, might actually be true. That he doesn't know, I mean.

But ignorance, as Grandmere is fond of saying, is no excuse.

I would also hazard a guess from the unconcerned tone of that email that the Drs Moscovitz have not been paying visits to Michael's room, telling HIM about birth control and the richness of the human sexual experience. Oh no. That kind of thing always ends up being the girl's problem. Even if your boyfriend, like mine, is a staunch supporter of women's rights.

Well, at least he wrote. That's more than can be said for my so-called best friend. You would think that Lilly might at least have called to apologize for ruining my party. (Well, really it was Tina who ruined it, with her stupid Seven Minutes in Heaven idea. But Lilly is the one who killed it spiritually by making out with a guy who is not her boyfriend in front of said boyfriend. Well, practically.)

But I have heard nary a word from that ungrateful Boris-dumper. Far be it for me to cast stones at anyone for dating one guy while liking another . . . I mean, didn't I do that just last semester? Still, I didn't MAKE OUT with Michael before formally parting ways with Kenny. I had THAT much integrity, anyway.

And of course, I can't really blame Lilly for liking Jangbu more than Boris. I mean, come on. The guy is hot. And Boris is so . . . not.

Still. It wasn't very nice of her. I'm dying to know what she has to say for herself.

So is everybody else, apparently. Since I logged on, I've been bombarded with instant messages – from everybody but the guilty party concerned.

From Tina:

Iluvromance
Mia, are you all right? I was SO EMBARRASSED for you last night when Mr G caught Lilly and Jangbu in the closet. Was he REALLY mad? I mean, I know he was mad, but was he HOMICIDAL? God, I hope you're not dead. Like that he didn't kill you. That would SUCK if you got grounded, with the prom next week.

What did he say, anyway? Michael, I mean? When the two of you were in the closet together?

By the way, have you heard from Lilly? That was SO WEIRD last night. I mean, with her and Jangbu, right in front of poor Boris. I felt so SORRY for him. He was practically crying, did you notice? And what was with her shirt? When she came out of the closet, I mean. Did you see that? Write back. T.

From Shameeka:

Beyonce_Is_Me
Oh, my God, Mia, that party last night was da BOMB!!!!!!!!! If only Jeff and I had got a turn in that closet, I might finally have got a little action in my Victoria's Secrets, if you know what I mean. Just kidding. LOL. Anyway, could you believe that Lilly/Jangbu thing? What was THAT about? Is Mr G going to tell her DAD? Oh, my God, if my dad found out I'd gone into the closet with a guy who'd already graduated from HS, I would be SO DEAD. Actually I'd be dead if I went into the closet with any guy . . . Anyway, have you heard from her? W/B with the DIRT!!!!!!!!!!!!!

~Shameeka~

PS Did you talk to Michael about the prom? WHAT DID HE SAY?????????????????????????

From Ling Su:

painturgurl
Mia, your mom is SUCH a good artist, her slides were INCREDIBLE. By the way, what HAPPENED while I was in her bedroom? Shameeka said Mr G caught Lilly and that busboy guy in the closet together? But surely she must have meant Lilly and Boris? What was Lilly doing in the closet with somebody other than Boris? Are they broken up, or something? – Ling Su

PS Do you think your mom would let me borrow her sable brushes? Just to try? I never used a really nice brush before and I want to see if it makes any difference before I go down to Pearl Paint and spend a year's allowance on them.

PPS Did Michael ask you to the prom yet??????????

But those were nothing compared to the email I got from Boris:

JoshBell2
Mia, I was wondering if you had heard anything today from Lilly. I have been calling her house all day, but Michael says she's not there. She isn't with you, is she (I hope)? I am really afraid I might have done something to upset her. Why else would she have picked that other guy to go into the closet with last night? Did she mention anything to you,

you know, about being upset with me? I know I stopped for that hot dog during her march, but I was really hungry. She knows I am slightly hypoglycaemic and need to eat every hour and a half.

Please, if you hear from her, let me know? I don't care if it turns out she's mad at me. I just want to know if she's all right. – Boris Pelkowski

I could kill Lilly for this. I really could. This is worse than that time she ran off with my cousin Hank. Because at least then there was no closet business.

God! It's so hard when your best friend is a genius riot-girl feminist/socialist champion of the common man.

It really is.

Monday, May 5, Homeroom

Well, I found out where Lilly was all day yesterday. Mr G showed me at the breakfast table. It was on the front page of the *New York Times*. Here is the article. I cut it out to save for posterity's sake. Also as a model for how my next article for *The Atom* should go, since I know Lesley is going to make me cover this story, as well:

CITY-WIDE BUSBOY STRIKE

Manhattan – Restaurant workers city wide have thrown down their dish towels in an effort to show solidarity with Jangbu Pinasa, a fellow busboy who was dismissed from the four-star uptown brasserie, Les Hautes Manger, last Thursday night after a run-in involving the Dowager Princess of Genovia.

Witnesses say Pinasa, 18, was passing through the restaurant bearing a tray laden with dishware when he tripped and inadvertently spilt soup on the Dowager Princess. Pierre Jupe, manager of Les Hautes Manger, says Pinasa had already received a verbal warning due to another tray he'd dropped earlier in the evening. 'The guy is a klutz, plain and simple,' Jupe, 42, told reporters.

Pinasa's supporters, however, tell a different story. There is reason to believe the busboy did not simply lose his balance, but tripped over a customer's dog. New York City Health Department regulations require that only service animals, such as Seeing Eye dogs, be allowed inside establishments in which food is served to the public. If Les Hautes Manger is proven to have allowed customers to bring their dogs into the dining area, the restaurant could be subject to fines and even shut down.

'There was no dog,' restaurant owner Jean St Luc told reporters. 'The rumour about a dog is nothing but that, a rumour. Our customers would never bring a dog into our dining room. They are too well bred.'

Rumours of a dog – or a large rat – persist, however. Several witnesses claim they spotted an apparently hairless creature, approximately the size of a cat or large rat, darting in and out of the dining tables. A few mentioned that they thought the animal was some sort of pet of the Dowager Princess's, who was at the restaurant to celebrate the fifteenth birthday of her granddaughter, New York City's own royal, Princess of Genovia, Mia Thermopolis Renaldo.

Whatever the reason behind Pinasa's dismissal, busboys throughout the city have vowed to continue their work-stoppage until his job is restored. While restaurateurs insist that their dining establishments will remain open, busboys or not, there is reason for concern. Most waiters and waitresses, used only to taking orders and serving food, not clearing the used plates, may find themselves overburdened. Already some are discussing a sympathy strike to support the busboys, many of whom are illegal immigrants who work off the books, generally for less than the minimum wage and without such benefits as vacation or sick days, health insurance or retirement plans.

Regardless, city restaurants will struggle to remain open – though strike sponsors would like nothing better than to see the Metro area's dining community suffer for what they see as decades of neglect and condescension.

'Busboys have long been the butt of everyone's jokes,' says strike supporter Lilly Moscovitz, 15, who helped organize an impromptu march on City Hall on Sunday. 'It's time the Mayor and everyone else in this city woke up and smelt the dirty dishwater: without busboys, this city's name is mud.'

I seriously can't believe this. This whole thing has got way out of control. And all because of Rommel!!!! Well, and Lilly.

I truly couldn't believe it when Hans pulled up in front of the Moscovitzes' building this morning, and Lilly was standing there next to Michael, looking as if butter wouldn't melt in her mouth. I actually don't know what that expression means, but Mamaw says it all the time, so it must mean something bad. And it does kind of fit how Lilly looked. Like she was just SOOOOOOOOO pleased with herself.

I glared at her and went, 'Talked to Boris yet, Lilly?' I didn't even say anything to Michael, on account of still being kind of mad at him over the whole prom thing. It was really hard to be mad at him because, of course, it was morning and he looked really, really good, all freshly shaved and smooth-faced, and like his neck would smell better than ever. And, of course, he is the best boyfriend of all time, since he wrote me that song and gave me the snowflake necklace and all of that.

But whatever. I have to be mad at him. Because that is the most absurd thing I've heard of, a guy not wanting to go to his own senior prom. I could understand if he didn't have a date or whatever, but Michael so totally DOES have a date. ME!!!!!!!!!! And doesn't he know that by not taking me to his senior prom he is totally depriving me of the one memory of high school that I might actually be able to recall without shuddering? A memory I might be able to cherish, and even show my grandchildren photos of?

No, of course Michael doesn't know this, because I haven't told him. But how can I? I mean, he should know. If he is my true soulmate, he should KNOW without my having to tell him. It is perfectly common knowledge throughout our set that I have seen the movie *Pretty in Pink* forty-seven times. Does he think I watched it all those times because of my fondness for the actor who played the Duck Man?

But Lilly totally blew off my Boris question.

'You should have been there yesterday, Mia,' she said. 'On the march on City Hall, I mean. We had to have been a thousand people strong. It was totally empowering. It brought tears to my eyes, seeing the people come together like that to help further the cause of the working man.'

'You know what else brought tears to someone's eyes?' I asked her pointedly. 'You making out in the closet with Jangbu. That brought tears to your boyfriend's eyes. You remember your boyfriend, BORIS, don't you, Lilly?'

But Lilly just looked out the window at all the flowers that had sprung as if by magic from the dirt in the median on Park Avenue (actually, there's nothing magic about it: NYC parks employees plant them fully grown in the dead of night). 'Oh, look,' she said innocently. 'Spring has sprung.'

Talk about cold. I swear, sometimes I don't even know why I am friends with her.

Monday, May 5, Bio.

So . . .

So what?

So did he ask you last night?????

Didn't you hear?

Hear what?

Michael doesn't believe in the prom. He thinks it's lame.

NO!!!!!!!!!!!!!!!!!!!!!

Yes. Oh, Shameeka, what am I going to do? I've been dreaming of going to the prom with Michael my whole life, practically. Well, at least since we started dating, anyway. I want everyone to look at us dancing and know once and for all that I am the property of Michael Moscovitz. Even though I know that's sexist and no one can ever be the property of another human being. Except . . . except I so want to be Michael's property!!!!!!!!!!!!!!!!

I hear you. So what are you going to do?

What CAN I do? Nothing.

Um . . . you could try talking to him about it.

ARE YOU CRAZY????? Michael said he thinks the prom is LAME. If I tell him it's always been my secret fantasy to go to the prom with the man I love, what does that make me? Hello. That would make *me* lame.

Michael would never think you're lame, Mia. He loves you. I mean, maybe if he knew how you really felt, he'd come around to the whole prom thing.

Shameeka, I'm sorry, but I really think you've seen too many episodes of *Seventh Heaven.*

It's not my fault. It's the only show my dad'll let me watch.

Monday, May 5, Gifted and Talented

I don't know how long I'm going to be able to take this. You could cut the tension in this room with a knife. I almost wish Mrs Hill would come in and yell at us or something. Anything, ANYTHING to break this awful silence.

Yes, silence. I know it seems weird that there'd be silence in the G and T room, considering that this is where Boris Pelkowski is supposed to practise his violin, usually with so much vigour that we are forced to lock him in the supply closet so that we are not maddened by the incessant scraping of his bow.

But no. That bow has been silenced . . . I fear forever. Silenced by the cruel blow of heartache, in the form of a philandering girlfriend . . . who happens to be my best friend, Lilly.

Lilly is sitting here next to me pretending like she doesn't feel the waves of silent grief radiating from her boyfriend, who is sitting in the back corner of the room by the globe, his head buried in his arms. She has to be pretending, because everybody else can feel them. The waves of grief emanating from her boyfriend, I mean. At least, I think so. True, Michael is working on his keyboard like nothing is going on. But he has headphones on. Maybe headphones shield you from radiating waves of grief.

I should have asked for headphones for my birthday.

I wonder if I should go over to the Teachers' Lounge and get Mrs Hill and tell her Boris is sick. Because I really do think he might be. Sick, I mean. Sick at heart and possibly even in the brain. How can Lilly be so mean? It is like she is punishing Boris for a crime he didn't commit. All through lunch, Boris kept asking her if they could go somewhere private, like the third-floor stairwell, to talk, and Lilly just kept saying, 'I'm sorry, Boris, but there's nothing to talk about. It's over between us. You're just going to have to accept it, and move on.'

'But why?' Boris kept wailing. Really loud, too. Like loud enough that the jocks and cheerleaders, over at the popular people's table, kept looking over at us and sniggering. It was a little embarrassing. But very dramatic. 'What did I do?'

'You didn't do anything,' Lilly said, throwing him a bone at last. 'I am just not in love with you any more. Our relationship has progressed to its natural peak, and while I will always treasure the memories of what we had together, it's time for me to move on. I've helped you achieve self-actualization, Boris. You don't need me any more. I have to turn my attention to another tortured soul.'

I don't know what Lilly means about Boris having reached self-actualization. I mean, it isn't like he's got rid of his bionater, or anything. And he's still tucking his sweater into his pants, except when I remind him not to. He is probably the least self-actualized person I know . . .

. . . with the exception of myself, of course.

Boris didn't take any of this too well. I mean, as far as kiss-offs go, it *was* pretty harsh. But Boris should know as well as anybody that once Lilly makes up her mind about something, that's pretty much it. She's sitting here right now working on the speech she wants Jangbu to give at a press conference she's having him hold at the Chinatown Holiday Inn tonight.

Boris might as well face it: he's as good as forgotten.

I wonder how the Drs Moscovitz are going to feel when Lilly introduces them to Jangbu. I am fairly sure my dad wouldn't let me date a guy who'd graduated from high school already. Except Michael, of course. But he doesn't count, because I've known him for so long.

Uh-oh. Something is happening. Boris has lifted his head from his desk. He is gazing at Lilly with eyes that remind me of hotly blazing coals . . . if I had ever seen hotly blazing coals, which I haven't, because coal fires are forbidden within the city limits of Manhattan due to anti-smog regulations. But whatever. He is gazing at her with the same kind of fixed concentration he used to stare at his picture of world-class violinist and role model, Joshua Bell. He's opening his mouth. He's about to say something. WHY AM I THE ONLY PERSON IN THIS CLASS WHO IS PAYING THE SLIGHTEST BIT OF ATTENTION TO WHAT IS GOING ON?

Monday, May 5, Nurse's Office

Oh, my God, that was so dramatic, I can barely write. Seriously. I have never seen so much blood.

I am almost surely destined for some kind of career in the medical sciences, however, because I didn't feel like fainting. Not even once. In fact, except for Michael and maybe Lars, I think I am the only person in the room to have kept my head. This is undoubtedly due to the fact that, being a writer, I am a natural observer of all human interactions, and I saw what was coming before anyone . . . maybe even Boris. The nurse even said that if it hadn't been for my quick intervention, Boris might have lost a lot more blood. Ha! How's that for princess-like behaviour, Grandmere? I saved a guy's life!

Well, OK, maybe not his *life*, but whatever, Boris might have passed out or something if it hadn't been for me. I can't even imagine what caused him to freak out like that. Well, yes, I guess I can. I think the silence in the G and T room caused Boris to go momentarily mental. Seriously.

I can totally see how it would, since it was bugging me, as well.

Anyway, what happened was, we were all just sitting there, minding our own business – well, except for me, of course, since I was watching Boris – when all of a sudden he stood up and went, 'Lilly, I can't take this any more! You can't do this to me! You've got to give me a chance to prove my undying devotion!'

Or at least it was something like that. It's kind of hard to remember, given what happened next.

I do remember how Lilly replied, however. She was actually somewhat kind. You could tell she felt a little bit bad about her behaviour towards Boris at my party. She went, in a nice voice, 'Boris, seriously, I am so sorry, especially about the way it happened. But the truth is, when a love like mine for Jangbu takes hold, there's no stopping it. You can't hold back New York baseball fans when the Yankees win the World Series. You can't hold back New York shoppers when Century Twenty-One has a sale. You can't hold back the floodwaters in the F train subway tunnels when it pours. Similarly, you can't hold back love like the kind I feel for Jangbu. I am so, so sorry about it, but seriously, there's nothing I can do. I love him.'

These words, gently as they were spoken – and even I, Lilly's severest critic, with the possible exception of her brother, will admit they were spoken gently – seemed to hit Boris like a fist. He shuddered all over. Next thing I knew, he'd picked up the giant globe next to him – which really was a feat of some athleticism, as that globe weighs a ton. In fact, the reason it's in the G and T room is that it's so heavy, nobody can get it to spin any more, so the administration, rather than throwing it away, must have figured, well, just stick it in the classroom with the nerds, they'll take anything . . . after all, they're nerds.

So there was Boris – hypoglycaemic, asthmatic, deviated-septum and allergy-prone Boris – holding this big heavy globe over his head, as if he were Atlas or He-Man or the Rock or somebody.

'Lilly,' he said in a strangled, very un-Borislike voice – I should probably point out that by this time everyone in the room was paying attention: I mean, Michael had taken off his headphones and was looking at Boris very intently, and even the quiet guy who is supposed to be working on this new kind of superglue that sticks to objects but not to human skin (so you won't have that stuck-together-finger problem any more after gluing up the sole of your shoe) was totally aware of what was happening around him for once.

'If you don't take me back,' Boris said, breathing hard – that globe had to weigh fifty pounds at least, and he was holding it OVER HIS HEAD – 'I will drop this globe on my head.'

Everyone sort of inhaled at the same time. I think I can safely say that there was no doubt in anybody's mind that Boris meant what he said. He was totally going to drop that globe on his head. Seeing it written down, it looks kind of funny – I mean, really, who DOES things like that? Threatens to drop a globe on his head?

But this WAS Gifted and Talented class. I mean, geniuses are ALWAYS doing weird stuff like dropping globes on their heads. I bet there are geniuses out there who have dropped weirder stuff than globes on their heads. Like cinder blocks and cats and stuff. Just to see what would happen.

I mean, come on. They're geniuses.

Because Boris is a genius, and so is Lilly, she reacted to his threat the way only another genius would. A normal girl, like me, would have gone, 'No, Boris! Put the globe down, Boris! Let's talk, Boris!'

But Lilly, being a genius, and having a genius's curiosity about what would happen if Boris did drop the globe on his head – and maybe because she wanted to see if she really did have enough power over him to make him do it – just went, in a disgusted voice, 'Go ahead. See if I care.'

And that's when it happened. You could tell Boris had second thoughts – like it finally sunk into his love-addled brain that dropping a fifty-pound globe on his head probably wasn't the best way to handle the situation.

But just as he was about to put the globe down, it slipped

– maybe accidentally. Or maybe on purpose. What the Drs Moscovitz call a self-fulfilling prophecy, like when you say, 'Oh, I don't want *that* to happen,' and then because you said that and you're thinking about it so much, you accidentally-on-purpose make it happen – and Boris dropped the globe on his head.

The globe made this sickening hollow thunking sound as it hit Boris's skull – the same noise that eggplant made as it hit the pavement that time I dropped it out of Lilly's sixteenth-storey bedroom window – before the whole thing bounced off Boris's head and went crashing to the floor.

And then Boris clapped his hands to his scalp and started staggering around, upsetting the sticky-glue guy, who seemed to be afraid Boris would crash into him and mess up his notes.

It was kind of interesting to see how everyone reacted. Lilly put both hands to her cheeks and just stood there, pale as . . . well, death. Michael swore and started towards Boris. Lars ran from the room, yelling, 'Mrs Hill! Mrs Hill!'

And I – not even really aware of what I was doing – stood up, whipped off my school sweater, strode up to Boris and yelled, 'Sit down!' since he was running all around like a chicken with its head cut off. Not that I have ever seen a chicken with its head recently cut off – I hope never to see this in my lifetime.

But you get what I mean.

Boris, to my very great surprise, did what I said. He sank down at the nearest desk, shivering like Rommel during a thunderstorm. Then I said, in the same commanding voice that didn't seem to belong to me, 'Move your hands!'

And Boris moved his hands off his head.

That's when I stuck my wadded up sweater over the small hole in Boris's head, to stop the bleeding, just like I saw a vet do on *Animal Precinct* when Officer Anne Marie Lucas brought in a pit bull that had been shot.

After that, all hell – excuse me, but it is true – broke loose.

- Lilly started crying in great big baby sobs, which I haven't seen her do since we were in second grade and I accidentally-on-purpose shoved a spatula down her throat while we were frosting birthday cupcakes to hand out to the class, because she was eating all the frosting and I was afraid there wouldn't be enough to cover all the cupcakes.
- The guy with the glue ran out of the room.
- Mrs Hill came running *into* the room, followed by Lars and about half the faculty, who'd apparently all been in the Teachers' Lounge doing nothing, as the teachers at Albert Einstein High School are wont to do.
- Michael was bent over Boris going, in a calm, soothing voice I am pretty sure he learned from his parents, who often get calls in the middle of the night from patients of theirs who have gone off their medication for whatever reason and are threatening to drive up and down the Merrick Parkway in a clown suit, 'It's going to be all right. Boris, you're going to be all right. Just take a deep breath. Good. Now take another one. Deep, even breaths. Good. You're going to be fine. You're going to be just fine.'

And I just kept standing there with my sweater pressed to the top of Boris's head, while the globe, having apparently come unstuck thanks to the fall – or perhaps the lubrication from Boris's blood – spun lazily around, eventually coming to rest with the country of Ecuador most prominent.

One of the teachers went and got the nurse, who made

me move my sweater a little so that she could see Boris's wound. Then she hastily made me press the sweater back down. Then she said to Boris in the same calming voice Michael was using, 'Come along, young man. Let's go to my office.'

Only Boris couldn't walk to the nurse's office by himself, since when he tried to stand up his knees sort of gave out beneath him, probably on account of his hypoglycaemia. So Lars and Michael half-carried Boris to the nurse's office while I just kept my sweater pressed to his head, because, well, nobody had told me to stop.

As we passed Lilly on our way out, I got a good look at her face, and she really had gone pale as death – her face was the colour of New York City snow, kind of pale grey tinged with yellow. She also looked a bit sick to her stomach. Which, if you ask me, serves her right.

So now Michael and Lars and I are sitting here as the nurse fills out an incident report. She called Boris's mother, who is supposed to come get him and take him to their family doctor. While the wound caused by the globe isn't too deep, the nurse thinks it will probably require a few stitches, and that Boris will need a tetanus shot. The nurse was very complimentary of my quick action. She went, 'You're the princess, aren't you?' and I demurely replied that I was.

I can't help feeling really proud of myself.

It is strange how even though I don't like seeing blood in movies and stuff, in real life, it didn't bother me a bit. Seeing Boris's blood, I mean. Because I had to sit with my head between my knees in Bio. that time they showed the acupuncture film. But seeing that blood spurt out of Boris's head in real life didn't cause me so much as a twinge.

Maybe I'll have a delayed reaction, or something. You know, like post-traumatic stress syndrome.

Although to be frank, if all of this princess stuff hasn't caused me PTSS, I highly doubt seeing my best friend's ex-boyfriend drop a globe on his head is going to do it.

Uh-oh. Here comes Principal Gupta.

Monday, May 5, French

Mia, is it true about Boris? Did he really try to kill himself during fifth period by stabbing himself in the chest with a protractor?

Of course not, Tina. He tried to kill himself by dropping a globe on his head.

OH, MY GOD!!!!!!!! Is he going to be all right?

Yes, thanks to the quick action of Michael and me. He'll probably have a bad headache for a few days, though. The worst part was talking to Principal Gupta. Because of course she wanted to know why he did it. And I didn't want Lilly to get in trouble, or anything. Not that it's Lilly's fault . . . Well, I guess it sort of is . . .

Of course it is!!!!! You don't think she could have handled the whole thing a little better? My God, she was practically Frenching Jangbu right in front of Boris! So what did you say to Principal UpChuck?

Oh, you know, the usual. Boris must have cracked under all the pressure AEHS teachers put on us, and why can't the Administration cancel finals like they did in Harry Potter Two. Only she didn't listen, because it's not like anyone is dead, or a giant snake was chasing us around, or anything.

Still, it is fully the most romantic thing I have ever heard. Only in my wildest dreams would a man be so desperate to win back my heart that he'd do something like drop a globe on his head.

I know! If you ask me, Lilly is totally rethinking the Jangbu thing. At least, I think so. I actually haven't seen her since it all happened.

My God, who knew that all this time, inside Boris's spindly chest beat the heart of a Heathcliff-like lover?

Tcha! I wonder if his spirit is going to roam around East 75th Street the way Heathcliff's roamed around the moor. You know, after Cathy died.

I kind of always thought Boris was cute. I mean, I know mouth-breathers annoy you, but you have to admit, he has very beautiful hands.

HANDS? Who cares about HANDS?????

Um, they are slightly important. Hello. They're what guys TOUCH you with.

You are sick, Tina. Very sick.

Although that might be the pot calling the kettle black, given my whole neck thing with Michael. But whatever. I have never ADMITTED that to anyone. Out loud.

Monday, May 5, in the limo on the way to princess lessons

I am so totally the star of the school. As if the princess thing were not enough, now it's going all around Albert Einstein that Michael and I saved Boris's life. My God, we are like the Dr Kovach and Nurse Abby of AEHS!!!!!!!!! And Michael even LOOKS a little like Dr Kovach. You know, with the dark hair and the gorgeous chest and all.

I don't even know why my mother is bothering with a midwife. She should just have me deliver the baby. I could so totally do it. All I'd need is like some scissors and a catcher's mitt. Jeez.

God. I am going to have to rethink this whole writer thing. My talents may lie in a completely different sphere.

Monday, May 5, Lobby of the Plaza

Lars just told me that to get into medical school you actually have to have good grades in maths and science. I can see why you'd have to know science, but why MATHS?????? WHY?????? Why is the American educational system conspiring against me to keep me from reaching my career goals?

Monday, May 5, on the way home from the Plaza

Trust Grandmere to burst my bubble. I was still riding high from the medical miracle I'd performed back at school – well, it WAS a miracle: a miracle I hadn't passed out from the sight of all that blood – when Grandmere was like, 'So when can I schedule your fitting at Chanel? Because I've put a dress on hold there that I think will be perfect for this little prom you're so excited about, but if you want it on time, you'll have to have it fitted in the next day or so.'

So then I had to explain to her that Michael and I still weren't going to the prom.

She didn't react to the news like a normal grandmother, of course. A normal grandmother would have been all sympathetic and would have patted my hand and given me some home-baked cookies or a dollar or something.

Not my grandmother. Oh no. *My* grandmother was just like, 'Well, then you obviously didn't do as I instructed.'

Jeez! Blame the victim, Grandma!

'Whaddaya mean?' I blurted out. So of course Grandmere was all, 'What do I mean? Is that what you said? Then ask me properly.'

'What . . . do . . . you . . . mean . . . Grandmere?' I asked her more politely, though inwardly, of course, I didn't feel very polite at all.

'I mean that you haven't done as I said. I told you that, if you found the right incentive, your Michael would be only too happy to escort you to the prom. But clearly you would rather sit around and sulk than take the sort of action necessary to get what it is that you want.'

I took umbrage at that.

'I beg your pardon, Grandmere,' I said, 'but I have done everything humanly possible to convince Michael to go to the prom.' Short, of course, of actually explaining to him *why* it was so important to me to go. Because I'm not so sure that even if I *did* tell Michael why it was so important to me he'd agree to go. And how much would THAT suck? You know, if I bared my soul to the man I love, only to have him decide that his desire not to attend something as lame as the prom was stronger than his desire to see my dream come true?

'On the contrary, you have not,' Grandmere said. She stubbed out her cigarette and, exhaling plumes of grey smoke from her nostrils – it is totally shocking how the weight of the Genovian throne rests solely on my slender shoulders, and yet my own grandmother remains unconcerned about the effects of her second-hand smoke on my lungs – went, 'I've explained this to you before, Amelia. In situations where opposing parties are striving to achieve détente, and yet are failing to reach it, it is always in your best interest to step back and ask yourself what the enemy wants.'

I blinked at her through all the smoke. 'I'm supposed to figure out what Michael wants?'

'Correct.'

I shrugged. 'Easy. He doesn't want to go to the prom. Because it's lame.'

'No. That is what Michael *doesn't* want. What does he *want*?'

I had to think about that one.

'Um,' I said, watching Rommel as he, seeing that Grandmere was otherwise occupied, leaned over and surreptitiously began licking all the fur off one of his paws. 'I guess . . . Michael wants to play in his band?'

'*Bien*,' Grandmere said, which means good in French. 'But what *else* might he want?'

'Um,' I said. 'I don't know.' I was still thinking about the band thing. It is the duty of the freshman, sophomore and junior classes to put on the prom for the seniors, even though we ourselves do not get to go, unless invited by a senior. I tried to remember what the Prom Committee had reported in *The Atom*, so far as the arrangements they'd made for music at the prom. I think they'd hired a DJ or something.

'Of course you know what Michael wants,' Grandmere said sharply. 'Michael wants what *every* man wants.'

'You mean . . .' I felt stunned by the rapidity with which my grandmother's mind worked. 'You mean I should ask the prom committee to let Michael's band play at the prom?'

Grandmere started to choke for some reason. 'Wh-what?' she demanded, hacking up half a lung, practically.

I sat back in my seat, completely at a loss for words. It had never occurred to me before, but Grandmere's solution to the problem was totally perfect. Nothing would delight Michael more than an actual, paying gig for Skinner Box. And I would get to go to the prom . . . and not just with the man of my dreams, but with *an actual member of the band*. Is there anything cooler in the world than being at the prom with a member of the band playing at the prom? Um, no. No, there is not.

'Grandmere,' I breathed. 'You're a genius!'

Grandmere was slurping up the last of the ice in her Sidecar. 'I don't have the slightest idea what you're talking about, Amelia,' she said.

But I knew that, for the first time in her life, Grandmere was just being modest.

Then I remembered that I was supposed to be angry with her, on account of Jangbu. So I went, 'But, Grandmere, be serious a minute. This thing with the busboys . . . the strike. You've got to do something. It's all your fault, you know.'

Grandmere eyed me over all the blue smoke coming out of the new cigarette she'd just lit.

'Why, you ungrateful little chit,' she said. 'I solve all of your problems, and this is the thanks you show me?'

'I'm serious, Grandmere,' I said. 'You've got to call Les Hautes Manger and tell them about Rommel. Tell them it was your fault that Jangbu tripped, and that they've got to hire him back. It isn't fair, otherwise. I mean, the poor guy lost his job!'

'He'll find another,' Grandmere said dismissively.

'Not without references,' I pointed out.

'So he can go back to his native land,' Grandmere said. 'I'm sure his parents miss him.'

'Grandmere, he's from *Tibet*, a country that has been under Chinese oppression for decades. He can't go back there. There are no jobs. He'll starve.'

'I no longer care to discuss this,' Grandmere said loftily. 'Tell me the ten different courses traditionally served at a royal Genovian wedding.'

'Grandmere!'

'Tell me!'

So I had no choice but to rattle off the ten different courses traditionally served at a Genovian wedding – olives, antipasto, pasta, fish, meat, salad, bread, cheese, fruit, dessert (note to self: when Michael and I get married, remember not to do it in Genovia, unless the palace'll do an all-vegetarian meal).

I don't understand how someone who has embraced the dark side as fully as Grandmere can come up with brilliant stuff like getting Michael's band to play at the prom.

But I guess even Darth Vader had his moments. I can't think of any right now, but I'm sure he had some.

Monday, May 5, 9 p.m., the Loft

Bad news:

I spent the whole evening pouring over back issues of *The Atom*, trying to figure out who was head of the Prom Committee, so I could email him/her with my request that Skinner Box be approached as a possible live entertainment alternative to the DJ I know they've got lined up. So you can only imagine my surprise and disappointment when I finally stumbled across the article I was looking for, and saw the horrifying answer right there in black and white:

Lana Weinberger.

LANA WEINBERGER is head of this year's Prom Committee.

Well, that's it. I'm dead. There is NO WAY I'm going to get to go to the prom now. I mean, Lana would sooner go off her Atkins diet than hire my boyfriend's band. I mean, Lana hates my guts, and always has.

And I can't say the feeling isn't mutual.

What am I going to do NOW? I CAN'T miss the prom. I just CAN'T!!!!!!!!!

But I guess I don't have the biggest problems in the world. I mean, there are people with worse ones. Like Boris, for instance. I got this email from him just now:

```
JoshBell2
Mia, I just wanted to say thanks for what you did
for me today. I don't know why I behaved so stu-
pidly. I guess I was just overcome with emotion. I
love her so much! But it is clear to me now that we
are not destined for one another, as I so long
thought (erroneously, I realize at last). No, Lilly
is like a wild mustang, born to run free. I see now
```

that no man – least of all someone like me – can ever hope to tame her.

Treasure what you have with Michael, Mia. It is a rare and beautiful thing, to love, and be loved in return.

Boris Pelkowski

PS My mother says she will get your sweater dry-cleaned so I can give it back to you at the end of this week. She says Star Cleaners think they can get the blood out without any permanent staining. B. P.

Poor Boris! Imagine thinking of Lilly as a wild mustang. Wild mushroom, maybe. But a *mustang*? I don't think so.

I figured I'd better check on how she was doing, since last time I'd seen her, Lilly'd been looking kind of green around the gills. I sent her a totally non-accusatory, completely friendly email, inquiring into her mental health after her ordeal earlier in the day.

You can imagine my outrage when this is what I got for my efforts:

WomynRule: Hey, P.O.G!

(Pog is the nickname Lilly decided to give me a few weeks ago. It stands for Princess of Genovia. I have asked her repeatedly not to use it but she persists, probably because I made the mistake of letting her know it bugs me.)

Whazzup? Missed you at tonight's SATWDOJPA press conference. Looks like we may actually get the hotel workers' union behind our cause. If we can get hotels 2 strike as well as the restaurant workers, we'll bring the city 2 its knees! Finally, people will start realizing that service industry personnel are not to be messed with! The common man deserves to be paid a living wage!

Wasn't that wild about Boris this afternoon? I have to say, it gave me quite a scare. I had no idea he was such a psycho. Then again, he IS a musician. I should have known. That was pretty cool the way you and Michael handled the situation, tho. You two were just like Dr McCoy and Nurse Chappell. Though you'd probably prefer it if I said you were like Dr Kovach and Nurse Abby. Which I guess you kind of were. Well, gtg. My mom wants me to put the dishes away.

Lil

PS Jangbu did the sweetest thing after the press conference tonight: he bought me a silk rose from a booth on Canal Street. Soooo romantic. Boris never did stuff like that. L

I have to admit: I was shocked. Shocked by Lilly's cavalier dismissal of poor Boris's pain. Shocked by her *whazzup* and her reference to the original *Star Trek*, which if *I'd* used Lilly would have rebuked me for being passé, the original *Star Trek* hardly being on the cutting edge of pop culture. And REALLY shocked at her implication that all musicians are psychos. I mean, hello! Her brother Michael, MY BOYFRIEND, is a musician! And yes, we certainly have our problems, but not because he is in any way a psycho. In fact, if anything, my problems with Michael have to do with the fact that he, as a Capricorn, has his feet planted TOO firmly on the ground, whereas I, a free-wheeling Taurus, want to bring a little more fun into our relationship.

I wrote back to her right away. I will admit I was so angry, my hands were shaking as I typed.

FtLouie

Lilly, it might interest you to know that Boris had to get two stitches AND a tetanus shot because of what happened in G and T today. Furthermore, he might even have concussion. Perhaps you could tear yourself away from your tireless work on behalf of Jangbu, a guy YOU ONLY MET THREE DAYS AGO, and spare a little sympathy for your ex, whom you dated for EIGHT WHOLE MONTHS.

M

Lilly's response was almost instantaneous.

WomynRule

Excuse me, P.O.G., but I can't say I really appreciate your condescending tone. Kindly don't pull your Royal Highness act on me. I'm sorry if you don't happen to like Jangbu or the work I am doing to help him and people like him. However, that does not mean I need to be held hostage to my old relationship by the juvenile theatrics of a self-delusional narcissist like Boris. I did not make him pick up that globe and drop it on his head. He made that choice all on his own. I would think you, as a faithful viewer of the Lifetime Movie Channel for Women, would recognize manipulative behaviour like Boris's as classic stalker stuff.

But then, maybe if you stopped watching so many

movies, and actually tried living life for a change, you might recognize this. You also might be writing something a little bit more challenging for the school paper than the cafeteria beat.

I could tell she was feeling guilty over what she'd done to Boris by how thoroughly she attacked him. That I could ignore. But her attack on my writing could not go unnoticed. I immediately fired back with:

FtLouie
Yeah, well, I may watch a lot of movies, but at least I don't go around with my face glued to a camera lens, the way you do. I prefer to WATCH movies not invent drama FOR the movies. Furthermore, I will have you know that Lesley Cho asked me to cover a hard news story for the paper just the other day.

This is what I just got in reply.

WomynRule
Yeah, a story I made possible. You are so weak. Go back to pining over the fact that you have to spend your summer in a palace in Genovia (wah-wah-wah) and that my brother doesn't want to go to the prom with you, and leave the REAL problem-solving to people like me, who are better equipped intellectually to handle it.

Well, that's the last straw. Lilly Moscovitz is no longer my best friend. I have taken all the abuse I can stand. I am thinking about writing back to her to tell her that.

But maybe that would be too childish, and not INTELLECTUAL enough.

Maybe I'll just ask Tina if she'll be my best friend from now on.

But no, that would be too childish, too. I mean, it's not like we're in third grade any more. We're practically women, like my mom said. Women like my mom don't go around declaring who is their best friend and who isn't. They just sort of . . . know. Without saying anything about it. I don't know how, but they do. Maybe it is an oestrogen thing, or something.

Oh, my God, I have such a headache.

Monday, May 5, 11 p.m.

I almost burst into tears just now when I checked my email one last time before bed. That's because this is what I found there:

LinuxRulz
Mia, are you sure you aren't mad at me about something? Because you hardly said three words to me all day. Except during the whole Boris thing. Did I do something wrong?

Then another one, a second later:

LinuxRulz
Nevermind that last email. It was stupid. I know if I'd done something to upset you, you'd have told me. Because that's the kind of girl you are. That's one of the reasons we're so good together. Because we can tell each other anything.

Then:

LinuxRulz
It's not that thing from your party, is it? You know, where I wouldn't beat up Jangbu for making out with my sister? Because getting involved in my sister's love life is never a good idea, as you might have noticed.

Then:

LinuxRulz
Well, whatever. Goodnight. And I love you.

Oh, Michael! My sweet protector!

WHY WON'T YOU TAKE ME TO YOUR PROM??????????????????????????????

Tuesday, May 6, 3 a.m.

I still can't believe the nerve of her. I have learned A LOT about writing from watching movies. For instance:

Valuable tips I, Mia Thermopolis, learned about writing from the movies:

Aspen Extreme

T. J. Burke moves to Aspen to become a ski instructor, but really he just wants to write. When he is done penning his touching tribute to his dead friend, Dex, he puts it in an envelope and sends it to *Powder* magazine. A hot-air balloon and two swans fly by. Then you see a mail carrier put a copy of *Powder* magazine in T.J.'s mailbox. On the cover is a blurb about T.J.'s story! It's *that* easy to get published!

The Wonderboys

Always keep a back-up disk.

Little Women

Ditto.

Moulin Rouge

When writing a play, do not fall in love with your leading lady. Especially if she has consumption. Also, don't drink anything green offered to you by a midget.

The Bell Jar

Don't let your mother read your book until *after* it's published (when there's nothing she can do about it).

Adaptation

Never trust a twin.

Isn't She Great, The Jacqueline Suzann Story

Publishers don't actually mind if you turn in a manuscript written on pink stationery. Also, sex sells.

How DARE Lilly suggest I've wasted my time watching TV?

And if I happen to choose a career in the medical profession, I am still golden, because I have seen practically every episode of *ER* ever made.

Not to mention *M*A*S*H*.

Tuesday, May 6, Gifted and Talented

Horrible day so far, in every way:

1. Mr G gave us a pop quiz in Algebra, which I flunked because I was too worked up over the whole Boris/Lilly/prom thing last night to study. You would think my own stepfather would be kind enough to drop me a hint or two when he's going to give a pop quiz. But apparently this would violate some teacher code of ethics.

As if. What about the stepfather code of ethics? Anyone ever thought about THAT?

2. Shameeka and I got caught passing notes again. Have to write a thousand-word essay on effects of global warming on ecosystems of South America.
3. I had no one to be my partner on the disease projects we are doing in Health and Safety because Lilly and I aren't speaking. She is doing the full-on avoidance thing. She even took the subway to school today instead of riding with Michael and me in the limo. Not that I mind. Plus when we drew diseases, I got Asperger's syndrome. Why couldn't I have got a cool disease, like Ebola fever? It is so unfair, especially as I am now considering a career in the health field.
4. At lunch I accidentally ate some sausage that was mistakenly baked into my supposedly cheese-only Individual Pizza. Also, Boris spent the whole period writing the word *Lilly* over and over again on his violin case. Lilly didn't even show at lunch. Hopefully she and Jangbu hopped a plane back to Tibet and won't

be bothering any of us any more. Michael says he doesn't think so, though. He says he thinks she had another press conference.

5. Michael did not change his mind about the prom. Not that I brought it up, or anything. Just that I happened to be walking with him past the table where Lana and the rest of the Prom Committee are selling tickets, and Michael went, "Sucka," under his breath when he saw the guy who hates it when they put corn in the chilli buying prom tickets for himself and his girlfriend.

Even the guy who hates it when they put corn in the chilli is going to the prom. Everyone in the whole world is going to the prom. Except for me.

Lilly still isn't back from wherever it is she went off to before lunch. Which is probably just as well. I don't think Boris could take it if she walked in here right now. He found some correcting fluid in the supply closet, and he is using it to make little curlicues around Lilly's name on his violin case. I want to shake him and go, 'Snap out of it! She's not worth it!'

But I'm afraid it might loosen his stitches.

Plus Mrs Hill, clearly due to yesterday's events, is fully sitting at her desk, flipping through Garnet Hill catalogues and keeping an eagle eye on us. I bet she got in trouble over the whole violin-virtuoso-globe-dropping thing. Principal Gupta is really very strict about bloodshed on school grounds.

Since I have nothing better to do, I am going to compose a poem that expresses my true feelings about everything that is going on. I intend to call *Spring Fever*. If it is good enough, I am going to submit it to *The Atom*. Anonymously, of course. If Lesley knew I wrote it, she'd never print it, since, as a cub reporter, I have not Paid My Dues.

But if she just FINDS it slipped under the door to *The Atom's* office, maybe she'll run it. The way I see it, I have nothing to lose. It's not like things can possibly get any worse.

Tuesday, May 6, St Vincent's Hospital

Things just got worse. Very, very worse.

It's probably all my fault. All my fault because I wrote that before. About things not possibly being able to get any worse. It turns out things most definitely CAN get worse than

- Flunking an Algebra quiz
- Getting in trouble in Bio. for passing notes
- Getting Asperger's syndrome as your Health and Safety project
- Your father trying to force you to spend most of your summer in Genovia
- Your boyfriend refusing to take you to the prom
- Your best friend calling you weak
- Her boyfriend needing stitches in his head from a self-inflicted globe wound
- Your grandmother trying to force you to have dinner with the Sultan of Brunei

What's worse is your pregnant mother passing out in the frozen-food department at the Grand Union.

I am totally serious. She landed face first in the Häagen Dazs. Thank God she bounced off the Ben and Jerry's and came to rest on her back, or my potential brother or sister would have been crushed under the weight of his or her own mother.

The manager of the Grand Union apparently didn't have the slightest idea what to do. According to witnesses, he ran all around the store, flapping his arms and yelling, 'Dead woman in Aisle Four! Dead woman in Aisle Four!'

I don't know what would have happened if members of

the New York Fire Department hadn't happened to have been there. I'm serious. Ladder Company Number 3 does all of its grocery shopping for the firehouse at the Grand Union – I know because Lilly and I, back when we were friends and first realized firemen are hot, used to go there all the time to watch them as they picked through the nectarines and mangoes – and they happened to be there stocking up for the week when my mom went horizontal. They checked her pulse right away and figured out she wasn't dead. Then they called an ambulance and whisked her to St Vincent's, the closest ER.

Too bad my mom was unconscious the whole time. She would so totally have loved to have ridden in an ambulance with all those hot guys. Plus, you know, the fact that they were strong enough to lift her . . . and at her current weight, which is a lot . . . that's pretty cool.

You can imagine when I was just sitting there, bored out of my skull in French, and my mobile phone rang . . . well, I freaked. Not because it was the first time anyone had ever called me, or even because Mademoiselle Klein fully confiscates any mobile phones that ring during her class, but because the only people who are allowed to call me on my mobile phone are my mom and Mr G, and then only to let me know that I need to get to home, because my sibling is about to be born.

Except that when I finally answered the phone – it took me a minute to figure out it was MY phone that was ringing: I kept looking around accusingly at everybody else in class, who just blinked confusedly back at me – it wasn't my mom or Mr G to tell me the baby was coming. It was Assistant Fire Chief Pete Logan, to ask me if I knew a Helen Thermopolis and, if so, could I come to St Vincent's hospital immediately. The firemen had found my mom's mobile phone in her purse, and dialled the only number she had in her address book . . .

Mine.

I about had a coronary, of course. I shrieked and grabbed my backpack, then Lars. Then he and I ran out of there without a word of explanation to anyone . . . like I had suddenly developed Asperger's syndrome or something. On our way out of the building, I skidded past Mr Gianini's classroom, then backed up and stuck my head in to scream that his wife was in the hospital and that he better put down that chalk and come with us.

I've never seen Mr G look so scared. Not even the first time he met Grandmere.

Then the three of us ran all out for the 77th Street subway station – because there was no way a cab was going to get us there fast enough in the midday traffic, and Hans and the limo are off duty every day until I get out of school at three.

I don't think the staff at St Vincent – who are totally excellent, by the way – ever encountered anything quite like a hysterical Princess of Genovia, her bodyguard and her stepfather before. The three of us burst into the ER waiting area and just stood there screaming my mom's name until finally this nurse came out of triage and was like, 'Helen Thermopolis is just fine. She's awake and resting right now. She just got a little dehydrated, and fainted.'

'Dehydrated?' I about had another coronary, but this time for different reasons. 'She hasn't been drinking her eight glasses of water a day?'

The nurse smiled and said, 'Well, she mentioned that the baby is putting a lot of pressure on her bladder . . .'

'Is she going to be all right?' Mr G wanted to know.

'Is the BABY going to be all right?' I wanted to know.

'Both of them are going to be fine,' the nurse said. 'Come with me, and I'll take you to her.'

Then the nurse took us into the ER – the actual ER of St Vincent's Hospital, where everybody in Greenwich Village who gets shot or has a kidney stone goes!!!!!!!!!! I saw tons of sick people in there. There was a guy who had all sorts of tubes sticking out of him, and another guy who was throwing up in a basin. There was an NYU student 'sleeping one off', and an old lady who'd had heart palpitations, and a supermodel who'd fallen off her stilettos, and a construction worker who had a gash on his hand and a bike messenger who had been hit by a taxi.

Anyway, before I got a good look at all the patients – patients like the ones I might have someday, if I ever pull up my Algebra grades and get into medical school – the nurse tugged a curtain back, and there was my mom, awake and looking pretty peeved.

When I noticed the needle in her arm, I saw why she was so peeved. She was hooked up to an IV!!!!!!!!!!!!

'OH, MY GOD!!!' I yelled at the nurse. Even though you aren't supposed to yell in the ER, because there are sick people there. 'If she's so OK, why does she have THAT???'

'It's just to get some fluids into her,' the nurse said. 'Your mom is going to be fine. Tell them you're going to be fine, Mrs Thermopolis.'

'It's *Ms*,' my mom snarled.

And I knew then that she was going to be just fine.

I threw myself on her and gave her the biggest hug I could, what with the IV and the fact that Mr G was hugging her too.

'I'm all right, I'm all right,' my mom said, patting us both on our heads. 'Let's not make a bigger deal out of this than has been made already.'

'But it IS a big deal,' I said, feeling tears trickle down my face. Because it is very upsetting, getting a phone call in the middle of French class from an assistant fire chief, telling you that your mother is in hospital.

'No, it's not,' my mom said. 'I'm fine. The baby's fine. And once they get the rest of this Ringer's lactate into me, I get to go home.' She shot the nurse a look. 'RIGHT?'

'Yes, ma'am,' the nurse said, and closed the curtain so that the four of us – my mom, Mr G, me and my bodyguard – could have some privacy.

'You have to be more careful, Mom,' I said. 'You can't let yourself get worn out like this.'

'I'm not worn out,' my mom said. 'It's that damned roast pork and noodle soup I had for lunch—'

'From Number One Noodle Son?' I cried, horrified. 'Mom, you didn't! There's like one million grammes of sodium in that! No wonder you passed out! The MSG alone—'

'I have an idea, Your Highness,' Lars said, speaking in a low voice in my ear. 'Why don't you and I go across the street and see if we can get your mother a smoothie?'

Lars always keeps such a level head in a crisis. That is no doubt on account of his intensive training with the Israeli Army. He is a distinguished expert marksman with his Glock, and pretty good with a flamethrower, too. Or so he once confided in me.

'That's a good idea,' I said. 'Mom, Lars and I will be right back. We're going to get you a nice, healthy smoothie.'

'Thanks,' my mom said weakly, but for some reason she was looking more at Lars than at me. No doubt because her eyes were still out of focus from the whole fainting thing.

Except that when we returned with the smoothie, the nurse wouldn't let us back in to see my mom. She said there was only one visitor per hour per patient in the ER, and that she'd only made an exception before because we'd all looked so worried and she'd wanted us to see for ourselves that Mom was OK, and I'm the Princess of Genovia, and all.

She did take the smoothie Lars and I had bought, and promised to give it to my mom.

So now Lars and I are sitting in the hard orange plastic chairs in the waiting room. We'll be here until my mom gets dismissed. I already called Grandmere and cancelled my princess lesson for the day. I must say, Grandmere wasn't very alarmed, once she heard my mom was going to be all right. You would think relatives of hers faint in the Grand Union every day. My dad's reaction to the news was much more gratifying. He got ALL worked up and wanted to fly in the royal physician all the way from Genovia to make sure the baby's heartbeat was regular and that the pregnancy wasn't putting undue stress on my mom's admittedly worn-out thirty-six-year-old system—

OH, MY GOD!!!!!!!!!! You'll never guess who just walked into the ER. My OWN royal consort, HRH Michael Moscovitz Renaldo to be.

More later.

Tuesday, May 6, the Loft

Michael is SO sweet!!!!!!!!! As soon as school let out he rushed over to the hospital to make sure my mom was all right. He found out what happened from my dad. Can you IMAGINE???? He was so worried when he heard from Tina that I had gone rushing out of French that he called MY DAD when he couldn't get an answer at the Loft.

How many boys would willingly call their girlfriend's dad? Hmmm? None that I know of. Especially if their girlfriend's dad happened to be a crowned PRINCE, like my dad. Most boys would be too scared to call their girlfriend's dad in a situation like that.

But not *my* boyfriend.

Too bad he still thinks the prom is lame. But whatever. Having your pregnant mother pass out in the refrigerated section of the Grand Union has a way of putting things into perspective.

And now I know that, much as I would have loved to have gone, the prom is not really important. What is important is family togetherness, and being with the ones you love, and being blessed with good health and—

Oh, God, what am I talking about? Of COURSE I still want to go the prom. Of COURSE it's still killing me inside that Michael refuses even to entertain the IDEA of going.

I fully brought it up right there in the St Vincent's ER waiting room. I was helped, of course, by the fact that there's a TV in the waiting room, and that the TV was turned to CNN, and that CNN was doing a story on proms and the trends towards separate proms in many urban high schools – you know, like one prom for the white kids, who dance around to Eminem, and one prom for the African-American students, who dance around to Ashanti.

Only at Albert Einstein, there is only one prom, because Albert Einstein is a school that promotes cultural diversity and plays both Eminem *and* Ashanti at its events.

So since we were still waiting for my mom to get through with her Ringer's lactate, and we were all three of us just sitting there – me, Michael, and Lars – watching the TV and the occasional ambulance that came rolling in, bringing yet another patient to the ER, I went, to Michael, 'Come on. Doesn't that look like fun?'

Michael, who was watching the ambulance and not the TV, went, 'Getting your chest cracked open with a rib spreader in the middle of Seventh Avenue? Not really.'

'No,' I said. 'On the TV. You know. Prom.'

Michael looked up at the TV, at all the students dancing in their formal wear, and went, 'No.'

'Yeah, but seriously. Think about it. It might be cool. You know. To go and make fun of.' This was not really my idea of a perfect prom night, but it was better than nothing. 'And you don't have to wear a tux, you know. I mean, there's like no rule that says you do. You could just wear a suit. Or not even a suit. You could wear jeans and one of those T-shirts that *look* like a tux.'

Michael looked at me like he thought I might have dropped a globe on my head.

'You know what would be even more fun?' he said. '*Bowling*.'

I heaved this enormous sigh. It was sort of hard to have this intensely personal conversation there in the St Vincent's ER waiting room, because not only was my bodyguard sitting RIGHT THERE, but so were all these sick people, some of whom were coughing EXTREMELY loudly right in my ear.

But I tried to remember the fact that I am a gifted healer and should be tolerant of their disgusting germs.

'But, Michael,' I said. 'Seriously. We could go bowling any old night. And frequently do. Wouldn't it be more fun, just once, to get all dressed up and go dancing?'

'You want to go dancing?' Michael perked up. 'We could go dancing. We could go to the Rainbow Room if you want. My parents go there on their anniversary and stuff. It's supposed to be really nice. There's live music, really great old-time jazz, and—'

'Yeah,' I said. 'I know. I'm sure the Rainbow Room is very nice. But I mean, wouldn't it be nice to go dancing some place with PEOPLE OUR OWN AGE?'

'Like from AEHS?' Michael looked sceptical. 'I guess so. I mean, if like Trevor and Felix and Paul were going to be there . . .' These are the guys from his band. 'But you know, they wouldn't be caught dead at something as lame as the prom.'

OH, MY GOD. It is EXTREMELY hard to be lifemates with a musician. Talk about marching to your own drummer. Michael marches to his own BAND.

I know Michael and Trevor and Felix and Paul are cool and all, but I still fail to see what is so lame about the prom. I mean, you get to elect a Prom King and Queen. At what other social function do you get to elect monarchs to rule over the proceedings? Hello, how about none.

But whatever. I am not going to let Michael's refusal to act like a typical male seventeen year old get in the way of my enjoyment of this evening. You know, the family togetherness my mom and Mr G and I are currently having. We are all having a nice time watching *Miracle Pets*. An old lady had a heart attack and her pet pig walked TWENTY miles to get help.

Fat Louie wouldn't walk to the corner to get help for me. Or he might, but he would soon be distracted by a pigeon and run off, never to be seen again, while my corpse rotted on the floor.

Asperger's syndrome

A Report
by
Mia Thermopolis

The condition known as Asperger's syndrome (also known as Pervasive developmental disorder) is marked by an inability to function normally in social interactions with others (wait a minute . . . this sounds like . . . ME!).

The person suffering from Asperger's exhibits poor non-verbal communication skills (oh, my God – this is ME!!!!!!!!!), *is unsuccessful in developing relationships with peers* (also me), *is incapable of expressing pleasure in the happiness of others* (wait – this is totally Lilly), *and does not react appropriately in social situations* (ME ME ME!!!!!!!). *There is a higher incidence of the syndrome in males* (OK, not me). *Frequently, sufferers of Asperger's syndrome are socially inept* (ME). *When tested, however, many score in the above average intelligence range* (OK, not me – but Lilly, definitely) *and will often excel in fields like science, computer programming and music* (oh, my God! Michael! No! Not Michael! Anyone but Michael!).

Symptoms may include:

- *Abnormal non-verbal communication – problems with eye contact, facial expressions, body postures or uncontrolled gesturing* (ME! Also Boris!).
- *Inability to develop relationships with peers* (totally me. Also Lilly).
- *Labelled by other children as 'weird' or 'freakish'* (this is creeping me out!!! Lana calls me a freak nearly every day!!!).
- *Atypical or noticeably impaired expression of pleasure in other people's happiness* (LILLY!!!! She is NEVER happy for ANYONE!!!!!!).

- *Lack of response to social or emotional feelings* (LILLY!!!!!!).
- *Inability to be flexible regarding minor trivialities, such as alterations to specific routines or rituals* (GRANDMERE!!!!!! ALSO MY DAD!!!!!!! Also Lars. And Mr G).
- *Continuous or repetitive finger tapping, hand wringing, knee jiggling or whole body movements* (well, this is totally Boris, as anyone who has ever seen him play Bartók on his violin could attest).
- *Obsessive interest or concern with subjects such as world history, rock collecting or plane schedules* (or possibly – PROM????????? Does being obsessed with the prom count? Oh, my God, I have Asperger's syndrome! I totally have Asperger's!!!! But wait. If I have it, so does Lilly. Because she is obsessed with Jangbu Pinasa. And Boris is obsessed with his violin. And Tina with romance novels. And Michael with his band. Oh, my GOD!!!!!!!! We ALL have Asperger's syndrome!!!!!!!! This is terrible. I wonder if Principal Gupta knows???????? Wait . . . what if AEHS is a special Asperger's syndrome school? And none of us know it? Until now, that is . . . I am going to bust the whole thing wide open! Like Woodward and Bernstein! Mia Thermopolis, forging a path for Asperger's sufferers everywhere!).
- *Obsessive concern or attention to parts of objects rather than the whole* (I don't know what this means, but it sounds like ME!!!!!!!!).
- *Repetitive behaviours, generally self-injurious in nature* (BORIS!!!!!!! Dropping globes on his head!!!!!!!!! But wait, he only did that once . . .).

Symptoms not included in Asperger's:

- *No indication of language retardation* (duh. We are all excellent talkers) *or of retardation in typical age-appropriate curiosity* (seriously. I mean, Lilly got to second base already and she is only in the ninth grade).

First identified in 1944 as 'Autistic Psychopathy' by Hans Asperger, the cause of this disorder is still unknown. Asperger's syndrome may possibly be related to autism. There is no known cure for Asperger's at this time, and indeed, some case subjects do not consider the disorder an impairment at all. To eliminate other causes, physical, emotional and mental evaluations are usually administered to suspected cases of Asperger's.

Lilly, Michael, Boris, Tina and I ALL need to take these tests!!!!! Oh, my God, we've had Asperger's all along and never knew!!!! I wonder if Mr Wheeton knows, and that's why he assigned me this condition!!!!! This is spooky . . .

Tuesday, May 6, the Loft

I just went into my mother's bedroom (Mr G is on an emergency run to Grand Union to secure more Häagen-Dazs for her) and demanded to know the truth about my mental health status.

'Mother,' I said. 'Am I, or am I not, a sufferer of Asperger's syndrome?'

My mom was trying to watch a bunch of episodes of *Charmed* she'd taped. She says *Charmed* is actually a very feminist show because it portrays young women who fight evil without the help of males, but I notice that a) they often fight while wearing halter tops, and b) my mother takes a special interest in the episodes where men take their shirts off.

But whatever. In any case, her reply to me was way cranky.

'For God's sake, Mia,' she said. 'Are you doing another report for Health and Safety?'

'Yes,' I said. 'And it is clear to me that you have been hiding from everyone the fact that I am a sufferer of Asperger's syndrome, and that, in fact, you send me to a special school for Asperger's sufferers. And the lying has got to stop now!'

She just looked at me and went, 'Are you seriously trying to tell me that you don't remember last month, when you were convinced you had Tourette's syndrome?'

I protested that this was totally different. Tourette's is a disorder characterized by multiple motor and vocal tics that begin prior to the age of eighteen, and at the time we were studying it in class, my constant use of words such as 'like' and 'totally' seemed totally characteristic of the disease.

Is it my fault that generally the tics are accompanied by

involuntary bodily movements, from which I apparently don't suffer?

'Are you trying to say,' I demanded, 'that I don't have Asperger's syndrome?'

'Mia,' my mother said. 'There is nothing wrong with you. You are one hundred per cent Asperger's syndrome-free.

I couldn't believe this, however, after everything I'd read.

'Are you SURE?' I asked. 'What about Lilly?'

My mom snorted. 'Well. I wouldn't go so far as to say that Lilly is normal. But I highly doubt she is suffering from Asperger's.'

Damn! I wish she were. Lilly, I mean. Because then I might be able to forgive her. For calling me weak, I mean.

But as she has no disease, there is no excuse for the way she's treated me.

I have to admit, I'm a little sad I don't have Asperger's. Because now my obsession with the prom is just that: my obsession with the prom. And not a symptom of a disease over which I have no control.

Just my luck!

Wednesday, May 7, 3:30 a.m.

I realize now what I am going to have to do. I mean, I think I knew it all along, and I was just blocking it. Which isn't surprising, considering that every fibre of my being is crying out against it.

But really, what choice do I have? Michael himself even said it: he'd go to the prom if the guys from his band were going too.

Oh, God, I can't believe it has come to this. My life really IS going down the toilet if this is the low to which I am forced to stoop.

I'll never be able to get to sleep now. I just know it. I am too filled with dread.

The Atom

The Official Student-Run Newspaper of Albert Einstein High School

Take *Pride* in the AEHS Lions

Week of May 12 *Volume 456/Issue 28*

Notice to all Students:
As we enter final exams in the next few weeks, school administrators would like us to review the AEHS mission statement and beliefs:

Mission Statement

It is Albert Einstein High School's mission to provide students with learning experiences that are technologically relevant, globally orientated and personally challenging.

Beliefs:

1. The school must provide a diverse curriculum that includes a strong academic programme enhanced by numerous electives.
2. A well-supported and diverse extra-curricular programme is an essential supplement to the academic programme in helping students explore a wide range of interests and abilities.
3. Students must be encouraged to develop responsible behaviour and accountability for their actions.
4. Tolerance and understanding of different cultures and viewpoints must be encouraged at all times.
5. Cheating or plagiarism will not be condoned in any form, and can lead to suspension or expulsion.

The administration would like the student body to be aware that in the coming exam period, it intends to enforce point 5 with vigilance. Forewarned is forearmed.

Incident at Les Hautes Manger
by Mia Thermopolis

Having been asked by this paper to provide an account of what occurred last week at the restaurant Les Hautes Manger, at which this reporter was present, it must be noted that the entire thing was the fault of this reporter's grandmother, who smuggled her dog into the restaurant. The said dog's ill-timed break for freedom caused busboy Jangbu Pinasa to drop a soup-laden tray on to the Dowager Princess of Genovia's person.

The consequent dismissal of Jangbu Pinasa was both unfair and possibly unconstitutional. Though this reporter isn't sure, due to her lack of familiarity with said constitution. It is this reporter's feeling that Mr Pinasa should be given his job back.

Editorial

While it is not the policy of this paper to print anonymous submissions, the following poem so neatly sums up what so many of us are feeling at this time of year that we decided to run it anyway. – Ed.

Spring Fever

By Anonymous

Sneaking away during lunch –
Taco salad, the kind with the meat in it, and the Green Goddess dressing.
God, why do they do that to us?
We find that Central Park beckons – Green grass and daffodils pushing their way out from underneath a blanket of cigarette butts and crumpled soda cans.
So we make a run for it – Did they see us? I don't think so.
Can we get In-School suspension for a first offence? I guess anything is possible.
Let's sit on the bench and try to get a tan . . .
Only to find, to our dismay, that we've left our sunglasses back in our lockers.

Please note: It is the policy of this administration to suspend any and all students who leave campus during school hours for WHATEVER REASON. Spring Fever is not an acceptable excuse for violating this school policy.

Student Injured by Globe

by Melanie Greenbaum

An AEHS student suffered an in-class injury yesterday due to a large globe that fell, or was dropped on his head. If it was the latter, this reporter feels it necessary to ask: where was the adult supervision at the time said globe was dropped? And if it was the former, why is this administration allowing dangerous objects such as globes to be placed at heights from which they might fall and cause injury to our students? This reporter demands a thorough investigation.

Letters to the Editor:

To Whom it May Concern:
The amount of malaise

evidenced by the student body of this establishment is a personal embarrassment to me and a disgrace to our generation. While the students of Albert Einstein High School sit around, planning their Senior Prom and whining about their finals, people in Tibet are DYING. Yes, DYING. Clashes continue between the rebels and the Chinese military, making it impossible for many Tibetans to make even a meagre living.

But what is our government doing to help the people of Tibet? Nothing more than advising tourists to stay away. People, the Tibetans make their *living* from tourists who come to climb the Himalayas. Please do not listen to our government's warnings to avoid Tibet. Encourage your parents to allow you to vacation there this summer – you'll be glad you did.
Lilly Moscovitz

AEHS Food Court Menu

compiled by Mia Thermopolis

Monday	Tuesday	Wednesday	Thursday	Friday
Spicy Chix	Nachos Deluxe	Italian Beef	Fish Stix	Soft Pretzel
Meatball Sub	Indiv. Pizza	Deli Bar	Pasta Bar	Buffalo Bites
Fr. Bread Pizza	Chicken Pattie	Burrito	Chicken Parm.	Grilled Cheese
Potato Bar	Soup & Sand.	Taco Salad Bar	Asian Bar	Bean Bar
Fish Fingers	Tuna in Pitta	Corndog/Pickle	Corn/FF	Curly Fries

Take out your own personal ad! Available to AEHS students at 50 cents/line

Happy Ad
From CF to GD: YES!!!!!!!!!!!

Happy Ad
JR, I am SO excited about the prom, I can't STAND it, we are going to have SO MUCH FUN. I feel SO SORRY for the rejects who aren't going to the prom. Isn't that just too bad for them? They'll be sitting around at home while you and I are DANCING THE NIGHT AWAY! I love you SOOOOOOOO much. LW

Happy Ad
LW – Right back atcha, babe – JR

Happy Ad

Shop at Ho's Deli for all your school supply needs! New this week: PAPER, BINDER CLIPS, TAPE. Also Yu-Gi-Oh cards, *Slimfast*

For Sale:

One Fender precision bass, baby-blue, never been played. With amp, how-to videos. Best Offer. Locker No. 345

Looking for Love:

Female frosh, loves romance/ reading, wants older boy who enjoys same. Must be taller than 5'8", no mean people, non-smokers only, musician preferred. NO METAL-HEADS, nice hands a must. Email: Iluvromance@aehs.edu

Happy Ad

Personal to from BP to LM – I'm sorry for what I did, but I want you to know that I still love you.

PLEASE meet me by my locker after school today and allow me to express my devotion to you. Lilly, you are my muse. Without you, the music is gone. Please don't let our love die this way.

Wednesday, May 7, Algebra

Well, I did it. I can't say it went over very well – in fact, it did not go over AT ALL well. But I did it. No one can say I didn't do EVERYTHING POSSIBLE to try to get my boyfriend to take me to his prom.

Oh, God, but WHY did it have to be LANA WEINBERGER???? WHY???? I mean, ANYBODY else – Melanie Greenbaum, even. But no. It had to be Lana. I had to grovel to LANA WEINBERGER.

Oh, God, my skin is still crawling.

She was so not receptive to my offer, either. You would have thought I was asking her to strip naked and sing the school song in the middle of lunch (no, wait – Lana probably wouldn't mind doing that).

I got to class early, because I know Lana usually likes to get there before the second bell to make a few calls on her mobile. There she was, all right, the only person in the room, yakking away to someone named Sandy about her prom dress – she really did get a black off-one-shoulder one with a butterfly hem from Nicole Miller (I so hate her). Anyway, I went up to her – which I think was VERY brave of me considering every time I fall under Lana's radar she makes some catty personal remark about my physical appearance. But whatever. I just stood there next to her desk while she yammered into the phone, until she finally realized I wasn't going away. Then she went, 'Hold on a minute, will you, Sandy? There's a . . . *person* who wants something.' Then she held the phone away from her face, looked up at me with those big baby blues of hers, and went, 'WHAT?'

'Lana,' I said. I swear, I have sat next to the Emperor of Japan, OK? I once shook the hand of Prince William. I even stood next to Imelda Marcos in line for the Ladies' Room at

The Producers. But none of those events ever made me as nervous as Lana does with a mere glance. Because of course Lana has made tormenting me a special personal hobby of hers. That kind of terror runs deeper than the fear of meeting emperors or princes or dictators' wives.

'Lana,' I said again, trying to get my voice to stop shaking. 'I need to ask you something.'

'No,' Lana said, and got back on to her mobile.

'I haven't even asked you yet,' I cried.

'Well, the answer is still no,' Lana said, tossing around her shiny blonde hair. 'Now, where was I? Oh yes, so I am fully getting body-glitter and putting it on my – no, not *there*, Sandy! You are so *bad*.'

'It's just . . .' I had to talk fast because, of course, there was a strong chance Michael was going to stop by the Algebra classroom on his way to AP English, as he does almost every day. I did not want him to know what I was up to. '. . . I know you're on the Prom Committee, and I really think this year's senior class deserves live music at their prom, and not just a DJ. That's why I was thinking you should ask Skinner Box to play.'

Lana went, 'Hold on, Sandy. That *person* still hasn't gone away.' Then she looked at me from between her thickly mascaraed eyelashes and went, '*Skinner Box*? You mean that band of geeks who played that stupid princess-of-my-heart song to you on your birthday?'

I said, taking umbrage, 'Excuse me, Lana, but you shouldn't speak so disparagingly of geeks. If it were not for geeks, we would not have computers, or vaccinations against many major diseases, or antibiotics, or even that mobile you are talking into—'

'Yeah,' Lana said briskly. 'Whatever. The answer is still no.'

Then she went back to her phone conversation.

I stood there for a minute, feeling colour rush into my face. I must really be making progress with my impulse control, since I didn't reach out and grab her mobile from her and crush it beneath my Doc Martens as I might once have. Being the proud owner of a mobile phone myself now, I know just how completely heinous doing something like that would be. Also, you know, considering how much trouble I got into the last time I did it.

Instead, I just stood there with my cheeks burning and my heart beating really fast and my breath coming out in these shallow little gasps. It seems like no matter what kind of strides I make in the rest of my life – you know, behaving with level-headed calmness in medical emergencies; knighting people; almost getting to second base with my boyfriend – I still can't seem to figure out how to act around Lana. I just don't get why she hates me so much. I mean, what did I ever DO to her? Nothing.

Well, except for the whole mobile phone stomping thing. Oh, and that time I stabbed her with a Nutty Royale. And that other time I slammed her hair in my Algebra book.

But I mean, besides all that.

Anyway, I didn't get a chance to get on my knees and beg her, because the second bell rang, and people started coming into the classroom, including Michael, who came up to me and gave me a bunch of pages he'd printed off the Internet about the dangers of dehydration in pregnant women – 'To give to your mom,' he said, kissing me on the cheek (yes, in front of everyone: *Tcha*).

Still, there are shadows over my otherwise exuberant joy: one shadow is, I was unsuccessful in getting my boyfriend's band booked for the prom, thus making it more likely than ever that I will never have my *Pretty in Pink* moment with Michael. Another shadow is that my best friend is still not speaking to me, nor I to her, because of her psychotic behaviour and mistreatment of her former boyfriend. Yet another shadow is the fact that my first actual published news story ever in *The Atom* reads so incredibly lamely (although they did publish my poem . . . *TRÈS TRÈS TCHA*. Even if I'm the only one who knows it's mine). It isn't exactly my fault my story sucks so much, though. I mean, Lesley hardly gave me enough time to come up with something truly Pulitzer-prize worthy. I'm no Nellie Bly or Ida M. Tarbell, you know. I had a lot of other homework to do, too.

Finally, everything is overshadowed by my fear that my mother might pass out again, next time not within sight of Assistant Fire Chief Logan and the rest of Ladder Company Number Three, and of course by my overall dread that, for two whole months this summer, I will be leaving this fair city and everyone in it for the distant shores of Genovia.

Really, if you think about it, this is all entirely too much for one simple fifteen-year-old girl to bear. It is a wonder I have been able to maintain what little composure I have left, under the circumstances.

When adding or subtracting terms that have the same variables, combine the coefficients.

Wednesday, May 7, Gifted and Talented

STRIKE!!!!!!!!!!

They just announced it on TV. Mrs Hill is letting us crowd around the one in the Teachers' Lounge.

I have never been in the Teachers' Lounge before. It is actually not very nice. There are weird stains on the carpet.

But whatever. The point is that the hotel-workers' union has just joined the busboys in their strike. The restaurant union is expected to follow suit shortly. Which means that there will be no one working in the restaurants or the hotels of New York City. The entire metro area could be shut down. The financial loss from tourism and conventions could be in the billions.

And all because of Rommel.

Seriously. Who knew one little hairless dog could cause so much trouble?

To be fair, it is actually not Rommel's fault. It is Grandmere's. I mean, she never should have brought a dog into a restaurant in the first place, even if it IS OK in France. It was weird to see Lilly on TV. I mean, I see Lilly on TV all the time, but this was a major network – well, I mean, it was New York One, which isn't exactly national or anything, but it's watched in more households than Manhattan Public Access, anyway. Not that Lilly was running the press conference. No, it was being run by the heads of the hotel and restaurant unions. But if you looked to the left of the podium, you could see Jangbu standing there, with Lilly at his side, holding a big sign that said LIVING WAGES FOR LIVING BEINGS.

She is so busted. She has an unexcused absence for the day. Principal Gupta will be so calling the Drs Moscovitz tonight.

Michael just shook his head disgustedly at the sight of his sister on a channel other than Fifty-Six. I mean, he is fully on the side of the busboys – they SHOULD be paid a living wage, of course. But Michael is disgusted with Lilly. He says it's because her interest in the welfare of the busboys has more to do with her interest in Jangbu than in the plight of immigrants to this country.

I kind of wish Michael hadn't said anything, though, because you know Boris was sitting right there next to the TV. He looks so pathetic with his head all bandaged and everything. He kept lifting up his hand when he thought no one was looking, and softly tracing Lilly's features on the screen. It was truly touching, to tell you the truth. I actually got tears in my eyes for a minute.

Although they went away when I realized that the TV in the Teachers' Lounge is forty inches, whereas all the TVs in the student media room are only twenty-seven.

Wednesday, May 7, The Plaza

This is unbelievable. I mean, truly. When I walked into the hotel lobby today, all ready for my princess lesson with Grandmere, I was completely unprepared for the chaos that met me at the door. The place is a zoo.

The doorman with the gold epaulettes who usually holds the limo door open for me? Gone.

The bellboys who so efficiently pile up everybody's luggage on to those brass carts? Gone.

The polite concierge at the reception desk? Gone.

And don't even ask about the line for high tea at the Palm Court. It was out of control.

Because of course there was no hostess to seat anybody, or waiters to take anybody's orders.

It was amazing. Lars and I practically had to fight off this family of twelve from like Iowa or whatever who were trying to crowd on to our elevator with the lifesize gorilla they'd just bought at FAO Schwartz across the street. The dad kept yelling, 'There's room! There's room! Come on, kids, squeeze.'

Finally Lars was forced to show the dad his sidearm and go, 'There's no room. Take the next elevator, please,' before the guy backed off, looking pale.

This never would have happened if the elevator attendant had been there. But this afternoon the porters' union declared a sympathy strike, and joined the restaurant and hotel workers in walking off the job.

You would think after everything we'd gone through just to get to my princess lesson on time, Grandmere would have had some sympathy for us when we walked through the door. But instead she was just standing in the middle of the suite, squawking into the phone.

'What do you mean, the kitchen is closed?' she was

demanding. 'How can the kitchen be closed? I ordered lunch hours ago, and still haven't received it. I am not hanging up until I speak to the person in charge of Room Service. He knows who I am.'

My dad was sitting on the couch across from Grandmere's TV, watching – what else? – New York One with a tense expression on his face. I sat down beside him, and he looked at me, as if surprised to see me there.

'Oh, Mia,' he said. 'Hello. How is your mother?'

'Fine,' I said, because, even though I hadn't seen her since breakfast, I knew she had to be OK, since I hadn't got any calls on my mobile phone. 'She's alternating between Gatorade and PediaLyte. She likes the grape kind. What's happening with the strike?' My dad just shook his head in a defeated way. 'The union representatives are meeting with the Mayor's office. They're hoping to work out a negotiation soon.'

I sighed. 'You realize, of course, that none of this would have happened if I had never been born. Because then I wouldn't have had a birthday dinner.'

My dad looked at me kind of sharply, and went, 'I hope you're not blaming yourself for this, Mia.'

I almost went, 'Are you kidding? I blame Grandmere.' But then I realized from the earnest expression on my dad's face that I had like this huge sympathy quotient going for me, and so instead I went, in this doleful voice, 'It's just too bad I'm going to be in Genovia for most of the summer. It might have been nice if I could have, you know, spent the summer volunteering with an organization seeking to help those unfortunate busboys . . .'

My dad so didn't fall for it, though. He just winked at me and said, 'Nice try.'

Geez! Between him wanting to whisk me off to Genovia for July and August, and my mother offering to take me to her gynaecologist, I am getting way mixed messages from my parental units. It's a wonder I haven't developed a multiple personality. Or Asperger's syndrome. If I don't already have it.

While I was sitting there sulking over my failure to keep from having to spend my precious summer months on the freaking Côte d'Azur, Grandmere started signalling me from the phone. She kept snapping her fingers at me, then pointing at the door to her bedroom. I just sat there blinking at her until finally she put her hand over the receiver and hissed, 'Amelia! In my bedroom! Something for you!'

A present? For *me*? I couldn't imagine what Grandmere could have got me – I mean, the orphan was enough of a gift for one birthday. But I wasn't about to say no to a present . . . at least, not so long as it didn't involve the hide of some slaughtered mammal.

So I got up and went to the door to Grandmere's bedroom, just as someone must have taken Grandmere off hold, since as I turned the knob she was hollering, 'But I ordered that cob salad FOUR HOURS AGO. Do I need to come down there to make it myself? What do you mean, that would be a public health violation? What public? I want to make a salad for *myself*, not the public!'

I opened the door to Grandmere's room. It is, being the bedroom of the penthouse suite of the Plaza Hotel, a very fancy room, with lots of gold leaf all over everything, and freshly cut flowers all over the place . . . although with the strike, I doubted Grandmere'd be getting new floral arrangements anytime soon.

Anyway, as I stood there, looking around the room for my present, and totally saying this little prayer – *Please don't let it be a mink stole. Please don't let it be a mink stole* – my gaze fell upon this dress that was lying across the bed. It was the colour of Jennifer Lopez's engagement ring from Ben Affleck – the softest pink imaginable – and was covered all over in sparkling pink beading. It was off the shoulder with a sweetheart neckline and this huge, filmy skirt.

I knew right away what it was. And even though it wasn't black or slit up the side, it was still the most beautiful prom dress I had ever seen. It was prettier than the one Rachael Leigh Cook wore in *She's All That*. It was prettier than the one Drew Barrymore wore in *Never Been Kissed*. And it was way, way prettier than the gunnysack Molly Ringwald wore in *Pretty in Pink*. It was even prettier than the prom dress Annie Potts gave Molly Ringwald to wear in *Pretty in Pink*, before Molly went mental with the pinking shears and screwed the whole thing up.

It was the prettiest prom dress I had ever seen.

And as I stood there gazing at it, a huge lump rose in my throat. Because of course, I wasn't going to the prom.

So I shut the door and turned around and went back to sit on the couch next to my dad, who was still staring, transfixed, at the television screen.

A second later, Grandmere hung up the phone, turned to me, and said, 'Well?'

'It's really beautiful, Grandmere,' I said sincerely.

'I know it's beautiful,' she said. 'Aren't you going to try it on?'

I had to swallow hard in order to talk in anything that sounded like my normal voice.

'I can't,' I said. 'I told you, I'm not going to the prom, Grandmere.'

'Nonsense,' Grandmere said. 'The Sultan called to cancel our dinner tonight – Le Cirque is closed – but this silly strike will be over by Saturday. And then you can go to your little prom.'

'No,' I said. 'It's not because of the strike. It's because of what I told you. You know. About Michael.'

'What about Michael?' my dad wanted to know. Only I really don't like saying anything negative about Michael in front of my father, because he is always just looking for an excuse to hate him, since he is a dad and it is a dad's job to hate his daughter's boyfriend. So far my dad and Michael have managed to get along, and I want to keep it that way.

'Oh,' I said lightly. 'You know. Boys don't really get into the prom the way girls do.'

My dad just grunted and turned back to the TV. 'You can say that again,' he said. He's one to talk! He went to an all-boys high school! He didn't even HAVE a prom!

'Just try it on,' Grandmere said. 'So I can send it back if it needs fitting.'

'Grandmere,' I said. 'There's no point . . .'

But my voice trailed off because Grandmere got That Look in her eye. You know the one. The look that, if Grandmere were a trained assassin and not a dowager princess, would mean somebody is about to get iced.

So I got up off the couch and went back into Grandmere's room and tried on the dress. Of course it fitted perfectly, because Chanel has all my measurements from the last dress Grandmere bought there for me, and God forbid I should grow or anything, particularly in the chest area.

As I stood there gazing at my reflection in the floor-length mirror, I couldn't help thinking how convenient the off-the-shoulder thing is. You know, in the event Michael and I ever wanted to get to second base.

But then I remembered we aren't actually going anywhere together where I would actually get to wear this dress, since Michael had put the whole kibosh on the prom, so it was kind of a moot point. Sadly, I peeled off the dress and put it back on Grandmere's bed. Probably there'll be some function I'll end up wearing it to in Genovia this summer. Some function Michael won't even be there to attend. Which is just so typical.

I came out of the bedroom just in time to see Lilly on TV. She was addressing a room full of reporters at what looked like the Chinatown Holiday Inn again. She was going, 'I would just like to say that none of this would be happening if the Dowager Princess of Genovia would publicly admit her culpability in her failure to control her dog, and in bringing said dog into a dining establishment.'

Grandmere's jaw dropped. My dad just kept staring stonily into the TV.

'As proof of this claim,' Lilly said, holding up a copy of today's edition of *The Atom*, 'I offer this editorial written by the Dowager Princess's own granddaughter.'

And then I listened in horror as Lilly, in a sing-song voice, read my article out loud. And I must say, hearing my own words thrown back at me in that manner really made me cognizant of just how stupid they sounded . . . far more so than, say, hearing them read in my own voice.

Oops. Dad and Grandmere are staring at me. They do not look happy. In fact, they look kind of . . .

Wednesday, May 7, 10 p.m., the Loft

I really don't get why they're so upset. It is a journalist's duty to report the truth, and that is what I did. If they can't take the heat, they both need to get out of the kitchen. I mean, Grandmere DID take her dog into that restaurant, and Jangbu DID only trip because Rommel darted out in front of him. They cannot deny this. They can wish it hadn't happened and they can wish that Lesley Cho had not asked me to write an editorial about it.

But they cannot deny it, and they cannot blame me for exercising my journalistic rights. Not to mention my journalistic integrity.

Now I know how the great reporters before me must have felt. Ernie Pyle, for his hard-hitting reportage during World War II. Ethel Payne, first lady of the black press during the civil rights movement. Margaret Higgins, the first woman to win a Pulitzer for international reporting. Lois Lane, for her tireless efforts on behalf of the *Daily Planet*. Those Woodward and Bernstein guys, for the whole Watergate thing, whatever that was about.

I know now exactly what it must have been like for them. The pressure. The threats of grounding. The phone calls to their mothers.

That's the part that hurt the most, really. That they would bother my poor dehydrated mother, who is busy trying to bring a *new life* into the world. God knows her kidneys are probably rattling around in her body like packs of desiccant right now. And they dare to pester her with such trivialities?

Plus, my mom is so on my side. I don't know what Dad was thinking. Did he really think Mom would be on GRANDMERE's side in all of this?

Although Mom did tell me that to keep peace in the family, I should at least apologize. I don't see why I should, though. This whole thing has resulted in nothing but heartache for me. Not only did it cause the break-up of one of AEHS's most long-term couples, but it caused me to have what looks to be a permanent falling-out with my best friend. I have lost MY BEST FRIEND over this.

I informed both Dad and Grandmere of this right before the latter imperiously ordered Lars to get me out of her sight. Fortunately, I had the foresight to snag the prom dress out of Grandmere's room and stuff it in my backpack before this happened. It's only a little wrinkled. A good steaming in the shower and it will be good as new.

I can't help thinking that they could have handled this little affair in a more appropriate manner. They COULD have called a press conference of their own, fessed up to the whole dog-in-the-restaurant thing, and had it all over and done with.

But no. And now it's too late. Even if Grandmere fesses up, it's highly unlikely the hotel, restaurant, and porters' unions are going to back down NOW.

Well, I guess it's just another case of people failing to pay heed to the voice of youth. And now they're just going to have to suffer.

Too bad.

Thursday, May 8, Homeroom

OH, MY GOD!!!!!!!!!!!!!!!!THEY'VE CANCELLED THE PROM!!!!!!!!!!!!!!!!!

The Atom

The Official Student-Run Newspaper of Albert Einstein High School

Special Supplementary Edition

PROM CANCELLED!!!!!!!!

By Lesley Cho

Due to the city-wide hotel, restaurant, and porters' unions strike, this year's Senior Prom has been cancelled. The restaurant Maxim's notified school officials that due to the strike, they would be closing, effective immediately. The Prom Committee's $4,000 deposit was returned. This year's senior class is left high and dry with no alternative but to have the prom in the school cafeteria, something Prom Committee members considered, but then dismissed.

'The prom is special,' said Prom Committee chairperson, Lana Weinberger. 'It's no ordinary school dance. We can't just have it in the cafeteria, as if it were another Cultural Diversity or Non-Denominational Winter Dance. We'd rather have no prom than a prom where we're stepping on old French fries or whatever.'

Not everyone in the school agrees with the Prom Committee's controversial decision, however. Said senior Judith Gershner, when she heard of Lana Weinberger's remarks, 'We've been looking forward to our prom since we were ninth graders. To have it taken away now, over something as trivial as stray French fries, seems a bit petty. I would rather have French fries stuck to my heel at the prom than no prom at all.'

The Prom Committee remains adamant, however, that it will have the prom off school grounds, or not at all.

'There's nothing special about coming to school dressed up,' ninth grader Lana Weinberger commented. 'If we're going to get dressed up to the nines, we want to be going somewhere other than where we have gone every morning all year long.'

The cause of the strike, which was summarized in this week's edition of *The Atom*, still appears to have been an incident which occurred at the restaurant Les Hautes Manger, where AEHS freshman and Genovian Princess Mia

Thermopolis dined last week with her grandmother. Says Lilly Moscovitz, former friend of the princess and chairperson of the Students Against the Wrongful Dismissal of Jangbu Pinasa Association, 'It's all Mia's fault. Or at least her grandmother's. All we want is Jangbu's job back, and a formal apology from Clarisse Renaldo. Oh, and vacation and sick pay, as well as health benefits, for busboys city-wide.'

Princess Mia was, at the time of going to press, unavailable for comment, being, according to her mother, Helen Thermopolis, in the shower.

We here at *The Atom* will attempt to keep all of you informed as strike negotiations progress.

Oh, my God. THANKS, MOM. THANKS FOR TELLING ME THE SCHOOL PAPER CALLED WHILE I WAS IN THE SHOWER.

You should SEE the dirty looks I got as I made my way to my locker this morning. Thank God I have an armed bodyguard, or I might have been in some serious trouble. Some of those girls on the Varsity Lacrosse team – the ones who smoke and do chin-ups in the third floor girls' room – made EXTREMELY threatening hand gestures towards me as I got out of the limo. Someone had even written on Joe the stone lion (in chalk, but still) GENOVIA SUCKS.

GENOVIA SUCKS!!!!!!!!! The reputation of my principality is being besmirched, and all because of a stupid dance being cancelled!

Oh, all right. I know the prom is not stupid. I mean, I, of all people, KNOW that the prom is not stupid. It is a vitally important part of the high-school experience, as Molly Ringwald can all too readily attest!

And yet, because of me, it is being ripped from the hearts and yearbooks of the members of this year's AEHS graduating class.

I've GOT to do something. Only what???? WHAT????????????

Thursday, May 8, Algebra

You will never believe what Lana just said to me. I completely kid you not.

LANA: (swivelling around in her chair and glaring at me) You did this on purpose, didn't you? Caused this strike and made the prom get cancelled.

ME: What? No. What are you talking about?

LANA: Just admit it. You did it because I wouldn't let your boyfriend's stupid band stink up the place. Admit it.

ME: No! That's not it at all. It wasn't me, anyway. It was my grandmother.

LANA: Whatever. All you Genovians are the same.

Then she whipped back around, before I could say another word.

All you Genovians? Um, excuse me, but I'm the only Genovian Lana has ever even met.

She has some nerve . . .

Thursday, May 8, Bio

Mia, are you all right?

Yes, Shameeka. It was just an apple core.

Still. That was way cool how Lars hit that guy. Your bodyguard has some sharp reflexes there.

Yeah, well. That's why he got the job. So how come you're speaking to me? Don't you hate me, too? I mean, after all, you and Jeff were going to go to the prom.

Well, it's not YOUR fault it got cancelled. Besides, I wouldn't have had that much fun at it anyway. I mean, not if the only other girl from my class was going to be LANA!!!!!!!!!

By the way, did you hear about Tina?

No. What?

Yesterday, when Boris was waiting at his locker for Lilly – you know, he put that Happy Ad in the paper, asking her to meet him there after school, so they could talk? Well, Tina decided to meet him, you know, and ask him if he wanted to grab a frozen hot chocolate at Serendipity, because she felt so sorry for him and all. Well, I guess he finally gave up on waiting for Lilly, since he said yes and the two of them went, and this morning, I swear I saw them holding hands beside the foamcore sculpture of the Parthenon outside the language lab.

WAIT A MINUTE. WHAT? YOU SAW TINA AND BORIS HOLDING HANDS. TINA AND BORIS. TINA and *BORIS PELKOWSKI*????

Yes.

Tina. Tina Hakim Baba. And Boris Pelkowski. TINA AND BORIS?????????

YES!!!!!!!!!!

Oh, my God. What is happening to the world we live in?

Thursday, May 8, Third Floor Stairwell

Shameeka and I cornered Tina after we came out of Bio. and dragged her up here to demand confirmation of the holding-hands-with-Boris thing. I am skipping Health and Safety, but who cares? I would only end up sitting there under the hostile gazes of my fellow Health and Safety practitioners, one of whom includes my ex-best friend Lilly Moscovitz, whom I have absolutely no desire to speak to anyway.

Besides, my Asperger's syndrome report is due, and I didn't exactly have a chance to finish it, due to the severe emotional problems I am suffering right now on account of my mother's bladder problems and my boyfriend's refusal to take me to the prom and the whole strike thing and all.

I cannot believe the stuff that is spilling out of Tina's mouth. About how all her life, she's just been looking for a man who could love her the way heroes in the romance novels she likes to read so much love their heroines. About how she never thought she would meet a man who could love a woman with the intensity of the heroes she admires most, like Mr Rochester and Heathcliff and Colonel Brandon and Mr Darcy and Spiderman and all.

Then she says that watching the way Boris fell apart after Lilly left him for Jangbu Pinasa made her realize that out of all the boys she had ever met, he was the only one who seemed close to fitting her description of the perfect boyfriend. Except, of course, for the whole looks thing. But other than that, he is everything Tina has ever wanted in a boyfriend:

- **Loyal**
  (Well, that goes without saying. Boris would never even LOOK at another girl after he hooked up with Lilly.)

- **Passionate**
  (Uh, I guess the whole globe thing proved Boris is deeply passionate. Or suffers from Asperger's syndrome.)
- **Intelligent**
  (4.0 GPA)
- **Musical**
  (As I can only too readily testify.)
- **In touch with popular culture**
  (He does watch *Buffy*.)
- **Fond of Chinese food**
  (This is true as well.)
- **Absolutely uninterested in competitive sports**
  (Except figure skating. Well, he *is* Russian.)

Plus, Tina adds, he is a really good kisser, once he takes out his bionater.

A REALLY GOOD KISSER, ONCE HE TAKES OUT HIS BIONATER.

You know what that means, don't you? IT MEANS THAT TINA AND BORIS HAVE KISSED! How would she know this if they hadn't????????

Oh, my God. I can't stop gagging. I like Boris – I really do. I mean, except for the fact that he is COMPLETELY INSANE I think he is a really nice guy. He is sensitive and funny and, if you can forget the asthma inhaler and the mouth-breathing and the violin playing and the whole sweater thing, yeah, OK I guess he is PASSABLY attractive.

I mean, at least he is taller than Tina.

BUT OH, MY GOD!!!!!!!!!!!! BORIS PELKOWSKI, TINA'S MR ROCHESTER?????

NO, NO, NO, A THOUSAND TIMES NO!!!!!!!!!!!!!!!!!!!!!

But as Shameeka just pointed out to me (while Tina was

checking her text messages), Boris doesn't necessarily have to be her Mr Rochester for all eternity. He could just be her Mr Rochester for, you know, now. Until her real Mr Rochester comes along.

Oh, my God. I just don't know. I mean, BORIS PELKOWSKI.

Well, at least Tina's right about one thing: he does feel things passionately. I have the blood-soaked sweater to prove it. Well, not really, because Mrs Pelkowski returned it and the dry cleaner really did get out all the stains.

But still.

Tina and BORIS PELKOWSKI?????????????

AAAAAAAAAAAAAAAAAAAAHHHHHHHHHHHH!!

Thursday, May 8, the Loft

After Lars had to shield me from yet another projectile – this one thrown with stunning accuracy by a senior rugby player – he called my dad and said he thought for safety reasons I should be removed from school premises.

So my dad said OK. So I get the rest of the day off.

Except not really, because Mr G is going over everything I haven't been paying much attention to in his class for the past week and a half, using the front of the refrigerator as a chalk board, and the magnetic alphabet as the coefficients in the problems I'm supposed to be solving.

Whatever, Mr G. Can't you see I have way bigger problems right now than a sinking grade in your class? I mean, hello, I cannot even set foot in my own school without being pelted with fruit.

I'm so depressed. I mean, after everything with the strike, and then with Tina, and now this thing with everybody hating me, I really don't see how I'm going to make it through the rest of the week. I already called my dad and was like, 'Tell Grandmere thanks a lot. Now I'm not even safe at my own institution of secondary education, and it's all her fault.'

I don't know if he told her, though. I'm not sure he and Grandmere are speaking any more.

I know I'M not speaking to Grandmere. It seems like I'm not speaking to a lot of people, actually . . . Grandmere, Lilly, Lana Weinberger . . .

Well, I've never really been on speaking terms with Lana. But you know what I mean. Wow, what if I can never go back to school again? Like, what if I have to be home-schooled? That would suck so bad! I mean, how would I keep up with all the gossip? Like who was going out with whom? And when would I ever see Michael? Just on weekends, and that's it. That would be so WRONG!!!! The high point of my day is seeing him waiting outside his building to be picked up by my limo on the way to school. I know that I am going to be deprived of this forever when he starts going to Columbia. But I thought I'd still be able to enjoy it for the rest of the school year, anyway.

Oh, my God, this is bumming me out so badly. I mean, I never really LIKED Albert Einstein High, but considering the alternatives . . . you know, home-schooling or, even worse, school in GENOVIA . . . my God, in comparison, AEHS is like Shangri-La. Whatever Shangri-La is.

How dare they try to keep me from it? AEHS, I mean. HOW DARE THEY?????????? Oh, someone is at the door. Please let it be Michael with the rest of my homework. Not because I'm desperate to do the rest of my homework, but because if I have ever needed to be comforted with the smell of Michael's neck, it's now . . .

PLEASE PLEASE PLEASE PLEASE PLEASE PLEASE PLEASE.

Thursday, May 8, later, the Loft

Well, it wasn't Michael. But it was close. It was a Moscovitz.

Just the wrong one.

I really think Lilly has some nerve coming around here after what she put me through. I mean, Asperger's or not, she has made my life a perfect hell these past few days, and then she shows up at my door, crying and begging to be forgiven?

But what could I do? I couldn't exactly slam the door in her face. Well, I could have, of course, but it would have been terribly unprincesslike.

Instead, I invited her in – but coldly. *Very* coldly. Who's the weak one NOW, I'd like to know????

We went into my room. I shut the door (I'm allowed to shut my bedroom door so long as anybody but Michael is inside there with me).

And Lilly let loose.

Not, as I was expecting, with the heartfelt apology I deserved for her dreadful treatment of me, dragging my good name and royal lineage across the airwaves in the manner she had.

Oh no. Nothing like that. Instead, Lilly is crying because she heard about Tina and Boris.

That's right. Lilly's crying because she wants her boyfriend back.

Seriously! And after the way she'd treated him!

I'm just sitting here in stunned silence, staring at Lilly as she rants. She's stomping around my room in her Mao jacket and Birkenstocks, shaking her glossy curls, her eyes, behind the lenses of her glasses (I guess revolutionaries working to empower the people don't wear their contacts), filled with bitter tears.

'How could he?' she keeps wailing. 'I turn my back for five minutes – five minutes! – and he runs off with another girl? What can he be thinking?'

I can't help but point out that perhaps Boris was thinking about seeing her, Lilly, his girlfriend, with another boy's tongue down her throat. In MY hallway closet, no less.

'Boris and I never vowed to see one another exclusively,' she insists. 'I told him that I am like a restless bird . . . I can't be tied down.'

'Well.' I shrug. 'Maybe he's more into the roosting type.'

'Like Tina, you mean?' Lilly rubs her eyes. 'I can't believe she could do this to me. I mean, doesn't she realize that she'll never make Boris happy? He's a genius, after all. It takes a genius to know how to handle a fellow genius.'

I remind Lilly, somewhat stiffly, that *I* am no genius, but I seem to be handling her brother, whose IQ is 179, quite well.

I don't mention the whole part about him still refusing to go to the prom and the fact that we haven't got to second base yet.

'Oh, please,' Lilly scoffs. 'Michael's gaga for you. Besides, at least you're in Gifted and Talented. You get to observe geniuses in action on a daily basis. What does Tina know about them? Why, I don't think she's even seen *A Beautiful Mind*! Because Russell doesn't take his shirt off enough in it, no doubt.'

'Hey,' I say harshly. I'd noticed this about *A Beautiful Mind*, too, and I think it's a valid criticism. 'Tina is my friend. A way better friend to me than *you've* been lately.'

Lilly has the grace to look guilty.

'I'm sorry about all that, Mia,' she says. 'I swear I don't know what came over me. I just saw Jangbu and I . . . well, I guess I became a slave to my own lust.'

I must say, I am very surprised to hear this. Because while Jangbu is, of course, quite hot, I never knew physical attraction was important to Lilly. I mean, after all, she's been going out with Boris for, like, ever.

But apparently, it was all completely physical between her and Jangbu.

God. I wonder what base they got to. Would it be rude to ask? I mean, I know that, considering we aren't best friends any more, it probably isn't any of my business. But if she got to third with that guy, I'll kill her.

'But it's over between Jangbu and me,' Lilly just announced very dramatically . . . so dramatically that Fat Louie, who doesn't like Lilly very much in the first place, and usually hides in the closet among my shoes when she comes over, just tried to burrow his way into my snow boots. 'I thought he had the heart of a proletarian. I thought, at last I had found a man who shared my passion for social causes and the advancement of the worker. But alas . . . I was wrong. So very, very wrong. I simply cannot be soulmates with a man willing to sell his life story to the press.'

It appears that Jangbu has been approached by a number of magazines, including *People* and *US Weekly*, who are vying for the exclusive rights to the details of his run-in with the Dowager Princess of Genovia and her dog.

'Really?' I was very surprised to hear this. 'How much are they offering him?'

'Last time I talked to him, they were up to six figures.' Lilly dries her eyes on one of Grandmere's Chanel scarves. 'He won't be needing his job back at Les Hautes Manger, that's for sure. He's planning on opening a restaurant of his own. A Taste of Tibet, he's planning on calling it.'

'Wow.' I feel for Lilly. I really do. I mean, I know how much it sucks when someone you thought was your spiritual lifemate turns out to be sell-out. Especially when he French kisses as well as Josh – I mean Jangbu – does.

Still, just because I feel sorry for Lilly doesn't mean I'm going to forgive her for what she did. I may not be self-actualized, but at least I have pride.

'But I want you to know,' Lilly is saying, 'that I realized I wasn't in love with Jangbu before all this stuff with the strike happened. I knew I had never stopped loving Boris when he picked up that globe and dropped it on his head for me. I mean, Mia, he was willing to get *stitches* for me. That's how much he loves me. No boy has ever loved me enough to risk actual, physical pain and discomfort for me . . . and certainly not Jangbu. I mean, he's WAY too caught up in his own fame and celebrity. Not like Boris. I mean, Boris is a thousand times more gifted and talented than Jangbu, and HE isn't caught up in the fame game.'

I really don't know quite how to respond to all this. I guess Lilly must realize this by the way she's narrowing her eyes at me and going, 'Would you please stop writing in that journal for ONE MINUTE and tell me how I can win Boris back?'

Though it pained me to do it, I was forced to inform Lilly that I think the chances of her ever winning Boris back are like zero. Less than zero, even. Like in the negative polynomials.

'Tina is really crazy about him,' I told her. 'And I think he feels the same way about her. I mean, he gave her his autographed eight-by-ten glossy of Joshua Bell—'

This information caused Lilly to clutch her heart in existential pain. Or maybe not so existential, since I'm not even really sure what existential means. In any case, she clutched her heart and fell back dramatically across my bed.

'That witch!' she keeps yelling – so loudly that I'm afraid

any minute Mr G is going to come busting in here, thinking we have *Buffy* turned up too loud. Also, she wasn't actually saying witch, but the other word that rhymes with it. 'That black-hearted, back-stabbing witch! I'll get her for stealing my man! I'll get her!'

I had to get very severe with Lilly. I told her that under no circumstances was she going to 'get' anyone. I told her that Tina really and sincerely adored Boris, which is all he has ever wanted – to love and be loved in return, just like Ewan McGregor in *Moulin Rouge.* I told her that if she really loved Boris the way she said she did, she would leave him and Tina alone, let them enjoy the last few weeks of school together. Then if, in the autumn, Lilly still found herself wanting Boris back, she could say something. But not before.

Lilly was, I think, a little taken aback by my sage – and very direct – advice. In fact, she still appears to be digesting it. She's sitting on the end of my bed, blinking at my Princess Leia screensaver. I am sure it must be quite a blow to a girl with an ego the size of Lilly's . . . you know, that a boy who had once loved her could learn to love again. But she will just have to get used to it. Because after what she put Boris through this week, I for one will see to it that she never, ever dates him again. If I have to stand in front of Boris with a big old sword, like Aragorn in front of that Frodo dude, I will totally do it. That is how determined I am that Lilly will never again mess with Boris Pelkowski's heavily bandaged, misshapen genius head.

I don't know if she could see how fiercely I was writing that, or if there was something particularly determined in my expression, or what. But Lilly just sighed and went, 'Oh, all *right.*'

Now she is putting on her coat and leaving. Because even

though she and Jangbu have parted ways, she is still chairperson of SATWDOJPA and has loads to do.

None of which apparently includes apologizing to me.

Or so I thought.

At my door, Lilly turned and said, 'Listen, Mia. I'm sorry I called you weak the other day. You're not weak. In fact . . . you're one of the strongest people I know.'

Hello! So true! I have battled so many demons in my day, I make those girls on *Charmed* look like the ones on freaking *Full House*. Really, I should get a medal, or at least the key to the city, or something.

Sadly, however, just when I thought my bravery was no longer going to be needed – Lilly and I had hugged, and she'd left, after a few words of apology to my mom and Mr G over the whole making-out-in-our-hall-closet-with-Jangbu-the-unemployed-busboy thing, which they'd graciously accepted – the buzzer in the vestibule went off AGAIN. I thought for SURE it had to be Michael this time. He'd promised to collect and bring over all of my remaining assignments.

So you can imagine my horror – my absolute revulsion – when I bounded over to the intercom, hit the Talk button, went, 'Hellooo-ooooo?' and the voice that came crackling over it in response was not the deep, warm, familiar voice of my one true love . . . but the hideous cackle of GRANDMERE!!!!!!!!!!!!!

Thursday, May 8, 1 a.m., the futon couch in the Loft

This is a nightmare. It has to be. Somebody is going to pinch me and I'm going to wake up and it's all going to be over and I'm going to be back snug in my own bed, not out here on this futon – how come I never noticed how HARD this thing is? – in the living room in the middle of the night.

Except that it's NOT a nightmare. I know it's not a nightmare, because to have a nightmare, you actually have to fall ASLEEP, something I can't do, because Grandmere is SNORING TOO LOUDLY.

That's right. My grandmother snores. Some scoop for *The Post*, huh? I should give them a call and hold up the phone to the door to my room (you can hear her even with the door CLOSED). I can just see the headline:

**DOWAGER PRINCESS
SNORES LIKE A
JACKHAMMER**

I can't believe this is happening. Like my life isn't bad enough. Like I don't have enough problems now my psychotic grandmother has *moved in* with me. I could hardly believe it when I opened the loft door and saw her standing there, her driver right behind her with about fifty million Louis Vuitton bags. I just stared at her for a full minute, until finally Grandmere went, 'Well, Amelia? Aren't you going to ask me in?'

And then, before I even had a chance to, she just barged right by me, complaining the whole way about how we don't have an elevator and did we have any idea what a walk up three flights of stairs could do to a woman her age (I noticed that she didn't mention what it could do to a chauffeur who had been forced to carry all of her luggage up the same aforementioned three flights of stairs)?

Then she started walking around the Loft like she always does when she comes over, picking up things and looking at them with a disapproving expression on her face before putting them down again, like Mom's Cinco de Mayo skeleton collection, and Mr G's NCAA Final Four drink holders.

Meanwhile, my mom and Mr G, having heard all the commotion, came out of their room and then froze – both of them – in horror as they took in the sight before them. I have to admit, it did look a bit scary . . . especially since by then Rommel had worked his way free from Grandmere's purse and was staggering around the floor on his spindly Bambi legs, sniffing things so carefully you would have thought he expected them to explode in his face at any given moment (which, when he gets around to sniffing Fat Louie, might actually happen).

'Um, Clarisse,' my mother (brave woman!) said. 'Would you mind telling us what you're doing here? With, er, what appears to be your entire wardrobe in tow?'

'I cannot stay at that hotel a moment longer,' Grandmere said, putting down Mr G's lava lamp and not even glancing at my mother, whose pregnancy – 'At her advanced age,' Grandmere likes to say, even though Mom is actually younger than many recently pregnant starlets – she considers an embarrassment of grand proportions. 'No one works there any more! The place is completely chaotic. You cannot get a soul to bring up a morsel of Room Service, and forget about getting someone to run your bath. And so I've come here.' She blinked at us less than fondly. 'To the bosom of my family. In times of need, I believe it is traditional for relatives to take one another in.'

My mom totally wasn't falling for Grandmere's poor-little-me act.

'Clarisse,' she said, folding her arms over her chest (which is quite a feat, considering how big her boobs have got – I can only hope that if I ever get pregnant, my own knockers will swell to such heroic proportions). 'There is a hotel workers' strike. No one is exactly lobbing SCUD missiles at the Plaza. I think you've lost your perspective a little bit . . .'

Just then the phone rang. I, of course, thinking it was Michael, dived for it. But alas, it was not Michael. It was my father.

'Mia,' he said, sounding a trifle panicked. 'Is your grandmother there?'

'Why, yes, Dad,' I said. 'She is. Would you care to speak with her?'

'Oh, God,' my dad groaned. 'No. Let me talk to your mother.'

My dad was totally in for it, and did he ever know it. I handed the phone to my mom, who took it with the expression of long-suffering she always wears in Grandmere's presence. Just as she was putting the phone to her ear, Grandmere said to her chauffeur, 'That will be all, Gaston. You can put the bags down in Amelia's room, then leave.'

'Stay where you are, Gaston,' my mom said, just as I yelled, 'MY room? Why MY room?'

Grandmere looked at me all acidly and went, 'Because in times of hardship, young lady, it is traditional for the youngest member of the family to sacrifice her comfort for the oldest.'

I never heard of this cockamamie tradition before. What was it, like the ten-course Genovian wedding supper, or something?

'Phillipe,' my mom was growling into the phone. 'What is going on here?'

Meanwhile, Mr G was trying to make the best out of a bad situation. He asked Grandmere if he could get her some form of refreshment.

'Sidecar, please,' Grandmere said, not even looking at him, but at the magnetic alphabet Algebra problems on the refrigerator door. 'Easy on the ice.'

'Phillipe!' my mother was saying, in tones of mounting urgency, into the phone.

But it didn't do any good. There was nothing my father could do. He and the staff – Lars, Hans, Gaston, et al. – were OK to rough it at the Plaza under the new, Room-Service free conditions. But Grandmere just couldn't take it. She had apparently tried to ring for her nightly chamomile tea and biscotti, and when she'd found out there was no one to bring it to her, she'd gone completely mental and stuck her foot through the glass mail chute (endangering the poor postman's fingers when he comes to collect the mail at the bottom of the chute tomorrow).

'But, Phillipe,' my mom kept wailing. 'Why *here*?'

But there was nowhere else for Grandmere to go. Things were just as bad, if not worse, at all the other hotels in the city. Grandmere had finally decided to pack up and abandon ship . . . figuring, no doubt, that as she had a granddaughter fifty blocks away, why not take advantage of the free labour?

So for the moment, anyway, we're stuck with her. *I* even had to give her my bed, because she categorically refused to sleep on the futon couch. She and Rommel are in *my* room – my safe haven, my sanctuary, my fortress of solitude, my meditation chamber, my Zen palace – where she already unplugged my computer because she didn't like my Princess

Leia screensaver 'staring' at her. Poor Fat Louie is so confused, he actually hissed at the toilet, because he had to express his disapproval of the whole situation somehow. Now he has hidden himself away in the hall closet – the same closet where, if you think about it, all of this started – amid the vacuum-cleaner parts and all the three-dollar umbrellas we've left there over the years.

It was an extremely frightening sight when Grandmere came out of my bathroom with her hair all in curlers and her night cream on. She looked like something out of the Jedi Council scene in *Attack of the Clones*. I was about to ask her where she'd parked her landspeeder. Except that Mom told me I have to be nice to her – 'At least until I can think of some way to get rid of her, Mia.'

Thank God Michael finally did show up with my homework. We could not exchange tender greetings, however, because Grandmere was sitting at the kitchen table, watching us like a hawk the whole time. I never even got to smell his neck!

And now I am lying here on this lumpy futon, listening to my grandmother's deep, rhythmic snoring from the other room, and all I can think is that this strike better be over soon.

Because it is bad enough living with a neurotic cat, a drum-playing Algebra teacher, and a woman in her last trimester of pregnancy. Throw in a dowager princess of Genovia, and I'm sorry: book me a room on the twenty-first floor of Bellevue, because it's the funny farm for me.

Friday, May 9, Homeroom

I decided to go to school today because:

1. It's Senior Skip Day, so most of the people who'd like to see me dead aren't here to throw things at me, and
2. It's better than staying at home.

I mean it. It is bad in Apt. 4, 1111 Thompson Street. This morning when Grandmere woke up, the first thing she did was demand that I bring her some hot water with lemon and honey in a glass. I was like, 'Um, no way,' which did not go over real well, let me tell you. I thought Grandmere was going to hit me.

Instead, she threw my Fiesta Giles action figure – the one of Buffy the Vampire Slayer's watcher, Giles, in a sombrero – against the wall! I tried to explain to her that he is a collector's item and worth nearly twice what I paid for him, but she was fully unappreciative of my lecture. She just went, 'Get me a hot water with lemon and honey or I shall destroy all of your Bippy the Monster Catcher characters!'

God. She can't even get the name of my favourite show right. I'd like to know how she'd feel, if *I* didn't pay attention next time she starts in about the Genovian bill of rights, or whatever.

So I got her her stinking hot water with lemon and honey, and she drank it down, and then, I kid you not, she spent about half an hour in my bathroom. I have no idea what she was doing in there, but it nearly drove Fat Louie and I insane . . . me because I needed to get in there to get my toothbrush, and Fat Louie because that's where his litter box is.

But whatever, I finally got in and brushed my teeth, and

then I was like, 'See ya,' and Mr G and I fully raced for the door.

Not fast enough, though, because my mom caught us before we could get safely out of the apartment, and hissed at us in this very scary voice, '*I will get you both for leaving me alone with her all day today. I don't know how, and I don't know when. But when you least expect it . . . expect it.*'

Whoa, Mom. Have some more PediaLyte.

Anyway, things here at school have calmed down a lot since yesterday. Maybe because the seniors aren't here. Well, all except for Michael. He's here. Because, he says, he doesn't believe in skipping just because Josh Richter says to. Also because Principal Gupta is giving ten demerits to every student with an unexcused absence for the day, and if you get demerits, the school librarian won't give you a discount at the end of year used-book sale, and Michael has had his eye on the school's collected works of Isaac Asimov for some time now.

But really I think he's here for the same reason I am: to escape his current home situation. That's because, he told me in the limo on the way up to school, Lilly's parents finally found out about how she's been skipping school and holding press conferences without their permission. The Drs Moscovitz supposedly went full-on Reverend and Mrs Camden and are making Lilly stay home with them today so they can have a nice long talk about her obvious dis-establishmentarianism and the way she treated Boris. Michael was like, 'I was so outta there,' for which who can blame him?

But things are definitely looking up because when we stopped by Ho's this morning before school to buy breakfast (egg sandwich for Michael; Ring Dings for me) he fully grabbed me while Lars was in the refrigerated section buying his morning can of Red Bull and started kissing me, and I got to smell his neck, which instantly soothed my Grandmere-frazzled nerves and convinced me that somehow, some way, everything is going to be all right.

Maybe.

Friday, May 9, Algebra

Oh, my God, I can barely write, my hands are shaking so badly. I cannot believe what just happened . . . cannot believe it because it is so GOOD. How is this possible? Good things NEVER happen to me. Well, except for Michael.

But this . . .

It is almost too good to be believed.

What happened was, I came into the Algebra classroom all unsuspectingly, not expecting a thing. I sat down in my seat and started taking out last night's homework – which Mr G fully helped me finish – when all of a sudden, my mobile rang.

Thinking my mom was going into labour – or had passed out in the ice-cream section of the Grand Union again – I hurried to answer it.

But it wasn't my mother. It was Grandmere.

'Mia,' she said. 'There's nothing to worry about. I've taken care of the problem.'

I swear I didn't know what she was talking about. Not at first, anyway. I was like, 'What problem?' I thought maybe she was talking about Verl and his noise complaints against us. I thought maybe she'd had him executed, or something.

Well, it's possible, knowing Grandmere.

Which is why her next words were such a total shock.

'Your prom,' she said. 'I spoke to someone. And I've found a place where you can have it, strike or no strike. It's all settled.'

I just sat there for a minute, holding the phone to my ear, barely able to register what I'd just heard.

'Wait,' I said. 'What?'

'For God's sake,' Grandmere said all testily. 'Must I repeat myself? I have found a place for you to have your little prom.'

And then she told me where.

I hung up in a daze. I couldn't believe it. I swear I couldn't believe it.

Grandmere had done it.

Oh, not fessed up to her role in causing one of the most expensive strikes in the history of New York City. Nothing like that.

No. This was more important.

She'd saved the prom. Grandmere had saved the Albert Einstein High School Senior Prom.

I looked at Lana sitting in front of me, resolutely not glancing in my direction, due to the fact that I was the one who'd caused the prom to be cancelled.

And that's when it hit me. Grandmere had saved the prom for AEHS. But I could still save the prom for me.

I poked Lana in the shoulder and went, 'Did you hear?'

Lana turned to stare at me in a very mean way. 'Hear what, freak?' she demanded.

'My grandmother found an alternative space to hold the prom,' I said.

And told her where.

Lana just stared at me in total shock. Really. She was so stunned, she couldn't talk. I'd stunned Lana into silence. Not like that time I'd stabbed her with a Nutty Royale, either.

That time, she'd had a LOT to say.

This time? Nothing.

'But there's just one condition,' I went on.

And then I told her the condition.

Which, of course, Grandmere hadn't brought up. The

condition, I mean. No, the condition was a little princess-of-Genovia manoeuvring all of my own.

But hey. I learned from a master.

'So,' I said in conclusion, in an almost friendly way, as if Lana and I were buddies, and not sworn mortal enemies, like Alyssa Milano and the Source of All Evil. 'Take it, or leave it.'

Lana didn't hesitate. Not even a second. She went, 'OK.'

Just like that. 'OK.'

And suddenly, it was like I was Molly Ringwald. I'm not kidding, either.

I cannot explain, not even to myself, why I did what I did next. I just did it. It was like for a moment I was possessed by the spirit of some other girl, a girl who actually gets along with people like Lana. I reached out, grabbed Lana's head, pulled it towards me and gave her a great big kiss, smack in the middle of her eyebrows.

'Ew, gross,' Lana said, backing away fast. 'What is wrong with you, freak?'

But I didn't care that Lana had called me a freak. Twice. Because my heart was singing like those little birds who fly around Snow White's head when she's hanging out by the wishing well. I went, 'Stay right here,' and ran out of my seat . . .

. . . much to the surprise of Mr G, who had just come into the room, his Starbucks Grande in hand.

'Mia,' he said bewilderedly as I darted past him. 'Where are you going? The second bell just rang.'

'Be back in a minute, Mr G,' I called over my shoulder as I raced down the hall to the room where Michael has AP English.

I didn't have to worry about making a fool of myself in front of Michael's peers or anything, since none of

Michael's peers were around, it being Senior Skip Day and all. I leaped into his classroom – the first time I had ever done such a thing: usually, of course, Michael visited me in MY classroom – and went, 'Excuse me, Mrs Weinstein,' to his English teacher, 'but may I have a word with Michael?'

Mrs Weinstein – who you could tell had been anticipating a light work day, since she'd come armed with the latest *Cosmo* – looked up from the Bedside Astrologer and went, 'Whatever, Mia.'

So I bounded over to an extremely surprised Michael and, slipping into the desk in front of his, said, 'Michael, remember how you said that you'd only go to the prom if the guys in your band went, too?'

Michael couldn't seem to fathom the fact that I was actually in *his* classroom for a change.

'What are you doing here?' he wanted to know. 'Does Mr G know you're here? You're going to get into trouble again . . .'

'Never mind that,' I said. 'Just tell me. Did you mean it when you said you'd go to the prom if the guys from your band went, too?'

'I guess so,' Michael said. 'But, Mia, the prom got cancelled, remember?'

'What if I told you,' I said all casually, like I was talking about the weather, 'that the prom was back on, and that they need a band, and that the band the Prom Committee has chosen is YOURS?'

Michael just stared. 'I'd say . . . get out of town.'

'I am totally serious,' I informed him. 'And I will not get out of town. Oh, Michael, *please* say yes, I want to go to the prom *so badly* . . .'

Michael looked surprised. 'You do? But the prom is so . . . lame.'

'I know it's lame,' I said, not without some feeling. 'I know it is, Michael. But that does not alter the fact that I have been dreaming of going to the prom for my entire life, practically. And I really believe that I could achieve total self-actualization if you and I went to the prom together tomorrow night . . .'

Michael still looked like he couldn't quite believe any of it – that his band was actually being booked for a real gig; that that gig was the school prom; and that his girlfriend had just confessed that her way up the Jungian tree of self-actualization might be speeded along if he agreed to take her to said prom with him.

'Uh,' Michael said. 'Well, OK. I guess so. If you feel that strongly about it.'

I was so overcome with emotion, that I reached out and grabbed Michael's head, just as I had grabbed Lana's. And just as I had done with Lana, I dragged Michael's head towards me and planted a great big kiss on him . . . only not between his eyebrows, like with Lana, but right square on the lips.

Michael seemed very, very surprised by this – especially, you know, that I'd done it right in front of Mrs Weinstein. Which is probably why he turned red all the way to his hair-line after I finished kissing him, and went, '*Mia,*' in a sort of strangled voice. But I didn't care if I'd embarrassed him. Because I was too happy. I went, 'See ya, Mrs Weinstein,' to Michael's stunned-looking English teacher and skipped out of there, feeling just like Molly when Andrew McCarthy came up to her at the prom and confessed his love to her, even though she was wearing that hideous dress.

And now I am sitting here – having told Lana that Skinner Box would definitely be performing at the prom – trembling with excitement over my own good fortune. I am going to the prom. I, Mia Thermopolis, am going to the prom. With my boyfriend and one true love, Michael Moscovitz. Michael and I are going to the prom.

MICHAEL AND I ARE GOING TO THE PROM!!!!!!!!!!!!!!!!

TO THE PROM!!!!!!!!!!!!

PROM!

Homework

Algebra: Who cares? Michael and I are going to the prom!!!!!
English: Prom!!!!
Biology: I'm going to the prom!!!!!!!!
Health and Safety: PROM!!!!!!!!!!!!!!!!!!!!!!!!!!
Gifted and Talented: As if
French: *Nous Allons Au Promme!!!!!!*
World Civ.: WORLD PROM!!!!!!!!!!!!!!!!!!!!!!!!

PROM!

Friday, May 9, 7 p.m., the Loft

I really do not have time for all of this bickering between my mom and Grandmere. Don't these women know I have more important things to worry about? I AM GOING TO THE PROM TOMORROW WITH MY BOYFRIEND. I am supposed to be getting plenty of rest and anointing my body with precious unguents right now, not refereeing fights between the post-menopausal and the hormonally-challenged.

WHY CAN'T YOU BOTH SHUT UP??????????? I want to scream at them.

But that, of course, wouldn't be very princesslike.

I am going to put on my headphones and try to drown out the noise with the mix Michael made for my birthday party. Perhaps the dulcet tones of The Flaming Lips will calm my fractious nerves.

Friday, May 9, 7:02 p.m.

Not even The Flaming Lips can drown out Grandmere's strident tones. Am switching to Kelly Osbourne.

Friday, May 9, 7:04 p.m.

Success! Finally, I can hear myself think.

Michael just emailed to let me know that he and the band would probably be up all night practising for their first big gig. But it is fully all right for the GUY to show up at the prom with dark circles under his eyes (look at that guy who ended up at the Time Zone dance with Melissa Joan Hart in *Drive Me Crazy*). It's just not OK for the GIRL to look less than petal smooth and daisy fresh.

The guys in the band aren't exactly stoked about the whole playing-at-the-prom thing. In fact, rumour has it Trevor even said, 'Oh, man, can't we just stick forks in our eyes, instead?'

But Michael says he told him a gig is a gig, and that beggars can't be choosers.

Michael signed off on his email with this:

See you tomorrow night. Love, M

Tomorrow night. Oh yes. Tomorrow night, my love, when I enter the prom on your arm, and see the jealous gazes of all of my peers. Well, just Lana, because she's the only freshman besides me who is going. Except for Shameeka. Only she would never look at me jealously, because she is my friend.

Oh, and Tina. Because it turns out Tina is going to the prom, too. Because of course Boris is in Michael's band, and since he is going to be there, he is allowed to bring one guest, and he chose Tina, because she, as he put it at lunch today, 'is my new muse, and sole reason for living.'

Oh, how thrilled Tina looked to hear those words uttered from the lips of her new love! I swear, she practically choked on her Fruitopia. She beamed across the table at Boris, and though I never thought I would write these words, I swear they are true:

Boris almost looked handsome as he basked beneath the hearthglow of her affection.

Seriously. Like, even his underbite didn't look that pronounced. And his chest kind of puffed out.

Either that, or he's been working out or something.

AHHHHH! The phone! Oh please God let it be my dad to say the strike is over and he's sending the limo down to pick Grandmere up . . .

Friday, May 9, 7:10 p.m.

It wasn't my dad. It was Michael, to ask if I agree with the line-up of songs Skinner Box plans on playing tomorrow. It includes many old prom standbys, such as The Moldy Peaches' 'Who's got the Crack' and Switchblade Kittens' 'All Cheerleaders Die', in addition to edgier stuff such as 'Mary Kay' by Jill Sobule and 'Call the Doctor' by Sleater-Kinney. This is not to mention Skinner Box's original songs, such as 'Rock Throwing Youths' and 'Princess of my Heart'.

I did feel compelled to suggest Michael substitute 'Rock Throwing Youths' with something a little less controversial, like 'When It's Over' by Sugar Ray or 'She Bangs' by Ricky Martin, but he said he would sooner show up in the middle of Times Square wearing nothing but a cowboy hat (oh, how I wish he would!). So I suggested some old school Spoon or White Stripes instead.

Then Michael went, 'What is all that shouting in the background?'

'Oh,' I said airily. 'That's just Grandmere and my mom arguing. Grandmere keeps insisting that my mom let her smoke in the Loft, but Mom says it's not good for me, or for the baby. Grandmere just accused my mother of being a fascist. She says when she had Hitler and Mussolini over to the palace for tea at the height of World War Two, they both let her smoke, and if it was good for those guys, it should be good enough for my mom.'

'Uh, Mia,' Michael said. 'You do realize that your grandmother just turned sixty-five.'

'Yeah,' I said, remembering Grandmere's birthday with all too much clarity: she had insisted on me going back to Genovia with her to celebrate it, only I had had midterms

(THANK GOD) and so was unable to. Don't think I didn't hear about THAT ad nauseam for weeks.

'Well, Mia,' Michael said. 'I know maths is not your strong point, but you do know that your grandmother could only have been about five years old during the height of World War Two. Right? I mean, she couldn't have had Hitler and Mussolini for tea at the Genovian Palace, because she wouldn't have even been living there yet, unless she married your grandfather when she was like, four.'

I was stunned into total and complete silence by that one. I mean, can you believe it? My own grandmother has been lying to me MY WHOLE LIFE. All Grandmere ever tells me about is how she saved the palace from being shelled by the Nazi hordes by having Hitler over for soup or something. All this time, I've thought about how brave she was, and what a diplomat, stopping the imminent military incursion into Genovia with SOUP and her charming (well, back then, maybe) smile.

AND NOW I FIND OUT IT'S NOT EVEN TRUE????????????????????????

Oh, my God. She's good. *Really* good.

Although – and I never thought I would say this – it's sort of hard to be mad at her.

Because . . . well . . .

She did save the prom.

Friday, May 9, 7:30 p.m.

Tina just called. She is kevelen over getting to go to the prom. It is, she says, like a dream come true. I told her I couldn't agree more. She asked me how I thought we'd come to be so lucky.

I told her: Because we are both kind and pure of heart.

Friday, May 9, 8:00 p.m.

Oh, my God. I never thought I would say this, but poor Lilly.

Poor, poor Lilly.

She just found out that Boris is taking Tina to the prom. She overheard Michael and I talking a little while ago. Lilly is on the phone with me now, barely able to speak, she is trying so hard to hold back her tears.

'M-Mia,' she keeps choking. 'W-What have I d-done?'

Well, it is very clear what Lilly's done: ruined her life, that's all.

But of course I can't tell her that.

So instead I went on about how a woman needs a man like a fish needs a bicycle and about how Lilly will learn to love again, blah blah blah. Basically all the same stuff Lilly and I said to Tina back when she got dumped by Dave Farouq El-Abar.

Except of course that Boris didn't dump Lilly: SHE dumped him.

But I can't point this out to Lilly, as it would be like kicking her when she was already down.

It is sort of hard dealing with Lilly's personal crisis when a) I am so happy, and b) my mom and Grandmere are still fighting in the background.

I just had to excuse myself for a moment and put the phone down. Then I went out into the living room and shrieked, 'Grandmere, for the love of God, would you please call Les Hautes Manger and ask them to hire Jangbu back so you can go return to your suite at the Plaza and leave us in PEACE?'

But Mr Gianini, who was sitting at the kitchen table, pretending to be reading the paper, went, 'I think it's going to take a little more than young Mr Pinasa getting his job back to end this strike, Mia.'

Which I must say is extremely disappointing to hear. Because I can barely find anything in my room, due to the fact that Grandmere's stuff is strewn everywhere. It is a little demoralizing to be looking around in my underwear drawer for a pair of Queen Amidala panties only to find the BLACK SILK AND LACE THONGS Grandmere wears. My *grandma* has sexier underwear than me. This is fully disturbing. I will probably be in therapy for years because of it, too.

But no one seems to worry about the mental health of the children, do they? So when I came back into my room just now and picked up the phone, Lilly was still going on about Boris. Really. It's like she doesn't even know I was gone. '. . . but I just never appreciated what we had together until it was gone,' she's saying.

'Uh-huh,' I go.

'And now I am going to grow old and die a spinster with maybe some cats or something. Not that there is anything wrong with that, because, of course, I don't need a man to be fulfilled as a human being, but still, I always pictured myself with a live-in lover at the very least . . .'

'Uh-huh,' I go. I just now noticed to my extreme annoyance that Rommel has decided to use my backpack as his own personal bed. Also that Grandmere has very cavalierly draped her sleep mask over one of my Disney Princess snowglobes.

'And I know that I took him for granted and never even let him get to second base, but seriously, he can't really think *Tina* is going to let him, can he? I mean, she is fully the type of girl who will demand a marriage proposal at the very least before she even lets him *look* under her shirt . . .'

Ooooh. This conversation suddenly got very interesting. 'Really? You and Boris never got to second base?'

'Well, it never really came up,' Lilly said, sounding very forlorn.

'What about you and Jangbu?'

Silence on the other end of the phone. *Guilty* silence, though. I could tell.

Still, it's good to know she and Boris never engaged in any full-frontal chestal activities. I mean, it will make Tina happy . . . as soon as I can get off the phone with Lilly and tell her, I mean.

I wonder if Michael and I will get to second base tomorrow night . . . after all, I'll be wearing my first strapless gown.

And it IS the prom . . .

Saturday, May 10, 7 a.m.

One would think that a PRINCESS would get to sleep in on the day of her first PROM.

BUT OH NO.

Instead of being wakened to the sound of birdsong, like princesses in books, I was wakened to the sound of Rommel shrieking as Fat Louie beat him senseless for getting into his bowl of Fancy Feast.

I am having a hard time summoning up any real sympathy for Rommel. After all, if it weren't for his behaviour on my birthday, he wouldn't be in this position right now. Although it is wrong to think Rommel could really have behaved any differently. He didn't exactly ASK Grandmere to bring him along to my birthday dinner. And it is clear to me now, having lived with him for several days, that Rommel, more than anyone I know, suffers from Asperger's syndrome.

Oh, God. I can hear the Gorgon stirring even now . . .

Maybe if I go grab my prom dress and run out of the door now, I can hightail it uptown to Tina's and prepare for my Big Night in the relative privacy of her place . . .

Oh, my God. That's it. That's *exactly* what I'll do! Why didn't I think of it before? I hate to leave my mom and Mr G alone with Grandmere all day again, but really, what choice do I have? THIS IS THE PROM!!!!!!!!!!!!!!!

If ever there was a time for emergency action, this is it.

Saturday, May 10, 2 p.m.

Well, I did it. I escaped from Casa Horrifico.

Tina and I are safely ensconced in her room, having our pores unclogged by heat-action mud masks. We just had our nails done at Miz Nail down the street (well, I basically just had my cuticles done, since I don't really have any nails) and, in a little while, Mrs Hakim Baba's hairdresser is coming over to do our coiffures.

This is *so* how you are supposed to spend your Prom Day: beautifying yourself instead of listening to your mother and your grandmother bicker over who drank the last of the PediaLyte (Grandmere, it turns out, likes it with a splash of vodka).

Of course, I feel badly that my mother doesn't get to share in this very important day in my formative development as a woman. However, she has more important things to worry about. Such as gestating. And doing her breathing exercises, to keep herself from killing Grandmere.

Reports from the strike negotiations are not promising. Last time we turned on New York One, the Mayor was urging all New Yorkers to stock up on staples such as bread and milk, since we were no longer going to be able to turn to our local Chinese restaurants or pizzerias for sustenance.

Really, I don't know what Mr G and Mom and Grandmere are going to eat without delivery from Number One Noodle Son. They'd better hope they can pick up some prepared food at Jefferson Market . . .

Not that any of that is my concern. Not today. Because today, the only thing I am going to worry about is looking beautiful for the prom.

Because today, I am just like any other girl on her prom day. Today, I am a

PROM

PRINCESS

!!!!!!!!

Saturday, May 10, 8 p.m., in the limo on the way to the prom

Oh, my God, I am so excited I can barely contain myself. Tina and I look FABULOUS, even if I do say so myself. When the boys see us – we are meeting them at the prom, as they had to go early to set up – they are going to PLOTZ.

Of course, it does suck a little that Tina and I, instead of just having adorable little beaded clutches at our sides, have to bring along a couple of bodyguards. Seriously. They never mention this in the *Seventeen Magazine* prom issue. You know: How to Accessorize Your Bodyguard.

You should have heard Lars and Wahim grousing about having to get into tuxes. But then I reminded them that Mademoiselle Klein was going to be there, and that to my certain knowledge she was going to be wearing a dress with a slit up the side. That seemed to spark their interest, and they didn't even complain when Tina and I pinned on their matching boutonnières. They look so cute together . . . kind of like Siegfried and Roy. Minus the tigers, and fake tans and all.

I didn't mention that Mr Wheeton was going to be there, too . . . and that, in fact, he'd be escorting Mademoiselle Klein. Somehow, I didn't think that information would be very well received.

Oh, my God, I am so nervous, I am actually SWEATING. I am telling you, fifteen is turning out to be the best age EVER. I mean, already I have got to play my first game of Seven Minutes in Heaven AND I'm going to my first ever prom . . . I truly am the luckiest girl in the world. Oh, my gosh. WE'RE HERE!!!!!!!!!!

May 10, 9 p.m., The Empire State Building Observation Deck

I never thought I would say this, but Grandmere rules.

Seriously. I am SO glad she brought Rommel to my birthday dinner, and that he escaped, and that Jangbu Pinasa tripped over him, and that Les Hautes Manger fired him, and that Lilly adopted his cause and created a city-wide hotel, restaurant, and porters' unions strike.

Because if she hadn't, the prom might never have been cancelled, and Lana and the rest of the Prom Committee would have gone ahead and had it at Maxim's instead of being forced to have it on the observation deck of the Empire State Building – something arranged entirely by Grandmere, who is like *this* with the owner – and Michael would have continued to refuse to go to the prom at all, and so instead of standing under the stars in my totally rocking Jennifer Lopez-engagement-ring pink prom dress, listening to MY BOYFRIEND'S BAND, I'd be stuck at home, instant messaging my friends.

So as I stare out at the twinkling lights of Manhattan, all I can say is:

Thank you, Grandmere. Thank you for being such a complete freak. Because without you, my dream of entering the prom on the arm of my one true love would never have come true.

And OK, it kind of sucks that we can't dance because the only time there's any music is when Skinner Box is playing.

But the band took a break a little while ago, and Michael came over with a glass of punch for me (pink lemonade with Sprite in it . . . Josh tried to spike it, but Wahim totally caught him and threatened him with his numb-chucks) and we went over to the telescopes and stood with our arms around each other, gazing out at the Hudson River, snaking silverly along in the moonlight, and . . .

Well, I'm not sure, but I think we got to second base.

I'm not sure because I don't know if it counts if a guy feels you up THROUGH your bra.

I will have to consult with Tina on this, but I think the hand actually has to get UNDER the bra for it to count.

But there was no way Michael was getting under MY bra, given as how I am wearing one of those strapless ones that are so tight it feels like you are wearing an Ace bandage around your boobs.

But he tried. I'm pretty sure, anyway.

There really is no doubting it now. I am a woman. A woman in every sense of the word.

Well, almost. Probably I should go into the ladies' room and take this stupid bra off so if he goes for it again I might actually be able to feel something . . .

Oh, my God, somebody's mobile is ringing. That is so rude. And in the middle of 'Princess of my Heart' too. You would think people would show some respect for the band and turn off their—

Oh, my God. That's MY mobile!!!!!!!!!!!!!!!!!!!!!!!!

Sunday, May 11, 1 a.m., St Vincent's Maternity Ward

Oh . . . my . . . God.

I can't believe it. I really can't. Tonight, not only did I become a woman (maybe) but I also became a big sister.

That's right. At 12:01 a.m., Eastern Standard Time, I became the proud big sister of Rocky Thermopolis-Gianini.

He is six weeks early, so he only weighed four pounds, fifteen ounces. But Rocky, like his namesake – I guess Mom was too weak to argue for Sartre any more. I'm glad. Sartre would have been a lousy name. The kid would have got beaten up all the time for sure with a name like Sartre – is a fighter, and will have to spend some time in an 'isolet' to 'gain and grow'. Both mother and Y-chromosomed oppressor, however, are expected to be fine . . .

Though I don't think the same can be said for the grandmother. Grandmere is slumped beside me in an exhausted heap. In fact, she appears to be half asleep, and is snoring slightly. Thank God there is no one around to hear it. Well, no one except for Mr G, Lars, Hans, my dad, our next-door neighbour, Ronnie, our downstairs neighbour, Verl, Michael, Lilly and me, I mean.

But I guess Grandmere has a right to be tired. According to my mother's extremely grudging report, if it hadn't been for Grandmere, little Rocky might have been born right there in the Loft . . . and with no helpful midwife in attendance, either. And seeing as how he came out so fast, and is so early, and needed a hit of oxygen before his lungs really started going, that could have been disastrous!

But with me away at the prom, and Mr Gianini having left the Loft to go 'buy some Lottery tickets down at the deli' (translation: he'd needed to get out of there for a few minutes, not being able to stand the constant bickering any more), only Grandmere was around when Mom's waters suddenly broke (thank God in her bathroom and not on the futon couch. Or else where would I sleep tonight????).

'Not now,' Grandmere apparently heard my mother wailing from the toilet. 'Oh, God, not now! It's too soon!'

Grandmere, thinking Mom was talking about the strike, and that she didn't want it to end so soon because it meant she'd be deprived of the delightful company of the Dowager Princess of Genovia, of course went bustling into my mom's room to ask which newscast she was watching . . .

Only to find that my mother wasn't talking about something she'd seen on TV at all. Grandmere said she didn't even think about what she did next. She just ran out of the Loft, screaming, 'A cab! A cab! Somebody get me a cab!'

She didn't even hear my mother's mournful cries of, 'My midwife! No! Call my midwife!'

Fortunately our next-door neighbour, Ronnie, was home – a rarity for her on a Saturday night, as Ronnie is quite the femme fatale. But she was just recovering from a bout of the flu and had decided to stay in for the night. She opened her door and stuck her head out and went, 'Can I help you, miss?'

To which my grandmother apparently replied, 'Helen's in labour and I need a cab! And that's Your Royal Highness to you, mister!'

While Ronnie ran downstairs to flag down a cab, Grandmere ducked back into the apartment, grabbed my mom, and went, 'Come on, Helen, we're going.'

To which my mother supposedly replied, 'But I can't be having the baby now! It's too soon! Make it stop, Clarisse. Make it stop.'

'I can command the Royal Genovian Air Force,' Grandmere supposedly replied. 'As well as the Royal

Genovian Navy. But the one thing in the world I have no control over, Helen, is your womb. Now come on.'

All of this activity was enough to wake up our downstairs neighbour, Verl, of course. He came running out of his apartment thinking that the mother ship was finally landing . . . only to find a mother of quite a different kind waddling down the stairs in front of him.

'I'll run to the deli and get Frank,' Verl said, when he learned what was going on.

So by the time Grandmere got my mom all the way down three flights of stairs, Ronnie had secured a cab, and Mr G and Verl were racing up the street towards them . . .

They all piled into the cab (even though there is a city ordinance that there are only five people, including the driver, allowed in a cab at one time – something the cabbie apparently pointed out, but to which Grandmere replied, 'Do you know who I am, young man? I am the Dowager Princess of Genovia and the woman responsible for the current strike, and if you don't do exactly as I say, I'll get YOU fired, too!') and sped off to St Vincent's, which is where Lars and Michael and I found them (in the maternity waiting area – minus my mom and Mr G, of course, who were in the delivery room) half an hour after they called me, waiting tensely to hear if my mother and the baby were all right.

My dad and Hans joined us a little while later (I called him) and Lilly showed up a little after that (Tina had apparently called her from the prom, feeling bad for her, I guess, sitting around at home) and the nine of us (ten if you count the cabbie, who stuck around demanding somebody pay for the damage Ronnie's stilettos did to his floor mats, until my dad threw a hundred dollar bill at him and the guy grabbed it and took off) sat there watching the clock – me in my pink prom dress, and Lars and Michael in tuxes. We were definitely the best-dressed people at St Vincent's.

If I had any fingernails before, I certainly don't now. It was a VERY tense two hours before the doctor finally came out and said, with a happy look on her face, 'It's a boy!'

A boy! A brother! I will admit that I was, for the teeniest second, a little disappointed. I had been hoping for a sister so hard! A sister I could share things with – like how tonight at the prom, I had maybe got to second base with my boyfriend. A sister I could buy those cheesy plaques for – you know, the ones that say, '*God made us sisters, but life made us friends.*' A sister whose Barbies I could still play with, and nobody could accuse me of being a baby, because, you know, they'd be HER Barbies, and I'd be playing with HER.

But then I thought of all the things I could do with a baby brother . . . you know, make him wait on line for *Star Wars* tickets, something no girl would ever be stupid enough to do (we'd use MoviePhone instead). Throw rocks at the mean swans on the palace lawn back in Genovia. Steal his *Spiderman* comic books. Mould him into a perfect boyfriend for some lucky girl of the future, like in the Liz Phair song 'Double Dutch'.

And suddenly, the idea of having a brother didn't seem so horrible.

And then Mr G came stumbling out of the delivery room, tears streaming down either side of his goatee, gibbering like those rhesus monkeys on the Discovery Channel about his 'son', and I knew . . . just knew . . . that it was right and good that my mom had had a boy . . . a boy named Rocky – after a man who, if you think about it, was really very respectful and loving of women ('Adrian!') . . . that my mom and I had somehow been divinely chosen for this. That together, Mom and I would raise the most kickass, non-sexist, non-chauvinistic, Barbie-AND-Spiderman loving, polite, funny, athletic (but not a dumb jock), sensitive (but not whiny), second-base-getting-to, non-toilet-seat-leaver-upper that there had ever been.

In short, we would raise Rocky to be . . .

Michael.

Only I hereby swear, on all I hold sacred – Fat Louie; Buffy; and the good people of Genovia, in that order – that I will make sure that when Rocky is old enough to attend his Senior Prom, he will NOT think it is lame to do so.

Sunday, May 11, 3 p.m.

Well, that's it. The strike is officially over.

Grandmere has packed up her things and gone back to the Plaza.

She offered to stay until Rocky comes home from the hospital, to 'help' my mom and Mr G with him until they get on some sort of schedule. Mr G couldn't seem to say, 'Um, thanks so much for the offer, Clarisse, but no,' fast enough.

I have to say, I'm glad. Grandmere would only get in the way of my moulding Rocky into the perfect boy. Like you can so tell she'll always be saying stuff to him like, 'Who's my big boy? Who's my gwate big widdle man?'

Seriously. You wouldn't think it of Grandmere, but when we finally got to see Rocky in his little incubator last night, that's exactly the kind of stuff she was saying. It was revolting.

I kind of know now why my dad has so many issues with forming lasting relationships with women.

Anyway, the restaurateurs finally caved in to the demands of the busboys. They will now all be receiving health benefits and sick leave and vacation pay. Well, all except for Jangbu, of course. He collected the money from his life story and flew back to Tibet. I guess city life didn't really work out all that well for him. Besides, in Tibet, all that money will provide him and his family with financial stability for life – not to mention a palatial mansion. Here in New York, it would have barely bought him a walk-up studio in a bad neighbourhood.

Lilly seems to be getting over her disappointment of not having gone to prom. Tina gave her a full report – about how after Michael unceremoniously abandoned the rest of the band in order to escort me to the hospital, Boris took over lead guitar, even though he'd never played the guitar before in his life.

But of course, being a musical genius, there is no instrument Boris can't pick up almost instantaneously . . . except for maybe like the accordion, or something. Tina says after we left, things got a little out of hand, with Josh and some of his friends leaning over the side of the observation deck and seeing if they could hit stuff below with their own spit. Mr Wheeton caught them though, and gave them all in-school suspension. Lana supposedly started crying and told Josh he'd ruined the most special night of her life, and that this was how she was going to be forced to remember him when he went off to college next year . . . hawking loogies off the Empire State Building.

Sweet.

As for me, well, I don't have to worry: when Michael goes off to college next year

a) it will be just uptown, so I'll still see him all the time, anyway. Or at least, a lot of the time, and
b) the memory I'll have of him is not hawking loogies off the Empire State Building, but of turning to my dad in the maternity waiting room and saying (after I'd asked Dad, for the millionth time, if, now that I had a baby brother, I could stay in New York for the whole summer and get to know him, and Dad, for the millionth time, replying that I had signed a contract and had to stick to it), 'Actually, sir, legally, minors can't enter into contracts and so, according to New York State law, you cannot hold Mia to any document she might have signed, as she was under sixteen at the time, making it invalid.'

WHOA!!!!!!!!!!!!!!!!! RIGHTEOUS!!!!!!!!!!!!!!!!!!

You should have seen my dad's face! I thought he was

going to have a coronary then and there. Good thing we were already at the hospital, just in case he keeled over. George Clooney could have rushed right over with the crash cart.

But he didn't keel over. Instead, Dad just looked Michael very hard in the face. I am happy to report that Michael just looked right back at him. Then Dad said, all grimly, 'Well . . . we'll see.'

But you could tell he knew he'd been beat. Oh, my God, it is so GREAT, going out with a genius. It really is.

Even if he hasn't, you know, mastered the art of strapless bra removal.

Yet.

So I've finally got my room back . . . and it looks like I'll be staying in the city for at least the majority of the summer . . . and I have a baby brother . . . and I wrote my first actual story for the school paper, AND had a poem published . . . and I *think* my boyfriend and I might have got to second base . . .

And I got to go the prom.

TO THE PROM!!!!!!!!!!!!

Oh, my God. I'm self-actualized.

Again.

The PRINCESS DIARIES

Sixsational

For Benjamin

'She will be more a princess than she ever was – a hundred and fifty thousand times more.'

A Little Princess
Frances Hodgson Burnett

Albert Einstein High School Fall Semester Course Schedule for:

Student: Thermopolis, Amelia Mignonette Grimaldi Renaldo, HRH Princess

Sex: F **Yr:** 10

Period:	**Course:**	**Teacher:**	**Room:**
Homeroom		Gianini	110
Period 1	PE	Potts	Gym
Period 2	Geometry	Harding	202
Period 3	English	Martinez	112
Period 4	French	Klein	118
Lunch			
Period 5	Gifted and Talented	Hill	105
Period 6	US Government	Holland	204
Period 7	Earth Science	Chu	217

Dear Students and Parents,

Welcome back from what I hope was a relaxing and yet intellectually stimulating summer vacation. The faculty and staff of AEHS look forward to spending another exciting and fruitful academic year with you. With this in mind, we'd like to share these few conduct reminders:

Noise

Please note that Albert Einstein High School is located in a residential – albeit vertical – community. It is important to remember that sound travels up, and that any excessive noise – especially on the steps at the front entrance of the school – which might be disruptive to our neighbours will not be tolerated. This includes shouting, screaming, shrill or explosive laughter, music and ritualistic chanting/drumming. Please be respectful of our neighbours and keep the noise level to a minimum.

Defacement

Despite what is often cited as Albert Einstein High School 'tradition' on the first day of classes, students are expressly forbidden from defacing, decorating or otherwise tampering with the lion statue, frequently referred to as 'Joe', outside the East Seventy-fifth Street entrance of the school. Twenty-four-hour surveillance cameras have been installed, and any student caught defiling school property in any way will be subject to expulsion and/or fines.

Smoking

It has been brought to the attention of this administration that, last year, large numbers of cigarette butts were daily swept up from the front steps of the Seventy-fifth Street entrance. In addition to the fact that smoking is strictly prohibited on school grounds, cigarette butts constitute a visual eyesore, as well as a fire hazard. Please note that any students caught smoking – either by a staff member or on the new video-surveillance cameras – will be subject to suspension and/or fines.

Uniforms

Please note that this year's standard AEHS uniforms include:

Female students:	*Male students:*
Long or short-sleeved white blouse	Long or short-sleeved white shirt
Grey sweater or sweater vest	Grey sweater or sweater vest
Blue-and-gold plaid skirt (or) grey flannel trousers	Grey flannel trousers
Blue or white knee-highs or blue or black tights or nude-coloured pantyhose	Blue or black socks
Blue-and-gold plaid tie	Blue-and-gold plaid tie
Navy-blue jacket	Navy-blue jacket

Please note that the wearing of shorts – including regulation gym shorts or athletic team uniform shorts – beneath skirts is prohibited.

Remember, classes commence the day after Labor Day, Tuesday, September 1, at 7:55 a.m. As always, tardiness will not be tolerated.

Welcome back!

Principal Gupta

Monday, August 31, Labor Day

WomynRule: Did you SEE it??? Did you get that hypocritical piece of garbage she sent out last week? Just who does she think she's kidding with that? You so know that that part about ritualistic chanting was directed at ME. Just because I organized a few student rallies last year. Well, we're going to show her. She might think she can stifle the voice of the people, but the student body of Albert Einstein High is NOT going to be intimidated.

>

FtLouie: Lilly, I—

>

WomynRule: Did you see that part about the surveillance cameras???? Have you ever HEARD of anything so fascist? Well, she can install all the surveillance cameras she wants, but that's not going to stop ME. It's just another example of how she's slowly turning this school into her own academic dictatorship. You know they used surveillance cameras in Communist Russia to keep the proletariat in line? I wonder what she'll bring in next. Ex-KGB militia, perhaps, as hall monitors? I so wouldn't put it past her. This is a total invasion of our right to privacy. That's why this year, POG, we're taking matters into our own hands. I have a plan—

>

FtLouie: Lilly—

>

WomynRule: —that will totally undermine her attempts to strip us of our sense of self and bend us to her will. Best of all, it's in complete compliance with school ordinances. When we're through, Mia, she won't even know what hit her.

>

FtLouie: LILLY!!! I thought the whole point of Instant Messaging was so that we could TALK.

>

WomynRule: Isn't that we're doing?

>

FtLouie: YOU are. I'm TRYING to. But you keep interrupting.

>

WomynRule: Fine. Then go ahead. What do you want to say?

>

FtLouie: I can't remember now. You made me forget. Oh, here's one thing: Stop calling me POG!

>

WomynRule: SORRY. God. You know, ever since that

little brother of yours was born, you have got way . . . sensitive.

>

FtLouie: Excuse me. I have ALWAYS been sensitive.

>

WomynRule: You can say that again, BL. Don't you want to hear my plan?

>

FtLouie: I guess so. Wait a minute. What's BL?

>

WomynRule: You know.

>

FtLouie: No, I don't.

>

WomynRule: Yes, you do . . . baby-licker.

>

FtLouie: STOP IT!!! I AM NOT A BABY-LICKER!!!

>

WomynRule: R 2. Just like the red panda.

>

FtLouie: Just because I didn't think it was appropriate for my mother to take her six-week-old newborn on a peace march across the Brooklyn Bridge does not make me a baby-licker!!!! ANYTHING could have happened during that march. ANYTHING. She could have tripped and accidentally dropped him and he might have bounced off the safety railing and fallen hundreds of feet into the East River and drowned . . . if the fall didn't crush all his little bones to pieces. And even if I dived in after him we might both have been swept out to sea by the current . . . OH, THANKS, LILLY!!! Why did you have to remind me????

>

WomynRule: Remember what the zookeeper had to do to the red panda?

>

FtLouie: SHUT UP!!!! NO ONE IS GOING TO TAKE AWAY MY BABY BROTHER BECAUSE I LICK HIM TOO MUCH!!! I HAVE NEVER ONCE LICKED ROCKY!!!!

>

WomynRule: Yes, but you have to admit you are a little obsessive-compulsive about him.

>

FtLouie: Well, SOMEBODY has to worry about him! I mean, between my mother wanting to lug him around to all sorts of inappropriate venues such as anti-war rallies – sometimes even taking him there on the SUBWAY, which you know is just a breeding ground for germs – and Mr G tossing him into the air and causing his head to smack against the ceiling fan, I frankly think Rocky is LUCKY to have a big sister like me who looks out for his welfare, since God knows no one else in the family is doing it.

>

WomynRule: Whatever you say . . . baby-licker.

>

FtLouie: SHUT UP, LILLY. Just tell me your stupid plan.

>

WomynRule: No. I don't want to now. I think you're better off not knowing. Baby-lickers like you, who worry too much, are probably better off not knowing things too far in advance, as it will just cause you to lick the baby harder.

>

FtLouie: Fine. I don't have time to hear your stupid plan anyway. Your brother's on the phone. I gotta go.

>

WomynRule: WHAT? Tell him to hold on. THIS IS IMPORTANT, MIA!

>

FtLouie: This may come as a surprise to you, Lilly, but talking to your brother is important too. At least to me. You know I've only seen him twice since I got back Friday—

>

Womynrule: I'm sorry I called you a baby-licker. Just wait one minute while I tell you—

>

FtLouie: —and once was dorm move-in day on Saturday, and hardly counts since he was all sweaty from carrying that mini-refrigerator up all those stairs after the elevators broke down—

>

Womynrule: MIA!!! ARE YOU EVEN LISTENING TO ME????

>

FtLouie: —and your parents were there and so was his Resident Adviser. And then on Sunday we went out, but I was still jet-lagged and I accidentally—

>

Womynrule: I'M—

>

FtLouie: —fell asleep while he was showing me his—

>

Womynrule: GOING—

>

FtLouie: —newest Magic deck, since Maya dropped his last one—

>

Womynrule: TO—

>

FtLouie: —and it got all mixed up with the decks he doesn't use any more—

>

WomynRule: KILL YOU!

>

FtLouie: terminated

Monday, August 31, Labor Day, 10 p.m., the Loft

Another school year. I know I should be excited. I know I should be thrilled at the prospect of seeing my friends again after having been on foreign soil for the past two months.

And I am. I *am* excited. I'm excited to see Tina and Shameeka and Ling Su and even – I can't believe I'm saying this – Boris.

It's just . . . well, it's going to be so DIFFERENT this year, with no Michael to pick up on the way to school and sit with at lunch and have drop by before Algebra – ACK! No Algebra this year either! Geometry! Oh, God. Well, I'll just think about that one later. Although Mr Gianini (FRANK. MUST REMEMBER TO CALL HIM FRANK) says people who do badly in Algebra always do really well in Geometry. Please, please let that be true.

And OK, it's not like Michael and I ever used to make out in front of my locker or anything, what with his lack of enthusiasm about PDA and my bodyguard and all.

But at least – because there was always a chance I could run into Michael in the hallway at any moment – I had something to look *forward* to at school.

And now, because Michael has graduated, there's *nothing* to look forward to. *Nothing*.

Except for the weekends.

But how much time is Michael even going to have to spend with me on weekends? Because he's in college now, and he has so much homework already there's no way we can see each other on week nights – not that, between princess obligations and my OWN homework, that was ever going to happen anyway. But still. It's like—

God, what is WRONG with my mother? Rocky was just crying there for like FIFTEEN MINUTES while she did absolutely NOTHING. I went out into the living room and there she was with Mr G, just sitting there watching *Law and Order*, and I was all, 'Hello, your son is calling you,' and Mom, without even looking up from the TV, was like, 'He's just fussing. He'll settle down and go to sleep in a minute.'

What kind of maternal compassion is THAT? Lilly can call me a baby-licker all she wants, but is it really any wonder I'm as maladjusted as I am if this is an example of how my mother treated *me* as a baby?

So then I went into Rocky's bright-yellow room and sang one of his favourite songs – 'Behind Every Good Woman' by Tracy Bonham – and he calmed right down.

But did anyone thank me? No! I walked out of his room and my mom actually looked at me (only because there was a commercial) and went, very sarcastically, 'Thanks, Mia. We're trying to get him to understand that when we put him down for the night he's supposed to go to sleep. Now he's going to think all he has to do is cry and someone is going to come in there and sing a song to him. I just got him over that while you were in Genovia this summer, and now we're going to have to start all over again.'

Well, EXCUSE ME! I may be a baby-licker, but is it really such a crime to have a little compassion for my only sibling? JEESH!

Let's see, where was I?

Oh, yeah. School. Without Michael.

Seriously, what is even the point? I mean, yeah, I know we're supposed to be going to school to learn stuff and all of that. But learning stuff was so much more fun when there was a chance of spotting Michael by the water fountain or whatever. And now I fully have nothing like that to look forward to until Saturday and Sunday. I'm not saying that life without Michael isn't worth living or whatever. But I will say that when he's around – or even when there's just a chance that he MIGHT be around – EVERYTHING is a lot more interesting.

The only bright spot in what appears to be a school year otherwise completely devoid of them, is English. Because it looks as if our teacher, Ms Martinez, might actually be enthusiastic about the subject. At least, if this note she sent around to all of us last month is any indication:

A letter to all members of Ms Martinez's Tenth Grade English Class:

Hello!

I hope you don't mind receiving a note from me before the new school year even starts, but as the newest teacher on the AEHS *staff, I just wanted to introduce myself, as well as get to know all of you.*

My name is Karen Martinez, and I graduated with a Masters in English Literature from Yale this spring. My hobbies include Rollerblading, tae-bo, visiting the many wonderful sights of New York City, and reading (of course!) literary classics such as Pride and Prejudice.

I hope to get to know each and every one of you this year, and to aid me in doing so, I'm asking that each of my students comes to our first class period with a previously prepared short bio as well as an expository writing sample (no longer than 500 words) on what you learned during your summer vacation – because, as you know, life's lessons don't discontinue during the summer months, just because school is not in session!

I'm sorry to be assigning homework before classes even begin, but I assure you that this will aid in my helping you to become the best writers you can be!

Thanks very much, and enjoy the rest of your summer!

Yours truly,
K. Martinez

Clearly Ms Martinez is extremely dedicated to her job. It's about time AEHS finally got some teachers who actually care about their students – Mr G excepted, of course.

Frank, I mean.

I am especially excited because Ms Martinez is the new adviser to the school paper, on which I am a staff member. I really feel, judging by how much Ms Martinez and I have in common – I really liked *Pride and Prejudice*, especially the version with Colin Firth, and I tried Rollerblading once – that I'm going to greatly benefit from her teachings. I mean, being an aspiring author and all, it's very important that my talent is appropriately moulded, and I already feel confident that Ms Martinez is going to be the Mr Miyagi to my Karate Kid – writing-wise. Not, you know, karate-wise.

Still, it's hard to figure out what to say in my bio, let alone my expository writing sample, on what I learned this summer. Because what am I going to write? 'Hello, my name is Amelia Mignonette Grimaldi Renaldo, HRH Princess. You might have heard of me, on account of there having been a couple of movies based on my life.'

Although to tell the truth, both of those movies took a lot of liberties with the facts. It was bad enough in the first one that they made my dad dead and Grandmere all nice and everything. Now, in the latest one, I supposedly broke up with Michael! Like *that*'s going to happen. That was entirely projection on the part of the movie studio – I guess to make the story more exciting or something. As if my life isn't exciting enough without any help from Hollywood.

Although I do have a lot in common with that

Aragorn guy from *The Return of the King*. I mean, we've both had the mantle of sovereignty thrust upon us. I would much rather be a normal person than an heir to a throne. I kind of got the feeling that Aragorn felt the same way.

Not that I don't love the land over which I will one day rule. It's just that it's really boring to have to spend the better part of your summer with your dad and your grandma when you'd LIKE to be spending it with your new baby brother, not to mention your BOYFRIEND, who is starting COLLEGE in the fall.

Not that, you know, Michael is going AWAY to college or anything, he's only going to Columbia, which is right in Manhattan, although it's way uptown, way further uptown than I usually go, except for that one time we went to Sylvia's for fried chicken and waffles.

Anyway, I wrote the following bio for Ms Martinez while I was still in Genovia last week. I hope that, when she reads it, she'll recognize in my prose the soul of a fellow lover of writing:

My Bio
by
Mia Thermopolis

My name is Mia Thermopolis. I'm fifteen, a Taurus, heir to the throne of the principality of Genovia (population 50,000), and my hobbies include being taught how to be a princess by my grandmother, watching TV, eating out (or ordering in), reading, working for AEHS newspaper, The Atom, *and writing poetry. My future career aspiration is to be a novelist and/or a rescue-dog handler (like when there's an earthquake, to help find people trapped under rubble).*

However, I will most likely have to settle for being Princess of Genovia (POG).

That was the easy part, really. The hard part was figuring out what to say about what I learned during my summer vacation. I mean, what DID I learn anyway? I spent most of the month of June helping Mom and Mr G adjust to having an infant in the house – which was a very difficult transition for them, since for so many years all inhabitants of our household were entirely bipedal (not counting my cat, Fat Louis). The introduction of a family member who will eventually – perhaps even for a year or more – get around mostly by crawling made me acutely aware of the entirely un-baby-safe environment in which we live . . . although it didn't seem to bother Mom and Mr G so much.

Which is why I had to get Michael to help me install safety plugs in all of the sockets, and baby guards on all of our lower cabinet drawers – something Mom didn't entirely appreciate, since she now has trouble getting out the salad spinner.

She'll thank me one day, though, when she realizes that it's entirely because of me that Rocky hasn't got into any devastating salad-spinner accidents.

When we weren't busy baby-proofing the Loft, Michael and I didn't do much. I mean, there's lots of things a couple deeply in love can do in New York City during the summer: boating on the Lake in Central Park; carriage rides along Fifth Avenue; visiting museums and gazing upon great works of art; attending the opera on the Great Lawn; dining at outdoor cafes in Little Italy; et cetera.

However, all of these things can get quite expensive (unless you take advantage of student rates), except for that whole opera-in-the-park thing, which is free, but you have to get there at, like, eight in the morning to stake out your place and even then those weird opera people are all territorial and yell at you if your blanket accidentally touches theirs. And besides, everyone in operas always dies and I hate that as much as the blanket thing.

And while it's true that I am a princess, I am still extremely limited in the funds department, because my father keeps me on an absurdly small allowance of only twenty dollars a week, in the hope that I won't become a party girl (like certain socialites I could mention) if I don't have a lot of disposable income to spend on things like rubber miniskirts and heroin.

Although Michael got a summer job at the Apple Store in SoHo, he is saving all of his money for a copy of Logic Platinum, the music software program, so he can continue to write songs even though his band, Skinner Box, is on hiatus while its members scatter across the nation to attend various colleges and rehab clinics. He also wants Cinema HD, a twenty-three-inch flat-panel display screen, to go with the Power Mac G5 he's also hoping to buy, all of which he can get with his employee discount, but which all together will still cost as much as a single Segway Human Transporter, something I've been lobbying for my dad to buy me for some time now to no avail.

Besides, it's no fun to go on a carriage ride through Central Park with your boyfriend and YOUR BODY-GUARD.

So mostly when we weren't at my place installing baby guards, we spent June just hanging out at Michael's place, since then Lars could watch ESPN or chat with the Drs Moscovitz when they were not with patients or at their country home in Albany, while Michael and I concentrated on what was really important: making out and playing as much Rebel Strike as was humanly possible before being cruelly separated by my father on July 1.

Sadly, that grim day rolled around all too quickly, and I was forced to spend the latter months of the summer in Genovia, where I saved the bay (at least, if all goes as planned) from being overrun by killer algae that was dumped into the Mediterranean by the Oceanographic Museum in next-door Monaco (even though they deny it. Just like they deny that Princess Stephanie was driving the car when she and her mom went over that cliff. Whatever).

Which is what I ended up writing about. For Ms Martinez, I mean. You know, about how I surreptitiously ordered (and charged to the offices of the Genovian defence ministry) and then released 10,000 *Aplysia depilans* marine snails into the Bay of Genovia after reading on the Internet that they are the killer algae's only natural enemy.

I honestly don't know why everybody got so angry about it. That algae was strangling the kelp that supports hundred of species in the bay! And those snails are as toxic as the algae, so it's not like anything down there is going to eat them and break the existing food chain. They'll die off naturally as soon as their only source of nutrients – the algae – is gone. And then the bay will be back to normal. So what's the big deal?

Seriously, it's as if they think I didn't consider all this before I did it. It's almost as if people don't realize that I am not like a normal teen, concerned solely with partying and *Jackass*, but am actually Gifted, as well as Talented. Well, sort of.

I left out the part in my writing sample, though, about how everybody got so mad about the snails. Still, I just know Ms Martinez is going to be impressed. I mean, I used a lot of literary allusions and everything. Maybe, with her support, I might even get to write something other than the cafeteria beat on the school paper this year! Or start a novel and get it published, just like that girl I read about in the paper who wrote that scathing tell-all about the kids in her school, and now no one will talk to her and she has to go to school online or whatever.

Well, actually, I don't think I'd like that.

But I wouldn't mind not having to write about buffalo bites any more.

Oh no, Lilly is IM-ing me again. Doesn't she realize it is past eleven? I need to get my sleep in order to look my best for—

Huh. I was going to say for Michael. But I won't even be seeing him at school tomorrow.

So what do I even care how I look?

FtLouie: What do you want?

>

WomynRule: God, touchy much? Are you done talking to my brother yet?

>

FtLouie: Yes.

>

WomynRule: You two make me sick. You know that, don't you?

Poor Lilly. She and Boris went out for so long that she still isn't used to not having a boyfriend who calls to say goodnight. Not that Michael was going to bed yet when he called, but he knew I was. Michael doesn't have to get to sleep early, because even though he is taking eighteen credit hours this semester – so that he can graduate in three years instead of four and take a year off before he starts graduate school and I start college, so we can work together with Greenpeace at saving the whales – he purposely only chose classes that start after ten so he can sleep in.

You have to admire a man who is so good at planning ahead. I can barely even figure out what I'm going to have for lunch every day, so this is extremely impressive to me.

But Michael is an excellent planner. It would only have taken about half an hour to move him into his dorm at Columbia over the weekend (if the elevators hadn't broken down), because he had everything so organized. I went with the rest of his family to help, and to see what his room was like, and to, you know, see him for the first time since getting back from Genovia and all. I don't know how much Columbia charges for its student housing, but I wasn't very impressed. Michael's room is very cinderblocky, with a view of an airshaft.

Not that Michael even cares. All he was concerned about was whether it had enough data jacks. He didn't even look in the bathroom to see if it had one of those smelly vinyl shower curtains or the even smellier rubber ones (I looked for him: rubber one. Ew).

Guys are so weird.

I didn't meet his room-mate, because he hadn't moved in yet, but the sign on the door said his name was Doo Pak Sun. I hope Doo Pak turns out to be nice and not allergic to cat hair or anything. Because I plan on being in their room a LOT.

Still, I felt bad for Lilly, on account of her not having a one true love and all, so I thought I'd try to cheer her up.

FtLouie: But it must be nice to have the apartment all to yourself now. I mean, isn't that what you always wanted? No Michael to drink all the Sunny D and eat all the Honey Nut Cheerios?

>

Womynrule: Whatever! Suddenly I have to do all MY chores AND Michael's too. And who do you think has to take care of Pavlov now?

>

FtLouie: Like Michael's not paying you.

>

Womynrule: Only twenty bucks a week. Hello, I worked it out, and that is only like a dollar a pooper-scooper-full.

>

FtLouie: TMI!!!!!!!!!!!!

>

WomynRule: Whatever. I suppose you LOVE scooping up after Fat Louie.

>

FtLouie: Fat Louie's poops are cute, just like he is. Same with Rocky's.

>

WomynRule: Um, NOW who is giving TMI, baby-licker?

>

FtLouie: I am choosing to ignore that. Hey, do you think the part in Dr Gupta's letter about not wearing shorts beneath your school skirt is because Lana always wore Josh's lacrosse uniform shorts under her skirt last year? You know, to show that Josh was her property?

>

WomynRule: I don't know and I don't care. Listen, about tomorrow—

>

FtLouie: What?

>

Womynrule: Never mind. Sleep tight.

>

FtLouie: ??????????????

>

Womynrule: terminated

Seriously. I can already tell that being a sophomore is not exactly going to be a picnic.

Tuesday, September 1, Homeroom

OH MY GOD.

So I thought it was going to be depressing to be back here. I mean, because school totally sucks anyway, but without Michael, it's REALLY going to suck.

And it *was* kind of sad to pull up in front of Lilly's building this morning and not see Michael there waiting for me, his neck all pinkly shaved. Instead there was just Lilly, not wearing any make-up and with her hair in 10,000 barrettes and her glasses on instead of contacts. Because now that Lilly has lost her one true love to another, she barely bothers to Make an Effort. Grandmere would be APPALLED.

And hello, I have even less reason than Lilly does to look good, but at least I washed my hair this morning. I mean, I still *have* a boyfriend, he's just going to another school. Lilly's the one who has yet to meet the man of her dreams.

Who is going to run from her the way people ran from the movie *Gigli* if she doesn't at least TRY to look a little more attractive.

But I didn't mention this to her, because it's not the kind of thing anyone wants to hear first thing in the morning.

Besides, as Lilly put it, we both have PE first thing. Why shower BEFORE PE when you're just going to have to shower again after?

Which is a good point.

Except that I think Lilly sort of regretted her decision not to bathe pre-PE when we stepped out of the limo in front of school and there was Tina Hakim Baba stepping out of HER limo. Tina was all, 'Oh my God!

It's so good to see you guys!', tactfully not mentioning anything about Lilly's glasses or hair. We were hugging when this guy walked up and at first I was like, *Whoa, hottie alert*, because even though I'm taken, I'm not DEAD, you know, and he was so big and tall and blond and everything . . .

. . . until he reached out and took Tina's hand and I realized he was BORIS PELKOWSKI!!!!!!!!!!!!!!!

BORIS PELKOWSKI GOT HOT OVER THE SUMMER!!!!!!!

I know it sounds completely insane but there really is no other way to put it. Tina says Boris's violin teacher told him he'd have more stamina and play better if he started lifting weights, and so he did and he must have put on like thirty pounds of pure unadulterated muscle.

Plus he had laser surgery to correct his myopia so he wouldn't have to keep pushing up his glasses as he plays.

Also he got rid of his bionater and must have grown like two inches or maybe more, because now he's as tall as Lars and almost as wide in the shoulders.

Plus his hair has these blond highlights in it – Tina says from the sun in the Hamptons.

Seriously, it's like he got one of those *Queer Eye* makeovers or something.

Except they left out the part about not tucking his sweater into his pants. That's the only way I recognized him. Well, that and he still breathes from his mouth. Seriously, I was all, 'Hi, who are – BORIS?'

But MY astonishment was NOTHING compared to LILLY'S! She stared at him for like a whole minute after he was all, 'Oh, hey, hi, you guys.' – Even his VOICE has changed. It's sort of deeper now, like that kid's who plays Harry Potter in the movies.

When Lilly heard it, then turned around and recognized him, she kind of sucked in her cheeks . . .

. . . and just headed into school without a word.

But then when I saw her in the ladies' just before the bell rang, she'd put on some lipgloss and had slipped her contacts in and taken some of the barrettes out.

As soon as Lilly was gone I totally grabbed Tina and was all, 'OH MY GOD, WHAT DID YOU DO TO BORIS????' but in a whisper in her ear because I didn't want Boris to hear.

Tina swears she had nothing to do with it. Also, she said not to say anything in front of Boris about it, because he totally hasn't realized he's hot yet. Tina is trying to keep him from finding out about his new hotness because she's afraid as soon as he does he'll dump her for someone thin.

Except that Boris would never do anything like that because you can see the love-light for Tina shining in his eyes every time he looks her way. Especially now that he doesn't have those thick lenses.

Jeez! Who knew someone could change so much in just a couple of months?

Although, come to think of it, Tina might have a point, because with last year's senior class gone there are a LOT of totally gorgeous girls who are completely boyfriendless now. Like Lana Weinberger, for instance. Not that I think Boris would EVER go for Lana, but I totally saw her giving him the *Hey! Come over here* finger-crook by the water fountain before she figured out who he was and instead of crooking her finger, pretended to be sticking it down her throat like she was barfing at the sight of him.

So I guess SOME people haven't changed over the summer.

Shameeka says she heard that Lana and Josh are totally over. Apparently their love could not withstand the test of distance since Lana spent her summer at her family's house in East Hampton and Josh was in South Hampton, and the four miles between the two was just too much, especially with him leaving for Yale in the fall and thong bikini bottoms being very popular in Long Island this summer.

Excuse me. Four miles is nothing. Try 4,000. That's how far Genovia is from New York, and Michael and I still managed to see each other over the summer.

Poor, poor Lana. I feel so sorry for her. NOT. For the first time in my life, I have a boyfriend and Lana doesn't. It is unprincesslike to gloat over the misfortunes of others, but TEE HEE.

Another plus about Josh being gone is that I can actually get INTO my locker this year, since he and Lana aren't splayed up against it with their tongues in each other's mouths.

Although I do have to say that the guy who's been assigned Josh's old locker is pretty good-looking. He must be an exchange student because I've never seen him before. But he can't be a freshman because he's got razor stubble. At eight in the morning. Also, when he said, 'So sorry,' after accidentally sloshing some of his latte grande on to my boot while he was wrestling a gym bag into his locker, he fully had a South American accent, like that guy Audrey Hepburn was going to run off with in that movie *Breakfast at Tiffany's* before she came to her senses (or lost her mind, in Grandmere's opinion).

This is so BORING, sitting here, listening to announcement after announcement. There's an assembly this afternoon, so we've got an abbreviated seventh period. Who cares? Mr G (FRANK, FRANK) looks as tired as I feel. I swear, I love Rocky with every fibre of my being – almost as much as I love Fat Louie even – but the lungs on that kid! Seriously, he will NOT stop crying unless someone sings to him.

Which is OK during waking hours, because ever since I saw *Crossroads* I've been kind of worried, you know, about what I'm going to sing if I ever have to do karaoke to earn motel money on a road trip, and so Rocky's obsession with song gives me good opportunity to practise. I really think I've got 'Milkshake' down pat, and I'm working on 'Man! I Feel Like a Woman' by Shania Twain.

But when he starts up with the crying thing in the middle of the night . . . whoa. I love him, but even I, the baby-licker – which is SO not fair of her to call me, because I have NOT licked all of Rocky's fur off like that red panda on *Animal Planet* did to HER baby – just want to stuff a pillow over my head and ignore it.

Only I can't. Because everyone else in the loft is doing that. Because Mom's theory is that we're just spoiling him, picking him up and singing every time he cries.

But my theory is that he wouldn't cry if there weren't something wrong. Like what if his blanket has got wrapped around his neck and he's CHOKING???? If no one goes in to check, he could be DEAD by morning!

So I have to drag myself out of bed and sing the fastest song I know to him – 'Yes U Can' by Jewel – and then as soon as he dozes off, dive back into my own bed and try to fall back asleep before he starts up again.

OOOOH! My cellphone just buzzed! It's a text message from Michael!

GOOD LUCK 2DAY. LOVE, M

He got up early, just to wish me luck!!!! Could there BE a better boyfriend?

Tuesday, September 1, PE

I understand that obesity is epidemic in the US and all of that. I know that the average American is ten pounds heaver than their BMI says they should be, and that we all need to walk more and eat less.

But seriously, is any of that an excuse for forcing teenage girls to have to CHANGE CLOTHES, much less SHOWER, in front of one another? I so think not.

Like it's not enough that I even have to TAKE physical education. And it's not enough I have to take it FIRST THING IN THE MORNING. And it's not enough I have to STRIP DOWN IN FRONT OF VIRTUAL STRANGERS.

No, I also have to do it in front of Miss Lana Weinberger. Who also happens to have first-period PE.

And who took the liberty of pointing out in front of everyone, as we were changing into our gym clothes before class, that she 'really liked' my Queen Amidala panties – which I only wore for good luck on my first day back to class, although evidently they don't work any more – in a tone that suggested she did not like them at all.

And then she wanted to know if Genovia was suffering from an economic crisis, since its royals seemed to be shopping for their underwear at Target. As if all of us can afford to get our underwear from Agent Provocateur like Lana and Britney Spears!

I hate her.

Lilly told me not to worry about it . . . that Lana will be 'getting what she deserves' shortly.

Whatever that means.

Tuesday, September 1, Geometry

OK.

I can do this. I can totally do this.

Converse:
The converse of a conditional statement is formed by interchanging its hypothesis and conclusion.

Contrapositive:
The contrapositive of a conditional statement is formed by interchanging its hypothesis and conclusion, then denying both.

Inverse:
The inverse of a conditional statement is formed by denying both its hypothesis and conclusion.

So:

Logically equivalent:
A conditional statement: a → b
The contrapositive of the statement: not b → not a

Logically equivalent:
The converse of the statement: b → a
Then inverse of the statement: not a → not b

I'm sorry. **WHAT?**

OK, once again I have managed to prove to be the exception to the rule. If people who are bad at Algebra are supposed to be good at Geometry then I should be the Stephen Freaking Hawking of Geometry, but guess what? I don't understand a WORD of this.

Plus Mr Harding? Yeah, could he BE any meaner? He already made Trisha Hayes cry over her isosceles triangles, and that's virtually impossible, since she's one of Lana Weinberger's cronies and also I'm pretty sure she's a female cyborg like in *Terminator 3*.

He's being totally nice to me, but that's just because one of his colleagues is my stepdad. Oh, and the princess thing, of course. Sometimes it actually doesn't hurt to have a six-foot-four Swedish bodyguard sitting behind you.

Tuesday, September 1, English

M - Could she be any cuter? - Tina

I know! When is the last time we had a teacher who wore anything that wasn't corduroy?

Totally! And her hair! That flippy thing it does on the ends!

That is so how I want my hair. So Chloe on *Smallville*.

I know! And her glasses!

Cat's eyes! With rhinestones! Could she be more Karen O?

Who's Karen O?

Lead singer for the Yeah Yeah Yeahs.

Oh right. I was thinking Maggie Gyllenhall.

I think it's Gylenhaal.

I think maybe it's Gellynhaal.

OH MY GOD, YOU IDIOTS, IT'S GYLLENHAAL! WOULD YOU TWO STOP PASSING NOTES AND FREAKING PAY ATTENTION? DO YOU WANT TO ALIENATE THE ONE TEACHER WHO ACTUALLY MIGHT TURN OUT TO BE ABLE TO TEACH US SOMETHING USEFUL????? – L

What's Lilly's problem today?

Um. I don't know, exactly. PMS?

Oh, sure. Anyway. So Maggie's brother's the one who went out with Kirsten Dunst, right?

RIGHT!

So cute!!!!!!!!!!

Oh, well. At least I have ONE good teacher. Ms Martinez is SO cool. It's so nice to have a teacher who is still close enough to our age to know about stuff like rubber spike bracelets and *The OC*.

As Ms Martinez was collecting our writing samples on how we spent our summer, she was like, 'And I just want you guys to know that you can come to me with questions about anything, not just English. I really want to get to know all of you as PEOPLE, not just as my students. So if there's anything – anything at all – you want to talk about, feel free to stop by. There is an open-door policy in my classroom, and I will always be here for you.'

Whoa! A teacher at Albert Einstein High who doesn't disappear into the Teachers' Lounge the minute class is over? Unbelievable!

Except I sort of wonder how long Ms Martinez is going to hang on to her open-door policy, because as I was leaving I noticed, like, ten people scurrying up to her desk to talk to her about their personal problems. Lilly was totally the first one in line.

I hope Ms Martinez counsels Lilly just to let the whole

Boris thing go. I didn't want to say anything to Tina, but her boyfriend's summer transformation into a hottie is fully why Lilly is wigging out today, not PMS, like I told Tina. It must totally suck to see the guy you dumped transforming into Orlando Bloom before your very eyes.

If Orlando Bloom had no fashion sense and breathed from his mouth, I mean.

I hope Lilly doesn't wear Ms Martinez out so much that she doesn't have time to read our writing samples tonight. Because I'm sure that when she's done with mine, she's going to want to submit it to a literary agent or something and get me a book deal. I realize fifteen is pretty young to have a multi-book deal with a major publishing house, but I've handled the princess thing pretty well so far. I'm sure I could handle a couple of book deadlines.

Euler diagram = relate two or more conditional statements to each other by representing them as circles

Tuesday, September 1, French

Mia – The new kid, second row from door, three seats down. Boy or girl? – Shameeka

Boy. He's wearing pants!

Hello. So am I. I forgot to shave my legs this morning.

Oh. OH.

Yeah. See what I mean?

Well, what's his/her name?

Perin. At least that's what Mademoiselle Klein said when she called roll.

Is Perin a boy's name or a girl's name?

I don't know. That's why I'm asking you.

Well, did Mademoiselle Klein say Per-run or Per-reen? Because if she's a girl, it would be Per-reen in French, right?

Yeah, but Mademoiselle Klein doesn't call role in French. She just said Perin, in English, with no accent.

So in other words . . . this is a mystery.

Totally. I just want to know whether or not to think he's cute.

OK. Here's what we'll do. We'll keep an eye on him/her, and see which bathroom he/she goes into before lunch. Because everyone goes to the bathroom before lunch, to put on lipgloss.

Not boys.

Exactly. If he doesn't go to the bathroom, he's a boy, and then you can like him.

But what if he's a girl who just doesn't wear lipgloss?

Argh! Mysteries are OK in books, but in real life they kind of suck.

Tuesday, September 1, Gifted and Talented

WHY? WHY, WHY, WHY did I think this year was going to be better – in spite of Michael not being around – than last year, just because at least Lana and Josh wouldn't be making out in front of my locker?

Because the thing is, when Josh was around, Lana was DISTRACTED and not actively seeking out targets to destroy.

But now that there's no man in her life, she has ample free time to torture me again. Like today at lunch, for instance.

It was all my fault in the first place for being greedy and going back to the jet line for a second ice-cream sandwich. Really, one ice-cream sandwich ought to be enough for a girl my size.

But there was something wrong with the three-bean salad. You would think with all the money the trustees invested in those surveillance cameras outside they'd have tossed just a LITTLE the cafeteria's way, so we could get something decent to eat in here beside frozen dairy products. But no. Lilly seems to have a point: apparently finding out who is stubbing their cigarettes out on Joe's head is more important than providing digestible sustenance for the student body.

So I was standing there waiting to get my ice-cream sandwich when I heard this voice behind me say my name and when I turned my head there was Lana and Trisha Hayes, who seemed to have recovered from Mr Harding's tongue-lashing – at least enough to join Lana in her quest to humiliate me publicly as often as possible.

'So, Mia,' Lana said, when I made the mistake of

turning around. 'Are you still going out with that guy? You know, that Michael guy, with the band?'

I should have known of course. That Lana wasn't trying to make up for all those years of being mean to me. I should have just put the ice-cream sandwich back and left the jet line then and there.

But I thought, I don't know, that maybe she was sorry for the whole underwear remark in the locker room that morning. I thought – don't ask me why – that maybe Lana really had changed over the summer too, just like Boris. Only instead of changing on the outside, Lana had changed on the inside.

I should have known something like that would be impossible, since in order to have a change of heart, Lana would actually have to HAVE a heart in the first place, and she obviously does NOT since when I said cautiously, 'Yeah, Michael and I are still going out,' she went, 'Isn't he in college now?'

And I said, 'Yeah. He goes to Columbia,' kind of proudly because, hello, at least MY boyfriend had chosen to go to a college in the same STATE as the one I live in, unlike Lana's ex.

'Well, have you two done it yet?' Lana wanted to know, as casually as if she were asking me where I'd got my highlights done.

And I was like, 'Done what?' Because I SWEAR I had no idea what she was talking about. I mean, who ASKS people things like that????

And Lana went, 'IT, you idiot,' and looked at Trisha and the two of them started laughing hysterically.

That's when I realized what she meant.

I swear I could FEEL my face turning red. Seriously. It must have turned as red as Lana's nail polish.

And then, before I could stop myself, I went, 'NO, OF COURSE NOT!' in a very shocked voice.

Because I WAS very shocked. I mean, this is a topic I barely discuss with my best FRIENDS. I certainly never expected to be discussing it with my MORTAL ENEMY. In the JET LINE.

But before I had a chance to recover from my paralysing astonishment, Lana went on.

'Well, if you want to hang on to him, you'd better hurry up,' she said, while Trisha giggled behind her. 'Because guys in college expect their girlfriends to Do It.'

Guys in college expect their girlfriends to Do It.

That is what Lana said to me. In the JET LINE.

Then, as I stood there staring at her in total and complete horror, Lana poked me in the back and went, 'Are you going to buy that, or are you just going to stand there?' and I realized the line had moved up so that I was standing in front of the cashier with my ice-cream sandwich melting in my hand.

So I handed the cashier my dollar and went back to my table with Lilly and Boris and Tina and Shameeka and Ling Su and just sat there not saying anything until the bell rang.

And no one even noticed.

Guys in college expect their girlfriends to Do It.

Can this possibly be true? I mean, I have seen a lot of movies and TV shows where guys in college seem to expect their girlfriends to do it. Such as *Fraternity Life*. And MTV's *Spring Break*. And *Revenge of the Nerds*.

But the guys in those movies and shows had girlfriends that were in college too. None of them were going out with sophomores in high school. Who will shortly be flunking Geometry. Who happen to be princesses of a small European principality. Who have six-foot-four bodyguards.

Oh my God, is Michael expecting to have SEX with me??? NOW????

Naturally I assumed we would have sex ONE DAY. But I thought ONE DAY was way, way in the future. As far into the future as the day we go out to sea together to stop those whaling ships for Greenpeace. I mean, we have only been to second base ONCE and that was at the prom and I'm pretty sure now it wasn't even on purpose and I didn't even FEEL anything because of my strapless bra having way too much metal in it.

Am I supposed to believe that all this time I have been supposed to be getting ready to DO IT? But I am NOT ready to DO IT. I don't think. I mean, I didn't even want Michael to see me in a BATHING SUIT this summer, let alone NAKED—

OH MY GOD!!!! Last night he asked me to come over on Saturday to see how he and Doo Pak have set up their dorm room!!!!

WHAT IF THAT WAS REALLY AN INVITATION TO COME OVER AND DO IT AND I DON'T EVEN KNOW IT BECAUSE I AM SO UNSKILLED IN THE WAYS OF LOVE?????

What am I going to do about this? Clearly I need to talk to someone. But WHO? I can't talk to Lilly, because Michael's her BROTHER. And I can't talk to Tina, because she already told me the most precious gift a woman can give to a man is the flower of her virginity and that's why she's saving herself for Prince William, who is only allowed to marry a virgin.

She says she will settle for giving her flower to Boris if the Prince William thing doesn't work out by the time our senior prom rolls around though.

I can't talk to my MOTHER about it, because she can barely concentrate on the things she's SUPPOSED to be concentrating on – like raising my baby brother – as it is, without the added distraction of her teenage daughter wanting to talk to her about sex.

Besides, I know what she'll do: she'll schedule an appointment with her gynaecologist. Excuse me, but EW.

And obviously I can't say a word to Dad, because he would just arrange to have Michael assassinated by the royal Genovian guard.

And Grandmere would just pat me on the head and then tell every single person she knows.

Who does that leave? I'll tell you who:

MICHAEL. I am going to have to talk to MICHAEL about having sex with MICHAEL.

What am I, NUTS??? I can't talk to a BOY about SEX!!!! Particularly not THAT BOY!!!!

WHAT AM I GOING TO DO????????????

Oh my God, I think I'm having a heart attack. Seriously. My heart is beating like a million times a minute and practically exploding out of my chest. I think I have to go to the nurse. I think I have to—

Mrs Hill just asked me if I'm all right. Since it's the first day of class, she is pretending like she actually intends to supervise us this year. She made us all fill out a form stating what our goal for the semester is. You know, in this class. I peeked at Boris's and he'd written, *To learn Antonin Dvořák's* Concerto Royale *by heart and win a Grammy like my hero, Joshua Bell.*

Frankly, I don't think that's a very realistic goal. But Boris is almost as hot as Joshua Bell now, so maybe it really is doable. If hotness counts to the Grammy judges.

I tried to peek at Lilly's goal, but she is being way secretive. She put her hand over her paper and went, 'Back off, baby-licker,' to me in a very rude way.

I doubt she would be so mean if she knew the intense emotional maelstrom currently swirling within me concerning the future of my relationship with her brother.

Since I didn't know what to put as my goal – I don't even know why I'm IN this class this semester – I just wrote down, *To write a novel, and to not flunk Geometry*.

I can't believe Mrs Hill noticed that I was having a heart attack. She never used to notice anything we did. Well, that's because she was always locked in the Teachers' Lounge. But still.

I told her I'm fine.

But the truth is, I don't think I'll ever be fine again, thanks to Lana.

Tuesday, September 1, US Government

THEORIES OF GOVERNMENT
DIVINE RIGHT:

Creation of government is divine intervention in human affairs. Religious and secular were interwoven. People were far less likely to criticize a government created by God.

In Christian civilization, kings maintained that with the blessing of the church, the monarch was the legitimate ruler.

(Um, hello, except in Genovia, where the king of Italy, not God, gave the throne to my ancestress Rosagunde because of her bravery in the field of battle. Or the bedroom, I guess, considering that's where she killed her people's mortal enemy, Alboin. It is good to know that at least one of my family members excelled in something bedroom-related, since I have a feeling I'm going to be sadly lacking in that area, as I don't even like to look at MYSELF naked, let alone permit anyone ELSE to look at me.)

John Locke, a seventeenth-century philosopher, opposed Divine Right. He and others said: Government is legitimate only to the extent that it is based on the consent of the people being governed.

(Ha! Good for you, John Locke! Psych on all you kings and pharaohs, going around saying GOD put you on the throne! IN YOUR FACE!!!!)

Tuesday, September 1, Earth Science

Great. As if my day hasn't been bad enough. Guess who I have to sit by in this class this semester? Well, let's see, what letter of the alphabet comes right before T? That's right, S. Kenny Showalter.

Seriously. Did I stumble into some bad karma today or WHAT?

Apparently, Boris isn't the only one who grew over the summer. Kenny also sprouted up a couple more inches. Except that Kenny doesn't appear to have been doing any sort of weight training. So he just looks like the Scarecrow from *The Wizard of Oz* instead of Legolas.

Minus the pointy ears, of course.

Unlike the Scarecrow, though, Kenny actually has a brain. So he remembers all too well that the two of us used to go out. And that I dumped him for Michael. Well, technically, Kenny dumped ME. A fact about which he seems all too eager to remind me. He just went, 'Mia, I hope you can put aside your personal feelings about me and allow us to work together in a professional manner this semester.'

I said I thought I could. The thing is, if I were still going out with Kenny, and Lana said something about him expecting me to DO IT with him, I'd have just laughed in her face.

But Michael is different.

The other thing is, what does Lana even know about college boys? I mean, she's never even gone out with one! She could be totally wrong about Michael. TOTALLY WRONG.

I wish I had thought of saying this to her back in the jet line.

Kenny just asked me if I intended to spend this semester writing in my journal during class and then expect him to do all the work like I did when we were lab partners in Bio last year. Excuse me. I think someone is rewriting history here. I did NOT write in my journal during class last year.

Well, OK, maybe I did. But Kenny OFFERED to do all the lab work for me. And write it up afterwards. I mean, he LIKES that kind of thing. And he's good at it too.

If everybody would just concentrate on their own personal strengths, the world would be a much better place.

I guess I'd better stop writing now or Kenny will think I'm taking advantage of him. And then maybe he will expect me to DO IT with him to make up for it.

EWWWWWWWWWWWWWWWWWWW!!!!!!!!!!!!!!

Orbital mechanics – systematic long-term changes

1. Shape of orbit not constant circle – extreme ellipse over 100,000 years
2. Angle of tilt of axis varies – wobbles from 22 degrees to 24 degrees 30 minutes over 48,400 years
3. Precession – 26,000 years

PE:	No Assignment
Geometry:	Exercises, pages 11–13
English:	Pages 4–14, Strunk and White
French:	*Ecrivez une histoire*
Gifted and Talented:	N/A
US Government:	What is the basis for Divine Right theory of gov.?
Earth Science:	Section 1, define perigee/apogee

Tuesday, September 1, Assembly

There really ought to be some kind of constitutional amendment to abolish high-school convocations. Seriously. While they are abolishing PE.

Because not only are they a huge waste of school resources (how many times can you sit and listen to some paralysed dude talk about how he wished he'd never driven drunk? Hello, we KNOW), but also I'm beginning to think convocations are just an excuse for teachers to take a break from teaching. I fully saw Mrs Hill sneaking a cigarette outside the gym doors just now. I guess the front of the school isn't the only place where we need surveillance cameras.

Any time you get 1,000 teens in one room together, you just know there's going to be trouble. Principal Gupta already had to yell at the varsity girls' lacrosse team for throwing Swedish fish at the kids from the Drama Club, who weren't even doing anything, for once. Except, you know, looking weird, with their dyed black hair and facial piercings.

And I saw a couple of members of the Computer Club sneak beneath the bleachers just now. They had expressions on their faces I can only describe as diabolical. I wouldn't be surprised if it turns out they're down there unpacking their killer robot and programming it to unleash a reign of terror upon the world.

Principal Gupta is telling us how happy she is to have us all back. Lilly's hand just shot up. Principal Gupta said, 'Not now, Lilly,' and just went right on talking. Lilly is now muttering to herself beside me.

Tina, on my other side, is playing hangman with Boris. So far she only has the letter E right and has already earned a head and body. The spaces are

_ _ _ _ _ _   _ E _ _

I can't believe she can't figure it out. But I'm not helping. Because what she does with her boyfriend is her own business. Just like what I do with MY boyfriend is MY own business. Or at least it WOULD be my business if, in fact, I was doing anything with him. Which I'm not. Which is apparently a huge problem, bound to lead to his breaking up with me for some college girl who WILL do it with him.

But why SHOULDN'T I Do It with him? People Do It all the time. I mean, I wouldn't be here if my mom and dad hadn't—

Oh, great, now I feel like barfing. Why did I have to think about that? My mom and dad Doing It. Ew. Ew ew ew ew ew ew. That's even worse than the thought of my mom and Mr G—

OK, now I'm TOTALLY going to barf. EWWWWW!!!!!!!!!!!

Now Principal Gupta is talking about the wonderful extra-curriculars that exist at Albert Einstein High, and how we should all really try to take advantage of them. Lilly put her hand up again, but Principal Gupta just said, 'Not now, Lilly.' Nobody else is paying any attention.

Tina got another letter. Now the spaces go

_ _ _ _ _ A   _ E _ _

But Boris has added two arms to his hangman. Why doesn't Tina try the letter L? This is so aggravating.

Now Principal Gupta is introducing the different student groups, to show how many extra-curriculars AEHS has to offer. It turns out the other new guy who got assigned Josh's old locker and who spilt his latte on my boot is an exchange student from Brazil named Ramon Riveras. He is going to be on the soccer team.

That ought to make all the soccer moms very happy. Especially if after he wins, he whips off his shirt and swings it around his head the way Josh used to.

Ramon is sitting with Lana and Trisha and all the rest of the popular people. How did he know? I mean, he isn't even FROM this country. How could he know who the popular people even are, let alone that he's one of them and should sit with them? Is this something popular people are just born with? Something they know innately?

Now Principal Gupta is talking about Student Council, and how we should all be eager to join, and what a wonderful opportunity it is to show your school spirit, and how it also looks good on your transcript. She is almost making it seem as if anybody who wanted to could run for Student Council and win. Which is so bogus, because everyone knows only popular people ever win elections for Student Council. Lilly runs every single year and has never once won. Last year the person who beat her wasn't even smart. No, last year she got soundly defeated by Nancy di Blasi, captain of the varsity cheerleading team (Lana Weinberger's mentor in evil), a girl who spent way more time organizing bake sales so that the cheerleaders could get a well-deserved trip to Six Flags than she did lobbying for real student reforms.

'Do we have any nominations for Student Council

President?' Principal Gupta wants to know. Lilly's hand just shot up. Principal Gupta is ignoring it this time.

'Anyone?' Principal G keeps asking. 'Anyone at all?'

Tina just said to Boris, 'Um, gee, let me see. Is there a Y?'

'Oh for God's sake.' I can no longer help myself. Maybe it's the looming threat of defloration. Or maybe it's just that I don't get to play hangman during school hours with the love of my life any more. In any event, I went, 'It's JOSHUA BELL, OK? JOSHUA BELL!'

Tina's all, 'Ooooooh! You're right!'

Ramon Rivera is laughing at something Lana has whispered in his ear.

Lilly's waving her arm around like a crazy person. Hers is the only hand in the air. Finally, Principal Gupta has no choice but to go, 'Lilly. We discussed this last year. You can't nominate yourself for Student Council President. Someone has to nominate you.'

Lilly stands up, and out of her mouth come the words, 'I'm not nominating myself this year. I NOMINATE MIA THERMOPOLIS!!!'

Tuesday, September 1, in the limo on the way to the Plaza Hotel

Seriously. Why am I even friends with her?

Tuesday, September 1, the Plaza

First princess lesson of the new school year, and – thank God – Grandmere is on the phone. She just snapped her fingers at me and pointed at the coffee table in the middle of her suite. I went over there and found these faxes all over it – letters of complaint from various members of the French scientific community and Monaco's Oceanographic Museum.

Huh. I guess they're kind of mad about the snails.

Whatever! Like I don't have WAY bigger problems right now than a bunch of angry marine biologists. Hello – apparently, if I want to keep my boyfriend, I have to Do It. As if that's not bad enough, I've been nominated for STUDENT COUNCIL PRESIDENT.

I honestly don't know what Lilly was thinking. Could she REALLY have thought I'd just sit there and be all, 'Student Council President? Oh, OK. Sure. Because, you know, I'm only the heir to the throne of an entire foreign country. It's not like *I don't have anything else to do.*'

WHATEVER!!! I fully grabbed her arm and pulled it down and was all, *'LILLY, WHAT DO YOU THINK YOU'RE DOING????'* under my breath, since of course every single head in the entire gym had swivelled in our direction and everyone was staring at us, including Perin and Ramon Riveras and the guy who hates it when they put corn in the chilli, who I thought had graduated. But I guess not.

'Don't worry,' Lilly hissed back. *'I've got a plan.'*

Apparently, part of Lilly's plan was to kick Ling Su in the shin very very hard until she squeaked, 'Um, I do, Principal Gupta,' when Principal Gupta asked in a confused voice, 'Does, uh, anyone second that nomination?'

I couldn't believe this was even happening. It was like a nightmare, only worse, because that guy who hates corn in his chilli is never in my nightmares.

'But I—' I started to protest, but then Lilly kicked ME really hard in the shin.

'Ms Thermopolis accepts the nomination!' Lilly called down to Principal Gupta.

Who totally didn't look as if she believed it. But who went, 'Well. If you're sure, Mia,' anyway, without waiting for any response from me.

Next thing I knew, Trisha Hayes had jumped to her feet and was screaming, 'I nominate Lana Weinberger for Student Council President!'

'Well, isn't that nice,' Principal Gupta said, when Ramon Riveras seconded Trisha's nomination of Lana, but only after Lana elbowed him . . . pretty hard, it looked like, from where I was sitting. 'Do any members of the junior or senior class care to enter a nomination? No? Your apathy is duly noted. Fine then. Mia Thermopolis and Lana Weinberger are your nominees for Student Council President. Ladies, I trust you'll run a good clean election. Voting will be next Monday.'

And that was that. I'm running for Student Council President. Against Lana Weinberger.

My life is over.

Lilly kept saying it's not. Lilly kept saying she has a plan. Lana running against me wasn't part of that plan – 'I can't believe she's doing that,' Lilly said as we were filing out of school after Assembly. 'I mean, she's only doing it because she's jealous.' – but Lilly says it doesn't matter, because everyone hates Lana, so no one will vote for her.

Everyone does NOT hate Lana. Lana is one of the

most popular girls in school. *Everyone* will vote for her.

'But, Mia, you're pure and good of heart,' Boris pointed out to me. 'People who are pure and good of heart always beat out evil.'

Um, yeah. In books like *The Hobbit*, for crying out loud.

And the fact that I'm so pure? That's probably why I'm about to lose my boyfriend.

And I think there are many historical examples of people who are very clearly NOT good at heart winning more elections than those that are.

'You're not going to have to lift a finger,' Lilly said as Lars handed me into the limo to Grandmere's. 'I'll be your campaign manager. I'll take care of *everything*. And don't worry. *I have a plan!*'

I don't know why Lilly thinks her constant assurances that she has a plan are in any way comforting to me. In fact, the opposite is true.

Grandmere just hung up the phone.

'Well,' she says. She's already on her second Sidecar since I got here. 'I hope you're satisfied. The entire Mediterranean community is up in arms about that little stunt you pulled.'

'Not everybody.' I found two or three very supportive faxes in the pile and showed them to her.

'Pfuit!' was all Grandmere said. 'Who cares what some fishermen have to say? They aren't exactly experts on the matter.'

'Yeah,' I said, 'but they happen to be *Genovian* fishermen. My countrymen. And isn't my first obligation to protect the interests of my countrymen?'

'Not at the expense of straining diplomatic relations with your neighbours.' Grandmere's lips are pressed so tightly together, they're practically disappearing. 'That was the President of France, and he—'

Thank God the phone rang again. This is pretty awesome. I'd have dumped 10,000 snails into the Genovian bay a long time ago if I'd had any idea doing so would get me out of having princess lessons.

Although it kind of sucks that everyone is so mad.

Jeez. I knew all about the French of course. But who knew marine biologists were so TOUCHY?

But seriously, what was I supposed to do, sit around and LET killer algae destroy the livelihoods of families who for centuries had made their living from the sea? Not to mention innocent creatures such as seals and porpoises, whose very survival depends on ready access to the kelp beds the *Caulerpa taxifolia* is totally strangling? Could anyone really imagine that *I* would allow an environmental disaster of those proportions to occur under my very nose, in my own bay – *me*, Mia Thermopolis? – when I knew of a way (albeit only theoretical) to stop it?

'That was your father,' Grandmere said, after slamming down the phone. 'He is extremely distraught. He just heard from the Oceanographic Museum in Monaco. Apparently some of your snails have drifted over to *their* bay.'

'Good.' I kind of like this environmentalist rebel thing. It keeps my mind off other stuff. Like that my boyfriend is going to dump me if I don't put out. And that I am currently running against the most popular girl in school for Student Council President.

'Good?' Grandmere jumped up out of her seat so fast she totally dumped Rommel, her toy poodle, off her lap. Fortunately Rommel is used to this kind of treatment and has trained himself to land on his feet, like a cat. '*Good?* Amelia, I don't pretend to understand any of this – all this fuss over a little plant and some snails. But I would think you of *all* people would know that . . .' She picked up one of the faxes and read aloud from it. '. . . "When you introduce a new species into a foreign environment, total devastation can occur." '

'Tell that to Monaco,' I said. 'They're the ones who dumped a South American algae into the Mediterranean in the first place. All I did was dump a South American snail in after it to clean up THEIR mess.'

'Have you learned NOTHING that I've tried to teach you this past year, Amelia?' Grandmere wants to know. 'Nothing of tact or diplomacy or even SIMPLE COMMON SENSE?'

'I GUESS NOT!!!!'

OK, probably I shouldn't have screamed that quite as loudly as I did. But seriously, WHEN is she going to GET OFF MY BACK????? Can't she see I have WAY BIGGER THINGS to worry about than what a bunch of stupid FRENCH MARINE BIOLOGISTS have to say????

Now she's giving me the evil eye. 'Well?'

That's what she just said. Just, 'Well?'

And even though I know I'm going to regret it – how can I not? – I go, 'Well . . . what?'

'Well, are you going to tell me what's got you so frazzled?' she wants to know. 'Don't try denying it, Amelia. You are as bad at hiding your true feelings as your father. What happened at school today that's got you so upset?'

Yeah. Like I'm really going to discuss my love life with Grandmere.

Although I have to say that the last time I did this – with the whole prom thing – Grandmere gave me some pretty kick-ass advice. I mean, it got me to the prom, didn't it?

Still, how can I tell my GRANDMOTHER that I'm afraid if I don't have sex with my boyfriend he's going to dump me?

'Lilly nominated me to be Student Council President,' I said, because I had to say SOMETHING or she'd hound me into an early grave. She's done it before.

'But that's wonderful news!'

For a minute, I thought Grandmere was actually going to kiss me or something. But I totally ducked and she pretended like instead she was going to lean down and pat Rommel on the head. Which is maybe what she meant to do all along. Grandmere is not a very kissy person. At least not with me. Rocky, she kisses all the time. And she is not even technically related to him.

I keep antibacterial wipes around for this very reason. To wipe Grandmere's kisses off Rocky, I mean. There is no telling where Grandmere's lips have been on any given day.

Anyway.

'It's not wonderful!' I yelled at her. Why am I the only person who sees this? 'I'm going to be running against Lana Weinberger! She's the most popular girl in the whole school!'

Grandmere swirled the swizzle stick in her Sidecar.

'Really,' she said thoughtfully. 'Interesting turn of events. There's no reason, however, that you shouldn't be able to defeat this Shana person. You're a princess, remember! What is she?'

'A cheerleader,' I said. 'And it's Lana, not Shana. And

believe me, Grandmere, in the real world – such as high school – being a princess is NOT an advantage.'

'Nonsense,' Grandmere said. 'Being a royal is ALWAYS beneficial.'

'Ha!' I said. 'Tell that to Anastasia!' Who, you know, got shot for being royal.

But Grandmere was totally not paying attention to me any more.

'A student election,' she was muttering to herself, looking far away. 'Yes, that might be just the thing . . .'

'I'm glad *you*'re happy about it,' I said, not very graciously. 'Because, you know, it's not like I don't have other things to worry about. Like I'm pretty sure I'm going to flunk Geometry. And then there's the whole thing with dating a college boy . . .'

But Grandmere was totally off in her own little world.

'What day are votes cast?' Grandmere wanted to know.

'Monday.' I narrowed my eyes at her. I'd wanted to throw her off the Michael scent, but now I wasn't so sure this had been such a good idea. She seemed WAY too into the election thing. 'Why?'

'Oh, no reason.' Grandmere leaned over, scooped up all the snail faxes, and dropped them into the ornate gilt trash can by her desk. 'Shall we proceed with your lesson for the day, Amelia? I believe a little brushing up on our public-speaking techniques might be in order, given the circumstances.'

Seriously. Is it not enough that I be burdened with a psychotic best friend? Must my grandmother be losing her mind AT THE EXACT SAME TIME????

Tuesday, September 1, the Loft

So as if this day hasn't been long enough, when I got home just now, it was to find utter chaos reigning. Mom was bouncing a screaming Rocky in her arms, tearfully singing 'My Sharona' to him, while Mr G sat at the kitchen table, yelling into the phone.

I could tell right away that something was wrong. Rocky hates 'My Sharona'. Not that I would expect a woman who took her three-month-old to a protest rally where someone ended up throwing a trash can through a Starbucks window to remember which songs he likes and doesn't like. But the 'M-m-m-my' part actually makes him spit up, if you accompany it with jiggling, as my mom was doing, and she seemed oblivious to the white stuff all over her back and shoulders.

'What's going on, Mom?' I asked.

Boy, did I get an earful.

'My mother,' Mom shouted above Rocky's screams. 'She's threatening to come here, with Papaw. Because she hasn't seen the baby.'

'Um,' I said. 'OK. And that's bad because . . .'

My mom just looked at me with her eyes all wide and crazy.

'Because she's my MOTHER,' she shouted. 'I do not want her coming here.'

'I see,' I said, as if this made sense. 'So you're—'

'—going there,' my mom finished, as Rocky's screaming hit new decibels.

'No,' Mr G was saying into the phone. 'Two seats. Just two seats. The third person is an infant.'

'Mom,' I said, reaching out and taking Rocky from her, careful to avoid the spit-up still spewing from his mouth like lava from freaking Krakatoa. 'Do you really think that's such a good idea? Rocky's a bit young for his first plane ride. I mean, all that recycled air. Someone with Ebola or something could sneeze and next thing you know, the whole plane could come down with it. And what about the farm? Didn't you hear about all those school kids who got E. coli from that petting zoo in Jersey?'

'If it will keep my parents from coming here,' Mom said, 'I'm willing to risk it. Do you have any idea what kind of minibar bill they racked up the time your father put them up at the SoHo Grand?'

'OK,' I said, between verses of 'Independent Woman', which always has a soothing effect on Rocky. He is much more into R & B than rock. 'So when are we going?'

'Not you,' Mom said. 'Just Frank and I. And Rocky of course. You can't go. You have school. Frank's taking a vacation day.'

I knew it had sounded too good to be true. Not the potential risks to my little brother's health but, you know, that I might get to escape to Indiana instead of facing election hell back at school, and the potential break-up with my boyfriend.

Which reminded me.

'Um, Mom,' I said, as I followed her into Rocky's room, where she'd apparently been engaged in putting away his clean laundry before Mamaw's blow fell. 'Can I talk to you about something?'

'Sure.' Although my mom didn't exactly sound like she was much in the mood to talk. 'What?'

'Uh . . .' Well, she HAD told me once that I could talk to her about ANYTHING. 'How old were you the first time you had sex?'

I fully expected her to say, 'I was in college,' but I guess she was so busy trying to cram all of Rocky's *My Mommy Is Mad as Hell and She Votes* sleepsuits into his tiny dresser that she didn't think about what she was saying beforehand. She just went, 'Oh God, Mia, I don't know. I must have been, what, about fifteen?'

And then it was like she realized what she'd just said and she sucked in her breath really fast and looked at me all wide-eyed and went, 'NOT THAT I'M PROUD OF IT!!!'

Because she must have remembered at the same time I did that *I* am fifteen.

The next thing I knew, she was blathering a mile a minute.

'It was Indiana, Mia,' she cried. 'It's not like there was so much else to do. And it was twenty years ago. It was the eighties! Things were different back then!'

'Hello,' I said, because I've fully seen every episode of *I Love the Eighties*, including *I Love the Eighties Strikes Back*. 'Just because people wore legwarmers all the time—'

'I don't mean that!' Mom cried. 'I mean, people actually thought George Michael was straight. And that Madonna would be a one-hit wonder. Things were DIFFERENT then.'

I couldn't think of anything to say. Except, moronically, 'I can't believe you and Dad did it for the first time when you were FIFTEEN.'

And then, noticing my mother's expression, I was like, 'Oh my God. That's right!' Because she didn't even meet Dad until she was in college. 'MOM!!! Who WAS it?'

'His name was Wendell,' my mom said, her eyes

going all dreamy, either because Wendell had been a total hottie or because Rocky had finally quit crying and was instead drooling all over the lion patch on my uniform blazer, so that for once the loft was filled with blissful silence. 'Wendell Jenkins.'

WENDELL???? The man my mom gave the precious flower of virginity to was named WENDELL????

I seriously would NOT have sex with someone named Wendell.

But then I am having grave reservations about having sex with anyone, so my opinion probably isn't worth much.

'Wow,' my mom said, still looking dreamy. 'I haven't thought of Wendell in ages. I wonder whatever happened to him.'

'You don't KNOW?' I cried, loudly enough that Rocky kind of gave a little start in my arms. But he calmed down after a quick verse of Pink's 'Trouble'.

'Well, I mean, I know he graduated,' my mom said quickly. 'And I'm pretty sure he married April Pollack, but—'

'Oh my GOD!' This was shocking. No wonder Mom is the way she is! 'He was two-timing you????'

'No, no,' my mom said. 'He started going out with April after he and I broke up.'

I nodded knowingly. 'You mean he loved you and left you?' Just like Dave Farouq El-Abar and Tina Hakim Baba!

'No, Mia,' my mom said with a laugh. 'Good grief, Mia, you have an uncanny ability to turn everything into a country and western song. I mean, he and I went out, and it was great, but I eventually realized . . . well, I wanted out of Versailles and he didn't, so I left and he stayed. And married April Pollack.'

Just like Dean married that other girl on *Gilmore Girls*! Only he and Rory never, you know, Did It.

'But . . .' I stared at my mom. 'You loved him?'

'Of course I loved him,' my mom said. 'Gosh, Wendell Jenkins. I really haven't thought of him in ages.'

JEEZ! I can't believe my mother is not still in contact with the boy who relieved her of her virginity! What kind of school did she GO to back then anyway?

'Why are you asking me all these questions, Mia?' my mom finally wanted to know. 'Are you and Michael—'

'No,' I said, hastily shoving Rocky back into her arms.

'Mia, it's perfectly all right if you want to talk to me about—'

'I don't,' I said fast. Real fast.

'Because if you—'

'I don't,' I said again. 'I have homework. Bye.'

And I went into my room and locked the door.

There must be something wrong with me. I'm serious. Because you could totally tell, when Mom was remembering having sex with Wendell Jenkins, that she'd had a good time. Doing It. Everyone seems to have a good time Doing It. Like in movies and on TV and everything. Everyone seems to think Doing It is just, like, the pinnacle of experiences.

Everyone except for me. Why am I the only person who, when she thinks about Doing It, feels nothing but . . . sweaty? This can't be a normal reaction. This has to be yet another genetic anomaly in my make-up, like the absence of mammary glands and size-ten feet. I am totally lacking in the Do It gene.

I mean, I WANT to Do It. I mean, I *guess* that's what I want, you know, when Michael and I are kissing and

I smell his neck and I get that feeling like I want to jump on him. Surely this is an indication that I want to Do It?

Except that to Do It you actually have to take your CLOTHES OFF. In FRONT OF THE OTHER PERSON. I mean, unless you're one of those Hasidic Jews who do it through a hole in the sheet like Barbra Streisand in *Yentl*.

And I do not think I am ready to TAKE MY CLOTHES OFF in front of Michael. It is bad enough taking them off in front of Lana Weinberger in the locker room first thing in the morning. I don't think I could ever take them off in front of a BOY. Especially not a boy I am actually in love with and hope to marry someday, if he ever asks me and if I ever get over this whole not-wanting-to-take-my-clothes-off-in-front-of-him thing.

Although I definitely wouldn't mind seeing Michael with HIS clothes off.

Is this a double standard?

I wonder if my mom felt the same about Wendell Jenkins. She MUST have or she wouldn't have Done It with him.

And yet here she is, twenty years later, and she doesn't even know where he IS now.

Wait, I bet I could find him. I could do a Yahoo! People search!

OH MY GOD!!! HERE HE IS!!!! WENDELL JENKINS!!! I mean, there's no picture, but he works for...OH MY GOD, HE WORKS FOR THE VERSAILLES POWER COMPANY!!!! HE IS THE GUY WHO FIXES THE POWER LINES WHEN YOUR LIGHTS GO OUT BECAUSE OF A TORNADO OR WHATEVER!!!!

I cannot believe my mom gave the flower of her virginity to a guy who now works for the VERSAILLES POWER COMPANY!!!!!!!!!!!!!!!

Not that there is anything wrong with someone who works for a power company. It is no different than being a high-school Algebra teacher, I guess.

But at least Mr G doesn't have to wear a JUMPSUIT to work.

I wonder if April Pollack, the girl who became Mrs Wendell Jenkins instead of my mom, is on here.

OH MY GOD! She is!!!! APRIL POLLACK WAS ELECTED CORN PRINCESS OF VERSAILLES, INDIANA, IN 1985!!!!!!!!!!!

My mom Did It with a guy who later went on to marry a corn princess.

Which is very ironic, considering my mom later went on to have the illegitimate child of a prince! Hello, I wonder if Wendell even knows this. That his ex, Helen Thermopolis, is the mother of the heir to the throne of GENOVIA. I bet he wouldn't feel so good about having dumped her for Miss Corn Princess April if he knew THAT, would he????

Although I guess he didn't really dump her if it's true what my mom said about her and Wendell wanting different things.

Could this happen to me and Michael? Could we want different things someday? In twenty years will Michael be married, not to the Princess of Genovia but to some CORN PRINCESS????

AHHHHHHHHHHHHHH!!!! SOMEONE IS IMing ME!!!! Who could it be NOW?

Help! It's Michael!

SkinnerBx: Hey!

Since going Mac, Michael's changed his IM address. It used to be LinuxRulz.

SkinnerBx: How was your first day back?

Oh my God. He hasn't heard. Well, how WOULD he? It's not like he was there. Or like Lilly would tell him. Since they don't live together any more.

FtLouie: It was . . . the usual.

Well, it WAS. My life is a constant roller-coaster . . . joy followed by crushing disappointments, with occasional patches where nothing at all happens and I just admire the scenery.

I figured I should change the subject.

FtLouie: How was YOUR first day?
>
SkinnerBx: Fantastic! Today in my Economics of Sustainable Development class the professor talked about how in the next ten to twenty years petroleum, the cheapest and most effective fuel on the planet – you know, what we use in cars and to heat our homes and in Chapstick and all – will run out. See, a hundred years ago, when petroleum was first discovered, the world population was only two billion. Now, with six

billion people – a population explosion almost directly caused by more easily accessible fuel – the earth cannot maintain that many people with the amount of petroleum it has left. Since the population isn't getting any smaller, oil consumption isn't going to decrease, so in about two decades – maybe more but probably less, at the rate we're going – we're going to run out, and if we don't find a way to get at the petroleum buried deep beneath the seas – without destroying the environment – or start converting to nuclear or hydro or solar power, everyone will be plunged back into the dark ages, and people worldwide will starve and/or freeze to death.

>

FtLouie: So, in other words . . . in about ten to fifteen years we're all going to die?

>

SkinnerBx: Basically. How about you? What did YOU learn today?

Um, that you are going to dump me if I don't put out.

But of course I couldn't SAY that. So I just told Michael about how this weekend my mom and Mr G are making an emergency trip to Indiana to introduce Rocky to his Hoosier grandparents. And how Lilly has stabbed me in the back ONCE AGAIN, this time by nominating me as Student Council President, but how she'd said not to worry about it since she 'has a plan'; also about how I hate Geometry already.

SkinnerBx: Wait . . . your parents are going to Indiana this weekend?

>

FtLouie: Not my parents. My mom and Mr G.

I love Mr G and all, I guess, but it still weirds me out when anyone refers to him as my parent or my dad. I already have a dad.

I forgive Michael for this common mistake, however, as he does not know – as I do – what it's like to come from a broken home.

FtLouie: What do you think your sister could be up to anyway? I mean, I would be the worst Student Council President EVER.

>

SkinnerBx: What day are they leaving?

Why is Michael fixated on the fact that Mom and Mr G are going out of town? This is totally the LEAST of my problems.

FtLouie: I don't know. Friday, I guess.

Which reminded me:

FtLouie: Do you still want me to come over

on Saturday to meet Doo Pak?

>

SkinnerBx: Sure. Or if you want I could come over there.

>

FtLouie: With Doo Pak?

>

SkinnerBx: No. I meant by myself.

>

FtLouie: Well, if you want to. But I don't know why you would. Nobody's going to be here but me.

Oh no. Rocky's crying again.

I'm not a baby-licker. I'm NOT.

SkinnerBx: Mia? Are you still there?

But how can they just sit there and listen to him cry like that? It's just WRONG.

SkinnerBx: Mia?

>

FtLouie: Sorry, Michael, I gotta go. I'll talk to you later.

I wonder if there's a Baby-lickers Anonymous I could join.

Wednesday, September 2, Homeroom

Well, Lana certainly didn't waste any time launching her campaign for Student Council President into overdrive.

When Lilly and I walked into school this morning, it was to find the hallways WALLPAPERED with giant full-colour glossy posters of Lana with the words *VOTE LANA* written underneath them.

Some of the posters are like just headshots, showing Lana tossing her long, shimmery gold hair back and laughing; or with her chin cupped in her hands, smiling with the angelic sweetness of Britney on her first album's cover. In the pictures, Lana doesn't look at all like someone who might grab the back of another girl's bra and hiss, 'Why do you bother to wear one of these when you have nothing to put in it?'

Or someone who might tell a girl in the jet line that college boys expect their girlfriends to Do It.

Some of the other posters show Lana in full-on action shots, like jumping into the air and doing the splits in her cheerleading uniform. One of them shows Lana in her prom dress from last year, standing at the bottom of some staircase. I don't know where, since there was no staircase like it at the actual prom. Maybe her apartment? I wouldn't know, of course, having never been invited there.

Lilly took one look at all the posters and then down at her own posters – yes, Lilly spent all last night, while I was learning about Wendell Jenkins, making campaign posters for me – and said a very bad word.

Because even though Lilly's posters are very nice – they say *Mia Rules* and *Pick The Princess* – they are only glitter poured over Elmer's glue on white foamcore (for rigidity). Lilly didn't exactly blow up any full-colour glossy headshots of me and plaster the school with them.

'Don't worry, Lilly,' I told her very sympathetically. 'I don't want to be President anyway, so maybe this is for the best.'

Even Boris noticed how sad Lilly was and felt badly for her, which I thought was really nice of him, given how she'd ripped his heart out of his chest and stomped all over it just last May.

'Your posters are much nicer than Lana's,' he told her. 'Because they come from the heart and not some photocopy shop.'

But Lilly ripped her posters in half and stuffed them into a trash can outside the administrative offices anyway. There was glitter *everywhere* by the time she was done.

She did say, kind of darkly, 'She wants war? She's got one.'

But Lilly may have been referring to the fact that they are serving brandade for lunch today in the caf. With cod, the main ingredient in brandade, being nearly extinct due to overfishing, Lilly's been conducting a very vocal campaign on her public-access show against its use in New York City restaurants.

I really wish those producers who optioned Lilly's show would hurry up and find a studio to buy it already. Lilly really needs a new project. She has WAY too much time on her hands.

I have not heard from Michael since I signed off last night. I'm hoping this means he is busy with the whole petroleum-running-out thing and not, you know, that he's breaking up with me because he's realized I'm not exactly the Do It type.

Wednesday, September 2, PE

There should be a law against dodge ball.

Also, what did I ever do to HER? I mean, she's clearly winning this stupid election.

What is the point of even HAVING a bodyguard if he is going to allow me to be pelted in the thigh with red rubber balls?

I definitely think that's going to leave a mark.

Wednesday, September 2, Geometry

'a if b' and 'a only if b'

The phrase 'if and only if' is represented by the abbreviations 'iff' and by the symbol <->

a <-> b means both a → b and b → a.

Is the converse of a true statement necessarily true?

Excuse me, but

WHAT???????????????

There is a Euler diagram appearing on my thigh where Lana hit me with that ball.

Wednesday, September 2, English

Don't you LOVE that pink sweater thing Ms M's wearing! She looks so totally Elle Woods in it! If Elle Woods had black hair, I mean. T.

Yes. It's nice.

R U OK? R U mad about what Lilly did? I think you'd make a really good Student Council Prez, 4 what it's worth.

Thanks, Tina. Actually, I'd sort of forgotten about that. So much other stuff is happening.

What other stuff? That thing with the snails?

You KNOW about that????

It was on the news last night. I guess those people in Monaco are kind of mad.

They have no right to be mad! It's all their fault!

Yeah, the reporter kind of mentioned that. Is that what's bothering U?

No. Well, partly. I mean – can you keep a secret?

Of course!

I know, but like a REAL secret. You CANNOT tell Lilly.

Pinky swear.

OR BORIS!!!!!!!!!!!!!!!!!!

PINKY SWEAR!!! I SAID PINKY SWEAR!!!!

OK. Well. It's just that yesterday in the jet line Lana told me that college boys expect their girlfriends to Do It, and that means Michael must be expecting ME to Do It, only I'm not sure I want to. I mean, I guess I WANT to, but not if it involves taking off my clothes in front of him. But I'm not sure there's any way around that. Also I thought college boys only Did It with college girls. But I'm not a college girl, I'm a high-school girl. But then I talked to my mom about it and she said she Did It when she was fifteen with this guy named Wendell Jenkins, but then he married this corn princess named April and my mom hasn't even seen him since. And what if that happens with me and Michael? Like what if we Do It and then we break up because it turns out we want different things and he marries a corn princess? I think that might kill me. Although my mom says she hasn't thought about Wendell in years. I don't know. What should I do?

Just because things didn't work out with Wendell and your mom is no reason to think that you and Michael are also going to break up. And what kind of name is WENDELL anyway?

So you're saying . . . I should Do It?????

I don't think Lana really knows what college boys do. She doesn't know any college boys. Or if she does they're probably frat boys. And Michael isn't even in a frat. Besides, Michael really loves you. It's obvious just in the way he looks at you. If you don't want to Do It, don't Do It.

Yeah, but what about what Lana said?????

Michael isn't one of those guys who would dump you just for not Doing It with him. I mean, maybe the guys LANA knows would do this. Like Josh Richter for instance. Or that Ramon guy. He looks kind of sketchy. But not Michael. Because he actually CARES about you. Besides, I really don't think Michael expects you to Do It. At least, not right now.

REALLY??????

Really. I mean, it would be kind of presumptuous of him. You guys have not even been going out for a year. I don't think anyone should Do It with a guy unless they've been going out for at least a year. And then they have to Do It for the first time on prom night. Because when you Do It for the first time, the boy should be wearing a tux. It's only polite.

Tina, I barely managed to get Michael to take me to the prom once. I highly doubt I'm ever going to be able to get him to go again.

Hmm. Well, coronations count. I'm sure it would be just as romantic to Do It for the first time after your coronation.

I'm not having a coronation until after my dad dies and leaves me the throne!!!! I could be as old as Prince Charles by the time that happens!!!!!!!!!!!!!! I do WANT to Do It before I'm ANCIENT, you know. Just not, you know, NOW.

Well, then you need to tell Michael that. You two really need to have The Talk. You need to get this all out in the open. Because communication is the key to success in a romantic relationship.

Have you and Boris had it? You know, The Talk. About DOING IT?

Of course!!!! I mean, providing things don't work out between Prince William and me, Boris knows that if he ever hopes to be bestowed the gift of my flower, he will need to do it after the prom

- on a king-sized bed with white satin sheets
- in a deluxe suite with Central Park views
- at the Four Seasons over on East Fifty-Second Street
- with champagne and chocolate-covered strawberries upon arrival
- an aromatherapy bath for after
- then waffles for two in bed the next morning

Oh. Tina, I don't know how to break this to you . . . but that sounds like a little more than Boris might be able to afford. I mean, he IS still in high school.

I know. That's why I suggested he start saving his allowance now. Also that he better have more than just that one condom he's been carrying around in his wallet for the past two years.

Boris has a condom in his wallet????

Right NOW??????????

Oh yes. He is very proactive. That is one of the reasons I love him.

WOULD YOU GUYS PLEASE QUIT PASSING NOTES AND PAY ATTENTION? THIS IS THE BEST TEACHER WE HAVE EVER HAD AND YOU TWO ARE TOTALLY EMBARRASSING ME WITH YOUR INABILITY TO PAY ATTENTION—

Wait. What's this about a condom?

Nothing! Eyes front!

Who are you guys talking about anyway?

No one, Lilly. Never mind. Look, she's passing back our expository writing samples.

I suppose you think that's going to distract me. I want to know who you guys are talking about. WHO carries around a condom??

Pay attention, Lilly!

Right! Talk about the pot calling the kettle black.
What did you get anyway? An A as usual, Miss I-Always-Get-an-A-in-English?

Well, I DID work really hard on it—

Ha! THAT's not an A!!!! Told you. You really should be paying attention in this class if you're serious about this writing thing.

Wednesday, September 2, French

I don't understand this. I DO NOT UNDERSTAND THIS.

I am a talented writer. I KNOW I am. I have been TOLD I am. By more than one person.

I mean, I'm not saying I don't have more to learn. I know I do. I know I'm no Danielle Steel. Yet. I know I have a lot of work to do before I can ever hope to win a Booker Prize or one of those other awards writers get.

But a B????

I have never got a B for an English assignment in my life!!!!

There must be some mistake.

I was in so much shock after I got my paper back that I think I just sat there with my mouth hanging open for a very long period of time . . . long enough for the line of people gathered around Ms Martinez's desk to thin out enough for her to finally notice me and go, 'Yes, Mia? Do you have a question?'

'This is a B,' was all I managed to choke out. On account of my throat had kind of closed up. And my palms were sweaty. And my fingers were shaking.

Because I have never got a B for an English assignment before. Never, never, never, never . . .

'Mia, you're a very good writer,' Ms Martinez said. 'But you lack discipline.'

'I do?' I licked my lips. They had got all parched, just while I was sitting there, it seemed to me.

Ms Martinez shook her head all sadly.

'I realize it isn't entirely your fault,' Ms Martinez went on. 'You've probably been getting As in your English classes for years using the same cartoonish slapstick humour and slick popular-culture references you used in your writing sample. I'm sure your teachers were too busy dealing with students who couldn't write at all to deal with one who clearly can. But, Mia, don't you see? This kind of self-conscious pseudo-zaniness has no place in a serious expositional work. If you don't learn to discipline yourself, you'll never grow as a writer. Pieces like this one you handed in to me only prove that you have a way with words, NOT that you are a writer.'

I had no idea what she was talking about. All I knew was, I had got a B. A B!!! IN ENGLISH.

'If I write a new one,' I asked, 'will you accept it in the place of this one and cancel out my B?'

'If it's good enough,' Ms Martinez said. 'I don't want you just dashing off something completely over the top again, Mia. I want you to put some thought into it. I want you to make me think.'

'But,' I protested weakly, 'that's what I tried to do in my piece about the snails—'

'By comparing your pouring 10,000 snails into the Bay of Genovia with Pink's refusal to perform for Prince William because he hunts?' Ms Martinez shuddered. 'No, Mia. That didn't make me think. It just made me sad for your generation.'

Thankfully, just then the warning bell went off, so I had to go.

Which is a good thing, because I was just about to throw up all over my desk anyway.

Wednesday, September 2, Gifted and Talented

Michael called during lunch. AEHS students are not supposed to make or receive cellphone calls during class, but at lunch it's OK.

Anyway, he was all, 'What happened to you last night? We were IM-ing, and then you just disappeared!'

Me: 'Oh, yeah. Sorry. Rocky woke up, crying, and I had go sing him back to sleep.'

Michael: 'Oh. So everything's OK?'

Me: 'Well, I mean, if you think the fact that two days into the school year I'm already flunking Geometry, I'm being forced to run for Student Council President against my will, and my new English teacher thinks I'm a talentless hack is OK, then yeah, I guess so.'

Michael: 'I don't think any of those things are OK. Have you talked to – who do you have? Harding? He's a decent guy – about getting some extra help in his class? Or if you want, we can go over the chapter together on Saturday, when I see you. And how could your English teacher think you're a talentless hack? You're the best writer I know. And as for the Student Council thing, Mia, just tell Lilly you don't care WHAT her plan is, you have enough to worry about and you don't want to run. What's the worst that could happen?'

Ha. That is all so easy for Michael to say. I mean, he is not afraid of his sister – not even a little bit, like I am.

And Mr Harding? A decent guy? My God, he threw a piece of chalk at Trisha Hayes's head today! Granted, I'd do the same if I thought I could get away with it. But still.

And how does Michael even know what kind of a writer I am? Except for a couple of articles in the school paper last year, and my letters, emails and Instant Messages to him, he has never read anything I've written. I certainly haven't given him any of my poems to read. Because what if he doesn't like them? My writer's spirit would be crushed.

Even more crushed than it is right now.

Me: 'I guess. How's YOUR day going?'

Michael: 'Great. Today in my Principles of Geomorphology we talked about how the ice cap has shrunk by two hundred and fifty million acres – that's the size of California and Texas put together – in the past twenty years, and how if it continues to erode at the rate it's going – about nine per cent per decade – it could vanish altogether by the end of this century, which will, of course, have devastating consequences for life on earth as we know it. Whole species will vanish, and anyone who owns seafront property is essentially going to own underwater property. Unless, of course, we do something to control pollutant emissions that are destroying the ozone layer and allowing this melt-off.'

Me: 'So essentially it doesn't even matter what kind of grade I end up getting in Geometry, since we're all going to die anyway?'

Michael: 'Well, not us necessarily. But our grandkids, for sure.'

Except I was pretty sure Michael didn't mean OUR grandkids, as in the children of kids he and I might have if, you know, we Did It. I believe he was referring to grandkids in the general sense. Such as grandkids he might have with a corn princess he marries later, after he and I have grown apart and gone our separate ways.

Me: 'But I thought we were all going to die in ten years anyway when easily accessible petroleum runs out.'
Michael: 'Oh, don't worry about that. Doo Pak and I have decided to come up with a prototype for a hydrogen-powered car. Hopefully that ought to do the trick. If, you know, the auto industry doesn't try to have us killed for it.'
Me: 'Oh. OK.'

It's nice to know that smart people like Michael are working on this whole petroleum-running-out thing. That leaves the more easily handled problems like, you know, killer algae and Student Council governance to people like me.

Michael: 'So are we all set for Saturday?'
Me: 'You mean my coming over to meet Doo Pak? I think so.'
Michael: 'Actually, what I meant was—'

This is when Lilly tried to wrestle the phone from me.

Lilly: 'Is that my brother? Let me talk to him.'

Me: 'Lilly! Let go!'

Lilly: 'Seriously. I need to talk to him. Mom changed her password again and I can't get into her email.'

Me: 'You shouldn't be reading your mother's email anyway!'

Lilly: 'But how am I going to know what she's telling people about me?'

Here is where I finally managed to wrench the phone out of her hands.

Me: 'Uh, Michael. I'm going to have call you back. After school. OK?'

Michael: 'Oh. OK. Hang in there. Everything's going to be fine.'

Me: 'Yeah. Right.'

It's easy for HIM to say everything's going to be all right. Everything IS going to be all right. For HIM. HE no longer has to be incarcerated in this hellhole for eight hours a day. He gets to take fun classes about how the polar ice cap is going to melt and we're all going to die, while I get to walk down the hall with twenty million posters of Lana Weinberger beaming down at me, going, *Loser! Loser! Princess of what? Oh yeah! Loserville!*

As we left the cafeteria to go put on lipgloss before our next class, I saw Ramon Riveras, the handsome new exchange student, demonstrating Brazilian ball-handling techniques to Lana and some fellow members of the AEHS soccer team, all of whom were paying rapt attention (good thing too, since last year they didn't win one single game). Only instead of a ball Ramon was using an orange, batting it back and forth between his feet. He was saying something too, but I couldn't understand a word, whatever it was. The other members of his team looked confused.

I saw Lana nodding like she understood though. She probably did too. Lana is very familiar with all things Brazilian. I know because I've seen her naked in the shower.

Wednesday, September 2, still Gifted and Talented

Mia. Let's make a list.

No! Lilly, leave me alone! I have too many problems right now to make a list.

What problems? You don't have any problems. You're a princess. You're not flunking Algebra. You have a boyfriend.

That's just it! I have a boyfriend, but apparently he expects me to—

To what?

Never mind. Let's make a list.

Lilly and Mia Rate the Reality Shows

Survivor

Lilly: A sickening attempt by the media to draw viewers by pandering to the lowest common denominator and appealing to the public's enjoyment of watching others being exploited and humiliated. 0/10

Mia: Yeah. And who wants to watch people eat bugs? Ew!!!! 0/10

Fear Factor

Lilly: Ditto. 0/10

Mia: More bugs. Yuck. 0/10

American Idol

Lilly: *This show is entertaining – if your idea of being entertained is watching young people being ridiculed for attempting to share their talents with the world. 5/10*

Mia: Having had my own dreams crushed all too recently, I am not a fan of watching other people get theirs stomped on. 2/10

Newlyweds: Nick and Jessica

Lilly: *If watching the pathetic ramblings of an uneducated chanteuse who doesn't know the difference between chicken and tuna is your idea of a good time, please feel free to watch this show. I won't try to stop you. 0/10*

Mia: Jessica is not dumb, just inexperienced! She's FUNNY. Also, Nick is hot. Best show EVA! 10/10

Rich Girls

Lilly: *Is anyone really interested in the musings of two young heiresses with nothing more on their minds than cargo pants and boys? 0/10*

Mia: Lilly is wrong about this one too! This is one of the best shows of all time. The Rich Girls care about a lot more than just cargo pants. They want to help people who are too poor to afford cargo pants! 10/10

The Bachelor/ette

Lilly: *Who cares about two stupid people getting together? All they'll end up doing is having kids, and then there'll be more stupid people on this planet. And we're encouraging them by watching this show! Disgraceful. 0/10*

Mia: Harsh! They're looking for love! What could be wrong with that? 5/10

Trading Spaces

Lilly: *I would so never let Hildy near my room. 10/10*

Mia: Have to agree. What is wrong with her? But it would be cool to turn her loose on LANA's room.10/10

The Real World

Lilly: *Perfection – if your idea of perfection happens to be watching young people cavort in hot tubs without parental supervision or any apparent morality. Which mine is. 10/10*

Mia: Why do they all have to be so mean to each other? Still, it IS kinda good. 9/10

Queer Eye for the Straight Guy

Lilly: *Five homosexuals give makeovers to hetero men who can't keep their rooms tidy and don't know any better than to wear acid-washed jeans. Some proponents of equal rights for the same-sex oriented fear this show will set their movement back decades. And yet . . . why WAS that guy wearing that hideous hairpiece for so long???? 10/10*

Mia: Yeah, and I happen to know someone who could still use a little help from the Fab Five, whom I'm sure frown on sweater-tucking in. 10/10

***The Simple Life* with Paris Hilton and Nicole Richie**

Lilly: *You're joking, right? I'm supposed to be entertained by an anorexic hotel heiress and Lionel Richie's cokehead kid as they rudely mock the people who were kind enough to take them in? I don't think so. 0/10*

Mia: Um. I kind of have to agree here. Those girls need some MAJOR princess lessons. Maybe next time the Hilton sisters and little Nicole could spend a week with Grandmere! I bet SHE'D have something to say about their piercings. Now that's a reality show I'd LOVE to see!!!!!!! 0/10

Wednesday, September 2, US Government

THEORIES OF GOVERNMENT (cont.)
SOCIAL-CONTRACT THEORY:

Thomas Hobbes, seventeenth-century English philosopher, wrote *Leviathan*, stating that:

Humans originally existed in a 'state of nature'.
In other words, ANARCHY.

(But anarchy is bad! With anarchy, people can just do whatever they want! With anarchy, for instance, a certain cheerleader who shall remain nameless could wear a pair of shorts that clearly belongs to a member of the men's soccer team under the skirt of her school uniform and make sure everyone notices that she's wearing them by crossing and uncrossing her legs in a very athletic and flamboyant way during her US Government class, as she might be doing RIGHT NOW in flagrant defiance of school regulations. And a certain other person who shall remain nameless might feel like telling on her, but will ultimately decide not to, because tattling is wrong unless someone's life is at stake.)

Hobbes maintained that the original contract between people and state was final, resulting in state's absolutism.

Fortunately John Locke modified this theory to say that the contract could be renegotiated.

GO, JOHN LOCKE!
GO, JOHN LOCKE!
GO, GO,
GO, JOHN LOCKE!

Wednesday, September 2, Earth Science

Kenny just leaned over to remind me that he has a new girlfriend, Heather, whom he met at Science Camp this summer. Apparently Heather is superior to me in every way (straight As, does gymnastics, doesn't employ slapstick humour or popular-culture references in her expositional essays, isn't a princess, etc.), so despite what I might think, Kenny is completely over me and I can go around flashing my big baby-blue eyes at him all I want, it won't make any difference, he is NOT going to do my Earth Science homework for me this semester.

Whatever, Kenny. First of all, get your prescription checked: my eyes are grey not blue. Second of all, I never asked you to do my Bio homework for me last year. You just started doing it on your own. I'll admit it was wrong of me to LET you, seeing as how I knew I didn't exactly like you in the same way you liked me. But rest assured that's not going to happen again. Because I'm fully going to pay attention in class and do my OWN work. I won't even NEED your help.

And I sincerely hope you and Heather will be happy together. Your children will probably be very, very smart. In the event that you two end up Doing It, I mean. And forget to use birth control. Although that is highly unlikely in the case of two science whizzes.

Kenny is so weird.

No, you know what? *Boys* are weird. Seriously. Maybe that's what I should write my make-up paper on for Ms Martinez. Boys and how weird they are.

For instance, my current top-five favourite movies include:

Dirty Dancing
Flashdance
Bring It On
The original *Star Wars*
Honey

All of which have a similar theme – girl must use her newly acquired talents (dancing) to save herself/relationship/team (well, OK, this is not the plot of *Star Wars* so much. Well, it is, but you have to substitute the word girl with boy. And dancing with the Force).

So you can see why I like them so much.

But Michael's top-five movies – not including the original *Star Wars*, of course – are totally different from mine. There is no single underlying theme to them at all! They're all over the place, theme-wise! And most of them, I don't even know WHY he likes them. There is not even any dancing in them.

Here is a glimpse into the Weird World of Boys and the Movies They Like:

Top-Five Movies Michael Likes (none of which I have seen or ever will):

The Godfather
Scarface
The Texas Chainsaw Massacre
Alien, Aliens, Alien Resurrection, etc.
The Exorcist

Top-Five Movies Michael Likes that I HAVE seen (not including the original *Star Wars*, of course):

Office Space
The Substitute
The Fifth Element
Starship Troopers
SuperTroopers

I would just like to point out that none of the above movies has dancing in it. Not one. In fact, there is no common underlying theme in any of them, with the possible exception of the fact that the guys in them all have super-cute girlfriends.

Basically, men and women have entirely different expectations in their movie-viewing fare. Really, given all that, it is a wonder any of them get together to Do It at all.

On second thoughts, this is probably not a topic Ms Martinez would care to read about. Although *I* find it educational, I doubt *she* will.

She probably never goes to the movies, because they are so pop-culturey. She probably only goes to *films*, like the ones they show at the Angelika. I bet she doesn't even own a TV.

My God. No *wonder* she's the way she is.

PE:	N/A
Geometry:	Exercises pages 20–22
English:	Don't know, was too flipped out to write it down
French:	*Ecrivez une histoire* Also, figure out if Perin boy or girl!!!!!!
Gifted and Talented:	N/A
US Government:	What is basis of government acc. to social-contract theory
Earth Science:	Ask Kenny

Wednesday, September 2, limo on the way home from the Plaza

Today when I got to Grandmere's for my princess lesson she announced that we were taking a field trip.

I told her I really don't even have time for a princess lesson today – that my English grade was at stake and that I needed to get home and write a new paper right away.

But Grandmere was completely unimpressed – even when I told her that my future career as an authoress was riding on it. She said royals shouldn't write books anyway – that people only want to read books ABOUT royals, not BY them.

Grandmere so doesn't get it sometimes.

I thought for sure our field trip was going to see Paolo – my roots are totally starting to show – but instead Grandmere took me downstairs to one of the Plaza's many conference rooms. About 200 chairs had been set up in this long room with just a podium in the front with a microphone and a pitcher of water on it.

Only the front row of chairs had people in them. And the people in them were Grandmere's maid, her chauffeur and various members of the Plaza Hotel staff in their green-and-gold uniforms, looking very uncomfortable. Especially Grandmere's maid, who was holding a trembling Rommel on her lap.

At first I thought I'd been set up and that it was a press conference for the snails or something. Except where were the reporters?

But Grandmere said no, it wasn't a press conference. It was to practise.

For the debate.

For Student Council President.

'Uh, Grandmere,' I said. 'There is no debate for Student Council President. Everybody just votes. On Monday.'

But Grandmere way didn't believe me. She went, exhaling a long stream of cigarette smoke, even though there is a Smoking-in-Your-Room-Only policy at the Plaza, 'Your little friend Lilly told me there's a debate.'

'You talked to LILLY?' I could hardly believe it. Lilly and Grandmere HATE each other. With good reason, after the whole Jangbu Pinasa incident.

And now Grandmere is telling me that she and my best friend are in CAHOOTS?

'WHEN DID LILLY TELL YOU THIS?' I demanded, since I didn't believe a word of it.

'Earlier,' Grandmere said. 'Just stand behind the podium and see how it feels.'

'I KNOW how standing behind a podium feels, Grandmere,' I said. 'I've stood behind podiums before, remember? When I addressed the Genovian Parliament on the parking-meter issue.'

'Yes,' Grandmere said. 'But that was before an audience of old men. Here I want you to pretend to be addressing an audience of your peers. Picture them sitting before you, in their ridiculous baggy jeans and backward baseball caps.'

'We wear uniforms to school, Grandmere,' I reminded her.

'Yes, well, you know what I mean. Picture them all sitting there, dreaming of getting their own television show, like that horrible Ashton Kutcher. Then tell me how you would answer this question: What improvements would you implement to help make Albert

Einstein High School a better learning facility, and why?'

Seriously, I don't get her sometimes. It's like she was dropped at birth. Only on to parquet, not on to a futon couch, like I dropped Rocky not too long ago. Except that that totally wasn't my fault on account of Michael walking in unexpectedly wearing a new pair of jeans.

'Grandmere,' I said. 'What is the point of this? THERE IS NO DEBATE.'

'JUST ANSWER THE QUESTION.'

God. She is impossible sometimes.

OK, all the time.

So just to placate her I went behind the stupid podium and said into the microphone, 'Improvements I would implement to help make Albert Einstein High School a better learning facility would include incorporating more meatless entrées into the lunch service for vegan and vegetarian students and, uh, posting homework assignments on the school website every night, so that students who might, er, have forgotten to write them down would know exactly what they have due the next day.'

'Don't hunch so over the podium, Amelia,' Grandmere said critically from where she was standing, blowing her smoke into a large potted rhododendron (Grandmere is so lucky. Because in ten years, when all the petroleum runs out and the polar ice cap is completely melted, she'll probably be dead already from lung cancer on account of all the cigarettes she smokes).

'Stand up straight. Shoulders back. That's it. You may proceed.'

I had totally forgotten what I was talking about.

'What about teachers?' called Grandmere's chauffeur, trying to sound like a baggy-panted Ashton Kutcher wannabe. 'Whadduya gonna do about them, huh?'

'Oh, yeah,' I said. 'Teachers. Isn't it their job to encourage us in our dreams? But I've noticed that certain teachers seem to feel that part of their job description includes crushing our spirit and . . . and . . . stifling our creative impulses! Just because they might, you know, be more entertaining than educational. Are those really the kind of people we want moulding our young minds? Are they?'

'No,' cried one of the maids.

'Damn straight,' yelled Grandmere's chauffeur.

'Oh,' I said, feeling more confident on account of their positive feedback. 'And the, er, video-surveillance cameras outside. I can see how, as a security measure, they are very worthwhile. But if they are being used as—'

'Amelia!' Grandmere screamed. 'Elbows off the podium!'

I took my elbows off the podium.

'—as a tool with which to monitor student behaviour, I have to say, should the administration have the right to essentially spy on us?' I was kind of getting into this debate thing. 'What happens to the tapes in the video cameras after they're full? Are they rewound and taped over or are they stored in some fashion so that the contents might be used against us at some future date? For instance, if one of us gets appointed to the Supreme Court, could a tape of our spraying Joe the Lion in Silly String be made available to reporters and used to bring us down?'

'Feet on the floor, Amelia!' Grandmere shrieked, just because I'd rested one foot on the little shelf in the podium where you're supposed to put your purse or whatever.

'And what about the issue of girls who wear their boyfriends' team athletic shorts beneath their skirts?' I went on. I have to admit, I was kind of enjoying myself. The Plaza maids were totally paying attention to me. One of them even clapped when I said the thing about the security video possibly being used against us if we ran for Supreme Court. 'As sexist as I find the practice, is it the administration's business what goes on beneath the skirts of its female-student population? I say no! No! Don't you dare mess with MY underwear!'

Whoa! This last part brought a standing O from the maids! They were on their feet, cheering for me, like I was . . . I don't know . . . J-Lo or somebody!

I had no idea I was such a brilliant orator. Really. I mean, the parking-meter thing had been nothing compared to this.

But Grandmere wasn't as impressed as everyone else.

'Amelia,' Grandmere said, exhaling a plume of blue smoke. 'Princesses do not beat on the podium with their fists when they make a point.'

'Sorry, Grandmere,' I said.

But I didn't really feel sorry. To tell the truth, I felt kind of stoked. I had no idea how much fun it was to address a roomful of hotel maids. When I'd addressed the Genovian Parliament on the parking-meter issue, hardly any of them had paid attention to me.

But tonight at the hotel, I had those women in the palm of my hand. Really.

Although it would probably be totally different if I really were addressing an audience of people my own age. Like if I really were standing in front of Lana and Trisha and the rest of them, that might be a little different.

Like I actually might throw up on myself.

But I'm not going to worry about it, because it's not like that's ever going to happen. I mean, that I'm actually going to be expected to debate with Lana. Because no one said anything about a debate.

And even if there is one, I'm not going to end up having to do it anyway.

Because Lilly said so. She has a plan.

Whatever that means.

Wednesday, September 2, the Loft

I walked in on utter chaos at 1111 Thompson Street again. Since Mom and Mr G are going to Indiana this weekend, Mom had to move Ladies' Poker Night from Saturday to tonight. So all of the feminist artists from Mom's poker group were sitting around the kitchen table eating moo goo gai pan when I walked in.

They were being really loud too. So loud that when I called Fat Louie he didn't come. I shook his bag of low-fat Iams and everything. Nothing. I actually thought for a minute that Fat Louie had run away – like he'd got out somehow in all the confusion of the feminists coming in. Because, you know, he hasn't been all that happy about sharing the Loft with a new baby. In fact, we've had to chase him out of Rocky's crib more than a few times, since he seems to think it's a bed we put there just for him, since it IS kind of Fat Louie-sized.

And I'll admit, I DO spend a lot of time with Rocky. Time I used to spend giving Fat Louie his kitty massages and all.

But I'm TRYING to be a good mother – a baby-licker to BOTH my brother AND my cat.

I finally found him hiding under my bed...but just his head, because he's so fat. The rest of him wouldn't fit, so his kitty butt was kind of sticking out in the air.

I didn't blame him for hiding, really. Mom's friends can be scary.

Mr G agrees apparently. He was hiding too, it turned out, in the bedroom he and Mom share, trying to watch a baseball game with Rocky. He looked up all startled when I came in to give Rocky a kiss hello.

'Are they gone yet?' he wanted to know, his eyes looking

kind of wild behind his glasses.

'Um,' I said. 'They haven't even started playing.'

'Damn.' Mr G looked down at his son, who wasn't crying for once. He is usually fine if there is a television on. 'I mean, darn.'

I felt a spurt of sympathy for Mr G. I mean, it is not easy being married to my mom. Aside from the whole crazy-painter thing, there's the fact that she seems to be physically incapable of paying a bill on time or even of FINDING the bill when she finally does remember to pay it. Mr G transferred everything to online banking, but it doesn't help, on account of all the cheques my mom gets sent for her art sales ending up wadded up somewhere weird, like in the bottom of her gas-mask container.

I swear, between my inability to divide fractions and her inability to assume any sort of adult responsibility – aside from attending political rallies and breastfeeding – it's a wonder Mr G doesn't divorce us.

'Can I get you anything?' I asked Mr G. 'Some spare ribs? Shrimps with garlic sauce?'

'No, Mia,' Mr G said, wearing a look of long suffering that I recognized only too well. 'But thanks anyway. We'll be fine.'

I left the menfolk to themselves and went into the kitchen to scrounge some food for myself before sneaking off to my bedroom to do all my homework. Fortunately none of my mom's friends paid any attention to me because they were too busy complaining about how male musical artists like Eminem are responsible for turning a generation of young men into misogynists.

Really, I could not stand idly by and allow that kind of

talk in my own home. Maybe it was the after-effects of my powerful speech-giving experience in the empty conference room at the Plaza, but I put down my plate of moo shu vegetable and told my mom's friends that their argument against Eminem was specious (I don't even know what this word means, but I've heard Michael and Lilly use it a lot) and that if they would just take a moment to listen to 'Cleaning Out My Closet' (one of Rocky's favourites by the way), they would know that the only women Eminem hates are his mom and the hos that be trippin' on him.

This statement, which I felt was quite reasonable, was met by utter silence by the feminist artists. Then my mom went, 'Is that the door? It must be Vern from downstairs. He gets so upset these days when he thinks we're having a party and we haven't invited him. I'll be right back.'

And she scurried to the door even though I hadn't heard the buzzer ring.

Then one of the feminists went, 'So, Mia, is your defence of Eminem the kind of thing your grandmother teaches you during your princess lessons?'

And all the other feminists laughed.

But then I remembered that I actually needed some advice on the feminist front so I was all, 'Hey, you guys, I mean, women, do you know if it's true that all college boys expect their girlfriends to Do It?'

'Uh, not just college boys,' said one of the women while the rest of them laughed uproariously.

So it IS true. I should have known. I mean, I'd kind of been hoping that Lana was just trying to make me feel bad. But now it looks as if she might actually have been telling the truth.

'You look worried, Mia,' commented Kate, the performance artist who likes to stand up on stage and smear chicken fat on herself to make a statement about the beauty industry.

'She's always worried,' said Gretchen, a welder who specializes in metal replicas of body parts. Particularly of the male variety. 'She's Mia, remember?'

All the feminist artists laughed uproariously at that too.

This made me feel bad. Like my mom's been talking about me behind my back. I mean, I talk about HER behind HER back of course. But it's different when your own mother has been talking about YOU.

Clearly Lilly is not the only one who thinks I'm a baby-licker.

'You spend way too much time freaking out about things, Mia.' Becca, the neon-light artist, waved her margarita glass at me knowingly. 'You should stop thinking so much. I don't remember thinking half as much as you do when I was your age.'

'Because you were already on lithium when you were her age,' Kate pointed out.

But Becca ignored her.

'Is it the snails?' Becca wanted to know.

I just blinked at her. 'The what?'

'The snails,' she said. 'You know, the ones you dumped in the bay. Are you worried about how everyone is upset about them?'

'Um,' I said, wondering if she, like Tina, had seen this on the news. 'I guess so.'

'That's understandable,' Becca said. 'I'd be worried too. Why don't you take up yoga?' she suggested. 'That always helps me to relax.'

'Or watch more TV,' suggested Dee, who enjoys creating totem poles and then dancing around them with pieces of liver strapped beneath her arms.

I couldn't believe this. I was being told by these intelligent women to watch MORE TV? Clearly they're not friends with Karen Martinez.

'Stop picking on Mia.' Windstorm, who happens to be one of my mom's oldest friends AND a midwife AND a minister AND a professional choreographer, got up to put more ice in the blender. 'She's got a right to think too much and freak out if she wants to. There isn't anything more stressful than being a fifteen-year-old, with the possible exception of being a fifteen-year-old princess.'

I had never thought of that before. DO I think too much? Do other people not think as much as I do? Except according to Ms Martinez, I don't think ENOUGH . . .

'I guess it must have been one of those delivery boys, slipping a menu under the door,' my mom said, coming back to the table. 'What'd I miss?'

'Nothing,' I said, taking my plate and hurrying off to my room. 'Have fun, you guys! I mean, women!'

I wonder if Windstorm is right. About my thinking too much. Maybe that's my problem. I can't shut my brain off. Maybe other people can, but I can't. I've never actually tried, of course, because who wants to have an empty head? Except for, you know, the Hilton sisters. Because it's probably easier to party all the time if you aren't worrying about killer algae or all the petroleum running out.

Still, maybe there's something to it. I can hardly sleep at night, my mind is so busy whirring away up there, wondering what I'm going to do if aliens come in the night and take over everything or whatever. I would LOVE to be able to shut my mind off the way other people seem to be able to. If Windstorm is right anyway.

Ooooo, Michael's Instant Messaging me now!

SkinnerBx: So are we still getting together on Saturday?

Right as Michael asked this, I got another Instant Message.

WomynRule: BL, what are you doing Saturday?

Seriously. Why me? WHY?

FtLouie: I can't talk to you right now. I'm IM-ing your brother.

>

WomynRule: Tell him Mom's turning his room into a shrine to the Reverend Moon.

>

FtLouie: LILLY! GO AWAY!

>

WomynRule: Just keep Saturday free, OK? It's important. It has to do with the campaign.

>

FtLouie: I already have plans with your brother on Saturday.

>

WomynRule: What, are you two going to Do It then or something?

FtLouie: NO WE ARE NOT GOING TO DO IT THEN. WHO TOLD YOU THAT?

>

WomynRule: No one! Jeez! Don't get the princess panties in a royal twist. Why would you even get so mad about that unless – wait – ARE YOU GUYS DOING IT???? AND YOU DIDN'T TELL ME??????????

>

FtLouie: NO, FOR THE LAST TIME WE ARE NOT DOING IT!!!!

>

SkinnerBx: Doing what? What are you talking about?

OH MY GOD.

FtLouie: Not you! I meant to send that to Lilly!

>

SkinnerBx: Wait, is Lilly IM-ing you right now too?

>

WomynRule: I can't believe you're Doing It with my brother. That is so gross. You know, he has hair growing out of his toes. Like a hobbit.

>

FtLouie: Lilly! SHUT UP!

>

SkinnerBx: Is Lilly giving you a hard time? Tell her if she doesn't cut it out

I'll tell Mom about the time she did the 'gravitational experiment' with Grandma's Hummel figurines.

>

FtLouie: BOTH OF YOU! STOP IT!!!! YOU'RE DRIVING ME INSANE!!!!

>

FtLouie: terminated

Seriously. I'm GLAD I'm a baby-licker if it means Rocky and I will never end up like those two.

Thursday, September 3, Homeroom

Oh.

My.

God.

That is all I have to say.

Thursday, September 3, PE

They're even in the gym. I don't know how she did it. But they're even HANGING FROM THE ROPES IN THE GYM.

Seriously.

They're in the showers too. Encased in plastic sheets, so they won't get wet.

I know we learned in Health and Safety that it's physically impossible to die from embarrassment, but I might turn out to be the exception to the rule.

Thursday, September 3, Geometry

THEY ARE EVERYWHERE.

GIANT FULL-COLOUR HEADSHOTS OF ME IN MY TIARA. WITH MY SCEPTRE. From when I got formerly introduced to the people of Genovia last December.

And underneath my photo, it says:

Vote for Mia.

Then underneath that:

PIT.

PIT. What does that even MEAN?????

Everyone is talking about them. EVERYONE. I was just sitting here, innocently going over my homework, when Trisha Hayes came in and was all, 'Nice try, *PIT*. But it won't make any difference. You may be a princess, but Lana is the most popular girl in school. She's going to decimate you on Monday.'

'Somebody's been studying up on their vocab,' is what I said to Trisha. Because of her use of the word decimate.

But that's not what I wanted to say. What I wanted to say was, 'IT WASN'T ME!!!! I DIDN'T DO IT!!!! I DON'T EVEN KNOW WHAT PIT MEANS!!!!!'

But I couldn't. Because everyone was looking at us. Including Mr Harding. Who took five points off Trisha's homework for not being in her seat by the time the bell rang.

'You can't do that,' Trisha had the bad judgement to say to him.

'Uh,' Mr Harding said. 'Excuse me, Miss Hayes, but yes, I can.'

'Not for long,' Trisha said. 'When my friend Lana is Student Council President, she's going to abolish tardy demerits.'

'And what do you have to say about that, Miss Thermopolis?' Mr Harding wanted to know. 'Is abolishing tardy demerits part of your campaign strategy as well?'

'Um,' I said. 'No.'

'Really?' Mr Harding looked way interested. Except that I think he was only interested because he found the whole thing vaguely hilarious. On some weird teacher level. 'And why is that?'

'Um,' I said, feeling my ears starting to turn red. That's because I could tell that everyone in the entire class was staring at us. 'Because I thought I might concentrate on stuff that actually matters. Like the lack of choice in vegetarian entrées in the cafeteria. And the cameras they've installed outside by Joe, which are a violation of our right to privacy. And the fact that some of the teachers around here don't grade objectively.'

And to my VERY great surprise, some of the people at the back of the room started to clap. Really. Like that slow clap they do in the movies, the kind where everybody eventually joins in, until it turns into fast clapping.

Only Mr Harding nipped it in the bud before it ever turned to fast clapping by going, 'All right, all right, that's enough of that. Turn to page fourteen and let's get started.'

Oh my God. This presidential thing has got WAY out of hand.

Syllogism = argument of the form $a \rightarrow b$ (first premise)
$b \rightarrow c$ (second premise)
Therefore: $a \rightarrow c$ (conclusion)

WHATEVER. Why did they have to use the one of me with my SCEPTRE??? I look like a total freak in that one.

Note to self: look up *decimate.*

Thursday, September 3, English

LILLY!!! WHERE DID YOU GET THOSE POSTERS????

Where do you think I got them? And stop yelling at me!

I'm not yelling. I'm very calmly asking . . . Did you get those posters from my grandmother?

Yes, of course I did. What do you think, I paid for them myself? Do you have any idea how much full-colour posters that size cost? I could have used up the entire annual budget for LILLY TELLS IT LIKE IT IS on the copy-setting alone!

But I thought you hated Grandmere! Why would you do something like that? Like let my grandmother be involved in this?

Because, in case you haven't noticed, this election is important to me, Mia. I REALLY want us to win. We HAVE to win. It's the only way we're going to save this school from becoming a completely fascist state under the tyrannical reign of Gutless Gupta.

But, Lilly, I DON'T WANT TO BE STUDENT COUNCIL PRESIDENT.

Don't worry. You won't be.

THAT MAKES NO SENSE! I mean, Lilly, I know everyone just assumes Lana is going to win because she wins everything, but things are getting really weird. In Geometry today, I said something about those cameras outside being a violation of our rights to privacy, and someone started CLAPPING for me.

It's happening. Just like I KNEW it would!

What's happening?????

Never mind. Just keep doing what you're doing. It's great. It's so NATURAL. I could never be that natural.

BUT I'M NOT DOING ANYTHING!

That's what's so great about it. Now come on, pay attention to this. You need to know this stuff if you're going to be a writer and all.

Lilly, is there going to be a debate? Because Grandmere said something about a debate.

Shhhh. Pay attention. Hey, what's going on with my brother anyway? Are you two really Doing It?

STOP TRYING TO CHANGE THE SUBJECT! IS THERE GOING TO BE A DEBATE?????

LILLY!!!!

LILLY!!!!!!!!!!!! ANSWER ME!!!!!!

I don't think Lilly's going to answer you. Is there anything I can do?

Oh. Hi, Tina. No. Just . . . well, you wouldn't be willing to get your bodyguard to shoot me, would you? Because I'd really appreciate it.

Um, Wahim's not allowed to shoot anyone unless they're trying to kidnap me. You know that.

I know. But I still wish I were dead.

I'm so sorry. The election thing?

That and Michael and everything else.

Did you and Michael have that talk like I told you to?

No. When could we have had a talk? I never get to see him any more because he's always in class, learning new ways we're all going to die. And you can't talk about Doing It – or, in this case, NOT Doing It – over the phone or IM-ing. It's kind of a face-to-face topic.

That's true. So when are you going to talk about it?

Saturday, I guess. I mean, that's the earliest we're going to see each other.

Good! Don't you love Ms M in those totally adorable culottes! Who knew culottes could even BE adorable?

You know, someone could be wearing culottes and still not be . . . um, right.

What do you mean? Ms Martinez is ALWAYS

right. She loves Jane Austen, doesn't she?

Um, yes. But maybe not for the same reasons we do.

You mean not because Colin Firth looks so hot every time he dives into that pond? But what other reason IS there to love Jane Austen?

Never mind. Pretend I didn't say anything.

Do you think Ms M knows how in real life Emma Thompson had the baby of the guy who played Willoughby???? Because even though he played a bad guy in *Sense and Sensibility*, I'm sure he's really nice in person. And besides, Emma needed to find love after that Kenneth Branagh left her for Helena Bonham Carter.

Sometimes I wish I could live inside Tina's head instead of mine. I swear. It must be very restful there.

Thursday, September 3, ladies' room, Albert Einstein High School

How do I always end up here? Writing in my journal in a stall of the ladies' room, I mean? It is becoming like a ritual or something.

Anyway, it all started innocently enough. We were talking about last night's episode of *The OC* when next thing I knew Tina was going, 'Hey, did you tell Lilly yet?'

And Lilly was all, 'Tell me what?'

And I totally thought Tina meant the thing about Doing It with Michael and I mouthed *PINKY SWEAR* at her until she went, 'About your parents going away to Indiana this weekend, I mean,' which I must have mentioned to her in a moment of weakness, although I don't remember doing so.

Lilly looked at me, all excited. 'They are? That's great! We can have another party!'

Hello. You would think Lilly of ALL people wouldn't want to come to another party at my place. Or at least would be a little more sensitive about the fact that her ex, whom she LOST forever at my last party, was sitting right there.

But she totally didn't seem to notice or care.

'So what time can we come over?' she wanted to know.

'Just because my mom and Mr G are going away does NOT mean I'll be having a party,' I yelled, all panicky.

'Yeah,' Lilly said, looking thoughtful. 'I forgot. You're heir to the throne of Genovia. It's not like they're going to leave you there alone. But that's OK. We can probably get Lars and Wahim to go off by themselves somewhere—'

'NO,' I said, 'that's not it. I'm not having a party because the last time I had one, it was a total disaster, in which SOME people thought it would be a good idea to play Seven Minutes in Heaven, and got CAUGHT at it by my stepfather.'

'Yeah,' Lilly said. 'But this time, Mr Gianini won't be there—'

'NO PARTIES,' I said in my most princessy voice.

Lilly just sniffed and went, 'Just because you got a B on an English paper, don't take it out on me.'

Oh, OK, Lilly, I won't. And just because YOUR parents don't trust you enough to let you stay alone in the house on account of that one time you set off the sprinkler system in the building with your home-made lighter-and-Rave-hairspray flamethrower, don't take it out on me.

Only of course I didn't say that out loud.

'Wait,' Boris said. 'YOU got a B on an English paper, Mia? How is that possible?'

So then I had no choice but to break the news to everyone at the lunch table. You know, about Ms Martinez being a big, huge über-phoney.

They were all shocked of course.

'But she has such cute clogs!' Tina cried, her heart clearly breaking.

'It just goes to show,' Boris said, 'that you can't tell what's in someone's heart by the way he or she dresses.' He shot a very significant look at me while he said this.

But I don't care. Tucking your sweater into your pants is not a good look for ANYONE.

'She probably means well,' Tina said, since she tries to find the good in everyone.

'There is never any justification for crushing the

artistic spirit,' Ling Su said – and, since she can draw better than anyone in our whole school, she would know. 'Lots of so-called critics and reviewers *meant* well when they ravaged the works of the Impressionists in the nineteenth century. But if artists like Renoir and Monet had followed their advice, some of the greatest works of art in the world would never have been created.'

'Well, I wouldn't exactly compare my writing to a Renoir painting,' I felt obligated to say. 'But thanks, Ling Su.'

'The thing is, even if Mia's writing DOES stink,' Boris said, in his usual blunt fashion, 'does a teacher really have the right to tell her so?'

'It does sort of seem anti-educational,' Shameeka said.

'Something's got to be done about this,' Ling Su said. 'The question is, what?'

But before we could come up with anything, this dark shadow fell over our lunch table and we looked up and there was . . .

Lana.

Our hearts sank. Well, mine did anyway.

Lana was accompanied by the new Grand Moff Tarkin to her Darth Vader, Trisha Hayes.

'Nice posters, *PIT*,' Lana said. Only of course she was being sarcastic. 'But they aren't going to do you any good.'

'Yeah,' Trisha said. 'We took a random poll of the cafeteria, and if the election were today you'd only get sixteen votes.'

'You mean there are sixteen people in this cafeteria,' Lilly said mildly as she peeled the chocolate coating off a Ho Ho, 'who were willing to tell you to your face that they aren't voting for you? God, I had no idea there were so many masochists in this school.'

'Keep sucking on that Twinkie, fatty,' Lana said. 'And we'll see who's the masochist.'

'It's a Ho Ho,' Boris pointed out, because that is what Boris does.

Lana didn't even look at him.

'And you know what else?' Lana said. 'I'm going to trounce you at Monday's debate during Assembly. Nobody at Albert Einstein wants a snail-dumper as President.'

Snail-dumper! That's almost as bad as being called a baby-licker!

But before I had a chance to defend my snail-dumping ways, Lana had flounced away.

Since I didn't want to humiliate Lilly by screaming at her in front of her ex, especially now that he's hot, I just looked at her and went, 'Lilly. Ladies' room. NOW.'

Somewhat to my surprise she followed me in here.

'Lilly,' I said, summoning all of the people skills Grandmere has taught me. Not, you know, that Grandmere has actually taught me any useful skills for dealing with people. It's just so hard dealing with Grandmere that I have sort of acquired some along the way. 'This has gone on long enough. I never wanted to run for Student Council President in the first place, but you kept telling me you had a plan. Lilly, if you really have a plan, I want to know what it is. Because I am sick of people calling me PIT – whatever that means. And there is NO WAY I'm going to debate Lana on Monday. NO FREAKING WAY.'

'Princess in Training,' was all Lilly had to say to that.

I just looked at her like she's a mental case. Which

I'm pretty sure she is.

'Princess in Training,' she said again. 'That's what PIT stands for. Since you asked.'

'I told you,' I said through gritted teeth, 'not to call me that any more!'

'No,' Lilly said. 'You said not to call you baby-licker or POG – Princess of Genovia. Not PIT – Princess in Training.'

'Lilly.' My teeth were still gritted. 'I do not want to be Student Council President. I have enough problems right now. I do not need this. I do not need to debate Lana Weinberger on Monday in front of the whole school.'

'Do you want to make this school a better place or not?' Lilly wanted to know.

'Yeah,' I said. 'I do. But it's hopeless, Lilly. I can't beat Lana. She's the most popular girl in school. No one is going to vote for me.'

At that moment, even though I'd thought we were alone in the ladies' room, a toilet flushed. The next thing I knew a tiny little freshman girl came out of a stall and over to the sinks to wash her hands.

'Um, excuse me, Your Highness,' she said to me after Lilly and I had stared at her in dumbfounded silence for several seconds. 'But I really admire that thing you did with the snails. And *I'm* planning on voting for you.'

Then she threw her paper towel in the trash and walked out.

'Ha!' said Lilly. 'HA HA! See? I TOLD you! Something's HAPPENING, Mia. It's like a groundswell of resentment towards Lana and her ilk. The people are sick of the reign of the popular crowd. They want a new queen. Or princess, as the case may be.'

'Lilly—'

'Just keep doing what you're doing and everything will be fine.'

'But, Lilly—'

'And keep Saturday during the day open. You can do whatever it is you're doing with my brother at night. Just give me the day.'

'Lilly, I don't WANT to be President,' I screamed.

'Don't worry,' Lilly said, giving my cheek a pat. 'You won't be.'

'But I also don't want to be humiliatingly beaten by Lana in a student election either!'

'Don't worry,' Lilly said, adjusting one of her many barrettes in the mirror above the sinks. 'You won't be.'

'Lilly,' I said. 'HOW CAN BOTH OF THOSE THINGS NOT HAPPEN???? IT'S IMPOSSIBLE!!!!'

But then the bell rang and she left.

I wonder if there's a disorder in Yahoo! Health for whatever it is that's wrong with my best friend.

Thursday, September 3, US Government

THEORIES OF GOVERNMENT (cont.)
THEORY OF FORCE:

Religion and economics play important roles in history. As a result, this theory says:

Governments have always forced the people within their reach to pay tribute or tax.

This became sanctioned by custom and people developed myths and legends to justify their rule.

(Sort of like the way people accept that the jocks and the cheerleaders run this school, despite the fact that they don't necessarily make the best grades, so it's not like they're the smartest group of people here, nor are they even very nice to those of us who don't eat, drink and breathe sports and partying. How are they even QUALIFIED to lead us? And yet their word is Law and everyone pays tribute to them by not calling them on their cruelty to others or by not telling on them when they flagrantly disregard school policy, such as smoking on school grounds and wearing their boyfriends' shorts beneath their skirts. This is just wrong. The misdeeds of a few are having a negative impact on the many, and that's not fair. I wonder what John Locke would have to say about it.)

Thursday, September 3, Earth Science

Why won't Kenny stop talking about his girlfriend? I'm sure she's nice and all, but really, does he HAVE to keep reciting every conversation he's ever had with her to me?

Magnetic field

1. Not constant – varies in strength but hardly detectable

2. Poles wander – number of times poles have reversed

3. Reversal of magnetic field – during times poles reverse, field disappears, allowing ions to hit earth, mutations, climatic ruin, etc.

Last major reversal, 800,000 years ago, magnetic particles that were pointing North about-faced to point South

PE:	N/A
Geometry:	Exercises, pages 33–35
English:	Strunk and White, pages 30–54
French:	*Lire L'Etranger pour Lundi*
Gifted and Talented:	N/A
US Government:	Definite force theory of gov.
Earth Science:	Orbital perturbations

Thursday, September 3, limo on the way home from the Plaza

So when I walked into Grandmere's suite at the Plaza for my princess lesson this afternoon, what did I find?

A pop quiz about seating arrangements for heads of state at a diplomatic banquet? Oh, no.

A waltz I needed to learn for some ball? Huh-uh.

Because those would be the kind of things you'd EXPECT at a princess lesson. And Grandmere likes to keep me on my toes apparently.

Instead, I found about two-dozen journalists gathered in her suite, all eager to discuss my Student Council Presidency campaign with myself and my campaign manager, Lilly.

That's right. Lilly. Lilly was sitting, cool as a cucumber, on a blue velvet settee, with Grandmere, answering the reporters' questions.

When the journalists saw me come in, they all jumped up and shoved microphones in my face instead of Lilly's and went, 'Your Highness, Your Highness! Are you looking forward to your debate on Monday?' And, 'Princess Mia, do you have anything you'd like to say to your constituents?'

I had one thing I wanted to say to one constituent. And that was, 'LILLY! WHAT ARE YOU DOING HERE?'

That was when Grandmere sprang into action. She hurried up and draped an arm around my shoulder and went, 'Your dear friend Lilly and I were just chatting with these nice reporters about your campaign for Student Council President, Amelia. But what they'd really like is a statement from you. Why don't you be a darling and give them one?'

The minute Grandmere calls you *darling*, you know something is up. But, of course, I already knew something was up because Lilly was there. How had she even got to the Plaza so fast? She must have taken the subway while I'd been tied up in traffic in the limo.

'Yes, *Princess*,' Lilly said, reaching out to take my hand, then pulling me – none too gently – down on to the settee beside her. 'Tell the nice reporters about all the reforms you're planning to make at AEHS.'

I leaned over, pretending I was reaching for a watercress sandwich from the tray Grandmere's maid had set out for the reporters, who are always hungry – and not just for a story. But then, as I grabbed one of the dainty little sandwiches, I hissed in Lilly's ear, 'Now you've gone too far.'

But Lilly just smiled blandly at me and said, 'I think the princess would like some tea, Your Highness.'

To which Grandmere replied, 'But of course. Antoine! Tea for the princess!'

The press conference went on for an hour, with reporters from all over the country peppering me with questions about my campaign platform. I was just thinking that it must be a REALLY slow news day if my running for Student Council President qualified as a decent story, when one of the reporters asked me a question that shed a little light on just why Grandmere was so keen on my making an ass of myself in front of Middle America – and not just my fellow AEHS students.

'Princess Mia,' a journalist from the *Indianapolis Star* asked. 'Isn't it true that the only reason you're running for Student Council President – and the only reason we were invited here today – is that your family is trying to distract the news media from the real story currently hitting headlines in Europe: your act of eco-terrorism concerning the dumping of 10,000 snails into the Genovian bay?'

Suddenly, two-dozen microphones were shoved into my face. I blinked a few times then went, 'But that wasn't an act of eco-terrorism. I did that to save the—'

Then Grandmere was clapping her hands and going, 'Who wants a nice glass of grappa? Come now, real Genovian grappa. No one can resist that!'

But none of the reporters was falling for it.

'Princess Mia, would you like to comment on the fact that Genovia is currently being considered for expulsion from the EU, thanks to your selfish act?'

Another one cried, 'How does it feel, Your Highness, to know that you're single-handedly responsible for destroying your own nation's economy?'

'Wh-What?' I couldn't believe it. What were these reporters talking about?

For once, Lilly came to my rescue.

'People!' she cried, leaping to her feet. 'If you don't have any more questions about Mia's campaign for school president, then I'm afraid I'm going to have to ask you to leave!'

'Cover-up!' someone yelled. 'That's all this is! A cover-up to keep us from the real story!'

'Princess Mia, Princess Mia,' someone else called as Lars began herding – or, to put it more accurately, bodily removing – all of the reporters from the suite. 'Are you a member of ELF, the Earth Liberation Front? Do you want to make a statement on behalf of other eco-terrorists like yourself?'

'Well,' Grandmere said, downing half a Sidecar in

one gulp as Lars finally closed the doors on the last of the reporters. 'That went well, don't you think?'

I couldn't believe it. I just sat there in total shock. Eco-terrorism? ELF? All because of some SNAILS????

Lilly picked up her Palm Pilot (when did she get one of those???) and strolled over to where Grandmere was standing.

'Right. So we've got *Time* magazine at six, and *Newsweek* at six-thirty,' Lilly said. 'I heard from NPR and I definitely think we should squeeze them in this evening – drive time, you know. It can't hurt. And we got a request from New York One for Mia to go on tonight's broadcast of *Inside Politics*. I've got them to swear there won't be any questions about the E word. What do you think?'

'Marvellous,' Grandmere said, taking another swig from her Sidecar. 'What about Larry King?'

Lilly tapped the headset she'd slipped on and said, 'Antoine? Have you got hold of Larry K yet? No? Well, get on it.'

Larry K? The E word? What was HAPPENING?

Which is exactly what I wailed.

Grandmere and Lilly looked at me as if only just realizing I was there at all.

'Oh,' Lilly said, taking off the headset. 'Mia. Right. The ELF thing? Don't worry about it. Par for the course.'

PAR FOR THE COURSE???? Since when has Lilly known anything about golf?

'We didn't want to trouble you, Amelia,' Grandmere said coolly as she lit a cigarette. 'It's nothing really. Tell me, is that really how you're wearing your hair these days? Wouldn't you like it better if it were a little . . . shorter?'

'What is going on?' I demanded, ignoring her hair question. 'Is Genovia REALLY going to get expelled from the EU for what I did with the snails?'

Grandmere exhaled a long plume of blue smoke.

'Not if I have anything to say about it,' she informed me casually.

My heart seemed to twist inside my chest. It's true!

'Can they do that?' I demanded. 'Can the European Union really kick us out because of a few snails?'

'Of course not.' This came from my dad, who'd wandered into the room, a cellphone clutched to his ear. I felt a momentary relief until I realized he wasn't speaking to me. He was talking into his cellphone.

'No,' he yelled at whoever was on the end of the line, bending to scoop up a handful of leftover sandwiches from the tray before heading back to his own suite. 'She was acting entirely on her own accord, not in the name of any global organization. Oh, really? Well, I'm sorry you feel that way. Maybe when you have a teenage daughter of your own you'll understand.'

He slammed the door on his way out.

'Well,' Grandmere said, stubbing out her cigarette and reaching for the rest of her Sidecar. 'Shall we talk about Amelia's platform then?'

'Excellent idea,' Lilly said and pressed some buttons on her Palm Pilot.

So now at least I know why GRANDMERE is so behind this presidency thing. It's the only thing she can think of to keep reporters distracted from the whole 'Genovia being kicked out of the EU for eco-terrorism' thing.

But what's LILLY's excuse? I mean, she's the LAST person I ever thought Grandmere could turn to the dark side.

Et tu, Lilly?

My dad came back into the room between my *Time* and *Newsweek* interviews. He looked way stressed. I felt really bad and apologized to him about the whole snail-dumping thing.

He seemed to take it in his stride.

'Don't worry too much about it, Mia,' he said. 'We'll probably get through this if I can manage to impress upon everyone the fact that you were acting on your own accord as a private citizen, and not on my behalf.'

'And maybe,' I added hopefully, 'when people see that the snails are only doing good and not anything bad, they'll change their minds.'

'That's just it,' my dad said. 'Your snails aren't doing anything at all. According to the latest reports I've had from the royal Genovian naval scuba squad, they're all just sitting down there. They are not, as you so passionately assured me they would, eating that damned seaweed.'

This was very disheartening to hear.

'Maybe they're still in shock,' I said. 'I mean, they were flown in from South America. They've probably never been that far from home before. It might take a while before they get acclimatized to their new environment.'

'Mia, they've been down there for almost two weeks. In two weeks you'd think they'd get a little hungry and eat something.'

'Yeah, but maybe they had a big meal on the plane,' I said, feeling desperate. 'I mean, I requested that they be kept as comfortable as possible during transport.'

My dad just looked at me.

'Mia,' he said. 'Do me a favour. From now on, if you

come up with any more grand schemes to save the bay from killer algae, run them by me first.'

Ouch.

Poor Dad. It's really hard being a prince.

I left right after that. But Lilly stayed. LILLY STAYED WITH MY GRANDMA. Because she still hadn't managed to get through to Larry. Lilly told me if she could get me on Larry King, I'd be a shoo-in to beat Lana on Monday.

But I disagree. If it were *TRL*, maybe. But no one at AEHS watches CNN. Except Lilly of course.

Anyway. Now I get why Grandmere is so into the idea of my running for Student Council President.

But what's LILLY getting out of it? I mean, you would think, mad as she is about the security-camera thing, SHE'D be the one running for President. What's up with that anyway?

Thursday, September 3, the Loft

So guess where I'm staying while my mom and Mr G are out of town? Yeah. That'd be at the Plaza.

WITH GRANDMERE.

Oh, they're getting me my own room. BELIEVE ME. No WAY am I sleeping in the same suite as Grandmere. Not after that time she stayed over at the Loft. I barely slept a wink the whole time she was there, she snored so loud. I could hear her all the way out in the living room.

Not to mention that she's a total bathroom hog.

I guess I kind of expected it. I mean, no way would Mom and Mr G let me stay alone at the Loft. Even if the entire Genovian national guard was positioned on the roof of our building, ready to take out any potential international princess hostage-takers. Not after what happened during my birthday party.

Not that I even care. Not now that I am responsible for making the country over which I will one day rule the most hated land in Europe. Which is pretty hard to do considering, you know, France.

I didn't actually think it was possible for me to get more stressed than I already was, considering that:

- I think I might be flunking Geometry after only three days of it.
- My best friend is making me run for Student Council President against the most popular girl in school, who is going to crush me like a bug in a humiliating defeat in front of the entire student body on Monday.
- My English teacher – the one I was so excited about and whom I was sure was going to help

mould me into the kind of writer I know in my heart I have the potential to be – seems to think my prose is so bad it should never be unleashed upon the unsuspecting public. Well, more or less.

- My boyfriend apparently expects me to Do It.
- I'm a baby-licker.

Thank God to all of that I get to add that I had 10,000 snails flown from South America and dumped into the Genovian bay in the hopes that they would consume the killer algae currently destroying our delicate ecosystem, only to discover that South American snails apparently don't like European food and that Genovia's neighbours now want nothing to do with us. Yay!

Why can't I do ANYTHING right?

Maybe Becca is right. Maybe I *should* take up yoga. Except that I tried it that one time with Lilly and her mom at the Ninety-Second Street Y, and they made you stick your butt up in the air the whole time. How is sticking your butt up into the air supposed to make you feel less stressed? It just made me feel MORE stressed because I kept wondering what everyone was thinking about my butt.

Ordinarily, to soothe my frazzled nerves, I might write a poem or something.

However, it is impossible for me to write poetry, knowing, as I do, that at this very moment Karen Martinez is poring over the piece of my soul that I handed to her. I hope she is aware that she is currently holding all my dreams of ever succeeding as a novelist – or at least a hard-hitting international journalist – in her black-nail-polished fingers. I sincerely hope she won't squash them like a bug under Fat Louie's massive paw.

I know, you know, that it's pretty unlikely I'll ever actually get to DO any writing once I take over the throne, since I'll be too busy begging the EU to let us back into it and all.

But I think I would have liked to see a book or even just a newspaper article with the words 'by Mia Thermopolis' on it.

Now I have to go make sure my mom is up on all the plane's safety regulations. I mean, it is not like they are buying a seat for Rocky. She is going to have to hold him the whole time. I hope, in the event that their plane goes down, she is prepared to use her body as a human shield to keep Rocky from being consumed in a fiery conflagration.

Also that Mr G knows he has to count the number of rows between his seat and the nearest emergency exit so that in the event of a water landing and the plane sinking and the lights going out, he will still be able to lead my mom and Rocky to safety.

Thursday, September 3 later, the Loft

Geesh! Talk about touchy! I don't know why they got so mad. It's important to know plane safety. I mean, that's why the airline companies print those cards they stick in the back of the seats. Hello. Good thing I have been collecting them for years, so I was able to use them as illustrations for my baby-safety talk just now.

You would think people would be a little more appreciative of my proactiveness.

Someone's IM-ing me . . .

Oooooooooooooo, it's Michael!

SkinnerBx: Hey! You're home! Saw you on New York One.

>

FtLouie: You SAW that??? OMG, how embarrassing.

>

SkinnerBx: No, you were good. Is that really true about the EU though?

>

FtLouie: Apparently. My dad says it will be all right though. He thinks. He hopes.

>

SkinnerBx: They should all be ashamed of themselves. Don't they know we were just trying to correct THEIR mistake?

>

FtLouie: Totally. How was your day?

>

SkinnerBx: Great. Today in my Policymaking

Under Uncertainty seminar we talked about how satellite imaging has revealed that Yellowstone National Park is actually a massive caldera, or crater, formed by a supervolcano, which is basically an underground reservoir for magma that has blown every 600,000 years, and is now about 40,000 years late for eruption. Also that when it does blow, volcanic ash from the explosion would travel as far away as Iowa and the explosion would be 2,500 times more forceful than that of Mount St Helens, killing tens of thousands immediately, and then millions more in the resulting nuclear winter. Unless, of course, we can figure out a way to relieve some of the pressure now and prevent what could be a global disaster.

OK, I HAVE to say it. *What kind of school is Michael going to anyway?*

SkinnerBx: So are your mom and Mr G still going away this weekend?

>

FtLouie: Yes. They're making me stay with GRANDMERE.

>

SkinnerBx: Harsh. Your own room?

>

FtLouie: OF COURSE! Same floor though. I hope I won't still be able to hear her snore through the walls.

>

SkinnerBx: Does your dad have bodyguards posted in the actual hallway on that floor? Or are they just in neighbouring rooms?

God, he asks the strangest questions sometimes. Boys are so WEIRD.

FtLouie: Lars and those guys stay on the floor below.

>

SkinnerBx: Are there security cameras?

The Moscovitz family is totally security-camera paranoid these days.

FtLouie: No, there are no security cameras. Well, I mean the hotel probably has them. Like in Maid in Manhattan. But not the RGG.

(RGG is short for Royal Genovian Guard, which is what Lars is a member of.)

FtLouie: What's with all the questions anyway? You planning on sneaking up there to steal the crown jewels? You already have a moon rock. What more do you want? Ha ha.

>

SkinnerBx: Ha ha. Yeah, no, I was just wondering. So you're still coming over Saturday, right?

>

FtLouie: It is the only thing I have to look forward to in my WHOLE LIFE RIGHT NOW.

>

SkinnerBx: I know. I miss you too.

Awwwwwwwwwwwwwww. I mean, seriously. It may not be very feminist of me, but I love it when he says – or writes – stuff like this. Actually writing is better because then I have actual proof, you know. That he loves me.

Then I heard a familiar sound.

FtLouie: Michael, I have to go. Rocky patrol.

>

SkinnerBx: Gotcha. Over and out.

You know, I really think Lana is wrong. Not ALL college boys expect their girlfriends to Do It. Because Michael hasn't said a SINGLE word to me about it.

And once after he paid for a couple of slices at Ray's Pizza he left his wallet on the table and I looked all through it – while he was in the men's room – because I was curious about what boys keep in their wallets, and here is what I found:

- Forty-eight dollars
- Metro card
- Hayden Planetarium membership card

- School ID
- Driver's licence
- Forbidden Planet Comic Superstore discount card
- NYC Public Library card

But no condom.

Which just goes to show my boyfriend clearly has other things on his mind than sex.

Such as the future energy crisis. And potential global disasters caused by supervolcanoes.

Which is a lot more than Lilly can say about Boris.

I mean Tina.

Whoever.

Maybe Michael and I won't ever even HAVE to have The Talk.

Friday, September 4, PE

I hate her so much.

Friday, September 4, Geometry

Seriously, where does she get off?

Theorem = statement that is proved by reasoning deductively from already accepted statements.

She only said it to get under my skin.

Right?

Because it can't be true. It CAN'T be.

Can it?

Friday, September 4, English

What was THAT about?????

What? Oh, the pom-pom squeezy thing? What do I want with a stupid squeezy thing shaped like a pom-pom that says *Vote for Lana* on it? I hate Lana. Do you have any idea what she said to me today in PE? IN FRONT OF LILLY????

What?????

She said college boys whose girlfriends won't Do It with them dump them for girls who will.

SHE DID NOT.

Oh, yes, she did. Right there in the shower. Right in front of everyone. In front of Lilly. Who'll tell Michael now.

She won't! Why would she?

Because he's her brother.

She won't. Some things you don't tell your brother.

Believe me, Mia, I have a brother. I know.

Tina, your brother is six years old.

OK, but whatever. Lilly won't tell Michael.

Anyway . . . what did she say when she heard?

She told Lana to cram it up her gym shorts.

See??? I told you.

Still!!!! You know what ELSE she said? Lana, I mean. She said boys HAVE to Do It, because if they don't it all backs up in there and they go crazy.

Wait . . . what backs up in where?

YOU KNOW. Think Health and Safety. Last year.

EWWWWWWWWWWWWWW!!!!!!!!!!!!
And it doesn't. Back up, I mean. Or Coach Wheeton would have said so.

But it would explain why boys whose girlfriends don't Do It have to dump them and find girls who will. Tina, what if it's true???? What if Lana knows something we don't know????

There's a simple way to find out.
Did you talk to Michael about it?

NOT YET!!! I TOLD YOU!!!!

Well, when you see him tomorrow you'll talk about it and you'll realize—

CAN YOU BELIEVE SHE IS STANDING OUT THERE GIVING AWAY THESE STUPID THINGS???? She must have spent a FORTUNE on them. And look how cheap they are. You can scrape the VOTE FOR LANA part right off. It's probably lead-based paint too, which is toxic. Anyway, Mia, don't feel inadequate. I put a call in to your grandmother and it's all under control. We're going to find something for you to give away too.

LILLY!!! I DON'T WANT TO GIVE ANYTHING AWAY!!! I DON'T EVEN WANT TO BE PRESIDENT!!!

Don't worry, you won't be.

YOU KEEP SAYING THAT, LILLY, AND YET EVERY TIME I TURN AROUND YOU'RE DOING SOMETHING ELSE TO HELP ME WIN, LIKE CALLING MY GRANDMOTHER AND GETTING HER TO GIVE AWAY FREE THINGS TO KIDS TO GET THEM TO VOTE FOR ME!!!!

Oooh, could you get Mia's grandma to give away free tiaras?

Because I would totally take one!

We can't give away tiaras, Tina. It's not in the budget.

I'm looking into tiara-shaped squeezy things like Lana has though.

WOULD YOU PLEASE LISTEN TO ME, LILLY????

I CAN'T TAKE THIS ANY MORE!!!! THE MADNESS HAS GOT TO STOP!!!!!!!!

Calm down, PIT. Everything's going to be all right. My brother's not going to dump you for not Doing It with him. At least, not if he wants to keep his stupid dog alive.

!

Whatever. Lana's on crack. Don't worry about it. You know Michael's not like that.

But he's in COLLEGE now, Lilly. He's CHANGING. Every time I talk to him he's learned some new, heinous thing. And what about . . . you know. THE BACK-UP.

Hello. It's the Ivy League. No one is having sex there. Believe me. Did you SEE those girls the day we went to help him move in? Um, hello, it's called shampoo. Try some.

It's true, Mia. You're MUCH cuter than all those genius Ivy League girls. Remember Elle's study group in *Legally Blonde*?

Can we please focus on what's important here? Tiara-shaped squeezy things. Yay or nay?

Oh my God. She's handing back my paper . . . and it's . . .

. . . covered in little red marks. Oh, Mia. I'm so sorry.

Mia? MIA?

Friday, September 4, nurse's office

I am lying here with a cool cloth over my forehead. Although it is very hard to write in your journal AND keep a cool cloth on your forehead, I am finding out.

The nurse says to try to keep still and not think so much. Ha! Who does that nurse think she's dealing with? It's ME, Mia Thermopolis! It is impossible for me not to think so much. Thinking is all I ever do.

Fortunately she can't me see disobeying her orders because she went into her cubicle to fill out some forms. Hopefully they're forms to have me committed. I can't debate Lana on Monday if I'm in a mental institution.

Nurse Lloyd says I'm not crazy though. She says everybody has their breaking point, and when I walked out into the hallway after receiving another B in English and saw my grandmother standing there in her tiara and ermine cape, handing out pens that say *Propriété du Palais Royale de Genovia* to everyone walking by, I reached mine.

Nurse Lloyd says it's not my fault I went mental, grabbed the box of pens out of Grandmere's hands and threw it at the security camera hanging outside the door to Principal Gupta's office.

The camera's not even broken. I mean, there are PENS all over the place.

But the camera is just fine.

I don't know why they had to call my mom and dad.

Nurse Lloyd says I should just rest quietly until they get here. She is keeping Grandmere out at my request. Not that it's Grandmere's fault really. I mean, she was just trying to help. Lilly must have called her and told her about Lana's pom-pom-shaped squeezy things. So

Grandmere felt obligated to rush over here with something she thought *I* could hand out.

Because who DOESN'T want a pen that says *Propriété du Palais Royale de Genovia* on it?

Really, none of this is anyone's fault. Except my own. I should never have handed that paper in to Ms Martinez. What was I THINKING? How could I for ONE MINUTE have thought that she would appreciate a paper comparing Romeo and Juliet's forbidden love with that of Britney Spears and Jason Allen Alexander? I mean, yeah, I poured my HEART and SOUL into it. I wanted the reader to feel Britney's pain at the way she and Jason were torn apart by the media and her management and record company. It's so clear to me that these two childhood sweethearts were meant for each other . . .

I should have known Ms Martinez wouldn't share my concern for Britney. It's quite clear she's never REALLY listened to 'Everytime'.

Oh no.

SOMEONE'S COMING!!! MUST GET CLOTH BACK ON HEAD!!!!

Friday, September 4, later, nurse's office

It was just my dad. I asked him how he got here so fast, and he said because he'd been on his way to the French mission to argue with them about voting Genovia out of the EU.

This just made me feel worse. Because it reminded me of how I'd let my own people down so very badly with the whole snail thing.

Dad said not to worry about it, that if anyone should be voted out of the EU it should be Monaco, for letting the museum, which was under Jacques Cousteau's supervision at the time, dump South American seaweed into the Mediterranean in the first place, and also France, for sitting on their hands about it for a decade afterwards.

I apologized to Dad for interrupting his busy day of politicking, but he just patted my hand and said everyone is entitled to a 'crying jag' now and then. I asked him if that was Nurse Lloyd's clinical diagnosis of what had happened to me and he said, 'Not exactly,' but that he's seen a lot of crying jags in his day. Although never in someone who hadn't had more Genovian prosecco than was good for her.

It's very embarrassing to blubber like a big baby in front of the whole school, not to mention doing it later in front of your dad. Especially when, you know, there's no Kleenex whatsoever around because I had used it all up already. So I had to blow my snot into my dad's silk show-hanky. Not that he looked like he minded too much. He'll probably just throw it away and buy a new one, like Britney Spears does with her underwear. It's nice to be a prince. Or a popstar.

Anyway, Dad was way concerned and kept asking me

what was wrong. *What's wrong, Dad?* Oh, you mean other than *everything*?

Of course the only thing I could TELL him about was the Ms Martinez thing. Because I knew if I told him about how much the whole election thing was bumming me out, he wouldn't understand and he'd just say something all fathery like, 'Oh, Mia, don't put yourself down. You know you'll do great.'

And God knows I couldn't tell him about the Michael thing. I mean, I love my dad. I don't want to cause his head to explode.

At first my dad totally didn't believe me. You know, that I could get a B on an English paper. I had to pull out my paper and SHOW him.

And then his eyes got all squinty – but I think mostly because he'd left his reading glasses back in the limo – and he cleared his throat a bunch of times.

Then he said some stuff about how *this* was what he was getting for his 20,000 dollars a year and what kind of world was it where a little girl's dream could get shot down like so much skeet, and that if this Ms Martinez person thinks she can get away with this, she has another think coming.

So, you know. That was kind of entertaining for a while: watching him hop around, all mad.

Finally the nurse heard him and she came in and shooed him out.

While Nurse Lloyd was shooing my dad out, though, my mom managed to sneak in, looking all flustered, with Rocky strapped to her. So I sat up and smelt his head for a while, because Rocky's head smells almost as good as Michael's neck, although in a much different way of course.

Although the smell of Rocky's head cannot soothe my fractious soul the way the smell of Michael's neck can.

While I smelt Rocky's head my mom said, 'Mia, this is a really bad time for you to have a breakdown. Our flight to Indiana leaves in two hours.'

I assured my mom that I wasn't having a breakdown, that it was just a crying jag. I didn't mention what had brought it on. You know, the part about what Lana had told me about college boys. And then Ms Martinez shooting down my dreams of being a writer. Instead I just said maybe I still had jet lag from my summer in Genovia and all.

'This isn't jet lag,' my mother said scornfully. 'This has Clarisse Renaldo written all over it.'

Well, I hadn't wanted to say so out loud. At least not to my mom, who has enough reasons not to like Grandmere.

But it IS true that the straw that broke the camel's back was seeing Grandmere passing out pens in the hallway.

'She means well,' I pointed out to my mom.

'Does she?' Mom looked dubious.

But I assured my mom that this time Grandmere had only the good of the crown at heart. After all, if my student-electoral campaign kept the press away from the story about Genovia being voted out of the EU, it was totally worth it.

Sort of.

Mom didn't look like she believed this though.

'Mia, if you want to quit this election thing, just say the word. I'll make it happen.'

My mom can look pretty fierce when she wants to – even with a baby as adorable as Rocky strapped to her chest. Really, if I had to make a choice between debating Lana and debating my mom about something, I'd pick Lana every time.

'No, Mom, it's OK,' I said. '*I'm* OK. Really. So . . . are you going to look up Wendell when you get back to Versailles?'

My mom was busy fussing with Rocky's foot, which had gotten all tangled up in the Tibetan prayer flags she had hanging from his carrier. 'Who?'

'Wendell Jenkins.' God! I can't believe she doesn't even remember the man to whom she gave the gift of the flower of her virginity. 'He still lives there. He and April. He works for the power company. And did you know April was a corn princess?'

Mom looked amused. 'Really? How do you know all this, Mia?'

'Yahoo! People search,' I said. 'If you run into April be sure to tell her, you know, how you're the mother of the princess of Genovia. That's a lot better than being a corn princess even if we ARE about to be thrown out of the EU.'

'I'll be sure to,' Mom said. 'You're positive you're going to be OK? Because I won't go to Versailles if you don't want me to.'

I assured Mom I would be fine. At which point Nurse Lloyd came back in and, finding my mother there, basically assured her of the same thing. Then, after letting Nurse Lloyd coo over Rocky for a while – because he is the cutest baby there ever was, and no one who sees him can HELP but coo over him – Mom left and I was all alone with Nurse Lloyd again.

Which, you know, reminded me that there was something I needed to know. And a member of the health profession was the perfect person to ask, since I couldn't go to Yahoo! Health as there wasn't a computer handy.

'Nurse Lloyd,' I said from around the thermometer she'd shoved under my tongue, to make sure I was well and truly cured and could be sent back to class.

'Yes, Mia?' She was looking at her watch as she took my pulse.

'Is it true that if college boys don't Do It it backs up?'

Nurse Lloyd snorted. 'Is that one still really going around? Mia, you should know better. You took Health and Safety, didn't you?'

'Then . . . it's not true?'

'It most certainly is not.' Nurse Lloyd let go of my wrist and took the thermometer out of my mouth. 'And don't let any of them try to tell you differently. And PS, any condom that's been in a wallet for an extended period of time should be discarded and replaced with a new one. Friction from movement while carrying the wallet in a pocket can cause tiny holes to develop in the latex.'

I just stared at her with my mouth hanging open. HOW HAD SHE KNOWN ABOUT THIS?

Nurse Lloyd just looked down at the thermometer and said, 'I've been in this job a long time. Oh, look, ninety-eight point six. You're cured. You can go now if you want. But before you do, Mia, just one more thing.'

I looked at her expectantly.

'You must stop bottling things up inside,' she said. 'I know you like to write a lot in your diary – yes, I've seen you – and that's great. But you've got to VERBALIZE your feelings as well. Especially if you're angry or upset with someone. The more you keep it buried inside, the more something like what happened today is going to happen. I know princesses are told to keep a stiff upper lip and all of that, but the truth is, if anyone shouldn't be letting things get backed up, it's you. Do you understand me?'

I nodded. Nurse Lloyd may be the smartest person I have ever met. And that includes all the geniuses I happen to be best friends with or go out with.

'Fine. Just let me write you a hall pass,' said Nurse Lloyd.

Which is what she's doing now.

Do you know what?

NURSE LLOYD IS THE BOMB!!!!!

Note to self: tell Tina to make Boris buy a new condom before they Do It on prom night.

Friday, September 4, third-floor stairwell

When I came out of the nurse's office Lilly was sitting there in the hallway, waiting for me. She had three detention slips in her hand because hall monitors had come around and found her there and written her up.

But she says she doesn't care because she HAD to make sure I was all right. She says she HAD to see me.

Remembering what Nurse Lloyd had said about not keeping things bottled up inside, I told Lilly I HAD to see her too.

So we escaped up here, where no one will find us, unless someone needs to get to the roof. But the only time anyone needs to do that is if some kid from the building next door has thrown his Pikachu or whatever out the window, on to the school's rooftop, and the custodian or the doorman from next door has to come up here to get it.

Anyway at first I have to admit I was kind of distant to Lilly because, hello, she is at least partially responsible for my crying jag. I mean, pens from the palace????

'But people love them,' was her big excuse. 'Seriously, Mia, people are, like, keeping them as souvenirs. Not everyone gets to go live in a castle every summer like you do.'

'That's not the point.' I can't believe that, even though Lilly is a genius and all, she needs to have stuff like this explained to her. 'The point is that you promised me I wouldn't have to go through with this.'

Lilly just blinked at me. 'When did I say that?'

'LILLY!' I couldn't believe it. 'You swore I wouldn't end up having to be Student Council President!'

'I know,' Lilly said. 'And you won't.'

'But you also promised me Lana wouldn't crush me in a humiliating defeat in front of everyone!'

'I know,' Lilly said. 'She won't.'

'LILLY!' I felt like the top of my head was going to blow off. 'If Lana doesn't beat me, I WILL be President.'

'No, you won't,' Lilly said. '*I* will.'

Now it was my turn to blink. 'WHAT? That doesn't make any sense.'

'Yes, it does,' Lilly said calmly. 'See, what's going to happen is, you're going to win the election – because you're a princess and you're nice to everyone and people like you. Then, after a suitable period of time – say two or three days – you're going to have to (regretfully, of course) step down from the presidency on account of being too busy with the whole princess thing. That is when I, whom you will have appointed your Vice-president, will have to assume the mantle of presidential responsibility.' Lilly shrugged. 'See? Simple.'

I stared at Lilly, completely dumbfounded.

'Wait a minute. You're doing all of this just so that YOU can be President?'

Lilly nodded.

'But, Lilly . . . why didn't you just run then?'

That's when something totally unexpected happened. Lilly's eyes, behind the lenses of her glasses, filled up with tears. Next thing I knew she was having a crying jag of her very own.

'Because there's no way I could ever win,' she said with a sob. 'Don't you remember how I got crushed in last year's election? Nobody likes me. Not the way they like you, Mia. I mean, you may be a baby-licker and all, but people seem to be able to relate to you, even with the whole princess thing. NOBODY can relate to me . . .

maybe because I'm a genius and that's intimidating to people or something. I don't know why really. I mean, you would think people would want the smartest leader they could find, but instead they seem perfectly content to elect total MORONS.'

I tried not to take Lilly's calling me a moron to heart. After all, she was in the middle of a full-blown personal crisis.

'Lilly,' I said in astonishment. 'I didn't know you thought of yourself that way. You know. As not popular.'

Lilly looked up from the detention slips she was weeping into.

'W-why w-would I ever consider myself popular?' she stammered sorrowfully. 'Y-you're the only real friend I've got.'

'That's not true,' I said. 'You have lots of friends, Shameeka and Ling Su and Tina—'

Lilly started to cry harder at the mention of Tina's name. Too late, I remembered Boris and his new hotness.

'Oh,' I said, patting Lilly on the shoulder. 'Sorry. What I meant was . . . Well, whatever. People DO like you, Lilly. It's just that sometimes . . .'

Lilly lifted her tear-stained face.

'W-What?' she asked.

'Well,' I said. 'Sometimes you're kind of mean to people. Like me. With the whole baby-licker thing.'

'But you ARE a baby-licker,' Lilly pointed out.

'Yes,' I said. 'But, you know, you don't need to SAY it all the time.'

Lilly rested her chin on her knees.

'I guess not,' she said with a sigh. 'You're right. I'm sorry.'

While I had her in a conciliatory mood, I added, 'And I don't like it when you call me POG or PIT either.'

Lilly looked at me blankly.

'Then what am I supposed to call you?'

'How about just plain Mia?'

Lilly seemed to think about this.

'But . . . that's so boring,' she said.

'But it's my name,' I pointed out.

Lilly sighed again.

'Fine,' she said. 'Whatever. You have no idea how good you have it, POG. I mean, Mia.'

'Good? *ME?* Please!' I practically burst out laughing. 'My life is TERRIBLE right now. Did you SEE what Ms Martinez gave me on my paper?'

Lilly wiped her eyes.

'Well, yeah,' she said. 'She WAS a little harsh. But a B isn't really that bad, Mia. Besides, I saw your dad heading towards her classroom a little while ago. He looked like he was going to read her the riot act.'

'Yeah, but what good is that going to do me?' I wanted to know. 'I mean, it's not going to change her mind about my writing talent . . . or lack thereof. It's just going to make her, you know, scared of my dad.'

Lilly just shook her head.

'Yeah,' she said. 'But at least you have a boyfriend.'

'Who's in COLLEGE,' I reminded her. 'And who apparently expects—'

'Oh, please,' Lilly said. 'Not that stupid Lana thing again. When are you going to get it through your head that Lana doesn't know what she's talking about? I mean, do you see HER dating a college boy?'

'No,' I said. 'But—'

'Yeah, well, there might be a REASON for that. And

if what it says all over the ladies'-room wall is true, it is NOT because Lana has any reservations about Doing It.'

We both sat there and thought about that for a while. Then Lilly said, 'So, are your mom and Mr G still going to Indiana for the weekend?'

'Yes,' I said and then added quickly, 'But there isn't going to be any party at my place because I'm staying at the Plaza.'

'In your own room?' Lilly asked. When I nodded, she said, 'Sweet.' Then she said, 'Hey, you should have a slumber party.'

I looked at her like she was crazy.

'At the *hotel*?'

'Sure,' Lilly said. 'It'll be fun. And we need to work on your debate skills anyway. We could do a mock run-through. How about it?'

'Well,' I said. 'I guess so.'

Although I'm not sure how Dad and Grandmere are going to feel about this. My having a slumber party at the Plaza.

But, oh well. If it'll make Lilly happy, I guess it's worth it. I seriously never knew she felt that way about herself. You know, that she's not popular. I mean, *I* know Lilly isn't very popular. But I never knew SHE knew it. She always ACTS like she thinks she's the queen of the school.

Who knew it was all for show?

Now we both have to sit here until the bell for sixth period rings and we can duck back downstairs and mingle with the rest of the hordes. We're missing Gifted and Talented, but I have my pass from the nurse to show Mrs Hill on Monday, so she won't count me absent from today.

I don't know what Lilly's going to do about it. She doesn't seem to care all that much either. Really, if you think about it, Grandmere and Lilly could BOTH teach the world a thing or two about acting like a princess.

Which is kind of scary if you *do* think about it.

Friday, September 4, US Government

THEORIES OF GOVERNMENT (cont.)
EVOLUTIONARY THEORY:

Darwin theory of evolution – applied government =

1. Family
2. Clan
3. Tribe

Groups formed to coordinate and manage enterprise of goods and services.

To maintain internal order and protect from external danger, governmental institutions were formed.

(Wow, this is just like cliques! Seriously! I mean, the way cliques are formed within a school – to protect from external danger. Like, for instance, all of us Geeks bonded together and formed a clique to protect ourselves from being picked on by the Jocks and Cheerleaders because there is safety in numbers. This explains so much:

- The Sk8terbois' clique formed to protect them selves from the Punks
- The Punks formed to protect themselves from the Drama Club
- The Drama Club formed to protect themselves from the Nerds
- The Nerds formed together to protect themselves from the Jocks
- And the Jocks formed to protect themselves from . . .

Well, I don't know who the Jocks formed together to protect themselves from. But otherwise it's all making sense now. This is why cliques exist! Darwin was right!!!)

Friday, September 4, Earth Science

Magnetic field surrounding earth due to interior convection currents

Discovered by Van Allen (radiation belts)

High radiation zone due to particles, some radioactive and charged, from space and sun

Aurora borealis caused by interaction of charged particles with the atmosphere

Kenny's new girlfriend Heather, according to Kenny:

1. Has naturally blonde hair and never needs to get her roots touched up
2. Gets straight As and is in all honours classes
3. Can do a back handspring
4. Often does them at parties
5. And in restaurants
6. Is totally popular at her school in Delaware
7. Is coming to see him at Thanksgiving
8. Has her own horse
9. Never wastes her time watching TV, because she is too busy reading books
10. Doesn't have an answering machine

Which is just as well, because probably no one ever wants to call her, since she doesn't watch TV and therefore has nothing to talk about.

PE:	N/A
Geometry:	Exercises, pages 42–45
English:	Strunk and White, pages 55–75
French:	????
Gifted and Talented:	????
US Government:	How is Darwin's theory applied to def. of gov.?
Earth Science:	Section 2, Nature of Energetic Environment

Friday, September 4, the Plaza

Grandmere felt so badly about having caused me to have a crying jag in the middle of the school day that she insisted on taking me to tea downstairs in the Palm to make up for it.

Of course I knew she didn't REALLY feel bad. I mean, she is GRANDMERE after all. And there WERE Press all over the place, trying to get pictures of us eating our scones with clotted cream so that tomorrow on the front of the *Post* there'll be a photo of us sitting there and a big headline that goes *Tea 4 2/Take that, EU!* or *FU, EU* or something.

But it *was* nice to sit there and eat tiny sandwiches with the crusts cut off while Grandmere nattered on about Lana's pom-pom-shaped squeezy things and how cheap they are and how much more superior our Propriété du Palais Royale de Genovia pens are. Especially, you know, since I hadn't had any lunch due to having spent all of that time in the nurse's office with a cool cloth on my forehead.

Grandmere was being so nice on account of the whole feeling-guilty thing (note to self: can someone with borderline personality disorder feel guilt? Check on this) that I finally just came out and went, 'Grandmere, can I have Lilly and Tina and Shameeka and Ling Su over for a slumber party in my room tonight, so we can do a mock debate?' and she went, totally calmly, 'Of course, Amelia.'

EEEEEEEEEEEEEEEEEEEEEEEEEEEEEE!!!!!!!!!!!!!!!!!!

So then I got on my cellphone and called them all and invited them. Mr Taylor had to speak to Grandmere before he would let Shameeka come, to make sure there was going to be adequate supervision and all, but Grandmere carried it off like a champ. By the time she handed the phone back to me Mr Taylor was asking if there was anything we wanted Shameeka to bring, like a popcorn popper or whatever.

But I assured him that the Plaza would see to all of our needs.

We sent Grandmere's maid back to the Loft to get my stuff and feed Fat Louie.

I hope he'll be all right on his own. It's going to be weird for him not to have Rocky around. He's got very used to licking all the leftover milk from Rocky's face every evening, as a sort of midnight snack.

Note to self:

Call Mom on cellphone as soon as her plane has landed and remind her to keep Rocky away from:

- hay threshers
- copperhead snakes (native to Indiana and highly poisonous)
- pitchforks
- black widow spiders (their bite is deadly to infants)
- unpasteurized milk (salmonella)
- Papaw's La-Z-Boy (Rocky could become wedged inside it and suffocate)
- farm animals (E. coli)
- Mamaw's tuna-potato-chip-macaroni casserole (it's just gross)
- the cellar (escapee from local mental institution could be hiding there)

Friday, September 4, Time ???? LATE!!!!!!!, the Plaza, room 1620

Oh my God, Ling Su found the coolest quiz online and brought it with her so that we can all do it and find out stuff about ourselves!!!!

QUIZ:

DO NOT CHEAT!!! NO reading ahead . . . just answer the questions in order!

First, get a pen and paper. When you choose names, make sure it's people you actually know. Go with your first instinct. DO THIS NOW!

1. First, write the numbers 1 through 11 in a column.
2. Beside numbers 1 and 2, write down any two numbers you want.
3. Beside the 3 and 7, write down the names of members of the opposite sex.
4. Write anyone's name (like friends or family) in the fourth, fifth and sixth spots.
5. Write down four song titles in 8, 9, 10 and 11.

DO THIS NOW, WITHOUT READING AHEAD TO THE ANSWERS!!!!!!!!

Mia Thermopolis's Answers:

1. Ten
2. Three
3. Michael Moscovitz
4. Fat Louie
5. Lilly Moscovitz

6. Rocky Thermopolis-Gianini
7. Kenny Showalter
8. 'Crazy in Love' – Beyoncé
9. 'Bootylicious' – Destiny's Child
10. 'Belle' – *Beauty and the Beast*
11. Theme song from *Friends*

Answer key:

1. You must tell (the numbers in spaces 1 and 2) people about this game.
2. The person in space 3 is the one that you love.
3. The person in 7 is one you like but can't work out.
4. You care most about the person you put in 4.
5. The person you name in number 5 is the one who knows you very well.
6. The person you name in 6 is your lucky star.
7. The song in 8 is the song that matches with the person in number 3.
8. The title in 9 is the song for the person in 7.
9. The tenth space is the song that tells you most about YOUR mind.
10. The eleventh answer is the song telling you how you feel about life.

Oh my God!!! THIS IS SO CRAZY!!!! IT'S ALL SO TRUE!!!!!!

Like Michael is totally the person I love! And Rocky is totally my lucky star! And Lilly is the person who knows me the best! And Fat Louie is the person (or cat) that I care about the most!

And I don't think I'll EVER figure out Kenny. 'Bootylicious' is an appropriate song for him, because one thing I *do* know: I don't think he's ready for this jelly.

And I am DEFINITELY 'Crazy in Love' with Michael! And the *Friends* theme song is TOTALLY my life: *Nobody told you life was gonna be this way* . . . Because nobody ever TOLD me I was going to be PRINCESS OF GENOVIA.

And as for the song 'Belle', Lilly can laugh all she wants, but it IS one of my favourite songs ever. And yeah, Ms Martinez would probably find that reprehesible . . . you know, a so-called writer liking a song from a Disney musical. But whatever! Belle and I have a LOT in common: we both always have our head in a book (well, mine's a journal, but whatever) and everyone thinks we're weird.

Except the men who love us.

Whatever. This is so much fun! We've ordered like EVERYTHING from room service. And a little while ago Lilly practically made us all wet ourselves from laughing so hard after Shameeka told her about Perin, from French, and how we can't tell if Perin is a boy or a girl, and Lilly said we should go into class on Monday and make a circle around Perin and chant, 'Pull . . . down . . . your . . . pants! Pull . . . down . . . your . . . pants!', so we could look and see.

Could you imagine the look on Mademoiselle Klein's face if we did that? Only, of course, I think that would be sexual harassment. And it wouldn't be very nice for Perin, that poor girl or boy.

So then we all jumped up and down on the bed and chanted, 'Pull . . . down . . . your . . . pants! Pull . . . down . . . your . . . pants!' at the top of our lungs until I thought I actually might WET my pants from laughing so hard.

Next, we're going to have a karaoke contest. Because

I told everyone about how if we are ever travelling across country and we have to sing for gas money and all, like Britney Spears in *Crossroads*, we'll need a good act. So we're gonna get on that right away.

Oh, and Michael called a minute ago, but I couldn't hear what he was saying on account of how Tina was screaming because we found a love note Boris left in her backpack and Ling Su was reading it out loud. Even Lilly was laughing.

This is the BEST NIGHT EVER. Except, of course, for the night of the Nondenominational Winter Dance.

And the night Michael and I watched *Star Wars* together and he told me he was IN love with me, not just loved me.

And the prom.

But except for those.

Note to self: remember to tell Mom to keep Rocky away from Papaw's chewing tobacco! Nicotine is toxic to babies if ingested! I saw it on *Law and Order*!

Lilly, Shameeka, Tina, Ling Su and Mia's List of Totally Hot Guys:

1. *Orlando Bloom, in anything, with or without shirt on.*
2. *Boris Pelkowski* (This is so WRONG! Boris should NOT be on this list. But Lilly and I were outvoted.)
3. *The cute guy from the most recent movie of Mia's life* (except that none of what happened in that movie could ever happen in real life since Genovia is a principality not a monarchy and it doesn't matter if the heir is married or not. Plus Skinner Box is unlikely to get a record deal since most of its members are too busy getting college degrees/thirty-day sobriety chips to practise).

4. *Seth from* The OC.
5. *Harry Potter* (Because even though he's still only fourteen or whatever, he's getting kind of hot.)
6. *Enrique Iglesias, now that he's had that mole removed.*
7. *Chad Michael Murray from* Freaky Friday *and* One Tree Hill. *Ooooh la la.*
8. *Samantha's hot boyfriend on* Sex and the City, *particularly when he shaved his head for her* (Shameeka had to abstain from voting on this one since her dad won't let her watch this show).
9. *Poor Jason Allen Alexander, Mr Britney Spears.*
10. *Ramon Rivera.*

Saturday, September 5, 1 p.m., the Great Lawn, Central Park

I'm so tired. WHY did I invite everybody over last night? And WHY did we stay up singing karaoke until 3 a.m.???

More to the point, WHY did I let Lilly talk me into going to an Albert Einstein High School SOCCER game today????

It's so boring. I mean, I've always thought sports were boring – God knows, Mrs Potts has yelled, 'Let's see some hustle, Mia!' at me enough times when I've let balls bounce right past me.

But *watching* sports is even more boring than *playing* them. At least when you're playing sports you get those sweaty-palmed, heart-pounding moments of, *Oh no! The ball's not coming towards ME, is it? Oh no. It IS coming towards me. What do I do? If I try to catch it I'll miss and everyone will hate me. But if I DON'T try to catch it everyone will hate me for THAT too.*

But when you're WATCHING sports there's none of that. There's just . . . boredom. Seemingly never-ending boredom.

When Lilly asked me to keep Saturday during the day free for her, I didn't know she meant so we could go to a school-related event. Why would I want to do school stuff (besides homework, I mean) on a WEEKEND?

But Lilly says it's important that I show myself at as many school functions as possible before the election on Monday. She keeps poking me and going, 'Stop writing in your journal and go mingle.'

But I'm not actually so sure mingling at a school soccer game is the way to get votes. You know? Because it's pretty much guaranteed that everyone here is going to vote for Lana.

And why SHOULDN'T they? Look at her over there, doing all those basket tosses or whatever. She's totally PERFECT. On the outside anyway. Inside, I know her heart is black as pitch and all. But outside – well, she's got that perfect smile with those perfect, gap-free teeth, and those perfectly smooth tanned legs with no razor nicks, and that shiny lipgloss her hair never gets stuck to – why WOULD anyone vote for me when they could vote for Lana?

Lilly says not to be stupid – that the election for Student Council President isn't a beauty or popularity contest. But then how come she wants ME to run in her place? And how come I'm HERE? The only people AT this game are the other jocks and cheerleaders. And none of them are likely to vote for ME.

Lilly says they for sure won't vote for me if I don't get my nose out of this book and go talk to them. TALK TO THEM? THE PERFECT, POPULAR PEOPLE?

They'll be lucky if I don't BARF on them.

Saturday, September 5, 3 p.m., Ray's Pizza

Well, THAT was a big waste of time.

Lilly says it wasn't. Lilly says that, actually, the day was extremely EDUCATIONAL. Whatever that means.

I'm not sure how Lilly would even KNOW this since she spent almost the entire game sitting behind Dr and Mrs Weinberger – who were in the stands – eavesdropping on their conversation with Trisha Hayes's parents. She didn't even WATCH the game so far as I know. *I* was the one who had to wander around, going up to people who wouldn't have looked twice at me if we'd passed in the hallway at AEHS, and going, 'Hi, we haven't met. I'm Mia Thermopolis, Princess of Genovia, and I'm running for Student Council President.'

Seriously. I have never felt like a bigger dork.

Nobody paid the least bit of attention to me either. The game was apparently a super-exciting one. We were playing the Trinity varsity men's team, who have basically kicked our butts every single year in, like, the history of AEHS soccer or something.

But not today. Because today AEHS produced its secret weapon: Ramon Riveras. Basically, once Ramon got hold of the ball it pretty much never left his feet, except when he was kicking it past the Trinity goalie into the big netty thing. AEHS beat Trinity four to nothing.

And it turned out I was right about Ramon. He fully whipped his shirt off and threw it into the air after the winning goal. I don't want to start a rumour or anything, but I saw Mrs Weinberger sit up a little straighter when that happened.

And of course Lana went running out on to the field and fell into Ramon's arms. The last time I saw her that day, he was carrying her around on his shoulders as if she were a trophy or something. For all I know, maybe she is: Win a game for AEHS, get one cheerleader, free.

Whatever. Ramon can have her. Maybe he'll keep her busy enough for her to leave ME alone. Me and my 'college boy'.

Which reminds me. I'm supposed to go over to Michael's dorm room after this, to meet his room-mate and 'catch up', since we haven't seen each other all week.

At least that's what Michael *said* we were going to do, when we managed to get hold of each other, earlier today. He sounded kind of annoyed when I finally remembered to turn my cellphone on and he got through at last.

'What was going on last night when I called?' he wanted to know.

'Um,' I said. I was kind of in the middle of buying a pretzel from one of those carts in the park when he called. A lot of people don't know this, but New York City pretzels – the kind you buy from a vendor on the street – have healing properties. It's true. I don't know what's in them, but if you buy one when you have a headache or whatever, as soon as you bite into one your headache goes away. And I had a pretty big headache on account of not having had any sleep.

'I had the girls over,' I explained to Michael, once I'd swallowed my first bite of hot, salty pretzel. 'For a sleep-over. Only, you know, there wasn't much sleeping.' And I told him how we jumped on the bed screaming, 'Pull . . . down . . . your . . . pants,' and all.

Only Michael didn't seem to think it was very funny. Of course I didn't mention the part about how later I sang 'Milkshake' into the TV remote for everyone while wearing the rubber shower mat as a minidress. I mean, I don't want him to think I am completely INSANE.

'You have a hotel suite all to yourself,' was all Michael said, 'and you invite my sister over.'

'And Shameeka and Tina and Ling Su,' I said, wiping mustard from my chin. Because you have to put mustard on your pretzel or the healing properties don't work.

'Right,' Michael said. 'Well, are you going to come over here later or not?'

Which some people might have found kind of, you know, rude. Except to me, the fact that Michael was annoyed with me – for whatever reason – was kind of a relief. Because if he was annoyed with me, it probably meant that Doing It wasn't foremost in his mind. And I really wasn't looking forward to having the Doing It conversation, even though I knew Tina was right and we were going to have to get that out in the open one of these days.

So now I'm just having a restorative slice of plain-cheese pizza with Lilly before I summon up my strength to get into the limo with Lars and head uptown to Michael's dorm. Really, after an evening of partying, it is very difficult to function the next day. I don't know how those Hilton sisters do it.

Lilly is now saying that we have this election in the bag. I don't have the slightest idea what she's talking about since

a) We never did end up doing that mock-debate thingy last night, so it's not like I ever had a chance to brush up on my answers for Monday, and

b) Most of the people I talked to in the stands at the game today just looked at me like I was a mental case and went, 'I'm voting for Lana, dawg.'

But whatever. Lilly spent the entire game sitting with people's PARENTS, so what does she even know?

I wish I could ask her about this Doing It thing though. I mean, Lilly's never Done It either . . . at least I don't think so. She only got to second base with her last boyfriend.

Still, I'm sure she'd have some valuable insights into the whole thing.

But I can't talk to Lilly about Doing It or not Doing It with her BROTHER. I mean, GROSS. If any girl wanted to talk to me about Doing It with Rocky, I would probably punch her lights out. Although he is, of course, my *younger* brother and only five months old.

Besides, I think I kind of know what Lilly would say: Go for it.

Which is very easy for Lilly to say, because she is very at ease in her body. She doesn't, like I do, change out of her school uniform and into her gym shorts as fast as possible before and after PE, and in the darkest, emptiest corner of the room she can find. She has even, upon occasion, strutted around the locker room COMPLETELY naked, going, 'Does anyone have any deodorant I can borrow?' And the remarks Lana and her friends make concerning Lilly's pot belly and cellulite seem not to bother her in the least.

Not that I'm worried Michael's going to make remarks about my nude body. I'm just not so sure I'm comfortable with him knowing anything about it at all.

Although I wouldn't mind, of course, seeing his.

Probably this means I'm inhibited and a prude and sexist and everything bad. Probably I don't deserve to be President of the Albert Einstein Student Council, even if only for a couple of days before I resign and let Lilly take over. Certainly I don't deserve to be princess of a country which I have managed to get thrown out of the EU . . . well, if it comes to that anyway.

Really, I don't deserve much of anything.

Well, I guess I'll go to Michael's now.

Someone, please shoot me.

Saturday, September 5, 5 p.m., Michael's dorm-room bathroom

OK, I thought Columbia was a hard school to get into. I thought they actually screened their applicants.

So what are they doing letting crazy people like Michael's room-mate in here?

Everything was going fine until HE showed up. Lars and I buzzed Michael from the lobby of Engle Hall, which is Michael's dorm, and Michael came down to sign us in, because they take their students' safety very seriously here at Columbia University. I had to leave my student ID at the security desk, so I wouldn't try to leave the building without signing out. Lars had to leave his gun permit (although they let him keep his gun when they found out I was the Princess of Genovia and he was my bodyguard).

Anyway, once we were all signed in Michael took us upstairs. I had been in Engle Hall before, of course, the day he moved in, but it looks very different now that all the moving carts and parents are gone. There were people running around in just towels up and down the hallway, screaming, just like on *Gilmore Girls*! And very loud music was blaring out of some open doorways. There were posters everywhere urging residents to come to this or that protest march, and invitations to poetry readings at various nearby coffee houses. It was all very collegiate!

Michael seemed to have got over being annoyed with me, since he gave me a very nice kiss hello, during which I got to smell his neck and immediately felt better about things. Michael's neck is almost as good as an NYC vendor pretzel, as far as healing properties go.

Anyway, we managed to ditch Lars in the student lounge on Michael's floor as there was a baseball game on the big TV there. You would think Lars would have had enough athletics for one day, seeing as how we'd just spent like three hours at one sporting event, but whatever. He took one look at the score, which was tied, and was glued to the set, along with a number of other people who were as slack-jawed as he was.

Michael went ahead and took me to his room, which looks a lot better than it did the last time I'd seen it, the day he'd moved in. There's a map of the galaxy covering most of the cinderblock, more computer equipment than they probably have at NORAD, covering every available flat surface (not counting the beds), and a big sign that says *Don't Even THINK About Parking Here* on the ceiling that Michael swears he didn't steal off the street.

Michael's side of the room is very tidy, with a dark-blue comforter over the bed and a tiny fridge as a night-stand and CDs and books EVERYWHERE.

The other side of the room is a little messier, with a red comforter, a microwave instead of a fridge and DVDs and books EVERYWHERE.

Before I even had a chance to ask where Doo Pak was and when I was going to get to meet him, Michael pulled me down on to his bed. We were getting very nicely reacquainted after our week apart when the door opened suddenly and a tall Korean boy in glasses came in.

'Oh, hi, Doo Pak,' Michael said very casually. 'This is my girlfriend, Mia. Mia, this is Doo Pak.'

I held out my right hand and gave Doo Pak my best princess smile.

'Hello, Doo Pak,' I said. 'It's very nice to meet you.'

But Doo Pak didn't take my hand and shake it. Instead he looked from Michael to me and back again very quickly. Then he laughed and said, 'Ha ha, that is very funny! How much is he paying you to play this joke on me, huh?'

I looked at Michael all confused, and he said, 'Uh, Doo Pak, I'm not joking. This really is my girlfriend.'

Doo Pak just laughed some more and said, 'You Americans are always playing jokes! Really, you can stop now.'

So then I tried.

'Um,' I said. 'Doo Pak, I really am Michael's girlfriend. My name's Mia Thermopolis. It's nice to finally meet you. I've heard a lot about you.'

This is when Doo Pak began laughing so hard that he doubled up and fell over on to his bed.

'No,' he said, shaking his head as tears of laughter streamed down his face. 'No, no. This is not possible. *You* . . .' He pointed at me. '. . . cannot be going out with *him*.' And he pointed at Michael.

Michael was kind of starting to look irritated.

'Doo Pak,' he said, in the same warning voice I've heard him use with Lilly when she starts in on him about his fondness for *Star Trek: Enterprise*.

'Seriously,' I said to Doo Pak, trying to help, even though I didn't have the slightest idea what was so funny. 'Michael and I have been going out for over nine months. I go to Albert Einstein High School, which is just down the street, and live with my mother and stepdad down in the Vill—'

'You stop talking now, please,' Doo Pak said to me – very politely, I have to admit. But still. It's kind of weird to be told to stop talking. Especially when Doo Pak then turned his back on me and started talking to Michael in a very urgent, low voice, and Michael responded in an equally low, but more annoyed than urgent voice.

It is extremely weird to be standing in a room watching two people have an urgent and annoyed conversation that you can't even eavesdrop on. So I went into the bathroom to give them some privacy.

I can hear Doo Pak whispering very urgently to Michael, who fortunately has stopped whispering his responses, so I can at least hear HIS part of the conversation.

'Doo Pak, I TOLD you who she is,' he just said. 'She's my GIRLFRIEND. Nobody is trying to play a joke on you.'

You know, their bathroom is actually quite clean, for boys. There's nothing in here I'm actually afraid to touch. I see they've exchanged the institutional rubber shower curtain for one with a map of the world on it. That must be to comfort Doo Pak, who clearly misses his native land. This way he can take a shower and gaze at his home country the whole time.

Oooooh, Doo Pak isn't whispering any more now either. They must both think I'm completely DEAF.

'But I don't understand, Mike,' Doo Pak is saying. MIKE????? 'Why would SHE go out with YOU?'

It's all becoming clearer now. Doo Pak must have recognized me. I *have* been in the press quite a lot lately on account of the whole snail thing and the election and all. Maybe he can't believe Michael is actually dating a princess.

I can't say I blame him. There really isn't anything in the world quite as dorky as being a princess. No wonder

Michael didn't warn him ahead of time. It must be excruciatingly embarrassing for him to have to admit to his college friends that not only is he dating a high-school girl, but she's also a PRINCESS.

Poor Michael. I never knew people actually TEASED him about the fact that he goes out with a royal. That, on top of the fact that his girlfriend has a bodyguard, is mammary-challenged and a baby-licker, makes Michael's devotion to me all the more extraordinary.

Ooooh, they've stopped talking. Maybe it's safe to come out now . . .

Saturday, September 5, 7 p.m., Cafe (212), John Jay Lerner Hall

I have to write this fast, while Michael is up paying for the food. Fortunately there's a horrendously long line at the cash register – this place is PACKED – so it should take him a while.

Anyway, I found out the reason Doo Pak thought Michael was pulling his leg about me being his girlfriend. And it has nothing to do with me being a princess. It has to do with Doo Pak thinking I'm too PRETTY for Michael.

I am not even kidding. Doo Pak told me so himself when I came out of the bathroom. He looked totally ashamed of himself. And he said, without Michael even hitting him first or anything, 'I am very sorry I did not believe you when you said you were Mike's girlfriend. You see,' he went on, in the same apologetic tone, 'you are much too pretty to be dating Mike. He is – what do you call it? Oh, yes – a nerd. Like me. And nerds like us don't get pretty girlfriends. So I thought he was pranking me. Please accept my very humble apologies for my mistake.'

I looked from Michael to Doo Pak to see if they were, um, pranking me, but I could tell from Doo Pak's red, embarrassed face and Michael's even *redder*, *more* embarrassed face that Doo Pak was telling the truth: he thinks I'm too pretty to go out with Michael!!!!! SERIOUSLY!!!!!!

They must have very different standards of prettiness in South Korea than they have here in the US.

Also, apparently, where Doo Pak is from, boys who play with computers all day just don't get girlfriends. At all.

Maybe this is why they are always drawing them. You know, through anime and manga.

But, as I explained to Doo Pak, being a nerd in America is actually quite stylish, and most sensible girls WANT to date a nerd – as opposed to a Jock or a Playa.

Doo Pak didn't look as if he dared believe me, but I pointed out that Bill Gates, who, of course, is the King of the Nerds, is in fact married. And that seemed to cinch it for him. He shook my hand and asked very excitedly whether I had any female friends I might bring over someday for him and the rest of the boys on the floor to meet.

I told him that I would certainly try.

Then Doo Pak excused himself to go to the computer store to buy the latest version of Myst, and Michael said irritably that he wished they would let freshmen have single rooms in the dorm, instead of forcing them to share with a room-mate.

Which reminds me about something I noticed in their bathroom right before Doo Pak let me out. Something that completely didn't register until JUST NOW. SOMETHING THAT MAY PERMANENTLY BURN ITSELF INTO THE SOFT TISSUE OF MY BRAIN:

THERE IS A BOX OF CONDOMS IN MICHAEL AND DOO PAK'S MEDICINE CABINET!!!!!!!!!!!!

Seriously. I SAW it. Oh my God, I TOTALLY SAW IT.

WHAT DOES THIS MEAN???? I mean, clearly DOO PAK isn't Doing It with anyone. I mean, he basically ADMITTED he's never had a girlfriend.

So whose condoms ARE those?????

Ooops, 'Mike' is back . . .

Sunday, September 6, 1 a.m., limo back to the Plaza

OH MY GOD. OH MY GOD OH MY GOD OH MY GOD. I just have to breathe. Really. Like they made me do in yoga that one time. In. Out. In. Out.

OK. I can do this. I can write this. I can just set it down on paper like I do every other little thing that happens to me, and then it will be all right. It HAS to be all right. It just HAS to.

We did it.

We had The Talk.

AND MICHAEL EXPECTS US TO HAVE SEX . . .

. . . SOMEDAY.

There. I wrote it.

So why don't I feel any better??????

Oh God, what am I going to DO???? How could it turn out that Lana is right? Lana has never been right about ANYTHING!!! I remember she told us if you sneezed and held your nose at the same time your eardrums would explode. And what about the great 'If you take a shower while you have your period, you could bleed to death' rumour she started? Even last year she had a couple of people going with the whole aspirin + Diet Coke = hole in your stomach thing.

The point is, none of those turned out to be true.

Why did THIS one have to be the one she was telling the truth about?????

College boys DO expect their girlfriends to Do It. At least, eventually. I mean, Michael was very sweet and understanding and almost as embarrassed as I was about it. It's not like, you know, he's going to dump me if we don't Do It tomorrow or whatever.

But he's DEFINITELY interested in Doing It.

Someday.

AAAAAAAAAAAAARRRRRGGGHHHHH!!!!!!!!!

I should have known of course. Because real men – like the *X-men*'s Wolverine and the Beast from *Beauty and the Beast* – ALL want to Do It. They may, you know, be polite about it. I mean, Wolverine might engage in witty repartee with Jean Gray while he lets Cyclops slobber all over her.

And the Beast might whirl Belle around that ballroom as if there is nothing on his mind but doing the box step.

But there is no getting around the fact that ultimately, deep down inside, ALL GUYS WANT TO DO IT.

I don't know why I thought Michael might be different. I mean, I have seen *Real Genius* and *Revenge of the Nerds*. I should know perfectly well that even smart boys like sex. Or *would* like it if they could find someone willing to have it with them.

And it's not like either of us belongs to a religion where it's, like, against the law to Do It before you get married or whatever. Well, I mean, Michael's Jewish but he's not THAT Jewish. He eats BLTs all the time.

Still. I mean, SEX. That is a BIG step.

Which is what I said to Michael when we were making out in his room after dinner tonight. Not like, you know, he Made a Grab or anything. He's never done that – although now I know he's WANTED to. It's just, you know, that someone's always around. Except for tonight, because Lars was totally glued to the TV in the lounge with the rest of the sports freaks. And Doo Pak had gone to the library to see if he could find any girls who might be looking for a nerd-for-the-night.

But we came in from dinner and Michael put on some retro Roxy Music and pulled me on to his bed and we were kissing and stuff, and all I could think was, THERE ARE CONDOMS IN HIS MEDICINE CABINET and COLLEGE BOYS EXPECT THEIR GIRLFRIENDS TO DO IT and WENDELL JENKINS and CORN PRINCESS, and I couldn't concentrate on kissing and finally I just pulled away from him and went, 'I AM NOT READY TO HAVE SEX.'

Which I have to say seemed to surprise him very much.

Not the part about me not being ready, but the part about even mentioning it.

Still, he seemed to get over it pretty quickly, because after blinking a few times he just went, 'OK,' and went straight back to kissing me.

But this wasn't very reassuring because I couldn't tell if he'd really heard me or not. And besides, Tina had said Michael and I really needed to have The Talk about this, and I figured if she could talk to *Boris* about it I should be able to talk to Michael.

So I pushed him away again and said, 'Michael, we need to talk.'

He looked at me all confused and went, 'About what?'

And I said – EVEN THOUGH IT WAS THE HARDEST THING I'VE EVER DONE, EVEN HARDER THAN THE TIME I HAD TO ADDRESS THE GENOVIAN PARLIAMENT ON THE PARKING-METER ISSUE – 'The condoms in your medicine cabinet.'

And he said, 'The what?' And his eyes seemed all swirly and unfocused. Then he seemed to remember and went, 'Oh, those. Yeah. Everybody got them. As we were moving in. They were in that welcome pack they handed everyone at check-in.'

And then his eyes seemed to get VERY focused – like laser beams – and he pointed them at me and went, 'But even if I'd bought them, what's the big deal? Is it wrong that I care about you and would want to protect you in the event we do make love?'

Which of course made me feel all melty inside, and it was VERY hard to remember that we were supposed to be having The Talk and not making out, especially when it occurred to me that:

As good as Michael's neck smells, the rest of him might smell EVEN BETTER.

Which is all the more reason why I knew we had to hurry up and have The Talk.

'No,' I said, moving his hand away from mine, because I knew it would be even harder to concentrate on having The Talk if he was touching me. 'I think that's a good thing. It's just that . . .'

And then it all came spilling out. What Lana had said in the jet line. Wendell Jenkins. What Lana had said in the shower (not the part about it backing up though. That was too gross). Corn princess. The fact that I love him but I'm not sure I'm ready to Do It yet (*I said* wasn't sure but, of course, I AM sure. I just, you know, didn't want to sound too harsh). The fact that condoms break (if it happened on *Friends* it could happen in real life). My mother's excessive fertility probably being an inheritable genetic tendency. EVERYTHING.

Because, you know, when you're having The Talk you have to put it ALL out there or what's the point?

Well, *almost* all of it anyway. I kind of left out the part about how I'm not so jazzed about the whole nudity thing. Well, MY nudity. His I'd be totally fine with. Plus, you know, on TV sex looks kind of . . . well, difficult. What if I mess it up? Or turn out not to be good at it? He might dump me.

Only, you know. I didn't mention any of that or anything.

Michael listened to the whole speech with a very serious look on his face. He even, at one point, got up to turn the music down. It was only when I got to the part about not being sure I was ready to Do It yet that he finally said something, and that was, in a very dry tone, 'Well, that's not actually a big surprise to me, Mia.'

Which was a surprise to ME anyway.

I went, 'Really?'

He said, 'Well, you made it fairly obvious where things stood when you invited all of your girlfriends, and not me, over the minute you found out you had a hotel room all to yourself for the weekend.'

HELLO. This is so not true. First of all, Lilly and those guys invited THEMSELVES over. And secondly—

Well, OK, he was right about this part.

'Michael,' I said, feeling completely horrible. 'I'm so, so sorry. I never even – I mean, I didn't even . . .'

I felt so awful I couldn't even VERBALIZE it. I felt like a total jerk. Kind of, like, how I felt at dinner when Michael was talking about his Sociology in Science Fiction class, and how in Orwell's *1984* the lottery is used as a way to control the masses, giving them false hope that they might one day be able to leave their dead-end jobs, and how in *Fahrenheit 451* Montague's wife is totally unsympathetic to his problems with setting books on fire for a living and how all she ever does is talk on the phone with her friends about some fictional TV show called *The White Clown*. I couldn't help remembering that all Lilly and Tina and I ever talk about half the time is *Charmed.*

But, hello, how can you NOT talk about that show?

But maybe that's all part of the government's strategy to keep us from noticing what they're up to with the clear-cutting of the national forests and the passing of laws that keep teens from being able to seek reproductive health care without their parents' consent . . .

Besides sometimes I think Michael won't ever stop talking about the shows he likes, like *Jake 2.0* and, lately, *60 Minutes.*

Anyway I did my best to make it up to Michael about the whole not-inviting-him-over-to-the-hotel thing. I put my hand on his and gazed deeply into his eyes and said, 'Michael, I really am sorry. Not just about that either. But the whole . . . well, everything.'

But instead of saying he forgave me or anything like that, Michael just went, 'Fine. The question is, when ARE you going to be ready?'

And I was like, 'Ready for what?'

And he said, 'It.'

It took me a minute to figure out what he meant.

And then, when it finally dawned on me, I turned bright red.

'Um,' I said.

Then I thought fast.

'How about after the prom,' I said, 'on a king-sized bed with white-satin sheets in a deluxe suite with Central Park views at the Four Seasons, with champagne and chocolate-covered strawberries upon arrival and an aromatherapy bath for after, then waffles for two in bed the next morning?'

To which Michael replied, very calmly, 'One, I'm never going to the prom again and you know it, and two,

I can't afford the Four Seasons – which you also know. So why don't you give that answer another try?'

Damn! Tina is so LUCKY to have a boyfriend she can push around. WHY isn't Michael as malleable as BORIS?

'Look,' I said, desperately trying to think of some way to get out of the whole situation. Because it wasn't going AT ALL the way I'd planned it in my head. In my head, I told Michael I wasn't ready to Do It and he said OK and we played some Boggle and that was the end of it.

Too bad things never work out the way they do inside my head.

'Do I have to decide this right NOW?' I asked, deciding DELAY was the best strategy at this point. 'I have a lot on my mind. I mean, it's possible that at this very moment my mom could be exposing Rocky to some very harmful stimuli, such as clog dancing or even funnel cakes. And I have this debate thing on Monday . . . did I mention that Grandmere and Lilly are working on it together? I mean, it's like Darth Vader joining forces with Ann Coulter. I'm telling you, I'm a wreck. Can I take a rain check on this whole thing?'

'Absolutely,' Michael said, with a smile that was so sweet it made me want to lean over to kiss him . . .

Until he added, 'But just so you know, Mia, I'm not going to wait around forever.'

This caused me to pause just as my lips were on the way to his.

Because he didn't mean that he wasn't going to wait around forever for my answer. Oh no. He meant he wasn't going to wait around forever to Do It.

He didn't say it like it was a threat or anything. He said it kind of lightly, even jokingly.

But I could tell it wasn't really a joke. Because boys really do expect you to Do It. Someday.

I didn't know what to say. Actually I don't think I could have spoken after that if I'd tried. Fortunately I didn't have to, because there was a knock on the door and Lars's voice called, 'The game is over. It's after midnight. Time to go, Princess,' which, of course, caused Michael and me to spring to separate sides of the room.

(I just asked Lars how he has such an uncanny knack for picking the wrong – or right, as the case may be – moment to interrupt me when I'm alone with Michael, and he went, 'As long as I hear voices I'm not worried. It's when things get quiet I start to wonder what's going on. Because – no offence, Your Highness – but you talk a *lot*.')

Anyway. So that's it.
Lana was right.
All boys want to Do It.
Including Michael.
My life is over.

The end.

Note to self: call Mom and remind her that she is still breastfeeding and that even though she might FEEL like drinking a lot of gin and tonics, seeing as how she's around her mother, this could be very dangerous to Rocky's cognitive development at this point.

Sunday, September 6, noon, my room, the Plaza

Why can't my life be like the lives of the kids on The N? None of them are princesses. None of them created eco-disasters in their native lands by pouring 10,000 snails into the local bay. None of them have boyfriends who expect them to Do It someday. Well, actually, some of them do.

But still. It's different when you're on TV.

Sunday, September 6, 1 p.m., my room, the Plaza

Why won't everyone leave me alone? If I want to wallow in my own grief, that should be my prerogative. After all, I AM a princess.

Sunday, September 6, 2 p.m., my room, the Plaza

I so wish I could talk to Michael right now. He called earlier, but I didn't pick up. He left a message with the hotel operator that said, 'Hey, it's me. Are you still there or have you gone home yet? I'll try you there too. Anyway if you get this message, call me.'

Yeah. Call him. So he can break up with me for my reluctance to Do It with him. I'm so not giving him the satisfaction.

I tried calling Lilly, but she's not home. Dr Moscovitz said she has no idea where her daughter is, but that if I hear from her I should let her know that Pavlov needs walking.

I hope Lilly isn't trying to secretly film through the windows of the Sacred Heart Convent again. I know she's convinced those nuns are running an illegal methamphetamine lab in there, but it was kind of embarrassing the last time, when she sent the video footage to the Sixth Precinct and all it turned out to have on it was shots of the nuns playing Bingo.

Oooooh, a *Sailor Moon* marathon . . .

Sailor Moon is so lucky to be a cartoon character. If I were a cartoon character I'm sure I would have none of the problems I am having right now.

And even if I did they would all be solved by the end of the episode.

Sunday, September 6, 3 p.m., my room, the Plaza

OK, this is just a violation of my personal rights. I mean, if I want to wallow in bed all day I should be allowed to. If that's what SHE felt like doing, and I went barrelling into HER private room and told her to stop feeling sorry for herself and sat down and started yammering away at her, you can bet SHE never would have gone along with it. She'd just have thrown a Sidecar at me or whatever.

But somehow it's all right for HER to do that to me. Come barrelling into my room, I mean, and tell me to stop feeling sorry for myself.

Now she's dangling this gold necklace in front of me. It's got a pendant almost as big as Fat Louie's head swinging from it. There are jewels all over the pendant. It looks like something 50 Cent might wear on his night off while he's working out or just hanging with his homies or something.

'Do you know what you are looking at here, Amelia?' Grandmere is asking me.

'If you're trying to hypnotize me into not biting my nails any more, Grandmere,' I said, 'it won't work. Dr Moscovitz already tried.'

Grandmere ignored that.

'What you are looking at here, Amelia, is a priceless artifact of Genovian history. It belonged to your namesake, St Amélie, the beloved patron saint of Genovia.'

'Um, sorry, Grandmere,' I said. 'But I was named after Amelia Earhart, the brave aviatrix.'

Grandmere snorted.

'You most certainly were not,' she said. 'You were named after St Amélie and no one else.'

'Um, excuse me, Grandmere,' I said. 'But my mom very definitely told me—'

'I don't care what that mother of yours told you,' Grandmere said. 'You were named after the patron saint of Genovia, pure and simple. St Amélie was born in the year 1070, a simple peasant girl whose greatest love was tending to her family's flock of Genovian goats. As she tended her father's herd, she often sang traditional Genovian folk songs to herself in a voice that was rumoured to be one of the loveliest, most melodic of all time, much nicer than that horrible Christina Aguilera person you seem to like so much.'

Um, hello. How does Grandmere even know this? Was she alive in the year 1070? Besides, Christina has like a seven-octave range. Or something like that.

'One fine day when Amélie was fourteen years old,' Grandmere went on, 'she was guarding the herd near the Italian/Genovian border when she happened to spy, billeted in a copse, an Italian count and the army of hired mercenaries he'd brought with him from his nearby castle. Fleet of foot as one of the goats she so loved, Amélie stole near enough to the miscreants to discover their dire purpose in her beloved land. The count planned to wait until nightfall, then seize control of the Genovian Palace and its populace and add them to his own already sizeable holdings.

'A quick-thinking girl, Amélie hurried back to her flock. The sun was already low in the sky, and Amélie knew she would not be able to return to her village and inform them of the count's dastardly plan until it was far too late and he would already be on the move. And so instead she began to sing one of her plaintive folk tunes, pretending to be oblivious of the scores of hardened soldiers just a few hillocks over . . .

'It was then that a miracle occurred,' Grandmere went on. 'One by one the loathsome mercenaries dropped off, lulled to sleep by Amélie's lilting voice. And when finally the count too sunk into the deepest of slumbers, Amélie scurried back to his side and – taking the little axe she kept with her for cutting away the brambles which often clung to the coats of her beloved goats – she whacked off his head and held it high for his suddenly wakeful army to see.

'"Let this be a warning to anyone who dares to dream of defiling my beloved Genovia,"' Amélie cried, waving the count's lifeless skull.

'And with that the mercenaries – terrified that this small, seemingly defenceless girl was an example of the kind of fighters they would encounter if they set foot on Genovian soil – gathered their things and rode quickly back whence they came. And Amélie, returning to her family with the count's head as proof of her astonishing tale, was quickly hailed the country's saviour and lived long and well in her native land for the rest of her days.'

Then Grandmere reached out and undid a latch on the pendant, causing the thing to spring open and reveal what was nested inside . . .

'And this,' she said all dramatically, 'is all that remains of St Amélie today.'

I looked at the thing inside the locket.

'Um,' I said.

'It's all right, Amelia,' Grandmere said encouragingly. 'You may touch it. It's a right reserved only for the Renaldi royal family. You may as well take advantage of it.'

I reached out and touched whatever was inside the

locket. It looked – and felt – like a rock.

'Um,' I said again. 'Thanks, Grandmere. But I don't know how my touching some saint's rock is supposed to make me feel better.'

'That is no rock, Amelia,' Grandmere said scornfully. 'That's St Amélie's petrified heart!'

EWWWWWWWWWWWWWWWWWWWWW!!!!!!!!!!!!!

THIS is what Grandmere busted in here to show me? THIS is how she tries to cheer me up? By having me pick up some dead saint's petrified HEART????

WHY CAN'T I HAVE A NORMAL GRANDMA WHO TAKES ME TO SERENDIPITY FOR FROZEN HOT CHOCOLATE WHEN I'M DOWN instead of making me fondle petrified body parts??????

And, OK, I GET it. I GET that I'm named after a woman who performed an incredible act of bravery and saved her country. I GET what Grandmere was trying to do: instil some of St Amélie's chutzpah into me in time for my big debate against Lana tomorrow.

But I'm afraid her plan totally backfired, because the truth is, except for a fondness for goats, Amélie and I have NOTHING in common. I mean, sure, Rocky stops crying when I sing to him. But it's not like anybody's rushing out to make me a saint.

Also, I highly doubt St Amélie's boyfriend was all 'I'm not going to wait around forever'. Not if she still had that meat cleaver on her.

It's all just so depressing. I mean, even my own grandmother thinks I can't beat Lana Weinberger without divine intervention. That is just so nice.

Oh great. Time to go home.

Sunday, September 6, 9 p.m., the Loft

I'm sooooooooo glad to be back. It feels like I've been gone for SO MUCH LONGER than just two days. Seriously. It feels like a YEAR since I last lay on this bed with Fat Louie curled around my feet, purring his head off, and the dulcet tones of Lash in my ears, since I don't have to listen for Rocky's mournful cry because my mom cured him of the crying-to-get-attention thing. Apparently she did it by leaving him with Mamaw and Papaw to babysit while she and Mr G went to a classic-car show in the parking lot of the Kroger Sav-on, because that was the closest thing to a cultural event that was actually going on in Versailles this past weekend.

By the time they got home – four hours later – Mamaw and Papaw were still sitting exactly where they'd been when Mom and Mr G had left (in front of the TV, watching *America's Funniest Home Videos*) and Rocky was sound asleep. All Mamaw said was, 'Well, he's got a set of lungs on him, I'll say that fer'im.'

Anyway Mom says Mr G was a real trooper, and that if she hadn't been sure he loved her before she definitely knows it now, because no other man would willingly have put up with as many indignities as he endured on her behalf, one of which included riding on Papaw's tractor (Mr G says the closest to a tractor he's ever been on before is the Zamboni at a Rangers game). Mr G says he was particularly impressed by the road signs he saw along the highway from Indianapolis Airport, urging him to repent his sins and be saved. Although he reports that sadly the Versailles County Bank appears to have taken down the 'If bank is closed, please slide money under the door' sign I loved so much.

I was very pleased to hear that they followed all of my advice and kept Rocky far away from hay threshers, copperhead snakes and Hazel, Mamaw's goat. Mom did say something about how it wasn't actually necessary for me to have called every three hours to let them know that there was no cyclone activity on Doppler Radar in their area, but that she appreciated my sisterly vigilance on Rocky's behalf.

Later, while Mr G was struggling to fit their suitcases back into the crawlspace, I asked Mom if she'd happened to look up Wendell Jenkins and she was all, 'Why would I?'

'Because,' I said. 'I mean, you loved him.'

'Sure,' Mom said. 'Twenty years ago.'

'Yeah,' I said. 'But you loved Dad fifteen years ago and you see still see *him*.'

'Because I have a child with him,' my mom said, looking at me sort of strangely. 'Believe me, Mia, if it weren't for you, your dad and I probably wouldn't have anything to do with each other. We've both moved on, just like Wendell and I moved on.'

Then my mom said, 'If I hadn't met Frank, maybe I'd regret breaking up with Wendell or your dad. But I'm married to the man of my dreams. So in answer to your question, Mia, no, I didn't look up Wendell Jenkins this weekend.'

Wow. That is just . . . I don't know. So *nice*. About Mr G being the man of my mom's dreams. I mean, I hope he realizes it. How lucky he is. Because whereas I strongly suspect there are a lot of women out there who might consider my dad, being a rich prince and all, the man of *their* dreams, I don't think there are a whole lot of ladies who are going, 'Hmmm, I wish I could meet a poor, flannel-shirt wearing, drum-playing

Algebra teacher named Frank Gianini,' like my mom evidently did.

Anyway that's kind of nice. That both my mom and I are with the men of our dreams at the same time . . .

Except that mine is about to break up with me.

But would the man of my dreams REALLY tell me he's not going to wait around for me forever? Wouldn't the man of my dreams be willing to wait around for all ETERNITY to have me? I mean, look at Tom Hanks in the movie *Castaway*. He TOTALLY waited for Helen Hunt. For FOUR years.

And OK, it's not like he had much of a choice since there weren't exactly any other girls running around on that island with him, but whatever.

Anyway when I got home I found a message from Michael on the answering machine. It was almost exactly like the one he'd left for me at the hotel, asking me to call.

And when I turned on my computer there was an email from him, too, saying basically the same thing he'd said in both phone messages: to call him.

No way am I falling for that one. I'm not calling him just so he can break up with me.

Ooooooo nooooooooo, Instant Message!

Let it be Michael.

No, don't let it be Michael.

Let it be Michael.

No, don't let it be Michael.

Let it be Michael.

No, don't let it be Michael.

Let it be Michael.

`Iluvromance:Hey! It's me!`

Oh. It's Tina.

FtLouie: Hi, T.

>

Iluvromance: Just wanted to say thanx again for the GR8 time on Friday nite. It was SO MUCH fun.

>

FtLouie: OK. Thanks.

>

Iluvromance: Hey, what's the matter?

>

FtLouie: Nothing.

>

Iluvromance: SOMETHING is the matter. You haven't used a single exclamation point yet! What's wrong? Did you and Michael have The Talk?

Sometimes I think Tina must be psychic.

FtLouie: Yes. And, Tina, it was AWFUL. He totally shot down the idea of doing it on prom night and says he can't afford the Four Seasons. He was nowhere NEAR as nice as Boris about it. He even said he wasn't going to wait around for me forever!!!!!!!!!

>

Iluvromance: NO! He did NOT say that!!!!

>

FtLouie: He totally did!!! Tina, I don't know what to do. My world is collapsing around me. It's like Lana was TOTALLY RIGHT.

>

Iluvromance: That is not possible, Mia. You must have misunderstood.

>

FtLouie: Believe me, I didn't. Michael wants to Do It and isn't going wait around forever for me to make up my mind about it either. I can't believe this. All this time, you know, I thought he was the man of my dreams!!

>

Iluvromance: Mia, Michael IS the man of your dreams. But just because you've found your one true love doesn't mean that your relationship isn't going to be fraught with hardship from time to time.

>

FtLouie: It doesn't?

>

Iluvromance: Oh, gosh, no! The road to romantic bliss is filled with many potholes and speed bumps. People think that once they've found that special someone everything is smooth sailing. But nothing could be further from the truth. Good relationships only stay that way through hard work and personal sacrifice on the part of both participants.

>

FtLouie: Then . . . what should I do?

>

Iluvromance: Well . . . I don't know. How did you leave things?

>

FtLouie: Um, Lars banged on the door and said it was time for me to go home. And I haven't spoken to Michael since.

>

Iluvromance: Well, what are you doing sitting there, writing to ME? Get on the phone and call Michael right now!!!

>

FtLouie: You really think I should?

>

Iluvromance: I KNOW you should. Let him know how much you love him and how hard this is for you and how much you're hurting inside. Then TALK to him, Mia. Remember, communication is the key.

>

FtLouie: Well, if you really think it'll help, I guess I could—

>

WomynRule: Hey, Mia. So tomorrow's the big day. Are you ready?

>

FtLouie: Lilly, where have you been? Your mother was looking for you. You haven't been messing around with those nuns again, have you? You know Sergeant McLinsky told you to leave them alone.

>

WomynRule: For your information, little missy, I have spent the entire day working tirelessly on YOUR behalf. You are going to ACE that debate tomorrow, thanks to some info I was just able to independently confirm. Although one of these days I WILL bring those nuns down. They are up to no good in there, of THAT I can assure you.

>

FtLouie: Lilly, what are you talking about? What info? And your mother wants you to walk Pavlov.

>

WomynRule: Already done. Hey, are you and my brother in a fight or something?

>

FtLouie: WHY???? DID HE ASK ABOUT ME????

>

WomynRule: Well, that answers THAT question. And yes, he did ask if I'd heard from you. But right now I want you to put whatever personal differences you're having with my brother OUT OF YOUR MIND. I need you to be at your best tomorrow for the BIG DEBATE. Go to bed early tonight – like right now, for instance – and eat a really good breakfast in the morning. AND THINK POSITIVE. There's an abbreviated fourth period tomorrow, with an assembly in the gym for the debate.

Then voting's right after, at lunch. NO PRESSURE. But if you don't do well at the debate everything we've done so far – the posters, the networking at the soccer game, all of it – will have been for nothing.

>

FtLouie: NO PRESSURE??? Lilly, I'm under NOTHING BUT pressure!!!! The country over which I will one day rule is being kicked out of the EU. My grandmother made me touch a dead saint's petrified heart. My boyfriend wants to Do It. My baby brother doesn't need to be sung to any more—

>

WomynRule: My brother wants to WHAT???????

>

FtLouie: OMG. I didn't mean to admit that.

>

WomynRule: YOU CAN'T DO IT BEFORE I DO IT!!! I WILL KILL YOU!!!!

>

FtLouie: I AM NOT DOING IT. YET. I said he WANTS to Do It. Someday.

>

WomynRule: Oh God. Then what's the problem? ALL guys want to Do It, you should know that by now. Just tell him to cool his jets.

>

FtLouie: You can't tell someone like your brother to cool his jets, Lilly. He is a MANLY man and has a manly man's needs. You wouldn't tell BRAD PITT to cool his jets. No. Because BRAD PITT is a manly man. LIKE YOUR BROTHER.

>

WomynRule: OK, only you, Mia, would call my brother a manly man. But whatever. Don't think about all that tonight. Tonight just concentrate on getting a good night's sleep, so you can be fresh for the debate tomorrow morning. And don't worry. You're gonna knock 'em dead.

>

FtLouie: LILLY!!! WAIT!!! I CAN'T DO IT!!! THE DEBATE, I MEAN!!! YOU HAVE TO DO IT FOR ME!!! YOU'RE THE ONE WHO WANTS TO BE PRESIDENT ANYWAY!!!!!!!! I HAVE A FEAR OF PUBLIC SPEAKING!!!! NONE OF THE GREAT WOMEN OF GENOVIA HAS BEEN GOOD IN FRONT OF CROWDS!!! WE'RE ONLY GOOD AT KILLING MARAUDERS!!! LILLY!!!!!!!!!!!

>

WomynRule: terminated

>

Iluvromance: If it's any consolation to you, Mia, I think you'll do great tomorrow.

>

FtLouie: Thanks, Tina. But I have to go now. I think I'm going to be sick.

Monday, September 7, 1 a.m.

I cannot do this. I canNOT do this. I am going to make the hugest fool of myself . . .

Why did I ever say I would do this?

Monday, September 7, 3 a.m.

This isn't fair. Haven't I endured enough for one person in my lifetime? Why must total humiliation in front of my peers – once again – be added to it?

Monday, September 7, 5 a.m.

Why won't Fat Louie stop sleeping on my head?

Monday, September 7, 7 a.m.

I'm going to die now.

Monday, September 7, Homeroom

Really, if you think about it, I'm worrying for nothing. I mean, if the world really is going to end in ten to twenty years due to all of the accessible petroleum running out, you have to ask yourself, What's the big deal?

And what about the ice caps melting? If that happens New York won't even exist any more.

And the supervolcano in Yellowstone? Hello, nuclear WINTER.

And what about the killer algae? If my snails don't work, the entire Mediterranean coast will be destroyed. It's really only a matter of time before every sea-floor in the entire world is carpeted with *Caulerpa taxifolia*. Life as we know it will cease, because there will no longer be any seafood . . . no shrimp scampi or lobster rolls or smoked salmon . . . since there won't be any shrimp or lobster or salmon. Or anything else living in the ocean. Except killer algae.

Really, considering all of this, isn't my debate with Lana just SLIGHTLY insignificant?

Monday, September 7, PE

WHY did we have to start our section on volleyball today of all days? I SUCK at volleyball. All that smacking the ball with the insides of your wrists . . . it really HURTS! I am totally going to have black-and-blue marks.

And also I don't appreciate Mrs Potts's little joke of making Lana and me team captains. Because, of course, it totally descended into a game of the Popular versus the Unpopular, with Lana picking Trisha and all of her heinous friends, and me picking Lilly and all of the uncoordinated rejects in the class on account of, well, I knew LANA wasn't going to pick them and I didn't want them to feel left out, because I KNOW what it's like to be the last person picked for a team. It's the most horrible feeling in the world, standing there while the person doing the picking flicks a glance your way then moves coolly past you as if you weren't even THERE!

And, of course, Lana won the coin toss, so she got to serve first and she whacked that ball straight AT ME, I swear. Good thing I ducked or it might have hit me and left a bruise.

And I don't care if Mrs Potts DOES say that's the point. Hasn't she heard of all those volleyball-related injuries that occur every year? How would SHE like to have an EYE put out by a BALL?

But then none of my teammates rushed forward to hit it because clearly ALL of them knew the volleyball-to-eye-related-injury ratio as well as I did.

Needless to say we lost every round.

Now Lana is prancing around the locker room in Ramon Riveras's soccer shorts, talking about what a

FABULOUS time they had this weekend after the game. Apparently she and Ramon went sailing around Manhattan on her dad's yacht. This is something she won't be able to do when the ice caps melt, because Manhattan won't exist any more since it will be under water, so I hope she appreciated it. Although I don't think she did because she said they had a fun time throwing bottle caps overboard and watching the seagulls swoop down to try to eat them, not realizing they were bottle caps and not food.

Obviously Lana is not very environmentally savvy if she doesn't realize those bottle caps could choke a not particularly intelligent seagull or fish.

Then her dad took them to the Water Club, a restaurant I have always wanted to go to, but which will probably be going out of business soon if something isn't done about the killer algae strangling all the other undersea plant life in the world.

Although I highly doubt that Lana has ever once in her life thought about what's going on UNDER the ocean. She only cares about what's going on ON TOP of the water. As in how she looks in a bikini.

Which, having seen her in a thong, I can honestly state is disgustingly good.

But that doesn't make her a good person.

Why won't someone shoot me?

Monday, September 7, Geometry

Two more periods until I make a fool of myself in front of the entire school.

Indirect proof = assumption made at the beginning that leads to contradiction. Contradiction indicates the assumption is false and the desired conclusion is true.

Because Lana is pretty, she must be nice. Because all things that are pretty are nice.

FALSE FALSE FALSE FALSE.

Killer algae is pretty, but it is also deadly.

Postulate = a statement that is assumed to be true without proof.

I can pretty much postulate that I will lose today's debate to Lana.

You know what? I think I might be getting the hang of this Geometry thing.

Oh my God, wouldn't it be weird if all this time I thought I was good at one thing and bad at another, and it turns out I was really bad at that one thing and good at another????

Except . . . I don't want to be a mathematician when I grow up. I want to be a WRITER. I want to be good at WRITING. I don't WANT to be good at Geometry.

Well, OK, I want to be good at it. Just not, you know, SO good that I start winning all these Geometry prizes and everyone is all, 'Mia! Mia! Solve this theorem!'

Because that would be boring.

Monday, September 7, English

One more period until I make a fool of myself in front of the entire school.

Look at her. Who does she think she is, in those Samantha Chang slippers?

I know! She fully thinks she's all that. You can so tell.

I bet she doesn't even need those glasses. She probably just wears them to distract from the fact that she has horrible, squinty little eyes.

Totally. And those cargo pants. Hello.

SO last year. I think.

MIA!!! ARE YOU PUMPED???? You don't look pumped. In fact you look as crappy as you did in PE. Did you get ANY sleep at all last night?

How was I supposed to sleep, knowing, as I did, that today I'm going to flayed alive in front of the entire student body – like that guy in *Horatio Hornblower*?

Nobody is going to get flayed alive. Except maybe Lana. Because you are going to flatten her.

LILLY! I'm NOT! I'm no good at public speaking, you KNOW that. And evolutionarily speaking, Lana has the advantage of both looks AND the fact that her socio-political group is the one to whom the rest of us willingly tithe.

What are you talking about?

Just trust me. I'm going to lose.

You aren't. I have a secret weapon.

YOU'RE GOING TO SHOOT HER?????

No, Tina, you FREAK, I am not going to shoot Lana during the debate. I have a little something up my sleeve that – if the student body looks unconvinced – I will pull out. But only if Mia looks as if she needs it.

I NEED IT!!!! I NEED IT!!!!

Patience, my young Padawan.

Lilly, PLEASE, if you know something you've got to tell me, I'm DYING here. Between your brother and this and the snails, I'm completely fried—

Mia! She wants to see you! In the hallway!

Breathe. Just breathe. And you'll be all right.
Just like Drew in EVER AFTER.

That's easy for you to say, Lilly. She didn't stomp all over YOUR dreams.

Monday, September 7, third-floor stairwell

Who does she think she is? I mean, REALLY? Does she think just because I'm BLONDE (well, OK, dishwater blonde, but still) and a PRINCESS that I'm STUPID too?

If so, she's going to have to WORK ON THAT POSTULATE.

'Mia,' she said, after dragging me out into the hallway 'so we can talk' in front of EVERYONE. 'I've spoken with your father. He came in on Friday to talk to me about your schoolwork. Mia, I had no idea you were so upset over your grades in my class. You should have said something . . .'

Um, hello, I believe I did. I asked to rewrite the paper. Remember, Ms Martinez?

'. . . you know you can come talk to me about anything, anytime.'

Um, oh, OK. Can I talk to you about how Justin just needs to get over it and take Britney back because this little fight between the two of them has gone on long enough? No, I don't believe I can, can I, Ms Martinez? Because you don't like slick popular-culture references.

'I know I'm a harsh grader, Mia, but really, a B is very good for my class. I've only given out one A so far this semester.'

Um, I know, because I saw it. On *Lilly's* writing sample.

'The only reason I didn't feel comfortable giving you an A is because I still don't think you're working up to your potential. You're a very talented writer, Mia, but you need to apply yourself and stick to topics that are a little more substantive than Britney Spears.'

THIS is what's wrong with this school. That people

don't understand that Britney Spears IS a substantive topic! She is a human barometer by which the mood of the country can be determined. When Britney does something outrageous people reach excitedly for their copy of *US Weekly* and *In Touch* magazine. Britney gives us all something exciting to look forward to. Yes, there might be murders and natural disasters and other downers in the news. But then there's Britney, French kissing Madonna on the MTV Music Video Awards, and suddenly things don't seem quite so bad as they did before.

I guess my outrage must have shown on my face because, a second later, Ms Martinez was all, 'Mia? Are you all right?'

But I didn't say anything. Because what COULD I say?

Great. The late bell for fourth period just went off. I'm going to get a tardy from Mademoiselle Klein when I finally get to French.

Not that I care. What's a tardy compared to what's going to happen to me in precisely forty minutes in front of the WHOLE SCHOOL?

Monday, September 7, French

0 periods until I make a fool of myself in front of the entire school.

WHERE WERE YOU???? YOU MISSED IT!!!!

Missed what? What are you talking about, Shameeka? WAIT – Did everybody circle around Perin and chant 'PULL DOWN YOUR PANTS'????

Of course not. But Mademoiselle Klein DID make us all read our histoires *out loud, and we had to say our name first when we did it – you know, like* 'Mon histoire, par Shameeka' *and when we got to Perin, who said,* 'Mon histoire, par *Perinne,' Mademoiselle Klein went, 'You mean Perin,' and Perin went, 'No, Perinne,' and Mademoiselle Klein went, 'No, you mean Perin because Perin is the masculine for Perin and you're a boy. Perinne is feminine,' and Perin went, 'I know Perinne is feminine. I'M A GIRL.'*

PERIN IS A GIRL???? OH MY GOD!!!!! Poor Perin! How embarrassing! I mean, that Mademoiselle Klein thought he was a he. I mean, that she was a he. Well, you know what I mean. What did she do? Mademoiselle Klein, I mean?

Well, she apologized of course. What else COULD she do? Poor Perin turned BRIGHT RED. I felt so sorry for her!

That's OK, Shameeka. We'll ask him – or her – to sit with us at lunch today. I saw him – her – sitting by herself all last week, over by the guy who hates it when they put corn in the chilli. I really think she needs us.

Oh! That's such a good idea! You're so good at things like that. Knowing how to make people feel better. It's kind of like—

What?

Well, I was going to say it's kind of like you're a princess, or something. But you ARE a princess! So of course you're good at that kind of thing. It's kind of like your job.

Yeah. It kind of is, isn't it?

Monday, September 7, Principal Gupta's office

You know what? I don't even care. I don't even care that I'm sitting here in the principal's office.

I don't care that Lana is sitting here beside me, shooting me evil looks.

I don't care that the lion-head badge is hanging off my blazer by a few threads.

And I don't care that the entire school is currently in the gym, waiting for us to arrive for our debate.

Where does she get off? That's what I want to know. Lana, I mean. HOW DARE SHE??? It is one thing to pick on me, but it is QUITE another to pick on someone who is completely defenceless, not to mention NEW TO OUR SCHOOL.

If she thinks I'm going to stand idly by and just let her make fun of someone that way, she is sadly, sadly mistaken. Well, I suppose she realizes that, seeing as how I'm still holding a chunk of her hair. Although I guess it's not actually her hair since it turned out to be a clip-on extension braid she'd added to show her school spirit (it's a blue ribbon braided into a lock of fake blonde hair).

Which would explain why it came out so easily in my hand when I lunged at her, intent on ripping out every strand of hair on her stupid head, after she told me to mind my own business and ripped off my AEHS Lion sew-on patch.

Still. I hope it hurt.

The sad thing is she doesn't know how lucky she is. I'd have inflicted a lot more damage if Lars and Perin hadn't held me back.

Perin may have turned out to be a girl, but she's a surprisingly strong one.

She's also very well-mannered. As Principal Gupta was dragging me off to her office I heard Perin call, 'Thank you, Mia!'

And although I may be mistaken in this – I was still in a rage-fuelled frenzy – I think a few people even applauded.

Except, of course, it would never occur to Principal Gupta that *Lana* might have done anything wrong. Please! She thinks the reason I lunged at Lana was 'nerves' over the debate. Yeah, that's right, Principal Gupta. It was nerves all right. It had NOTHING to do with the fact that as we were coming out of French Lana walked by and leaned over to Perin and said, 'HERMAPHRODITE.'

Or that I, in response, told Lana to shut her stupid mouth.

Or that Lana, in retaliation, reached out and yanked off my AEHS Lion patch.

The part where I, totally instinctively, yanked off Lana's clip-on braid was the only part Principal Gupta heard about.

Principal Gupta says I'm lucky she doesn't suspend me on the spot. She says the only reason she's not is because she knows I have a lot of problems at home right now. (HELLO??? WHAT IS SHE TALKING ABOUT? THE SNAILS? THE FACT THAT I'M A BABY-LICKER? THAT MY BOYFRIEND WANTS TO DO IT SOMEDAY? WHAT?????)

She says she thinks it would be better for Lana and me to take out our differences with one another in a more civilized manner than brawling in the second-floor hallway. She's making us go through with the debate after all. She says, 'Mia, will you please lift your head out of that journal and pay attention to what I'm saying?'

Jeez. What does she THINK I'm writing about? *Star Wars* fan fic?

Lana's laughing of course.

I don't think she'd be laughing quite so hard if she found out that I happen to be named after someone who cut off another person's head with a meat cleaver.

Monday, September 7, the gym

Oh God. How did I ever get into this? They're ALL here. All 1,000 students at Albert Einstein High School, grades nine through twelve, sitting there in the bleachers in front of me, LOOKING at me, STARING at me, because there's nothing else to stare at, except for Lana and the two podiums and this potted palm they pulled out to make it look homier or something – or maybe to provide me with oxygen if I start to pass out – and Principal Gupta, standing in between our two folding chairs like a referee at a prize fight.

I'm totally going to barf into the potted palm.

Principal Gupta is going on about how this is just a friendly debate so that Lana and I can let the voters know where we stand on the issues.

Friendly. Right. That's why I'm still holding Lana's braid in my hand.

And hello, issues? There are ISSUES???? NOBODY TOLD ME THERE WERE GOING TO BE ISSUES!!!

I can see Lilly, her video camera pointed and ready, in the front row of bleachers – sitting with Tina and Boris and Shameeka and Ling Su and, oh look, isn't that sweet, Perin – signalling me. What is Lilly trying to tell me? She can't be getting ready to pull out her secret weapon. Not yet anyway. The debate hasn't even started! What is she doing with her hands??? Why is she making that folding motion?

Oh, I get it. She wants me to sit up straight and stop writing in my journal. Yeah, fat chance, Lilly. I—

OH MY GOD. That smell. I recognize that smell. Chanel Number Five. Only one person I know of wears Chanel Number Five – or at least slathers on so much of it that you can smell it from miles off before she even enters the room.

WHAT IS SHE DOING HERE????

Oh God. Why ME? Seriously. They should NOT allow people's families to just saunter on to school grounds whenever they feel like it. I would not have half the amount of problems I currently have if there were some kind of security at this school, keeping my parents and grandparents OUT of it.

Oh no. Not my dad too.

And Rommel.

Yes. My grandmother brought her DOG to my debate.

And a phalanx of reporters.

Good grief? Is that LARRY KING????

Great. All I need now is for my mom and Rocky to show up, and it'll turn into a Thermopolis-Gianini-Renaldo family reunion—

Oh. And there she is. Waving Rocky's little arm at me from the bleachers. Hi, Rocky! So glad you could come! So glad you could come watch your sister be totally and systematically annihilated by her mortal enemy—

Oh no. It's starting.

WHERE IS MICHAEL WHEN I NEED HIM????

Monday, September 7, ladies' room

Well, here I am. In the ladies' room. How unusual.

I don't think I'll be coming out for a while. A long, long while. As in . . . maybe never.

The whole thing was so surreal. I mean, I saw Principal Gupta tap on the microphone. I heard the murmuring from the people in the bleachers suddenly stop. Every single eye in the place was on us.

And then Principal Gupta welcomed everyone to the debate – making a special effort to thank Larry King for coming, with his cameras – and explained the importance of the Student Council and the vital role the President plays in its governance. Then she said, 'We have two very different young ladies – each with her own uniquely, er, *strong* personality – running for office today. I hope you will give them all your attention while each of our candidates tells us why she is suited to the role of President, and what she intends to do to make Albert Einstein High School a better place.'

And then – I guess as punishment for the whole braid-ripping-out thing – Principal Gupta let Lana go first.

The applause that went up as Lana swished her way to her podium could only be called thunderous. The whoops and catcalls, the chants of 'La-na, La-na', were almost deafening, especially since it was the gym, after all, and the sound really carried, what with the metal rafters.

Then Lana – looking coolly unconcerned over the fact that she was addressing 1,000 of her peers and another seventy-five or so members of the AEHS faculty and staff (if you count the lunch ladies), my entire family and a number of CNN correspondents – began to speak.

Suffice it to say that what those 1,000 peers of hers

wanted to hear – well, most of them anyway – Lana gave them. Not surprisingly Lana turned out to be a strong supporter of better cafeteria food, a longer lunch hour, larger mirrors in the girls' bathrooms, less homework, more sports, guaranteed admission from the guidance office to such Ivy League schools as AEHS graduates might want to attend, and more diet and low-carb options in the candy and soda machines. She was against the outdoor security cameras and vowed to have them removed. She promised a cheering student populace that if they elected her as President she would make all of these things happen . . .

. . . even though I happen to know that she can't. Because those security cameras may infringe upon the rights of the people who like to smoke outside the school and litter the steps with their gross cigarette butts, but mostly they help keep the school safe from vandalism and break-ins.

And the food distributor for the cafeteria is the same one who services all the schools and hospitals in the area, and offers the lowest prices for the highest-quality food that can be found in the Tri-State area.

And, if the trustees approve a longer lunch period, they'll have to shorten classes, which are already only fifty minutes.

And where does Lana think she's going to get the money for bigger mirrors in the ladies' room? And has she considered the fact that:

- less homework will leave us less prepared for the college courses some of us might want to take later on?
- more sports will result in less money for enrichment programmes in the arts?

- no one can be guaranteed admission to an Ivy League school, not even people whose parents went there?
- our choices in the candy and soda machines are limited to what the vendors are able to offer?

Obviously not.

But I guess that didn't matter to her. Or to her constituents, since by the time she finished they were screaming their heads off and pounding their feet on the bleachers to show their approval. I saw Ramon Riveras stand up and whip his school blazer around his head a few times to pump up the crowd even more.

Principal Gupta looked a little tight-lipped as she stepped up to the microphone and said, 'Er, um, thank you, Lana. Mia, would you like to respond?'

I thought I was going to barf. I really did. Although I don't know what I possibly could have thrown up, since I hadn't been able to eat breakfast this morning, and only had five Starbursts Lilly had given me, half a Bit-O-Honey mooched off Boris, three Tic Tacs from Lars and a Coke in my system.

But as I started walking towards that podium – my knees shaking so badly I'm surprised they even managed to hold me up – something happened. I don't know what exactly. Or why.

Maybe it was the intermittent booing.

Maybe it was the way Trisha Hayes pointed at my combat boots and snickered.

Maybe it was the way Ramon Riveras cupped his hands over his mouth and shouted, *'PIT! PIT!'* in a manner that could hardly be called flattering.

But as I looked out at the sea of humanity before me

and saw bobbing amidst it Perin's bright and shining face as she clapped her guts out for me, it was like the ghost of my ancestress Rosagunde, the first princess of Genovia, took over my body.

Either that or my patron saint, Amélie, did some swooping down from the clouds to lend me some of her meat-cleavering attitude.

In any case even though I still wanted to barf and all, when I got to the podium and remembered the way Grandmere had harangued me about leaning my elbows on it I did something totally unheard of in the history of Student Council presidential debates at Albert Einstein High School.

I ripped the microphone off its stand and, holding it in my hand, went to stand in FRONT of the podium.

Yeah. In front. So there was nothing for me to shield my body behind.

Nowhere for me to hide.

Nothing separating me from my audience.

And then, when they fell into a stunned silence because of this unusual move, I said – not having the slightest idea where the sudden tide of words flowing from me was coming from:

'"Give me your tired, your poor/Your huddled masses yearning to breathe free." That's what it says on the Statue of Liberty. That's the first thing millions of immigrants to this country saw when they stepped on to its shores. A statement assuring them that into this great melting pot of a nation, *all* would be welcome, regardless of socio-economic status, what colour hair she has, whom she might be dating, whether she waxes, shaves or goes au naturel, or whether or not she chooses to play a sport.

'And isn't a school a melting pot unto itself? Aren't we a group of people thrown together for eight hours a day, left to fend as best we can?

'But despite the fact that we here at Albert Einstein are a nation unto ourselves, I don't exactly see us acting like one. All I see are a bunch of people who've split off into cliques for their own protection and who are totally afraid to let anybody new – any of the huddled masses yearning to breathe free – into their precious, selective little group.

'Which totally sucks.'

I let this sink in for a minute as before me I saw a ripple of disbelief pass over my audience. Larry King murmured something into Grandmere's ear.

But it was like I didn't even care. I mean, I still felt like projectile vomiting all over the Jocks, who were sitting directly in front of me.

But I didn't. I just kept going. Like . . .

Well, like St Amélie.

'History has tried and rejected many forms of government over time, including governance of divine right, something this country abolished hundreds of years ago.

'And yet for some reason, at this school, the divine right of governance still seems to exist. There's a certain set of people who seem to believe they have an inherent right to office because they are more attractive than the rest of us – or better at sports – or get invited to more parties than we do.'

As I said this, I looked very pointedly back at Lana, then eyed Ramon and Trisha too, for good measure. Then I looked again at the crowd before me, most of whom were staring at me with their mouths open – and not, like Boris, because of deviated septums either.

'These are the people who are at the top of the evolutionary ladder,' I went on. 'The people with the nicest complexions. The people with the bodies that are shaped most like the models we see in magazines. The people who always have the hottest new bag or sunglasses. The popular people. The people who want to make you wish you were more like them.

'But I'm standing here before you today to tell you that I've been there. That's right. I've been to the popular side. And guess what? It's all a scam. These people, who act as if they have a right to govern you and me, are completely unqualified for the job due to the simple fact that they don't believe in the most fundamental precepts of our nation, and that's that we are ALL CREATED EQUAL. Not a single one of us is better than any other person here. And that includes any princesses who might be in the room.'

This got a laugh, even though the truth is, I wasn't trying to be funny. Still, the laugh made me feel a little less like barfing for some reason. I mean . . . I had made people laugh.

And not, you know, AT me. But at something I'd said. And not in a mocking way either.

I don't know. But that felt kind of . . . cool.

And suddenly, even though I could still feel my palms sweating and my fingers shaking, I felt . . . good.

'Look,' I said. 'I am not going to stand up here and promise you a bunch of junk you and I both know I can't deliver.' I looked back at Lana, who had crossed her arms over her chest and now made a face at me. I turned back to the crowd. 'Longer lunch periods? You know the board of trustees will never approve that. More sports? Is there anyone here who really feels his or her sports needs aren't being met?'

A few hands shot up.

'And is there anyone here who feels that his or her *creative* or *educational* needs aren't being met? Anybody who thinks that this school needs a literary magazine, or new digital video, photography and editing technology for the film and photography clubs, or a kiln for the art department, or a new stage-lighting system for the drama club more than it needs another soccer district championship trophy?'

Many, many more hands shot up.

'Yeah,' I said. 'That's what I thought. There is a real problem in this school, and that's that for too long a group that is in the minority has been making decisions for the majority. And that is just *wrong*.'

Someone whooped. And I don't even think it was Lilly.

'Actually,' I said, encouraged by the whoop, 'it's *more* than just wrong. It's a total violation of the principles upon which this nation was founded. As the philosopher John Locke put it, "Government is legitimate only to the extent that it is based on the consent of the people being governed." Are you really going to give your consent to the privileged few to make your decisions for you? Or are you going to entrust those decisions to someone who actually understands you – someone who shares your ideals, your hopes and your dreams? Someone who will do her very best to make sure YOUR voice, and not the voice of the so-called popular minority, is heard?'

At this there was another whoop, and this one came from way on the other side of the bleachers – definitely not one of my friends.

The second whoop was followed by a third. And then there was a smattering of applause. And a voice that shouted, 'Go, Mia!'

Whoa.

'Um, thank you, Mia.' Out of the corner of my eye, I saw Principal Gupta take a step towards me. 'That was very enlightening.'

But I pretended like I hadn't heard her.

That's right. Principal Gupta was giving me the OK to sit down – to get out of the limelight – to shrink back down into my chair.

And I blew her off.

Because I had some more stuff to get off my un-endowed chest.

'But that's not all that's wrong with this school,' I said into the microphone, enjoying the way it made my voice bounce around the gym.

'How about the fact that there are people working here – people who call themselves teachers – who seem to feel that theirs is the only legitimate form of expression? Are we really going to tolerate being told by instructors in a field as subjective as something like, oh, English, for example, that the subject matter of our essays is inappropriate because it might be considered – by some – not substantive enough in topical importance? If, for instance, I choose to write a paper about the historical significance of Japanese anime or manga, is my paper worth less than someone else's essay on the caldera in Yellowstone Park that might one day explode, killing tens of thousands of people?

'Or,' I added, as everyone started buzzing because they didn't know that Yellowstone Park is nothing more than a deadly magma reservoir and probably a lot of them have been unknowingly going there on family vacations and whatnot, 'is my paper on Japanese anime or manga

JUST AS IMPORTANT as the paper on the caldera at Yellowstone because knowing, as we do now, that such a caldera exists, we need something entertaining – such as Japanese anime or manga – to get our minds off it?'

There was a moment of stunned silence. Then someone from somewhere in the middle of the bleachers yelled, '*Final Fantasy!*' Someone else yelled, '*Dragonball!*' Another person, from way at the top, shouted, '*Pokémon!*' and got a big laugh.

'Maybe things like the lottery and television were invented to sell products, bilk workers of their hard-earned cash and lull us all into a false sense of complacency, distracting us from the true horrors of the world around us. But maybe we NEED those distractions so that during our leisure time we can enjoy ourselves,' I went on. 'Is there something wrong with, after our work is done, hanging out and watching a little *OC*? Or singing karaoke? Or reading comic books? Does something have to be complicated and hard to understand to be culture? A hundred years from now, after we're all dead from the Yellowstone caldera, or the ice caps melting, or no more petroleum, or killer algae taking over the planet, when whatever remains of human civilization looks back at early-twenty-first-century society, which do you think is going to better describe what our lives were really like – an essay on the ways in which the media exploits us or a single episode of *Sailor Moon*? I'm sorry, but as far as I'm concerned, give me anime or give me death.'

The gym exploded.

Not because the Computer Club had finally succeeded in building a killer robot and setting it loose amongst the cheerleaders.

But because of what I'd said. Really. Because of what

I, Mia Thermopolis, had said.

The thing was, though, I wasn't done.

'So today,' I said, having to shout to be heard over the applause, 'when you're casting your vote for Student Council President, ask yourself this question: What is meant by "the people" in the phrase "governance of the people, by the people"? Does it mean the privileged few? Or the vast majority of us who were born without a silver pom-pom in our mouths? Then vote for the candidate who you feel most represents you, the people.'

And then, my heart slamming into my ribs, I turned, tossed Principal Gupta the microphone and ran from the gym. To thunderous applause.

And into the safety of this bathroom stall.

The thing is I feel so WEIRD. I mean, I have never in my life stood up and done anything like that. Well, except for the parking-meter thing, but that was different. I wasn't asking people to support ME. I was asking them to support less damage to the infrastructure and higher revenue. That was kind of a no-brainer.

This, though.

This was different. I was asking people to put their trust – their vote – in me. Not like in Genovia where that support is kind of automatic because, um, there IS no other princess. It's just me. What I say goes. Or will, you know, when I take over the throne.

Uh-oh. I hear voices in the hallway. The debate must be over. I wonder what Lana said in her rebuttal. I probably should have stuck around to rebut her rebuttal. But I couldn't. I just couldn't.

Oh no. I hear Lilly . . .

Monday, September 7, Gifted and Talented

Well, that was fun. Lunch I mean. Everybody kept stopping by our table to congratulate me and tell me I had their vote. It was kind of cool. I mean, not just people from my clique – the Nerds – but the Sk8terbois and the Punks and the Drama kids and even a few of the Jocks. It was bizarre to be talking to all these people who normally look right past me in the hallway.

And all of a sudden it was like they wanted to sit at MY lunch table for a change.

Only they couldn't, because now that Perin's sitting there, in addition to the regular crowd, there's no more room.

We were a particularly festive bunch today on account of a couple of pieces of good news. At least *I* thought it was good news. And that is that, after I ran from the gym, Lana attempted a rebuttal and she was booed down and couldn't even get a word in edgeways. Principal Gupta had to turn up the sound system until the feedback became so unbearable that people finally calmed down. And by then Lana had left the gym in tears (serves her right. I don't know how I'm going to get my school patch back on. My mom certainly doesn't sew. Maybe I can ask Grandmere's maid).

But that's not the only good thing that happened. After Lilly finally managed to drag me out of the bathroom I ran into my mom and dad and Grandmere. Mom gave me a big hug – and Rocky beamed at me – and told me I'd done her proud.

But Dad had the really big news. He'd heard from the Royal Genovian scuba team, and the *Aplysia depilans* have actually started eating the killer algae! Really and truly! They've already polished off thirty-seven acres practically overnight, and will probably eradicate the entire crop by October, when the waters of the Mediterranean will become too cold to support them and they'll die.

'But that's all right,' Dad said, smiling at me. 'I've already introduced a bill to parliament that calls for another 10,000 snails to be transported to the bay next spring, in case any of our neighbouring country's algae creeps into our territory.'

I could barely believe my ears.

'So does this mean we aren't going to be voted out of the EU?' I asked.

My dad looked shocked.

'Mia,' he said. 'That was never going to happen. Well, I mean, I know a few countries might have *wanted* us ejected from the EU. But I believe they're the same ones who caused this eco-disaster in the first place. So no one was actually giving their calls for our expulsion serious consideration.'

Now he tells me. Nice one, Dad. Like I wasn't up all night, worrying about this. Well, among other things.

It was right about then that I noticed Ms Martinez standing there too, looking kind of . . . well, sheepish is the only way I can think of to describe it.

'Mia,' she said, when I'd finally stopped hugging my dad (in my joy at hearing that my snails had saved the bay). 'I just want to say that that was a great speech. And that you're right. Popular culture isn't necessarily lacking in value or merit. It has its place, just like high culture. I'm very sorry if I made you feel that the things you enjoy writing about were less worthy than more serious subjects. They aren't.'

Whoa!!!!

The fact that my dad was giving Ms Martinez the old eye as all this was going on kind of diminished my joy over my victory somewhat however.

But whatever. I think it's highly unlikely my dad's going to start dating someone who actually knows what a gerund is. His last girlfriend thought gerunds were mean, foul-smelling rodents.

Speaking of which, Grandmere came up to me right after that, took me by the arm and led me a little bit away from everyone.

'You see, Amelia,' she said in a raspy, Sidecar-scented whisper. 'I told you that you could do it. That was inspired in there. Truly inspired. I almost felt as if the spirit of St Amélie was amongst us.'

The freaky thing about this was – I'd kind of felt the same.

But I didn't say so. Instead, I said, 'So, uh, Grandmere? What's this secret weapon you and Lilly came up with? And when are you going to launch it?'

But she just lifted my half-torn-off AEHS patch between her thumb and index finger and said, 'What happened to your coat? Really, Amelia, can't you take better care of your things? A princess really ought not to walk about looking like such a slattern.'

But anyway. The whole thing was still pretty cool. Especially the part where Grandmere said she had to cancel our princess lesson for the day so she could go have a facial at Elizabeth Arden. Apparently, all the stress of helping Lilly with the election has caused her pores to expand.

All in all it was almost enough to make me think things – I don't know – might actually go my way for a change.

But then I remembered Michael. Who, by the way, hasn't once called or even text-messaged me today to say good luck with the debate or ask how I'd done or anything. In fact I haven't talked to him at all since the whole Doing It talk.

And I'll admit, that talk didn't actually go as well as I'd hoped it would.

But still. You'd think he'd call. Even if, you know, I'm the one who hasn't returned HIS calls or emails.

Boris is playing 'God Save the Queen' on his violin on my behalf. I told him it's a little early for that. After all, the votes collected over lunch are still being tabulated. Principal Gupta's going to make the announcement over the loudspeaker last period.

Lilly just went, all softly, to me, 'Then, when you win, next week you can make an announcement of your own. You know, about your stepping down and leaving the presidency to me.'

Huh. Isn't it funny? But up until that moment I had kind of forgotten about that part of our plan.

Monday, September 7, US Government

Mrs Holland congratulated me on my speech today and said it made her proud. PROUD! OF ME!!! A teacher is proud of me!!!

ME!!!!!!!

Monday, September 7, Earth Science

Kenny just said the strangest thing to me. Just blurted it right out as we were drawing our diagrams of the Van Allen radiation belts.

'Mia,' he said. 'I want to tell you something. You know my girlfriend, Heather?'

'Yeeee-ah,' I said reluctantly, because I thought he was getting ready to tell me another long, boring story about Heather's gymnastic prowess.

'Well.' Kenny's face turned as red as the radiation belt I was colouring. 'I made her up.'

!!!!!!!!!!!!!!!!!!!!!!!!

Yes, that is right. Kenny has spent the past seven days telling me MADE-UP stories about his MADE-UP girlfriend, Heather. A girlfriend who, I will admit, I actually felt threatened by! Because she's so perfect! I mean, blonde and sporty AND she gets straight As????

Actually, now that I think about it, I should probably be grateful Heather turns out not to be real. She was making me feel pretty inadequate to tell the truth.

But anyway. I just looked at him and was like, 'Kenny. Why would you do that?'

And he said, all shamefaced, 'I just couldn't stand it, you know? You having this whole perfect princess life, with Michael, your perfect princely boyfriend. It . . . I don't know. It just got to me.'

Yeah. Right. My perfect life. My perfect princess life, with Michael, my perfect princely boyfriend. Let me tell you something, Kenny. You want to know how NOT perfect my perfect princess life is? My perfect princely boyfriend is getting ready to dump me because I don't want to Do It. How's that for perfect, Kenny?

Except, of course, I couldn't say that. Because that's none of Kenny's business. Also because I don't much want the whole Michael-wants-to-Do-It thing getting around school. Thanks to the many movies based – however loosely – on my life that are floating around out there, enough people already think they know everything there is to know about me. I don't need any MORE info leaking out.

But whatever. I just assured Kenny that my life isn't as perfect as he might think. That, in fact, I have a LOT of problems, among them the fact that I am a baby-licker and very nearly got my own country kicked out of the EU.

Surprisingly, this information seemed to cheer him up excessively. So much so, in fact, that I'm feeling kind of annoyed.

Wha—

Oh no. The classroom loudspeaker just crackled. Principal Gupta is coming on to announce the results of today's votes.

Oh God. Oh God. Oh God.

Here it is:

Lana Weinberger, 359 votes.

Mia Thermopolis, 641 votes.

Oh my God.

OH MY GOD.

I'M THE NEW STUDENT COUNCIL PRESIDENT OF ALBERT EINSTEIN HIGH.

Monday, September 7, 5 p.m., Ray's Pizza

OK. That was . . . that was just totally surreal.

I don't even know how else to describe it. I'm in a total and complete daze. Still. And it's been two hours since Principal Gupta declared me the winner. And I've had half a plain-cheese pizza and three Cokes since then.

And I'm STILL in shock.

Maybe it's not so much winning the election as what happened *after* I found out I won the election. Which was . . .

. . . a LOT actually.

First off, everyone in my Earth Science class, including Kenny, started jumping all over the place, congratulating me then asking me if I could please ask the trustees to buy the bio lab an electrophoresis kit, something for which they'd unsuccessfully lobbied the last President.

So, obviously, in no time at all, I understood the full weight of the responsibility I would bear as President.

And . . .

I welcomed it.

I know. I *KNOW*.

I mean, like it's not enough I'm

- the Princess of Genovia
- sister to a defenceless infant whose mother and father are somewhat lacking in the parenting department, if you know what I mean
- a budding writer who still has to get through sophomore Geometry this year
- a teen, with all that that word implies, such as mood swings, insecurities, and the occasional zit

• in love with a college boy. •

Now I'm actually entertaining the idea of being all that AND President of my school Student Council???

But. Well. Yeah.

Yeah, I am. Because winning that election against Lana?

That totally RULED.

But anyway. That was just the FIRST thing that happened.

The next thing was that after the bell rang, letting us out for the day, I was making my way down to my locker – slowly . . . very slowly, because everyone kept stopping me to congratulate me – when I ran into Lilly, who leaped into my arms (even though I'm a lot taller than she is, she still weighs more. She's lucky I didn't drop her. But I guess I had, like, that adrenaline thing you get when your baby is stuck under a car or you win the presidency of your school's student council or something, since I was able to hold on to her until she climbed down again).

Anyway, Lilly was all, 'WE DID IT!!! WE DID IT!!!!'

And then Tina and Boris and Shameeka and Ling Su and Perin showed up and started jumping up and down along with us. Then we all made our way down to my locker, singing that 'We Are the Champions' song.

Then, as everybody else was chatting excitedly, and I was working the combination to my locker, I noticed something very odd going on at the locker next door to mine. And that was that Ramon Riveras, flanked by Principal Gupta and Lana Weinberger's DAD, of all people, was taking everything – and I do mean EVERYTHING – out of his locker and putting it glumly in his gym bag.

And standing a little way behind him, tears streaming down her face, was Lana, who kept stomping her foot and going, 'But, Daddy, WHY???? Why, Daddy, WHY???'

Except that Dr Weinberger wasn't answering her. He just stood there, looking very solemn, until Ramon had got the last of his stuff out of the locker. Then Principal Gupta said, 'Very well. Come along.'

And she, Ramon, Dr Weinberger and Lana all trailed back to the principal's office.

But not before Lana swung a decidedly nasty look over her shoulder at me and hissed, *'I'll get you back for this if it's the last thing I do! You'll be sorry!'*

I thought she meant she'd get back at me for winning the election over her. But when Shameeka went, 'Hey, where are they taking Ramon?' Lilly smiled in an evil way and said, 'The airport probably.'

While we all asked, in a chorus, what she was talking about, Lilly said, 'My secret weapon. Only after that speech you gave, Mia, I knew we didn't need it. Looks like that grandmother of yours dropped the dime on the Weinbergers anyway, even though she didn't have to. I have to hand it to that Clarisse. She is one old dame you don't want to get on your bad side.'

Since this didn't exactly clear the matter up any – at least as far as I was concerned – I asked Lilly just what the heck she was talking about, and she explained. It turns out that day at the soccer game, when Lilly had been sitting behind Lana's parents, she'd totally eavesdropped on their conversation and found out that Ramon is a wringer!

Yes! He is already a high-school graduate! He graduated last year, back in his native Brazil, where he'd led his school district to claim the national championship!

Dr Weinberger and a couple of the other trustees got the brilliant idea to PAY him to come to this country and enroll at AEHS, so we'd have a chance at actually winning some games for a change.

Lilly and Grandmere had planned on using this information as part of a smear campaign against Lana in the event that it looked as if, after the debate, she was going to win.

But my pulling out *Sailor Moon* and that John Locke quote convinced them I had the election in the bag. So Grandmere ended up not calling Principal Gupta's office to tell her about Ramon until *after* the election results were announced.

I must say this information caused me to look at Lilly in a new light. I mean, I've always known that Lilly is capable of some underhanded things. And I'm not saying the Weinbergers had a right to use poor Ramon that way or to dupe the other trustees.

But, jeez! I would not want to be on the wrong side of Lilly – much less Grandmere – in a fight.

Lilly was standing there, looking all pleased with herself while everyone else patted her on the back and said what a cool thing she had done.

And I guess it *was* cool in a way, if you agree – which I most definitely do – that anything that makes Lana cry is a good thing.

'So,' Lilly said, when I'd got together all my stuff and was standing there, ready to go. 'Since Clarisse let you out of princess hell for the day, want to go celebrate OUR victory?'

She put a very significant emphasis on the word OUR that only a moron would have missed.

I got it all right.

And felt my stomach lurch.

'Um,' I said. 'Yeah, Lilly. About that. Something kind of happened when I was giving that speech today . . .'

'You're telling *me* something happened,' Lilly said, patting me on the back. 'You struck a blow for unpopular kids everywhere, is what happened while you were giving that speech today.'

'Yeah,' I said. 'I know. About that. I just don't know how I feel about it now. I mean, Lilly, don't you think your plan is kind of unfair? Those people voted for *me*. *I'm* the one they expect—'

I saw Lilly's eyes widen at something she saw behind my back.

'What's HE doing here?' she wanted to know. Then, to whoever was standing back there, she said, 'In case you forgot, you GRADUATED, you know.'

Something gripped my heart at her words. Because I knew – just KNEW – who she was talking to.

The LAST person I wanted to see just then.

Or maybe the person I MOST wanted to see just then.

It all depended on what he had to say to me.

Slowly I turned around.

And there stood Michael.

I guess it would sound super dramatic to say that everything else in the hallway seemed to vanish, until it was as if it were only Michael and me alone, standing there, just looking at each other.

If I wrote that in a story, Ms Martinez would probably write CLICHÉ on it or something.

Except that it's NOT a cliché. Because that's really what it was like. Like there was no one else in the whole world except us two.

'We need to talk,' is what Michael said to me. No *Hello.* No *Why didn't you call me?* or *Where have you been?* And certainly no kiss.

Just *We need to talk.*

And those four words were all it took to make my heart feel as shrivelled and hard as St Amélie's.

'OK,' I said, even though my mouth had gone completely dry.

And when he turned around to leave the school, I followed him, after throwing a warning glance over my shoulder – letting Lars know to stay FAR behind me, and Lilly know there wasn't going to be any celebrating.

At least not just yet.

Lars took it like the professional he is. But I heard Lilly scream, 'Fine! Go with your BOYFRIEND! See if we care!'

But Lilly didn't know. Lilly didn't know about how shrivelled and small my heart had suddenly got. Lilly didn't know I suspected that my life – my perfect princess life – was about to explode into fifty billion pieces. That supervolcano under Yellowstone? Yeah, when that thing finally blows, it'll be NOTHING in comparison.

I followed Michael down the steps of the school – right under the watchful eye of the security cameras – and away from the crowds gathered around Joe. I followed him across two avenues, neither of us saying a word. I certainly wasn't going to speak first.

Because everything was different now. If he was going to break up with me because I wouldn't Do It – well, I didn't care.

Oh, I CARED of course. My heart was breaking ALREADY, and all he'd said was, 'We need to talk.'

But hello. I am the Princess of Genovia. I am the newly elected President of the AEHS Student Council.

And NO ONE – not even Michael – is going to tell me when to Do It.

Finally we got here – to Ray's Pizza. The place was empty because school hadn't been out long enough for it to fill up, and it was way past lunchtime and not quite dinner.

Michael pointed to a booth and said, 'You want a pie?'

'*We need to talk.*'

'*You want a pie?*'

That's all he'd said to me so far.

I said, 'Yes.' And because my mouth still felt as dry as sand, I added, 'And a Coke.'

He went to the counter and ordered both. Then he came back to the booth, slid into the seat across from mine, looked me in the eye and said, 'I saw the debate.'

This was NOT what I'd expected him to say.

It was SO not what I'd expected him to say that my jaw dropped. I didn't remember to shut my mouth again until I felt cool, pizza-scented air on my tongue, and realized I was breathing out of it, just like Boris.

I snapped my mouth shut. Then I asked, 'You were *there*?'

AND YOU DIDN'T COME UP AND SAY HI??????????? Only I didn't say that last part.

Michael shook his head.

'No,' he said. 'It was on CNN.'

'Oh,' I said. Seriously, who else but ME would get their school debate aired on CNN?

And who else but MY BOYFRIEND would happen to catch its broadcast?

'I liked what you said about *Sailor Moon*,' he said.

'You DID?' I don't know why this came out so squeaky.

'Yeah. And the John Locke quote? That kicked butt. You get that from Holland's government class?'

I nodded, unable to speak. I was so astonished he'd known this.

'Yeah,' he said. 'She's cool. So.' He leaned an arm against the back of his side of the booth. 'You're the new President of AEHS.'

I folded my hands on the table top, hoping he wouldn't notice the damage I'd done to my fingernails since the last time I'd seen him. Damage that was almost entirely due to worry about HIM.

'Looks like it,' I said.

'I thought Lilly wanted to be President,' Michael said. 'Not you.'

'She does,' I said. 'But now . . . well, I sort of don't want to give it up.'

Michael raised his eyebrows. Then he let out a low whistle.

'Wow,' he said. 'Mind if I'm not around when you explain that to her?'

'No,' I said. 'That's OK.'

Then I froze. Wait . . . if he didn't want to be around when I explained to Lilly that I had no intention of stepping down from the presidency, did that mean . . .

That had to mean that . . .

Suddenly my poor, shrivelled heart seemed to be showing some signs of life.

'Pie's up,' the guy behind the counter said.

So Michael got up and got the pizza and our three sodas – he'd also got one for Lars, who was sitting at a table on the other side of the restaurant, pretending to be very interested in the *Dr Phil* episode the guy behind the counter was watching on the TV hanging from the ceiling – and brought them back to the booth.

I didn't know what else to do. So I pulled a slice from the pie, slapped it on to a paper plate and took it over to Lars, along with his soda. It's no joke, having to worry about your bodyguard all the time.

Then I went and sat back down and pulled my own slice on to a plate and carefully sprinkled hot-pepper flakes all over it.

Michael, as was his custom, merely picked up a slice – seemingly oblivious to the fact that it was steaming hot – folded it in half and took a big bite.

His hands, as he did this, looked alarmingly . . . large. Why had I never noticed this before? How large Michael's hands are?

Then, after he'd swallowed, he said, 'Look. I don't want to fight about this.'

I glanced up at him kind of sharply on account of having been staring at his hands. I wasn't sure what he meant by 'this'. Did he mean about Lilly and the presidency? Or did he mean—

'All I want to know is,' he went on, in a sort of tired voice, 'are we EVER going to Do It?'

OK. Not Lilly and the presidency.

I practically choked on the tiny bite of pizza I'd taken and had to swallow about a gallon of Coke before I was able to say, 'OF COURSE.'

But Michael looked suspicious.

'Before the end of this decade?'

'Absolutely,' I said, with more conviction that I necessarily felt. But, you know. What else could I say? Plus my face was as red as the pizza sauce. I know because I saw my reflection in the napkin holder.

'I knew going into this that it wasn't going to be easy, Mia,' Michael said. 'I mean, aside from the age difference and your being my sister's best friend, there's the whole princess aspect to it . . . the constant-hounding-by-paparazzi/can't-go-anywhere-without-a-bodyguard thing. A lesser man might find all that daunting. I, on the other hand, have always enjoyed a challenge. Besides which, I love you, so it's all worth it to me.'

I practically melted right there on the spot. I mean seriously. Has any guy EVER said anything so sweet?

But then he went on.

'It's not that I'm trying to rush you into something you aren't ready for,' Michael said, as matter-of-factly as if he were discussing the next move he planned on making in Rebel Strike. How do boys do this by the way? 'It's just that I know it takes you a while to get used to things. So I want you to start getting used to this: you're the girl I want. One day, you WILL be mine.'

Now my face was REDDER than the pizza sauce. At least, that's what it felt like.

'Um,' I said. 'OK.' Because what else COULD I say to that????

Besides it wasn't like I was displeased. I WANT Michael to want me.

It's just, you know, for him to SAY it like that was actually kind of . . . I don't know.

Hot.

'So long as that's clear,' Michael said.

'Crystal,' I said, after I'd choked for a while.

Then he said as far as Doing It went, I was off the hook for the time being, but he expected periodic re-evaluation of our stances on that issue.

I asked how often he thought we should re-evaluate

our stances, and he said about once a month, and I said I thought six-month evaluations might be better, and then he said two, and I said three, and then he said, 'Deal.'

Then he got up and went to offer Lars another slice and got sucked into a conversation Lars is having with the guy behind the counter about the Yankees chances in the World Series this year even though, to my knowledge, Michael has never watched a baseball game in his life.

He did, however, design a computer model in which you can input all the statistics concerning a team and it will then tell you what their chances are of beating another team to within a six-point spread.

The fact is, I love him. He's the boy I want. And one day, he WILL be mine.

And now he wants to know if I want to go get a gelato.

I said, 'I most certainly do.'